P9-DYE-233

BLOOD AND BROTHERHOOD

Other Books by Eugene Stovall

FICTION
Frank Yerby: A Victim's Guilt

NONFICTION
Stovall's Guide to Media Pins
Stovall's Guide to Disney Pins of the Twentieth Century

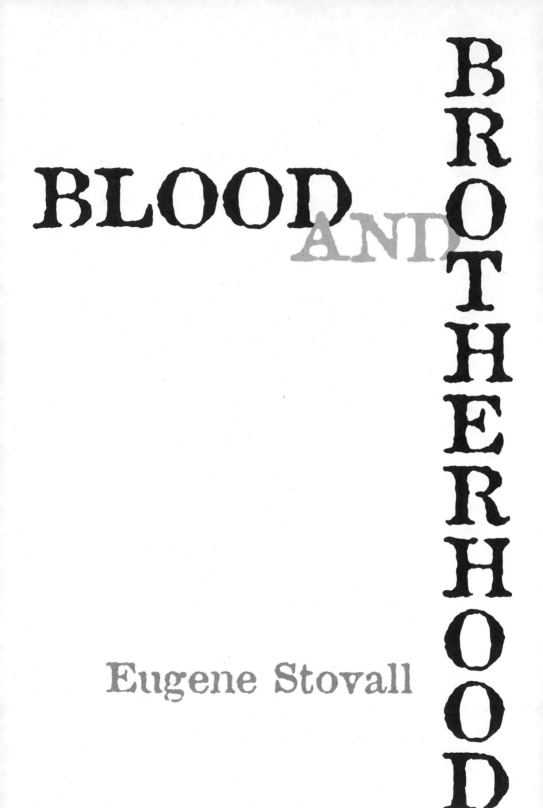

BLOOD AND BROTHERHOOD

Eugene Stovall

Copyright © 2007 Dr. Eugene A. Stovall III

All rights reserved. No parts of this book may be reproduced
or transmitted in any form or by any means, electronic or mechanical,
including photocopying, recording, or by any information storage
and retrieval system, without permission in writing from the author.

ISBN: 978-0-9716691-2-3

Produced by Wilsted & Taylor Publishing Services

Copyediting: Andrew Patty
Design and composition: Susan E. Kelly
Proofreading: Andrew Joron

*This book is dedicated to my beloved grandmother
Maggie Shepard Stovall*

Prologue

Everything is ready. The woman is dressed in a modest grey suit and a white blouse with lace around the neck. All has been prepared. Her rimless glasses, which make the woman look somewhat older than her forty-one years, lend that air of dignity the government, as well as the NAACP, wants to convey. It is seven in the morning and the woman is not simply on her way to work. As Rosa Parks strides purposefully out the door into the brisk December morning, Sid Jenkins knows that there still remains much to be done.

Actually, Irene Morgan, the Virginia woman who refused to relinquish her seat on the segregated Greyhound bus more than ten years earlier, has already played this role. When the pregnant Morgan, returning home from a doctor's visit in the next town, refused to relinquish her seat to a white man, the bus driver took her to the Gloucester County Sheriff's Department, where a dirty, foul-smelling sheriff's deputy dragged Morgan from the Greyhound bus and into jail. The defiant woman did not go without a struggle. She clawed at the deputy's face and tore at his shirt. When a rednecked white man pulled out his nightstick, Morgan delivered a well-placed kick between his legs. Another deputy grabbed the pregnant woman from behind, wrestled her through the jail doors and threw her into a holding cell. The deputies cursed and screamed at the black woman each step of the way. For her part, Morgan continued to resist all the way—screaming back and kicking viciously. When she was brought before the judge, Morgan was convinced by her attorney, Thurgood Marshall, to plead guilty to resisting arrest. The battered and bruised woman was fined $100. In addition, the judge found Morgan guilty of violating Virginia's segregation law. He fined her an additional

$10. Marshall appealed Morgan's case all the way to the U.S. Supreme Court. In a 6-to-1 decision, the high court overturned Morgan's conviction for refusing to yield her bus seat to a white man. Thus, it was Morgan who was responsible for the landmark decision striking down state laws segregating interstate travel. But Morgan was not the NAACP's idea of a black heroine. They have chosen to reenact the event with Rosa Parks in the starring role. This time there will be no resistance, no violence, no cursing cops and no angry colored woman. Everything will be dignified and cordial. It has all been arranged.

This evening, a white bus driver will ask Mrs. Parks, the secretary of Montgomery's NAACP, to give up her seat to a white man. Mrs. Parks will refuse. The bus will come to a halt and two uniformed officers will escort Mrs. Parks to a waiting police car. From there she will be taken to the Montgomery jail, where she will be charged with violating the city's ordinance segregating intrastate public transportation facilities. After being formally charged, Mrs. Parks will be fingerprinted, photographed and taken to a holding cell. Her husband, Ray Parks, will bail her out. It has all been arranged. It will be nonviolent and civilized, the kind of sanitized event the white folks insist upon—not that Marshall and the NAACP disagree. This event will usher in a new era of race relations. It will be done without rancor or bitterness and without any surprises. In the courtroom, the most important legal cases unfold in an orderly, well-planned manner. So shall racial segregation come to an end. At least that is the plan.

Sid smiles. "Chat would never have understood the importance of this event," he thinks. Chat would have done everything he could to expose the fraud and deceit. Sid couldn't understand Chat. "It's good he's not around to ruin it for me," Sid thinks. "If everything goes as planned, there is no telling how far I'll go." Sid knows this is the assignment of a lifetime. Ray Walker, the FBI special agent in charge, guarantees that the Montgomery Police Department will cooperate completely. As a representative for the NAACP Legal Defense Fund, Sid's job is to ensure that the Negroes in Birmingham cooperate as well. There can be no violence. The fate of a race and a nation depends upon it. *No violence.*

What disturbs Sid, though, is the pictures. Why do they insist on having pictures taken of Mrs. Parks being booked by a lieutenant in the Montgomery Police Department? They are using studio cameras and professional lighting. The booking area looks like the kind of Hollywood set his mother used to work on. Is he the only one that believes this picture-taking will cause someone to suspect that this entire affair is a put-up job? Sid had thought about mentioning something to his boss, but then he had thought better of it. The coloreds in the NAACP don't want the white folks to know the truth. They don't want them to know that some Negroes—a few, anyway—can think and figure things out. "These dumb niggers will never figure out this scheme," Sid concedes, "not in a million years. Why should I rock the boat?" What was it that Marcus Garvey had said: "*The ordinary Negro newspaperman who is only able to see the surface of things is an illiterate,*" or something like that. It was something his mother had told him. She was always talking about Garvey and the African Blood Brotherhood and the Ku Klux Klan. Sid got sick and tired of hearing about it. But Chat, that little kiss ass, just ate it up. It was just another reason why his mother preferred Chat to him. But Sid had his grandparents.

Realizing that he is daydreaming about the past again, Sid pulls himself out of it. "Whites are choosing the future Negro leaders," Sid thinks. "And, if everything goes right, I'll be one of them. There's no telling how far I can go, Congress, the Supreme Court, who knows." No, Sid decides that it is not his place to criticize the plan now. The best thing is for Sid to keep his mouth shut and follow orders. Washington has planned everything, and Sid couldn't change it even if he wanted to.

Checking around the apartment, the NAACP operative makes certain everything is in order. Mrs. Parks is on her way. Sid will go over to the NAACP office and set up his vigil. Ed Nixon needs help to keep up his courage and see this affair through. "Chat," Sid says, almost as a prayer, "neither you nor Dad could have gotten this far. Neither of you had what it takes."

PART ONE

Chapter One

Peter Jenkins sits in the straight-backed wooden booth of Candy's Café, facing the front. He wants to see whoever comes through the door. It is a quarter to one in the morning. The supper-club crowd has not yet started to arrive, so Pete has his choice of booths. In an hour or so, Candy's will be packed with partygoers from downtown slumming in Harlem. When the rush of white swells, platinum blonde floozies, slick pimps and ladies of the evening make it uptown later on, there won't be a seat left in the place.

Pete is in an unfamiliar environment. He is normally asleep in his cramped two-room Peach Street apartment at this time in the morning. Pete is one of thousands of messenger boys delivering letters and parcels all over Lower Manhattan, maintaining the flow of information critical to the functioning of the financial juggernaut known as Wall Street. Pete reports to Alfred Cronin—the white man in charge of the mailroom of a medium-sized commercial bank—each day at six AM sharp. Mr. Cronin is a friendly sort, but very strict about time and punctuality.

"One hour and no more for each delivery round," are Pete's instructions. "You're one of my best messenger boys," Mr. Cronin tells Pete almost every day. "I wish the others were as good as you." All the other messengers are white and boys of high school age. Even though Mr. Cronin gives them fewer deliveries and shorter distances, they seldom, if ever, complete their rounds within the allotted hour. Pete is twenty-three years old, a man who fought in the Great War. Nonetheless, Pete knows that if he fails to meet his schedule, Mr. Cronin will fire him on the spot. The Garveyites got Pete his job. He had replaced another black man who was fired for failing to keep his delivery schedule. Pete is determined to keep this job until he can find something better. He is saving up to buy a bicycle. He saw a J.C. Higgins in a Sears catalogue for $25. But this job barely pays enough for Pete to pay for food and rent, not to mention the cost of riding the subway each day to and from work. Pete dreams that one day he will work for the Post Office as a letter carrier. "I'll deliver mail right in Harlem," he vows, even though Pete knows that, in 1920, the United States Post Office does not hire Negroes to deliver the mail, not even in Harlem.

Pete considers himself fortunate to have a job at all. "It's because Marcus Garvey is looking out for us," he tells himself. "And I'm not going to let Mr. Garvey down." That was why Pete took it as an obligation to be in bed by eight o'clock—that is, when his duties at Garvey's Liberty Hall permitted it. Pete really needs his sleep. Fortunately, his job allows him to keep "banker's hours." Rarely does he have to work past four PM. Sometimes, however, Mr. Cronin has a late delivery, and it is always Pete he calls on. Mr. Cronin says that his late deliveries are always important. That's why he depends on his Negro messenger boy. Pete likes the fact the Mr. Cronin depends on him to make those late deliveries. So it is very unlike Pete to be sitting in Candy's Café, nursing a cup of coffee, at one o'clock in the morning.

The after-midnight crowd begins filing in. Pete notices three street hustlers making a grand entrance, talking loud and flashing their jewelry. Their clothes are immaculate, sharp suits, cashmere topcoats and Stetson hats: they look just like the department store dummies, whose dress they try so hard to emulate. One of the hustlers brandishes a walking stick with a carved ivory handle. Pete follows the trio with his eyes as they make their way to a table at the back, making lewd remarks to Big Mabel on their way. "Man, I sure wish I had clothes like that," Pete thinks, aware that his only suit was purchased from one of Father Divine's thrift shops on Lenox Avenue. Pete is so completely engrossed in the attire of the three pimps that he is unaware of the man who slides into his booth and settles next to him.

"Hi there, fella!"

Looking up and recognizing his Army buddy, Pete shouts out "Grady!" and, reaching over, gives the newcomer a great hug. "Grady, Grady Jones!"

"I see you got my note," the conservatively dressed, light-skinned colored man says. Then turning to a woman standing next to the booth, he announces, "Julia, I want you to meet Pete Jenkins. Pete, here, saved my life. Pete, this is Julia Duncan."

Pete tries to stand but is stopped by the cramped booth as well as by the woman herself. Staring back at him with seductive green eyes is the most beautiful woman Pete has ever seen. Although to say that she is a beautiful *woman* might be somewhat of an overstatement. This tall, green-eyed goddess is nineteen, possibly twenty, at most. Whatever her age, Julia is drop-dead gorgeous. Beautiful, yet poor. Julia wears a threadbare coat that has seen many winters and probably had several owners. The coat opens to reveal Julia's voluptuous front, narrow waist and tapering hips. Her golden brown hair curls from under a tight-fitting hat, out of fashion, but adequate for keeping out the New York chill. Around her long, smooth neck is wrapped a yellow scarf, beneath which Pete can see the frayed edges of a laced blouse. Julia has the face of an angel; her skin is almost ivory, with a golden glow. Despite her dowdy attire, Julia strikes the pose of a princess, reminiscent of the heroine, Lorna Doone, from the novel Pete borrowed from the public library on 135th Street.

"Happy to meet you, Julia," Pete stammers. He is aware of how ridiculous he looks, half standing like some awkward schoolboy, gawking at the Jamaican beauty. Julia flashes her mysterious green eyes in Pete's direction before turning away with an air of complete indifference.

"I thought we were going to a rent party," Julia says to Grady in a lilting West Indian accent. "You know that I've got to be back home soon!"

"Don't worry, baby," Grady says, patting Julia's gloved hand. "Cora is throwing a party on West 137th Street. I just came to fetch my old Army buddy, Pete, here."

"Your note said that it was important," Pete says, turning toward Grady, trying not to stare a Julia.

"It is important," Grady laughs. His eyes twinkle and his lips curl into an infectious smile. Pete and Grady were very close in France, despite the fact that the light-skinned slickster was always getting into trouble and Pete always had to come to Grady's rescue. Like the time Grady got drunk and went out to that French farm looking for his mademoiselle. She was Grady's girl and always willing. Except this time, instead of a young French lady, Grady had found two Southern crackers waiting to string him up. "First we're going to cut your dick off, boy," a big, sandy-haired American soldier had boasted. Pete and a couple of other soldiers in their outfit saved Grady's life—as well as his masculinity —that night.

"How long has it been since we mustered out of the Army, Pete?" Grady asks.

"Haven't seen you in six months."

"That's a long time," Grady says, "and I don't intend to lose touch with the man that saved my life. I'm here to take you with us to Cora's rent party."

Even though Pete has to be at work at six AM and isn't interested in jumping and strutting all night with people who don't have jobs and are living from hand to mouth, Pete can't pass up the opportunity to spend more time in the company of Julia. The smooth-talking, good-looking Grady takes one look at the hound-dog, slack-jawed expression on his friend's face and knows he has him hooked. Julia is that kind of woman, the kind of woman that Pete wants to take home to meet his mama even if—as far as Grady knows—Pete doesn't have a mama. Guys like Pete don't stand a chance with women like Julia. They can look, but they can't touch. Pete, Grady decides, will want to look at Julia. Pete can't know that a fire burns behind those smoldering green eyes and desire beats within that exquisite body. Julia is the perfect bait to help Grady complete his mission. After all, Pete saved his life, and no good deed goes unpunished.

Chapter Two

J. Edgar Hoover to George Cross Van Dusen,
Military Intelligence Division

Washington, D.C.

I desire that there be prepared at once a summary
memorandum upon the activities of Marcus Garvey, giving
particular attention to utterances either by word, or
mouth, or in writing, advocating the overthrow of the
government of the United States by force or violence,
or urging the unlawful destruction of property. The
files of the Military Intelligence Division and State
Department should be thoroughly gone into and the
memorandum prepared in final form not later than Monday,
March 21st at noon.

Very truly yours,

J.E. Hoover

George Cross Van Dusen,
Military Intelligence Division,
to J. Edgar Hoover

Washington, D.C.

Little information is contained in the Military
Intelligence Division files as to the actual

organization of this association. It is essentially a
propaganda agency through which Garvey carries on his
agitation. Its official publication is the "Negro
World." I will not go into detail in regard to the
Negro Factories Company, the Universal Negro
Improvement Association or the "Negro World" as they
are fully covered by Department of Justice files.

Geo. C. Van Dusen

"Come in, private." The steely-eyed lieutenant motions for Grady to sit in the wooden chair across from the plain flat-top desk in the drab room of military green. "I guess you're happy to be leaving this man's Army?"

Grady and the other soldiers of the Services Supply Battalion of the 93rd Division are being mustered out from Ellis Island in New York's harbor under the vigilant eyes of the Statue of Liberty, a gift to the United States from the people of France. The people of France also gave many of these colored war veterans the first idea of liberty and equality they had ever known.

"Yessir," Grady replies. He knows some of the soldiers are being interviewed before being discharged. But most of them had been sergeants whom the Army wanted to keep. There is no reason for the Army to keep Grady, which is fine because Grady has no reason to stay in the white man's Army.

"I see here that you went to college," the lieutenant continues. "What college did you attend?"

Grady has never seen the inside of a college. He passed by Tuskegee Institute when his parents brought him and his sisters to New York from Alabama. Both his parents attended Booker T. Washington's industrial school, where they each learned trades. His mother learned to sew and landed a job in New York's garment industry. His father studied metallurgy, but in New York, he became a doorman, an elevator operator and a dishwasher—but mostly he was unemployed. Grady did not even graduate from high school. But he is smart, and he likes to read when he isn't hustling on the streets of Harlem. More than once he and his father got into arguments about Grady going to school and learning a skill.

"What for?" Grady asked his father. "Where has your 'skill' gotten you?"

But Grady liked to read. As a kid, Grady spent afternoons at the New York Public Library on 135th Street in Harlem. This is what he and Pete have in common and why Pete looks out for Grady. Pete is the only Negro that Grady respects. As a youngster, Grady liked to hang out with the hustlers in the park who played chess. Grady was a fair chess player, but not in the league with some of those guys. They lived and breathed chess. To Grady, chess was just a whetstone to sharpen his wits for the game of life. When he was drafted, he told the sergeant at the induction center that he had attended college, hoping to get a soft assignment. But like the other 200,000 black draftees in France, he was put into a service unit that went to the battlefields, picked up the corpses of American soldiers—or the pieces of what is left of dead Americans soldiers—and buried them.

So what that Grady lies about attending Tuskegee Institute? "What difference does it make?" he asks himself.

The lieutenant stares at the file. Then, pushing back from the desk, he stares straight at Grady. "What if I told you that you're a liar, that you never attended Tuskegee Institute? What would you say to that, private?"

Grady flinches, but he isn't afraid. If anything, Grady is amused. "I guess I would say that you caught me, sir," he replies with a grin.

"And what if I were to say that while you were in France, you were seen molesting white women in violation of the general order that colored troops were not to keep company with or even speak to white women?"

The grin disappears from Grady's face. He remains silent.

"Furthermore, we have evidence that on several occasions you forced these women to have sex with you."

"That's a lie," Grady says. "Whoever told you that, lied. I never forced any woman to have sex. They wanted me. They offered it to me."

"Is that so, private?" the lieutenant sneers. "Well, what if I was to tell you that we know what happened at Romagne on July 17, 1918? You killed an American soldier after he caught you raping a white woman."

Grady's mind starts racing. He stares at the smug intelligence officer. "He's fishing," Grady thinks. There were two white soldiers, not one. And there were four of us. Pete brought Willie and Sam along that night. The three of them got the drop on those crackers just as they were about to start slicing on me. Sam and Pete sneaked up from behind and opened up with their forty-fives. Two rounds fired simultaneously caught the tall sandy-haired one square in his back, lifting him almost a foot off of the ground. Another two rounds also found their mark and the man's body buckled, falling like a sack of potatoes, the full moon capturing the surprised look etched on his dead face. When the second soldier tried to escape, he ran right into Willie, whose forty slug buried itself into the fleeing man's forehead, making a rather small hole in front but blowing most of the back of his head off. After that the four of them took the bodies back and buried them with the other Americans killed in action. Sam, Willie and Pete have all been mustered out of the Army. "This guy's just fishing," Grady says to himself. "He doesn't know anything."

"I didn't kill anybody in France," Grady tells the Army officer. "I just buried the ones you white folks killed."

"Is that so?" the lieutenant says quietly. "Well, your lies don't matter to me. I have enough evidence to court-martial your black ass and then hang you. What do you think about that?"

Looking around the room, Grady doesn't know what to think. He knows that it doesn't matter what actually happened; he is caught. There is nowhere to run and nowhere to hide. "Well, I'm not too happy about the hanging part," Grady replies with a bravado he doesn't really feel.

"Guard," the lieutenant shouts. Instantly the door flies open and an MP the size of Mount Rushmore fills the doorway. "Take this man prisoner!"

Three weeks later, Grady finds himself in the same drab room, sitting at the same flat wooden desk, facing the same steely-eyed lieutenant. This time he is not as cocky and a lot more wary about what he says. It isn't as if Grady has suffered any physical abuse. He was taken to a small room with a solid-iron door. The door had a sliding hole. Once a day he was given a tray with water, a slice of bread and some tasteless gruel that contained lumps that might have been meat, but Grady couldn't be certain. Once a day, the hole opened and he could replace his slop jar. The only other item in the room was a steel bed with a thin mattress and a tattered blanket. A steel-covered bulb glowed continually, flooding the cell with light. At the top of the iron door was a peephole. Every once in a while the peephole would slide open and a single blue eye peered at Grady for several minutes before the hole closed again. During the first few days of his imprisonment, anticipation kept Grady in a state of nervous anxiety. He jumped at every sound. He watched the iron door constantly. He listened to the muffled sounds behind the walls. He couldn't sleep under the harsh glare of the light. His nerve left him and he began to feel less like a man and more like a thing. Then, gradually, almost imperceptibly, he began to hear a voice. It was quiet, yet insistent. Grady wasn't certain whether the voice was inside his head or outside his cell. It really didn't matter. The voice soothed him; it comforted him; it helped him maintain his sanity. Then he tried to remember some of the books he had read, tried to find something to hang on to, tried to remember something meaningful. He couldn't remember anything, but trying to remember helped pass the time. Now he finds himself facing the lieutenant once again. It is as if the past three weeks didn't even happen; it is as if they were a dream, a really bad dream. But Grady knows it actually happened because he smells like something from a garbage dump, an itchy, scraggily beard covers almost all of his face, and his body has become a playground for a colony of lice.

"So private," the steely-eyed lieutenant begins, "where were we? Oh yes, I think we were talking about that incident on July 17, 1918, at Romagne. Would you care to tell me about it now?"

Briefly considering his situation, Grady decides to tell the entire story down to the last detail without reservation. The steely-eyed lieutenant takes notes. When Grady finishes his narrative, the Army intelligence officer asks Grady to clarify certain points in his story. Then he begins grilling Grady over and over again, checking and rechecking the story. When, finally, after several hours, the lieutenant seems satisfied, he calls for a guard. Once again, Grady finds himself in his cell. This time, in addition to a bed, there is a table and chair and a meal. Sliced beef, mashed potatoes and gravy, Army peas and a green salad rounded off by a cup of coffee. An Army newspaper lies across the steel cot bed, now fitted with sheets, a second blanket and a pillow. After his meal, an MP comes into his cell and clears away the steel mess plate. Sometime later, the light is turned off and Grady drifts off into a dreamless sleep.

"Yessir, the problem is far worse than we imagined," the lieutenant reports to his superior. Captain Elmer Hansen is chief of population section in Army intelligence. He has the responsibility of collecting intelligence on the thousands of colored troops being released from the Army. "Not only have we confirmed reports that Negro soldiers have killed white Americans in France during the war, but several of them have worked together to conceal their crimes."

"How widespread do you think the problem is, lieutenant?" Captain Hansen asks. Hansen had graduated from the United States Military Academy at West Point. He did not see action in the great European war but worked in counterespionage, where he not only successfully uncovered plots hatched by the Kaiser's spies but also by the Bolsheviks, socialists and Negroes. During the Great War, Captain Hansen oversaw the capturing and hanging of America's enemies here at home. Now Captain Hansen has a mission of the highest priority in military intelligence. His job is to determine the magnitude of the threat posed by colored soldiers leaving the army. The information Hansen receives from his subordinate is the kind of military intelligence he needs to convince his superiors that there is a potential for an upcoming race war. At the academy, Hansen studied population control, a major concern of the American military since the time of Andrew Jackson. As president, Jackson assigned the military the task of containing and controlling native populations inside as well as outside America's borders. If there is one department in the fledgling nation that took seriously De Tocqueville's warnings about whites being overwhelmed by the inferior races, it is the military, particularly military intelligence. Fully a third of Hansen's fellow West Point graduates specialize in intelligence activities. But none are as keen or as capable as he; Hansen is top in his class. In intelligence circles, Hansen, even at the age of thirty, is considered an expert in population control. His department, headquartered on the Army post on Ellis Island, is responsible for domestic intelligence throughout the Eastern seaboard. Hansen has complete freedom of operation and reports only to the post commander, whose boss is the chief of Army intelligence in Washington. Even Joel Spingarn is Hansen's subordinate.

"From what we have learned from discharge reports, a significant number of Negro soldiers would fight against whites," the lieutenant concludes. "Not only those who served in combat units, but also those assigned to labor battalions would take up arms if given the opportunity."

"Do we have any idea how many that would be, lieutenant?"

"Sir, of the 200,000 Negroes making up the 92nd Division, 40,000 were in combat regiments, the 367th, 368th, and 369th. Despite the best efforts of the general staff, these regiments sustained only a 60 percent casualty rate. The most conservative estimates show that 70 percent of those 16,000 would willingly kill white Americans."

"I had hoped that the planners would have taken my advice to retain them and send them to Russia to fight the Bolsheviks. But somehow the brass doesn't believe colored soldiers are a threat. Now, all of a sudden, they're concerned about releasing those niggers into the general population."

"Yessir," the lieutenant sighs, "they should have listened to you. We'll have a war on our hands for certain now."

"What about those in the labor battalions," Hansen asks, "the cooks, road gangs and grave diggers? You're certain they'll fight?"

"It is estimated that even 40 percent of service personnel assigned to the most menial jobs would fight, sir." The lieutenant put the summary of the report on his superior's desk. "I have identified several Negroes from a number of units as potential operatives, as you instructed. Each of them received psychological tests, but only one seems suitable for your purposes. His name is Private Grady Jones. His file is on top."

Captain Hansen picks up the file and casually scans Grady's entire life history.

"Will that be all, sir?"

"Yes, lieutenant, that will be all," Hansen says. Staring at the reports, the intelligence expert sighs. Hansen must review this information and submit a summary to his superiors in Washington. This is not good news. "First," Hansen decides, "I'd better have a chat with this Private Grady Jones."

"Okay, private come on out of there," the MP barks. Grady is taken from his cell to another section of the post, where he is deloused and ordered to shower and shave. They give him a clean Army uniform that, Grady notes, does not have a P/fc chevron on the sleeve. The MP ushers Grady into the mess hall, where he is seated at one of the dining tables. A dining hall attendant gives him a tin mess plate filled with scrambled eggs, hash browns, French toast, bacon and sausage, along with a steaming cup of coffee. The MP leaves. Just as Grady begins sampling the Army chow, an officer grabs the chair on the opposite side of the table. It takes all of Grady's self-control to resist the urge to jump up and salute.

"Private, my name is Captain Hansen, and for the time being, you belong to me."

"What about my discharge?" Grady asks hesitantly.

"Well, boy, the Army intends to keep you around awhile," the captain says, smiling. "That is, unless you prefer the gallows."

In 1920, Harlem teems with migrants and veterans and Grady Jones is both. Once he completes his training in spy craft, under the tutelage of Captain Elmer Hansen, Grady has no problem blending in and plying his new trade as an agent for military intelligence on the lively streets of Harlem. His parents still live in their apartment on West 67th in the San Juan Hill area that they rented in 1910 after leaving Tuskegee. But subsequently, the Rockefellers and other wealthy land speculators built great tenements for blacks across 110th Street into Harlem. The landlords charge their Negroes tenants exorbitant rents. Most of Harlem's residents have no gainful employment. Some, like Pete, work jobs paying starvation wages and consider themselves middle class. These upwardly mobile Negroes, brimming with optimism, work as domestics, janitors, doormen, cooks, waiters, chauffeurs, longshoremen, elevator operators and messengers. Many of those returning from the Great European War live in the squalid Harlem tenements and are unemployed. They would fight willingly, had they only known where and when. These Negroes worry military intelligence most. Some of them become Garveyites; others join more militant organizations, such as the African Blood Brotherhood. None of them are welcome in organizations like the NAACP or the Urban League. They are not members of DuBois' "talented tenth." Neither are they welcome in socialist-inspired organizations or in labor unions, whose unwritten rule is "niggers need not apply." But despite the economic hardships, Harlem is alive with music and song. And those who can't pay their rent throw rent parties that last all night long, every night.

Chapter Three

Cora's apartment is not far from Candy's Café. Pete, Grady and the luscious Julia march down Seventh Avenue, across Lenox and over West 137th Street. They pass by the famous Pabst restaurant that just recently has been turned into a Kress five and dime store. Kress takes the Negroes' dimes and nickels but will not hire any Negro sales clerks. Occasionally, the store manager hires a black day laborer to sweep the street in front of the store and take out the garbage. He considers himself a liberal on racial matters. On the way to the party, Pete and Grady say very little. Julia clutches at Grady's arm. But once inside Cora's, Grady disappears and Pete and Julia are left alone with each other.

Cora's party is jumping. It is happening not only in Cora's apartment, but also in every apartment on her entire floor. Jazz music, hot licks and a steady beat accompanying a wailing saxophone, a screeching trumpet and a rhythmic banjo resonate from across the hall. The smell of hot links, fried chicken, chit'lins, greens and potato salad wafts over the partygoers, who are everywhere, cramming into each apartment, overflowing into the hall and continually going up and down the stairs. People of all types and colors jostle each other, spilling cups of alcohol, beer, wine and bathtub gin. Downtown "swells" with their platinum blonde "molls" salute the working stiffs from Queens and Long Island aristocrats. Uptown numbers runners and dope peddlers hustle midtown bohemians while the political crowd tests its liberal sentiments by indulging in the fanciful games that dusky-hued ladies of the evening are experts at playing. Suddenly Grady reappears.

"Here, take this," Grady says to Pete, pressing a ten-dollar bill into his friend's hand. "Buy Julia something to eat and get her something to drink."

"Where you going now?" Pete shouts at his friend's retreating back.

"I'll be back," comes the reply, barely audible over the noise.

"Can I get you something?" Pete tries to avert his eyes as he speaks. She is just so beautiful that to look at her is embarrassing.

Julia shoots Pete a disdainful look. "Where did Grady go?" she asks.

"Out," he shrugs.

"You got a cigarette?" It is more of a command than a request, her imperious West Indian accent loaded with contempt.

"Anything else?" he asks. The party is so crowded and the noise is so loud that, even though they are right next to each other, they must shout at each other to be heard. Shouting makes Pete feel even more uncomfortable. The music is hot. Everyone else is laughing and having a good time. Pete feels miserable. "Do you want anything else?" he asks again, knowing that Julia heard him the first time.

"No," she says, "I'll wait for Grady."

"Grady asked me to see that you got something to eat before he came back," Pete says, shoring up his courage to look directly at this island goddess.

"Oh," she says, raising her eyebrows ever so slightly.

"Yes!" Pete replies emphatically. "I'm responsible for you now. I'm here to make sure you have a good time."

Pete has been with beautiful women before. White women even. But they never affected Pete like this. In France, Pete had been as successful as any of the fellows when it came to the ladies. The French women loved his shy, boyish manner. Even here in New York, some women like him despite his shy manner. Pete's handsome face appeals to many women, white as well as black. He is almost six feet tall with a well-developed physique, wide shoulders and muscular arms. His hair is coarse and dark, but has a certain texture that makes women want to run their fingers through it. His nose reminds one of a pug; it turns up just as the nostrils widen. Pete's eyes seem sad, but at times they twinkle with merriment as if he is happy just to be alive. His skin is the color of chocolate, a shade that leaves no doubt that he is a member of that outcast and most despised Negro race. But its smoothness and its color are appealing. Even the most bigoted or, in the case of members of his own race, the most "color struck"—which is what he believes Julia to be—find Pete's color attractive. But Pete can tell that Julia prefers someone like Grady, someone with lighter skin. Still, Pete is determined to make an impression. He even decides to get to know her better. At least that is what he hopes to do. It doesn't matter to Pete that she is obviously attached to Grady. After all, Grady owes Pete.

"You might as well try to make the best of the situation while Grady's gone," Pete shouts at Julia over the noise.

"I am not here for you to show me a good time," Julia snaps back. But after awhile, probably thinking better of it, she says, "If you want, you may get me a cigarette and something to eat and something to drink, too."

"A drink?" Pete replies in mock disbelief. "You're not old enough to be drinking."

"I'm old enough," Julia says demurely, looking around at all the partygoers with drinks in their hands. "Since the government has passed a law prohibiting alcohol to everyone, there's no reason why I can't drink. That's why people come to parties like these, isn't it?" She stares at him defiantly, actually seeing him for the first time. And to her surprise Julia likes what she sees. Before she knows it, Julia begins to relax, her indifference gradually yields to curiosity and her disdain turns into interest.

"Okay! Let's get you some food and something to drink," Pete says, flashing a little boy's smile that many women find irresistible.

After Julia eats and has a couple of drinks, she mellows considerably. Grady has been gone for an hour. Julia and Pete do several "struts." They dance down the hall and into one of the other apartments, laughing and frolicking with the other partygoers. When Julia almost falls, Pete reaches out and catches her. She is soft to the touch, but not too soft. Pete wants to hold her close. He has had a couple of drinks. So has Julia. She doesn't mind his arms around her at all. Or is it just the alcohol, Pete asks himself. Anyway, it doesn't matter.

After awhile they even try to talk, but any conversation other than a series of shouts followed by "What?" is nearly impossible. So they go back to what they came to do, dancing and bumping and eating and drinking and making noise and having fun like everybody else at Cora's rent party. Pete has all he can do to keep the wolves from grabbing Julia. Even her shabby clothes don't prevent Julia from being one of the most stunning women there. White men leer and pimps scheme—good reasons for Julia to stay close to Pete, at least that is what Pete thinks. By now it is three o'clock in the morning. Pete must get home to catch a short nap before getting downtown to his messenger job. But Julia shouts at Pete over the music, "Look there's Fats Waller! He's going to play, he's going to play," she screams with delight, joining the others who press around the famous piano player. Then, just like everyone else, she becomes disappointed when she realizes that there is no piano at Cora's rent party.

"What time do you have to be home," Pete asks Julia a little later. She is still in ecstasy over seeing Fats Waller and some of the other big name musicians like Claude Hopkins and Corky Williams.

Julia looks at him with an impish smile. "I should have been home before I met you at Candy's," she says shyly. "I'm going to be in big trouble when I get home."

"Well, I've got to be at work in the morning, so maybe we ought to leave now."

Julia looks around; the party is still going, but she says, "Yes, of course, you're right. My mother will be worried and my father will be furious."

"Where do you live?"

"On Tinker Street."

"Where's that?"

"It's over by East 117th Street. The 110th Street cross-town trolley will take us there."

On the ride to her home, Pete hopes to cement a relationship with the beautiful West Indian, but freed from the gaiety and fun-loving atmosphere of Cora's party, Julia relapses into a quiet, almost sullen demeanor. When Pete tries to talk, Julia freezes up and puts so much distance between them that once again they become total strangers. The only thing Julia says is that Grady played a trick on her, leaving like that. And that Pete was probably in on it.

"I won't forget it, you know!" she tells Pete. Her words come out without her even looking his way.

They arrive at a commercial section in East Harlem and stop in front of a small thrift shop. Without a word, Julia darts around the side. Pete can hear her footsteps running up some stairs, a door opening, slamming shut. Then comes the night-shattering noise of a man's voice yelling and screaming words that are hardly intelligible and a woman's cries mixed with anger and relief. Pete shakes his head and, taking out his pocket watch, decides that sleep is out of the question. He barely has time to don his messenger uniform and go downtown to the bank.

Chapter Four

"What happened to you?" Grady slides into the booth at Candy's Café, a lopsided smile plastered across his face.

It is a blustery Sunday in March, one of those early spring days that New Yorkers love. Winter's departure leaves the city alive with flowers, fragrances and birds. Pete decides to treat himself to a good "soul-food" dinner at Candy's before going down to Liberty Hall where this evening's teen social is being held. Pete promises Captain E. L. Gaines, Minister of Legions, that he and his squad of legionnaires will provide security for the affair.

With the success of the Universal Negro Improvement Association's first convention, held in Madison Square Garden, a number of Negro organizations, following the NAACP's lead, begin attacking Garvey. More than 2000 delegates representing forty states, twenty-five countries and four continents declare their intention to wage a relentless struggle against white supremacy. Hired thugs attack attendees of many of the Association's Liberty Hall activities. The police offer no protection. In the face of increasing provocations from Negroes as well as whites, Garveyites must depend on the African Legion to provide security service for the Association. The African Legion is Garvey's internal police, responsible for protecting members against attacks from outsiders and for resolving internal dissensions. Pete's military background as well as his own personal bearing brought him to the attention of Captain Gaines, who is not only Minister of Legions but also Garvey's close confidant. When Pete joins the UNIA, he signs on for the Association's African Legion. The imposing former serviceman makes an ideal candidate. Gaines offers Pete the opportunity to form his own squad of legionnaires and shoulder some of the security responsibilities at Garvey's Liberty Hall headquarters on West 138th Street. Pete and his squad earn a reputation for being one of Garvey's most reliable security units.

Pete personally chooses each man in his squad. He looks for maturity, preferring ex-servicemen who saw action in the great European war. Hundreds of former Negro veterans, with few job opportunities, join Garvey's African Legion in hopes of finding employment. The Association tries to provide every member of the African Legion a job, even though, in most cases, it is menial labor. Thus Pete has hundreds of legionnaires to choose from.

Pete drills his men twice a week at Liberty Hall. They are expected to be on time and properly dressed in the uniform provided by the association. Pete conducts an inspection, close order drill, code- and hand-signal training and firearm practice. Though there are problems with standards and ammunition, each of Pete's men is responsible for providing their own weapons. The Association does have a small armory. Its whereabouts, and even its existence, is a closely guarded secret. Even Pete is not aware of it until he has gained the confidence of the Minister of Legions as well as the President-General, Marcus Garvey, himself. After training, each member of his squad is given his weekly assignment, such as providing security for this evening's social. Infractions, such as tardiness, are disciplined. Pete will dismiss any legionnaire guilty of multiple infractions. Dismissal from the squad means loss of the Association job. But because of Pete's success as a leader, it is necessary for him to dismiss only one man. Pete, himself, is never late and never falters in training or on assignment. Pete makes no excuses to his captain, nor does he accept excuses from his men. Pete's unit is tops in the New York division and tops in the country. The Chaplin-General, Bishop McGuire, even cites Pete's squad for its effectiveness in handling a disruption at one of the public meetings by some of A. Philip Randolph's socialist thugs. After the incident, the Chaplin-General specifically requests Pete's squad to provide security for McGuire's Sunday services at Liberty Hall. Once in awhile, Pete and the bishop will share a cup of coffee and a bit of philosophy after the service. When there is a possibility of trouble, as is the case today, Pete's unit is usually on hand. So, Pete has very little time for Grady on this particular Sunday afternoon.

"What do you mean, what happened to me?" Pete asks. "What happened to you?"

Grady just sits there with a grin on his face. Big Mabel ambles over and asks, "What can I get you, honey chile?"

"Bring me your chicken special," Grady replies. "Does that come with peach cobbler?"

"It sure does, honey."

"Then that's what I want."

"Coming right up. Want something to drink?"

"I'll take some of that special tea." Grady winks at Big Mabel. Even though Prohibition has been in effect for almost two years, it is no problem getting a beer with Sunday dinner at Candy's.

Grady grins at Pete. "How did you like Julia?"

"I liked her fine, but . . ."

"But what?"

"She thinks that I was in on whatever you were up to. She's says that she's going to get even with you and me. Why did you leave us like that? Where did you disappear to? What are you up to?"

"Disappear? I was trying to leave the field open for you," Grady says, feigning innocence.

"She wasn't interested in me; she's interested in you!" Pete replies. "Besides which, there's plenty of women around. I just don't have time for them right now. So I really don't need you to give me your leavings."

Pete's angry. But his anger has nothing to do with Grady trying to fix him up. It has to do with Julia's rejection. Pete went back to the thrift shop on Tinker Street the next day after work. Inside, the owner of the thrift shop, a light-skinned Jamaican, Julia's father, was puttering around, rearranging his second-hand goods while pontificating to his wife about the state of the world in general and the state of the Jamaican community in particular. When Pete entered, Ed Duncan looked over and said, "Let me know if you need something you don't see, young man."

"I will," Pete replied.

Then the shop owner shouted out, "Julia, Julia!" Looking over at his wife, he complained, "Where is that girl? Lying in bed all day, staying out all night. It's your fault, she being so loose, now."

"Just you be quiet now, Edward," Sharon Duncan scolded. "Enough of your talk. Leave the girl be. She has to make her way. You don't think she'll find a man around here, do you?"

Julia's mother wore a friendly smile. Pete could see where Julia got her beauty. Though a good deal plumper, Sharon had the same golden skin with high cheekbones, narrow features and green eyes. Pete began to stare. Before he realized it, Sharon was standing directly in front of him.

"I said, can I help you, young man?" Julia's mother said, breaking into Pete's thoughts.

Fumbling about in embarrassment, Pete picked up a set of porcelain coffee cups that he did not need and could not afford. "How much?" he asked.

"Three dollars for the set," Julia's mother replied. She eyed Pete suspiciously. "Are you buying these as a gift?" she asked.

Pete mumbled something incoherent and produced three dollar bills that Sharon quickly accepted. While Julia's mother wrapped up his demitasse cups, Pete casually tried to look into the curtained-off area at the rear of the shop. But he saw nothing. So he took his newly acquired porcelain ware and departed, leaving Julia's mother happy about the three dollar sale as well as about the possibility that Julia might have a handsome young suitor as well. Sharon mentioned nothing to her husband, who continued to putter about, fuming to himself about his daughter.

Pete couldn't get Julia out of his mind. Several days later, he returned to Tinker Street. This time, however, he watched from across the street, hoping for he didn't know what. Possibly to catch a glimpse of Julia, maybe. Again Pete was disappointed.

Julia and her mother spotted Pete. "Who was that boy mooning about the shop?" Sharon asked her daughter later that evening.

"No one important," Julia replied. "Just a friend of Grady's."

"Well, I hope you're not giving him any ideas," Julia's father huffed. "I don't trust that Grady Jones fellow, and I don't trust any friend of his, either."

"Leave the girl alone, Edward," her mother intervened. "She knows what she's doing."

After all of that, Pete is doubly embarrassed and is in no mood to discuss the matter. "There may be plenty of women around, but none like Julia," Grady says, giving Pete a knowing wink. "I saw how you looked at her, like some love-struck school boy. Besides which, Julia and I are quits."

"Quits?"

"Yeah man, that Julia is one fine mama, but she's not for me."

"Why not?" Pete asks, trying to affect disinterestedness while his stomach churns. Suddenly he loses his appetite. In his mind's eye, Pete can see Julia's face and feel the warmth of her body pressing against his. His mouth goes dry, forcing him to reach for a glass of water, draining it completely.

Grady smiles. "I've got another woman, Nadine, Nadine Eastman. She lives midtown, near DeLancy Street. She's the jealous type. And you know me. I'm a straight shooter when it comes to my women. I never try to play more than one at a time. Besides which, Julia's father keeps giving me the eye when we go out but he ain't got a dime. Nadine's got plenty of money and she don't mind spending it on a poor nigger like me."

"Nigger!" Pete cries out. "Is that what you call yourself? A *nigger*! Don't you have any self-respect? We're no longer the white man's slaves or boys or *niggers*. If that's what you think about yourself, you need to get some education, my brother."

"Oh, I'm sorry, man," Grady says. "I forgot that you're one of those Garveyites, one of those 'New Negroes.'"

"That's right," Pete snaps back. But then Pete asks himself, "How does Grady know that?" He tries to remember ever discussing his membership in the Association with Grady. Pete is positive that he hadn't. All Garvey's people, especially the legionnaires, are warned not to discuss their activities with nonmembers. Too much information has already leaked out about the Association to their enemies. The UNIA is discussed in the Negro press all across the country, and lot of it is unfavorable. Negro weeklies like T. Thomas Fortune's *New York Age*, one of the oldest Negro newspapers in America, and Cyril Briggs' *Crusader* treat the movement fairly evenhandedly. But others—like Robert Abbott's *Chicago Defender*, DuBois' *Crisis* and, above all, A. Philip Randolph's

Messenger—print personal attacks, half-truths and outright lies about the Association, its leadership and Marcus Garvey himself. What's more, Pete knows that Grady is still in the Army. Willie told him that Grady hadn't been mustered out like the others. Even the note Grady sent asking Pete to meet him at Candy's had been posted from Ellis Island. Willie started to tell Pete something more, something hush-hush, the last time they had talked, but decided not to say anything more about it. At the time, Pete thought nothing of it. Now he wondered. Pete always sees both Sam and Willie at least a couple of times a week, but lately neither of them has been around. It's as if they both just disappeared.

"How much do you know about the New Negroes in the Association?" Pete asks Grady.

Laughing it off, Grady tries to make a joke.

"I can tell by the way that you walk that you're still drilling. It's like someone stuck a poker up your butt." He starts wiping his nose and pulling at his chin, a habit Grady picked up in France, Pete remembers. "Anyhow, I didn't mean to offend your race consciousness. I know you're a race man. You've always been a race man. That's why you saved my black ass over in France that time and I'm never going to forget it. You've got a friend for life, ole buddy, whether you want one or not. And that's why I'm here."

"Why are you here?" Pete asks. Big Mabel brings Grady's meal—several pieces of fried chicken, mashed potatoes, and green peas with peach cobbler on the side.

"I came to help get you and Julia together."

"How do you propose doing that?"

"Well, Nadine is taking me to see a new musical called *Shuffle Along*. She's got two extra tickets. I thought maybe you and Julia would like to 'shuffle along' with us."

Grady pauses to laugh at the pun that Pete doesn't find very amusing.

"I'm not interested in seeing whites in blackface ridiculing our people," Pete says.

"You've got it wrong," Grady replies between bites of fried chicken and gulps of beer. "This is going to be a Negro musical with an all-colored cast. You'll like it, you'll see. It'll show that Negroes can produce something that's worthwhile. Nadine thinks it can make it to Broad-way."

"Negroes don't play on Broadway!" Pete says.

"Not yet," Grady says, chuckling. "But this musical will be a first, it'll play at the Garden Theater. That's what Nadine says, and she should know. She's in with the theater crowd. But first it's going to be shown right here in Harlem next week at Hurtig and Seamon's New Theater. What do you say?"

"How am I going to get Julia to go with me?"

"Don't worry about that. It's all been arranged," Grady says. "But there is one thing."

"What's that?" Pete asks, thinking to himself, I knew there's a catch.

"You've got to pick Julia up at her apartment."

"I can do that," Pete responds.

"And bring her a corsage."

"No problem."

"And wear a nice suit. I don't want you looking like the poor ass nig' . . . I mean like the broke Negro that you are."

On the night of the production, Pete calls for Julia at six o'clock. He goes around to the side of her parents' thrift shop, taking the same route she took the night, or morning, rather, that Pete brought her home. A set of narrow wooden stairs leads to the second floor. Both Julia's father and mother meet Pete at the door.

"Come in, young man," Julia's mother beams. "I'm Sharon Duncan, Julia's mother. This is Edward Duncan, Julia's father."

"Happy to meet you, Mrs. Duncan," Pete replies, and, reaching over, he shakes Julia's father's hand. "Sir."

They escort him through an abbreviated hallway and into a surprisingly well-furnished parlor. Glancing about, Pete sees a style of living and an appreciation for neatness that one seldom finds in Harlem, except maybe among the middle class of Striver's Row or Morningside Heights. The Duncans' flat has an easy, comfortable feel to it as Pete strides across a delicately designed Persian rug setting off the well-varnished hardwood floor. In the living room, an overstuffed armchair ottoman and a comfortable sofa surround an ornately carved coffee table. Two straight-backed chairs boast matching laced doilies on arms and backs. Through glass partitions, Pete can see a gleaming dining room table complete with a laced tablecloth, a silver candelabra and place settings for four.

"Mrs. Duncan," Pete announces shyly, "this is for you." Pete hands her a small bouquet of daisies and carnations surrounding a single red rose.

"How thoughtful of you, Peter!" Julia's mother exclaims. "I'll put them in some water right away. And I'll hurry Julia along." The beaming Jamaican lady hurries through the dining area into the rear of the apartment.

"Have a seat, young man." Julia's father motions Pete to one of the straight-backed chairs and sinks himself into the armchair, propping his feet upon the ottoman. Then, without bothering with preliminaries, Ed asks, "How do you know my daughter?"

The question is hostile, and Ed's manner is even more so. He is unimpressed by flowers. Pete searches his mind for a good answer. Telling Julia's father that he met his daughter at Candy's and took her to an all-night rent party doesn't seem an appropriate response. The West Indian community has a low opinion of the American Negro's nocturnal adventures. West Indians adhere to the same Protestant work ethic that Pete applies to himself.

"Didn't Julia tell you?" Pete replies. "I thought you might remember me. I bought the set of coffee cups in your shop several weeks ago."

"Yes, I do remember you," Ed concedes. Ed will remember anyone who spends three dollars in his shop. "But . . ."

"Did Julia tell you that I saw action in France? But I never got to England," Pete continues quickly. He spots a framed picture of a distinguished white man occupying a dominant position on the parlor wall. The aristocratic figure poses in an immaculately tailored dress uniform covered in gold braid. Across his chest gleam numerous medals.

"Isn't that the King of England?" Pete asks.

A smile flashes across Ed's face.

"Yes, indeed," the Jamaican replies. "That's his royal highness, George the Fifth. I had that picture sent to me from England after his coronation."

Pete guesses that the picture of the King of England—cousin to Kaiser Wilhelm, the German ruler whose greed for colonial possessions caused the Great War—is Ed's prized possession.

But before anything more is said, much to Pete's relief, Julia's mother reappears with Pete's flowers arranged in a vase. And behind her stands Julia.

Julia walks, or rather glides, effortlessly into the parlor. Pete jumps to his feet. "So we meet again," she says, searching his face for a hint of what he and her father were discussing. Her white evening gown flows over her body like waves washing over the Jamaican coast.

"This is for you," Pete says, thrusting out a corsage, a white gardenia.

"How perfect!" she exclaims. "Mother, see how well it goes with my dress? Help me put it on."

Julia's mother beams as she pins the corsage to Julia's gown. Pete continues to stare. Even the goddess Isis cannot be more stunning. But then he asks himself a more practical question, "What kind of mood is she in?" Her entry is encouraging. Maybe she's over Grady. What Pete doesn't realize is that it might be far better for him if Julia were emotionally involved with his friend. But, in reality, Julia is not emotionally tied to Grady; she's not emotionally committed to anyone or anything, except herself. The only thing that interests Julia is getting off of Tinker Street. And if Pete can help her do it, he will get her attention, at least for the time being. Grady promised her the moon and stars, and Julia means to have them. Her mother understands, but her father doesn't and neither does Pete, not that understanding Julia will do Pete any good. Pete just doesn't have what it takes to get Julia's attention.

"Don't you think we should be going?" Julia remarks. "We don't want to be late, and it's a long trolley ride to the Hurtig and Seamon's New Theater."

The pomp and the ceremonial trappings of Garvey's organization impress Pete, as it does most of Garvey's followers. The pageantry, the parades, the uniforms, the martial music, all that accompanies the UNIA's public events is as compelling as it is dramatic. Even Sunday worship is accentuated by the joyous sounds of youth choirs, brass bands and full choral accompaniment. In addition, the UNIA serves its members' needs to belong, to be a part of something big, something meaningful, something historic. In New York, Garveyites can boast of cooperative grocery stores, restaurants, laundries, garment factories, dress shops, a greeting card company, a millinery, a phonograph record company and a publishing house. Then there is Garvey's crowning achievement, the Black Star Steamship Line. Some of Garvey's more vocal critics declare that the Black Star Line is nothing more than a riverboat steamer that Garvey uses to smuggle whiskey from ships arriving in the New York Harbor to bootleggers. But like all true Garveyites, Pete believes that Garvey leads an association of New Negroes whose goal is to usher in a new social order where black people in the United States and around the world will find their rightful and exalted place among the affairs of men. Garvey's ideals, pageantry, enterprises and music inspire Pete as well as thousands of other Negroes across the United States and around the world. These Negroes pledge their hearts, souls and minds to Garvey's Universal Negro Improvement Association. Yet on this wondrous evening, none of Garvey's pageantry and accomplishments, none of his rousing speeches and exuberant followers, nothing before or afterwards comes as close to the awe-inspiring magic that Pete and Julia experience, along with the cream of Harlem society, when Noble Sissle and Eubie Blake debut their musical production of *Shuffle Along*.

Music, glamor, a meaningful story—*Shuffle Along* has all the ingredients necessary to fill the hearts of the Harlem theatergoers, in need of self-esteem, with joy and gladness. It gives New York's New Negroes—who are continually caricatured as *sambos* and *pickininnies* and belittled as pickpockets and chicken thieves—a thrilling experience and pride in their racial identity. *Shuffle Along* is magical and transformative. It mesmerizes its audience with images of beauty and grace, inspires them with its message of optimism, hope and, above all, it thrills them with the power of love. And in that brief period that Sissle and Blake's production holds its audience spellbound, the Harlem Renaissance is born. For certainly no other event could have inspired so many Negroes to achieve such artistic feats. No one remains unaffected by the experience. Certainly not Pete, nor even Julia. The musical strains, voices and dances so captivate Julia's imagination that she must struggle to remain the selfish, self-centered person she has always been. And, though it will take a long time before she admits it, even to herself, this is the night Julia falls deeply in love with Pete.

To say that Shuffle Along *is an instant hit is an understatement. Not only does Sissle and Blake's production make it to Broadway, it becomes a landmark production for all time. Conceived, composed and directed entirely by Negroes with an all-black cast and music performed by all black musicians,* Shuffle Along *demonstrates that the Negro race is emerging as a cultural entity capable of not only adding to but, in some ways, dominating cultural expressions that all Americans will adopt and value. From the standpoint of the Negro race, it is a triumph. To the proponents of white supremacy,* Shuffle Along *is a surprise. Sissle and Blake open an entirely new and unexpected front in the war of racial domination.*

"I can't remember when I was so thrilled by a show," Nadine gushes.

Julia and Pete join Nadine and Grady at the Kentucky Club, a Greenwich Village nightspot hosting the show's afterparty. The club is a favorite watering hole of Mabel Dodge's group, to which Nadine and her uncle, Max, the editor of the avant-garde *Liberator* newspaper, belong. Dodge has assembled the coterie of literary and artistic intellectuals, from throughout the Eastern seaboard, who have launched America's early 20th century renaissance in literature and culture. Her group—whose members include the founder of the NAACP, William English Walling, playwright Eugene O'Neill, journalist Walter Lippman, and writer Sinclair Lewis—came to Hurtig and Seamon's New Theater to sneer. Carl Van Vechten, the Dodge group's resident Negro expert, remarked, "I hardly expect anything more than a minstrel show with the black faces being real black faces." The Dodge group got a real laugh out of that. But *Shuffle Along* took them by surprise, causing these elitists, who consider themselves arbiters of American culture, to twinge with more than a touch of envy.

Nadine continues her praises. "I can still hear the music. Wasn't it just dreamy, Grady?"

Grady Jones isn't paying Nadine much attention. He is too absorbed with his plans for Pete and Julia. Now Grady has Pete where he wants him. "Julia's got his nose wide open," the Army's somewhat unwilling spy thinks to himself. "The old boy just can't help himself. Time for Plan B."

Julia sits at the table like an ice princess, her face frozen into a look of permanent boredom, as if she is a member of some noble family making a rare social appearance among the hoi polloi. The men pay homage to her with their eyes, with the winks and nods they give each other, with the way they glower at Pete as if his presence is keeping Julia outside of their reach. Grady watches Julia, calculating his payoff, thinking how fortunate he is to control a woman every man in Harlem covets.

The Kentucky Club is jam-packed with celebrities. The *Shuffle Along* cast prances about, seeing and being seen. Blake and Sissle are being feted with toasts and speeches. So are the musical's writers, Flournoy Miller and Aubry Lyles. More cast members arrive fashionably late. A roar goes up when Florence Mills, now an instant star, makes her entrance. Chorus girls, including the fifteen-year-old Josephine Baker, rush about, exciting the crowd even more. But all this excitement notwithstanding, eyes from all around the Kentucky Club stay glued to the ravishing West Indian beauty sitting at Max Eastman's table.

Julia flutters her green eyes about, never settling on any one person, giving each of her many admirers the illusion that she waits just for him, and him alone. It is her white gown, Grady decides. Without any other adornment, it gives the illusion of virginal purity, like a vestal virgin dedicated to Jupiter. Would-be suitors, black and white, maneuver about her table. Each tries to get a better look at the apparition that seems to be some figment of his own imagination, too beautiful to be real. But Julia is real all right, and she plays the crowd like Cleopatra played Julius Caesar and Mark Antony.

"Didn't you think the music was dreamy, Grady?" Nadine asks once again. "I just loved *Love Will Find a Way*. I can still hear the music." And, enticed by alcohol, Nadine begins to hum to herself. She is only slightly off key, but it is enough to annoy everyone else at the table.

Julia turns to Pete and, mimicking her hostess, asks, "Didn't you think the music was just dreamy?"

Pete is surprised. It is one of the few things Julia says to him all evening. He feels more like Julia's chaperone than her date. But when she turns those green eyes to fully gaze at him, her honey-colored skin accentuating the red blush of her full lips, Pete feels like an elevator has just dropped and his heart has landed in the pit of his stomach.

But as much as Julia tries to hide it from herself as well as from Pete, *Shuffle Along* affected her as much as anyone else. When Florence Mills, as Jessie, sang *Everything Reminds Me of You*, Julia trembled ever so slightly. Pete had felt it, leaving Julia embarrassed and angry at her own rebellious feelings.

But Pete is under no illusion. Even if Julia is moved, Pete knows her feelings are certainly not for him; she's probably thinking of Grady, at least, that's what Pete believes. Pete reproaches his own feelings for this woman, which seem to have deprived him of his manhood and self-control. "Why did I go along with this farce in the first place?" he asks himself, wishing he were back at Liberty Hall with the good, solid black folks building a new society for the New Negro.

Pete realizes his anger is misplaced. The woman is drop-dead gorgeous; he can't help the way he feels. Pete has fallen in love and he is enough of a man to admit it. He turns to gaze fully into Julia's lovely green eyes, those eyes that mock him and his feelings, and in his most debonair voice, replies, "I don't know whether or not the music was dreamy, but I am certain that, from this night on, whenever I hear it, I will always dream of you."

Pete's remark takes Julia totally by surprise. His look, his mocking smile, his penetrating stare all take Julia's breath away. Something inside her thrills to his voice: the certainty of his response, the look in his eyes, the power of his presence. Something inside her gives way, and Julia feels an involuntary quiver of excitement. And for a second time, Julia sees Pete as the man that can make her own dreams come true.

"Rubbish," she shouts silently to herself. The moment passes, as rare moments of candor and honesty often do. Once more Julia directs her attention elsewhere.

Members of the band begin arriving. Pete recognizes some as former members of Jimmy Europe's 369th Infantry Jazz Band. The Hellfighters not only played music in France, but fought and died with the famous Fighting 69th. After the war, a disgruntled Hellfighter shot Jimmy Europe. Supposedly the bandleader was killed over a wage dispute, but Pete hears that Jimmy Europe's death was an assassination. Once again, Pete recalls the strange disappearances of his two wartime buddies. A lot of the Negro servicemen returning from Europe have begun to disappear and die under mysterious circumstances. Some of the musicians come over to Pete's table. Before they can say anything, one of the white guests, who had been staring at Julia all evening, barges up, drink in hand and, still staring at Julia, blurts out, "Nadine, I simply must meet this ravishing Negress."

"Oh, Carl," Nadine chirps. "It's so nice to see you. Julia, this is Carl Van Vechten. And Carl, this is Julia Duncan and her escort . . ."

But Nadine does not finish the introductions. Carl waves her off, saying, "Don't bother, don't bother." Then reaching out his arm across Pete, the self-assured white man grabs Julia's arm and pulls her out of her seat, saying, "Come dear, there are people here just dying to meet you." Before Pete or anyone else can say a word, Carl has whisked Julia off into the crowd.

Pete feels like he's been shot in the gut and his life is oozing away. But it's not his life that is oozing away, it's his pride, his dignity, his manhood. In their place, Pete finds something else. He finds rage. Pete had prepared himself for Julia's eventual return to Grady Jones, or possibly her choosing some other light-skinned Negro. But Pete was not prepared to have this pasty-faced white man come up and grab Julia as if it was his right, and to see her not offer any resistance. Pete is furious. And his rage will stay with him for a very long time.

Chapter Five

During the opening decades of the twentieth century, a cultural renais-
sance radiates throughout the Western world, ridiculing, satirizing and
challenging the fundamental concepts of the existing world order. Art
and literature begin breaking out of the constraints imposed by archaic
religious concepts and intolerant social values; scientific discovery pro-
claims the need for a new division of labor; democratic pretensions open
up the possibilities for individualism and self-expression. Nowhere does
this renaissance express itself more fully than in the voices of an idle class
whose artistic gestures extol the need for new freedoms. These idlers
vainly attempt to justify their own worthless existence by mocking ev-
eryone and everything. Nowhere is this idle class better represented than
at Mabel Dodge's famous Fifth Avenue apartment, near Washington
Square, where the Greenwich Village bohemian movement functions as
an agent of change and reaction.

"America is all machinery, money-making and factories," Dodge
says. "It's ugly, ugly, ugly." So she gathers together creative intellectuals
who will free America from the clutches of the economic and political
vampires gorging themselves with the blood, sweat and tears of the un-
fortunate masses. These bohemians, as they are called, decry the process
of industrialization that transforms citizens into unthinking, unfeeling
zombies, barren of mind and soul, unaware of their own existence and
unable to resist the equally false cries of religious superstition and pa-
triotic warmongering. These left-leaning commentators predict the dire
consequences awaiting a society, regulated by market forces, that cre-
ates thousands of orphan children, homeless and destitute, so that a few
dozen industrialists might luxuriate in wanton opulence.

Dodge gathers an eclectic assortment of thinkers and artists, who discuss the efficacy of radical political activity. Meanwhile, government agents eavesdrop on the radical conversations. Many of the most important intelligence and national security assessments gathered for the State Department, the Justice Department and Military Intelligence, even before the Great War, owe their existence to discussions held at Dodge's soirees.

"Private, we gave you a simple assignment," Captain Hansen says in a low growl. "You were supposed to get information about Garvey's African Legion a month ago."

"Yessir," Grady replies with military precision. Captain Hansen is a spit and polish officer. Grady learns that the more spit and polish he shows, the more Captain Hansen likes it.

"Well, private, where is my information?"

"Sir, the information is being compiled and being forwarded to your office, sir!"

Hansen doesn't like working with enlisted men, and he especially doesn't like working with Negroes. Privately, he doubts that any information this darkie provides will be of any of value. At West Point, Hansen learned that the Negro has little of what the Army considers intelligence. Hansen frequently reminded his superiors of this fact.

"Captain," he was told, "your job is to recruit assets from among the coloreds and not to question orders."

"Yessir."

"These coloreds need to be trained. They need to be trained to follow orders. When the time comes, we're going to need them. What you're doing is drilling them. You can't get soldiers to charge a machine gun before you train them to march on a parade ground, can you?"

"No sir," Hansen replied.

"Neither can you get these people to betray their own without training."

Hansen follows orders. "When can I expect to see your report, private?"

"I am working on it, sir," Grady replies.

It isn't as if Grady has any qualms about getting the information military intelligence wants. If those Garveyites have anything to hide, well, so much the worse for them. It isn't his business. But Grady knows that there is no way he can just go up to Pete and ask him about his business. Pete is too smart for that. Pete was the one that everyone trusted over in France. He took care of all the fellows. During the war, the Army didn't like Pete; he was too race conscious. He knew what the white boy was planning before it ever happened. Pete never even wanted to get laid by one of those French mademoiselles. He is on a completely different level and there is no going up to him and asking about this Garvey business. That is why Grady came up with the plan to use Julia. She will do anything for him. And Pete is just the type to fall dopey in love with someone like her. I'm going to get all the information I need, Grady believes, I just need that Van Vechten out of the way. What a thing to have happened. Julia was supposed to make Pete jealous by having a drink with Van Vechten, not leave with him. Now Grady has to stall Hansen to get more time.

"That's not good enough," the Captain roars out. "Report back to Lieutenant Smitz for reorientation, immediately."

"But sir," Grady says weakly.

"Immediately, private!"

"Yessir."

After another two weeks of reorientation, Grady finds himself back in Nadine's apartment. "You know I love you to death, Grady," she pouts. "Why don't you let me help you?"

Just as Hansen doesn't trust Grady, neither does Grady trust Nadine. There's something about her, something secretive. No, that isn't it. Something alien, something . . . Grady can never put his finger on it. But the more time he spends with Nadine, the less Grady knows about her. Nadine is too smug, too secure, as if she is above it all, as if nothing can touch her. Moreover, she takes Grady for granted. She anticipates his every move, even his every thought, as if he were some lower form of existence, some pet. The whole scene is bizarre. He always feels out of sorts, like he is a third-class passenger on a luxury liner who's hobnobbing on the first-class deck, and the ship is the *Titanic*. Grady often considers giving Nadine a good beating to knock some of the smugness off of her face, but he knows that would be a one-way ticket to the gallows. So Grady decides to make the best of a bad situation. Besides which, being with Nadine has certain advantages.

Grady has his own apartment in the Village, he wears nice clothes, he has access to transportation, and he has plenty of pocket change.

Nadine is Grady's link to the government's intelligence community. She also comforts him. And Nadine knows how to comfort Grady just the way he likes to be comforted. Also, Nadine is *white*. What else could Grady want? Every once in awhile, Grady smokes a little reefer; it helps get his head straight, like now, when he is trying to shake the effects of Lieutenant Smitz's reorientation session. Nadine even supplies that. But Grady worries. Sooner or later, if he doesn't give Hansen what he wants, the captain will find someone who will, and then that will be the end of Grady Jones.

"I just don't know what to do," Grady admits to Nadine. "I haven't seen Julia in a couple of weeks."

"Why don't you let me help you?" Nadine stretches out on her bed, completely naked, her white body glistening with moisture. "Someone in Mabel Dodge's group ought to be able to tell you whatever it is you need to know. I can contact them for you."

"The Mabel Dodge group," Grady says. "Who are they?"

"They're the most important people around," Nadine replies. "Van Vechten is a member, that's probably why he grabbed Julia."

"Oh, him!" Grady's eyes narrow and he starts tugging at his chin.

"It wouldn't hurt for you to get to know *him*," Nadine suggests.

"Why?" Grady asks. "What can he do for me?"

"Because you don't want to be on the wrong side of those people; they're the ones who are rounding up all the Communists."

"What's that mean to me?"

"Let me tell you a little story," Nadine answers.

"Okay," Grady sighs, lighting up a cigarette. "I hope it's not too long."

Ignoring Grady's remark, Nadine begins. "Mabel Dodge came to New

York before the war. She was bored with her very wealthy husband, a Boston merchant, I believe."

"How long before the war?" Grady asks.

"About 1913," Nadine replies. "Now let me finish the story, will you?"

"Okay."

"Mabel came to Greenwich Village, looking for the 'Bohemian Movement.'"

"Bohemian Movement?" Grady interrupts again. "What's that?"

"It's a movement where anything goes. Bohemians believe they can live a free lifestyle, where anyone can have sex with anyone else regardless of who's married to whom."

"Like you and me?" Grady asks, trying to keep a straight face.

The bohemians, like Mabel Dodge herself, are attracted to New York by the sex. Indeed, the bohemians of Greenwich Village believe in "free love" between married and unmarried partners, between married partners who are not married to each other and between partners of the same sex. Bohemians experiment having sex with multiple partners; these often degenerate into orgies. The bohemian lifestyle encourages open promiscuity and homosexuality. The bohemians include some of America's most avant-garde personalities in the arts and letters as well as in the social and political movements.

Upon her arrival in Manhattan, Dodge joins the recently reconstituted Liberal Club. The Liberal Club is an old New York institution, but when it relocates to its new Macdougal Street location, off Washington Square and within blocks of Dodge's Fifth Avenue apartment, it becomes the hub for the emerging bohemian movement spurred on by unorthodox women who flaunt their unorthodox behavior. Emma Goldman, Max Eastman, Jack London, Upton Sinclair, Lincoln Steffens, and Sinclair Lewis all belong. And when she applies, the Liberal Club immediately welcomes the rich and raunchy Dodge into its ranks.

Blessed with a talent for throwing great parties, Dodge plunges into the spirit of bohemianism with wild abandon. Her apartment becomes more popular than the Liberal Club headquarters. Dodge finds sexual freedom, becoming a companion and a great admirer of the anarchist Emma Goldman. Goldman's lover, Ben Reitman, then takes Hutchins Hapgood as his homosexual partner, while Alameda Sperry, a lesbian acquaintance of Reitman, frequents Dodge's soirees hoping to sleep with Goldman as well. Goldman reads love letters written to her by Reitman at Dodge's parties. The letters, filled with graphic details and sexual expressions, reveal the lurid activities for which the bohemian movement becomes known.

Edna St. Vincent Millay, whom everyone calls Vincent, becomes a regular at Dodge's parties. With the publication of her poem "Renascence" in a 1912 anthology, Vincent becomes a celebrity at age 20. She begins having a series of affairs with prominent men from New York's social elite, including Edmund Wilson. Vincent becomes addicted to making men fall in love with her. She enhances Dodge's reputation as a party giver with the question "With whom will Vincent sleep tonight?" An ever-widening circle of celebrities make Dodge's salon the place to be, attracting the likes of Eugene O'Neill, Carl Van Vechten, J.C. Stokes, William English Walling and the enigmatic Jack Reed.

Jack Reed was a fixture in Greenwich Village's bohemian community even before Dodge's arrival. He is a big man with powerful muscles and a quick temper. Though professing pacifism, Reed is known as a brawler and only too eager for a fight. And that is not his only contradiction. While haranguing anyone who will listen about the plight of the worker, Reed has the unsettling habit of looking away from the person or group he is addressing. Reed seems incapable of looking a person in the eyes, as if he is terrified that, somehow, someone might peer into his soul.

Walter Lippman, Lincoln Steffens and Max Eastman are Reed's close friends. In 1913, Reed, along with his friends, joins the Young Socialists, and starts to publish The Masses *magazine. The same year, Reed becomes involved in the long and bloody I.W.W.-led strike of silk workers in Paterson, New Jersey. Reed is jailed for a short time. After his release, Reed directs a mass pageant that he claims will benefit the striking silk workers. The pageant is held in Madison Square Garden and includes more than 1,000 of the strikers, with speeches by I.W.W. organizers Bill Haywood and Elizabeth Gurley Flynn. In front of a great painted canvas depicting a mill building, the pageant shows workers going to and from the mill, and then, during the strike, the workers begin picketing and the police start clubbing and the union leaders continue exhorting and the people are dying, all in grandiose and heroic magnitude. While Reed puts on the pageant, Dodge becomes his close companion, collaborator and lover.*

Even as the pageant is being well attended by the downtown crowd, Elizabeth Gurley Flynn complains that Reed's play is destroying worker unity and diverting worker attention from the strike.

"The first scabs got into the Paterson mills while workers trained for the pageant," Flynn says. "Up to that time, no one dared cross our picket lines. We were in control. But while a thousand of our most dedicated members are down in Madison Square Garden, the bosses bring scabs inside the mill."

No one ever says that Reed, the first American to become a genuine Communist Party hero, deliberately sabotages the Paterson workers' strike. But the workers receive none of the money Reed promises. And when the Paterson strike begins to crumble, Reed and his millionaire Fifth Avenue mistress, Dodge, leave New York on a luxurious first-class ocean liner for Europe . . . without telling the strikers.

"There must be a point to all of this history," Grady says.

"Yes, there is a point," Nadine replies, "And you'd better try to get it."

"Okay, what is it?" Grady asks.

"Have you ever heard of J. Edgar Hoover?" Nadine asks.

"No, I haven't."

"In 1917, the attorney general of the United States gave Hoover the responsibility of gathering evidence on 'revolutionary and ultra-revolutionary groups': socialists, communists, and anarchists. On the seventh of November, 1919, Hoover has over 10,000 suspected communists and anarchists arrested in twenty-three different cities."

"This must be very interesting to someone," Grady yawns, "but . . ."

"In order to round up these people," Nadine continues, "Hoover creates a card index with the names of 450,000 people suspected of left-wing or radical views; 60,000 are identified as active subversives."

Nadine watches Grady to see if he understands the significance of any of this. Grady doesn't have a clue. "Do you know how Hoover got all of those names?" she asks quietly.

"No, I don't," Grady says, "but I'm sure you're going to tell me."

"Hoover is a bohemian and a member of Dodge's group," Nadine explains quietly. "He is a homosexual and likes to have sex with boys."

"Okay, so what?"

"So, those names came from the wobblies, the socialists, the communists and every other left-wing group that Jack Reed and his friends, including Carl Van Vechten, can get their hands on."

Nadine takes a cigarette from a handsome silver cigarette case, giving Grady an opportunity to evaluate the information she has shared with him. But she can tell that he just doesn't get it.

"Do you know who Hoover went after first?" Nadine asks with the dry sarcasm of someone trying to teach a child to read.

"Not a clue."

"Emma Goldman," Nadine says. "And what do you think happened to Jack Reed?"

Grady just looks bored.

"After returning from his European trip with Dodge, he traveled to Russia to be feted as a hero. Reed died of typhus in Moscow."

Nadine continues to watch the same bored look on Grady's face. She pulled the switch but the lights just didn't turn on. After awhile, deciding to forgo all subtlety, Nadine says, "Look, Walling sends his intelligence on the NAACP to the Justice Department through the Dodge group. Possibly he can help you get information on Garvey."

"Who is Walling?" Grady asks without enthusiasm.

"William English Walling is one of those southern patricians who claims to have seen the light. He's like J. G. Graham Stokes, the millionaire socialist," Nadine says.

"This is not going to be another long story, is it?"

"Walling is a descendant of a slave-owning family and is interested in protecting his status. So now he has become a leader in the socialist movement. But more importantly for you, Walling is the chairman of the NAACP executive committee."

"Why is that important for me?" Grady asks.

"Walling used to be a supporter of Booker T. Washington, but Washington's economic radicalism alarmed him. Walling was especially concerned over Washington and his followers purchasing property in the North in cities like New York. Walling chartered the NAACP to give him and his fellow aristocrats a means for steering the colored community away from economic activities. Booker T. Washington was one of Garvey's sponsors. So I'm certain that Walling is willing to help you get the information you need."

"How do I get the information from Walling?" Grady asks.

Nadine smiles at her lover. He is certainly very naïve, she thinks to herself. "Well darling, you don't. Mabel Dodge doesn't care for Negroes. Your friend, Van Vechten, has been the only one able to convince Mabel to admit Negroes to any of her parties, and they are entertainers. Van Vechten is developing a group of acceptable Negroes."

"Acceptable Negroes!" Grady says. "What are acceptable Negroes?"

"Why, Negroes like you, darling," Nadine says, blowing cigarette smoke in his direction.

"Okay, okay," Grady says. He has neither the patience nor the tools to become an efficient intelligence agent. "So how do I get the information?"

"Don't worry, Max is a member of the group. He'll help you. Trust me."

Several days later, Nadine and Grady sup at a midtown bistro. One of the advantages Grady enjoys because of his light skin and wavy hair is that the maitre d', who normally wouldn't even consider seating a Negro in his establishment, assumes that Grady is a Latino. Nadine can barely contain herself. "Have you ever heard of the African Blood Brotherhood?" she asks her Latin lover excitedly.

"No," Grady replies.

"Well, you have now, my dear," she says gaily. "And they are about to give you all the information you need about Garvey and his organization."

"Why will they give me this information?" Grady asks suspiciously.

"Oh, they're not going to give it to you," Nadine smiles, "they're going to give it to one of our editors at the *Liberator*."

"The *Liberator*?" Grady says. "So that's how information is passed directly to the government?"

"Not only that," Nadine replies, "there's also a *quid pro quo*."

"A *quid pro quo*?"

"They tell us what they want known and in return they tell us what we want to know."

Once again, Grady realizes that there is a lot more to this than what Nadine is saying. Who is this *we* to whom she continually refers? Grady thinks about asking Nadine, but decides not to. "All I'll get is another long story," he tells himself. And one thing Grady has learned is never to look a gift horse in the mouth. He needs to play along with this intelligence game as if his life depended upon it, which, in fact, it does.

Nadine continues, "We use the *Liberator* to redirect socialist thinking as well as send intelligence information to the Justice and State Departments."

"How does that work?" Grady asks.

"Well, when Spingarn and Walling needed socialist *bona fides* for the NAACP, Max published an article in the *Liberator* by James Weldon Johnson about what the Negro is doing for himself. From then on *real* socialists and others believe that the NAACP is being run by Negroes to help their race instead of by Walling, Spingarn and our group."

"Your group?"

"Yes, our group, dear!" Nadine replies. "Since we gather intelligence for the Justice Department, they trust us to tell your people what we want them to know. That way we can identify loyal coloreds for the government from those Negroes who are likely to be radicals and malcontents. It really works very well. The government identifies those who pose a threat and we identify the ones we can trust."

"Coloreds, Negroes, what's the difference?"

"The British showed us the benefits of separating you Negroes by caste, but it was actually Dr. DuBois who taught us how to do it. Originally, we thought we could put West Indians in leadership positions instead of the Negro Americans. But color works even better, and the benefits, according to Dr. DuBois, is that no more than a tenth—the 'talented tenth' of Negroes—need to be supported with full citizenship rights. When our people learned about his system they jumped at the opportunity. Booker T. Washington had begun flooding the North with all kinds of Negroes, looking to compete for jobs and looking to own property. Look at what is happening in Harlem. We just couldn't control Washington. Anything could happen. In case of a Negro uprising we needed a group of coloreds who we could depend on, people we could trust would always do as they were told no matter what, especially now that over 200,000 Negroes have returned from Europe, *all trained to kill white people.*"

When Grady had completed his orientation in Army intelligence under Lieutenant Smitz, he was ordered to report to Nadine every day without fail. But Grady's natural male chauvinism made him believe that he had seduced Nadine and that she was under his control. Grady slowly begins to realize that he was never in control.

"Am I a part of this process?" he asks.

"You see, darling," Nadine smiles, "I chose you from a number of likely candidates." Nadine rubs her leg against his under the table, unconcerned by onlookers. "But now, since Max has agreed to give you access to the information you want, you need to be off."

"Off? Where?" Grady asks.

"One of our editors, Claude McKay, is going to interview some members of the African Blood Brotherhood today. Maybe you know some of them."

"I doubt it," Grady says. "Who are they?"

"Hubert Harrison, Cyril Briggs . . ."

"No, I don't know them."

"What about Otto Huiswoud, Richard Moore, Grace Campbell?"

"No, not them either."

"What about Domingo? He's our man."

"No, not him either," Grady says.

"Well, no matter," Nadine tells him as she stuffs a piece of filet mignon into her mouth. "You've got an hour to get to the *Liberator*'s offices over on 7th and St. Nicholas. Ask for Claude McKay. You met him that night at the after-party for the cast of *Shuffle Along.*"

Grady nods. He remembers the West Indian gushing all over the white guests at the Kentucky Club.

"He's been told that you will attend the 'Brotherhood' meeting. Don't make any comments or say anything," Nadine instructs. "Do you understand?"

"Yes."

"Just pretend that you're a fly on the wall and you'll do fine," she says. "McKay will ask all the questions. All you have to do is take notes. You can write, can't you?"

Nadine's question is only half in jest.

Grady is ecstatic. The interview with the "Brotherhood" goes exactly as Nadine promises. Grady gets all the information he needs about Garvey's organization. He doesn't even have to write a report—Max Eastman provides McKay with a stenographer. Nadine is even able to give Grady a copy of the original notes.

Nadine suggests that Grady supplement his notes with the transcribed copies. "Don't revise them or make them too literate," she advises. "You don't want the captain to think that you're one of those 'smart niggers,' do you?" She loves chiding him.

But Grady can afford to overlook her sarcasm. He has accomplished his mission and he doesn't care what the white folks, including Nadine, think of his intelligence. The job is done. It doesn't matter to Grady whether this was a test of his ability, his loyalty or his intelligence. The monkey is off of his back. Now he can go back to Nadine's Greenwich Village apartment and celebrate.

Chapter Six

Talk about war being hell, this war beats everything. Caloocan contained 17,000 inhabitants. The 20th Kansas swept through it, and now Caloocan contains not one living native. The village of Maypaja is where our first fight occurred. The village had 5,000 people. Now not one stone remains on top of another but the bodies are stacked up high. War is worse than hell.

The troops are ordered to kill all they can find. I ran off from the hospital where I was on duty and joined the scouts. I didn't cross that ocean not to have some fun. The first one I found was in a house, down on his knees fanning a fire. I pulled my rifle to my shoulder and left him to burn in that fire. I left the house and another one jumped out of a window and ran. I brought him to ground like a jackrabbit. I killed seven that I know of, and one more, I am almost sure of. That evening the boys out in front of our trenches found one with his arm shot off at the shoulder and dead as hell. I had lots of fun that morning.

*Eyewitness Account of the U.S. Army's Suppression
of the Revolt in the Philippines, 1899–1916*

"Private, we're satisfied with your report," Captain Hansen tells Grady, "so that will be all for now."

What the Army intelligence officer does not say is that the Justice Department and J. Edgar Hoover are pleased with Grady's report. Hoover is especially pleased with the information about the African Blood Brotherhood. The Justice Department knew nothing about the organization. On the other hand, Hansen believes Grady is a waste of the Army's time and money. The only way for him to repay his debt is to be swinging from the gallows. But Hansen has his orders.

"What do you think of this?" Hansen asks as he flips Grady's report over to Lieutenant Smitz.

"He still hasn't given us a reliable inside person," Smitz says, looking at Grady's notes. "We need agents. He hasn't given us anyone we can turn." Hansen wants Grady to turn Pete into an informant for Army intelligence.

"You just can't trust them," Hansen sighs.

"I don't know why we are bothering with all of this; why don't get rid of all of them at once?" Smitz grimaces.

"Well, lieutenant, right now, we've got a bunch of niggers around with guns and they know how to use them," Hansen says. "Furthermore, they are organizing. This report says that Garvey's African Legion is drilling right here in New York. What's next, rifle practice?"

"Damn," Smitz swears.

"Watch your language, lieutenant,"

"Sorry, sir, but these niggers just infuriate me. We can put a stop to all of this if we want," Smitz says. "Using Army intelligence officers to coddle them seems a waste of time. If this country is going to be secure for the white race, sooner or later, sir, you know that we're going to have to get rid of them. And that's what we should begin planning right now."

"The brass see it otherwise," Hansen replies. "And right now they're worried about the Bolsheviks, socialists and labor organizers. They're even concerned about the women. They say that they've got enough on their hands without having to deal with a bunch of coons holed up in the tenements of every big city in America *with guns*. I think they're right on this one. You saw the reports on the Chicago incident, a lot more white people died than was reported. They want assets inside these organizations. That way we can control them from inside their groups. We don't want them all to join up with one another, especially now that we've got that coon in the White House."

Smitz nods, becoming somewhat more appreciative of the Army's dilemma. "Boy, if word got out about that, there's no telling what the white people of this country might do."

"Not only that," Hansen observes, "I've heard that he doesn't even deny that he has Negro blood. What if he took a notion to rally all the niggers together? We'd have a real mess on our hands."

Smitz remains silent. Things have really gotten out of hand. But they had dealt with the redskins, hadn't they? They can deal with the coons the same way. Time is on their side. He recalls a speech given by Congressman Lindbergh, the famous aviator's father: *All coons look alike, and, without trying to be original, it is safe to add that all coons act alike. He is the happiest of all the races. The future worries him not in the least. This gay, happy contentment is the strong sustaining influence of the Negro, for it offsets the cloud of race prejudice that holds him down politically and socially. The happy-go-lucky way of the Negro is but evidence of a lower organization. What to do about the Negro is a problem that is practically settled. He will be kept down. There is no question about it. His future is simply to merge into the white race. It may not elevate the white race but it will eventually lift the black.* This sentiment angers Smitz.

"Liberals believe that the Negro problem will take care of itself," Smitz tells himself. "Well it won't. We need to do something before it's too late."

And Smitz knows that the Army brass feel the same way. "It's the damn politicians," he concludes. But the lieutenant decides that he had better keep quiet; his superior has spoken.

"Tell me, Smitz," Hansen asks, "how many of those Garveyites do we have working for us in New York, so far?"

"Ten, sir!" Smitz replies.

"Our orders are to get as many as we can," Hansen states, in a tone that indicates to his subordinate that the discussion is over. "We need a lot more. At this rate, the jigs will have taken over before we can do anything about it. Get on it!"

"Yessir!" Smitz replies. Giving a smart salute, the stocky lieutenant turns about and immediately departs Hansen's office.

Watching the retreating figure of his subordinate, Hansen knows that many agree with Smitz. The American dilemma, the code name for the Negro problem, can be easily solved, they say. But Hansen isn't so certain. These reports are troubling. Negroes drilling and training in fighting units. His job is to not let it get out of hand. But Smitz is right about one thing: everything is getting confused. Right now he has his orders. "Keep an eye on the Garveyites in Harlem; report all their activities to the Justice and State Departments; turn as many of them into assets as you can." Those are his orders. As a West Point graduate, Captain Elmer Hansen knows how to give orders. But no one rises through the military ranks without understanding how to obey them as well.

William Howard Taft is in an expansive mood. Being expansive is not difficult for him since the former president of the United States is enormously large. Being expansive is a problem. Weighing well over 300 pounds, Taft, currently the chief justice of the Supreme Court, the only man in the history of the United States to hold both posts, crams his gigantic body into the great armchair even though the chair has been modified and adjusted especially to fit his bulging frame. Nevertheless, Taft wears an angelic look on his face. His eyes twinkle with merriment. Indeed, his mood is expansive because the master schemer is pleased with how his master plan is unfolding.

Despite his massive size, Taft is not unattractive. Complementing his dimpled chin and rosy cheeks, Taft wears a dashing mustache and keeps his hair well groomed. It is a trick he uses to divert attention away from his enormous head and bulging neck. Taft is a fastidious dresser. His starched wing-collared white shirt, held together by a fashionable cravat complete with a pearl stickpin, contrasts smartly with a striped vest, Prince Albert morning coat, pinstriped trousers and patent leather shoes. Earlier that morning the manicurist, accompanying Taft's personal barber, saw to it that the nails on his pudgy fingers were trimmed neatly and well polished. Someone who doesn't know better could easily mistake Taft for a kindly grandfather, even jolly old Saint Nick, instead of the monster Taft really is. The man who ordered women raped, children murdered and homes burned as part of a master plan for conquering the Philippines and subjugating the Filipino people. The man who conquered the Philippines in order to become president of the United States.

Taft squats behind a great oaken desk finely crafted and inscribed by German masons in the inner sanctum of an office suite located along the same great hall that houses the offices of Arthur Hadley, president of Yale University. As a matter of fact, Taft's office suite occupies a far larger section of the second floor than President Hadley's own suite of offices. Hadley personally orders Taft's desk and oversees the details of its construction. He grants the commissions to a skilled German craftsman whose family lineage is associated with a secret operative lodge that goes back generations, a scion to a medieval guild that served royal monarchs and crowned heads of Europe. The desk is inlaid with leather, gold and precious stones. It is engraved with the insignias and symbols of that secret order, over which Taft reigns as supreme grand master. Inside the desk's secret compartments, Taft keeps, among other things, mementos of his Philippine adventures. One of the mementos, the editorial cartoon from Hearst's *New York Journal* published on May 5th, 1902, concerning the Philippine war, never fails to bring a smile to Taft's face. It reads:

"KILL EVERYONE OVER TEN"

Under these words a firing squad of American soldiers towers over four little Filipino boys, white blindfolds draped over their faces and hands tied behind their backs. An American officer is issuing the command and the firing squad is shooting the Filipino children in the back. This is how Taft, as governor general of the Philippines, concluded the Filipino war and secured the Philippines as an American colony and military base. After concluding his activities, there is no more insurrection in the Philippines, nor will there be for decades to come. Taft's genocide against the Filipino people was worthy of a grand master.

I think I'll go down to the Tomb, Taft says to himself. The cartoon causes Taft to reflect upon what mementos of his Philippine adventures he will leave Yale's Skull and Bones Society. Bonesmen dearly love their trophies, Taft knows, and he wants to bring them something special. Members of Yale's Skull and Bones Society know Taft as Magog. When Taft is in town, he never passes up an opportunity to visit the Society's chambers, known simply as the Tomb. It is the only place where he feels comfortable. The Bonesmen understand his mission and admire his tactics. They understand why he ordered General Smith to "kill them all." Taft is Nietzsche's "blond beast." Taft's role is to regenerate western civilization with the blood of its victims. He and his fellow Bonesmen are the inheritors of the mantle of Arian supremacy. Never may they shirk their responsibility for upholding white rule *"über alles."* Taft loves to regale members of his sinister secret society with tales of his exploits since he is not merely another Bonesman, he is the Tomb's exalted grand master.

Taft's father, Alphonso Taft, had been a charter member of the Skull and Bones Society as well as a close personal friend of William Russell, the society's founder. Russell received his charter in Germany from the Teutonic Knights. The charter directs Russell to establish an American scion of the Knights' Death Head's Society, a society dedicated to the furtherance of worldwide Arian supremacy. Originally, Russell calls his society the Brotherhood of Death; however, the merging of the Scottish rite with Tudor rule in England paves the way for Russell's society to use the name long associated with the international Arian brotherhood, the Skull and Bones, otherwise known as the Jolly Roger. When Russell calls together the original group of Bonesmen, including Taft's father, he adopts the secret number 322 for his society, signifying that it is the second chapter of the Brotherhood of Death formed in 1832. By the time Taft takes charge of this bloody organization, members of the Skull and Bones have outstripped even Germany's Brotherhood of Death in the execution of bloody deeds. In the Tomb, Bonesmen boast of the lives taken, the property expropriated and trophies claimed, like the head of Geronimo. In the Tomb, Taft becomes Magog, master and guardian of graves.

Suddenly the door to his inner sanctum swings open, forcing Taft to set aside his reveries. The secret service agent who serves as Taft's personal valet ushers in the chief justice's visitor, a squat young man with determined bulldog jowls and bulging frog eyes. Over the years, this man's face will strike fear in hearts of many, but now it is bowed in deference and awe to the massive mound of bulging flesh that is Taft. Flashing the familiar sign and making the required obeisance signifying his utter submission, the young man takes the chair indicated by a nod from his supreme grand master.

"Ah, Edgar," Taft beams at his guest, "have you brought me something interesting?"

J. Edgar Hoover reaches into the satchel cuffed to his wrist and withdraws a parcel of government documents marked Top Secret. Behind his desk, Taft's eyes twinkle in anticipation.

"Yes, most worshipful master," Hoover replies. "Here are the reports that you requested from military intelligence, the State Department, as well as from the Justice Department."

"Excellent," Taft says. "Now we will see if we can't get your department back to doing what it was originally created to do: defending the white race and America from its enemies, both foreign and domestic."

"Yessir," Hoover agrees enthusiastically.

"So what do we have here, Edgar?"

"As you requested, I have compiled information about this Negro leader, Marcus Garvey, and his organization, called the Universal Negro Improvement Association."

"Ah, our UNIA," Taft repeats contentedly.

"Yessir, they claim to have a million members here in the United States and 400,000,000 around the world."

"Wonderful," Taft says.

"You are pleased, sir?" Hoover asks. "I thought you would be concerned."

"Concerned?" the big man asks. "No, I am not concerned. I am surprised that our plans have gone so well."

"Gone well, sir?" Hoover stutters, thinking that the supreme master must be overly tired. "How can you be pleased with a nigger organization that intends to disrupt our plans to keep them in their place?"

"That's just the point, Edgar," Taft says pleasantly. "That organization has grown precisely because of our activities in defense of the race. Let me share something with you. Garvey approached our brothers in the Anglo-Saxon Clubs of America and applied for membership."

Astonished, Hoover manages to stutter, "They refused him, of course?"

"To the contrary, Edgar," Taft chuckles. "They accepted him."

"But that would mean that . . ."

"That's right," the big man laughs, "that would make Marcus Garvey a member of the Ku Klux Klan!"

J. Edgar Hoover is speechless. He knows that the supreme grand master likes making deft moves among the lower races. When Taft left the Philippines, the Filipinos hailed Taft as a hero, at least that is what the American press reported, even after he virtually exterminated them over a sixteen-year period. But Garvey a Klansman! Hoover manages to ask, in as respectful a tone as possible, "But why, most all-knowing sovereign, do we want that nigger in the Klan?"

"Because, Edgar, it will further our interests."

The future head of the FBI knows that the supreme grand master speaks the truth. The supreme grand master is infallible, just as for Catholics the Pope of Rome is infallible. And just like Catholics, who have maintained the Pope's infallibility for millennia, it is up to loyal masons to make certain that the supreme grand master remains infallible.

Hoover must wait patiently as his grand master's head lolls back and a slight bit of drool trickles from the corner of his mouth. Those close to Taft expect him to doze off in the middle of a conversation, even in mid-sentence. Taft is afflicted with narcolepsy, otherwise known as sleeping sickness. The malady is brought about by his enormous weight. Hoover will wait all day if need be, but within minutes Taft is awake once again. He wipes the corners of his mouth with a lace handkerchief and resumes the discussion, as if nothing had happened.

"Where was I?" Taft asks his young protégé. "Ah, yes. Do you remember that as president, I appointed Edward Douglass White as chief justice of the Supreme Court?"

"Yes, master," Hoover replies, "but he was a former Confederate soldier and the head of a local Klavern."

"But did you know that White was a Jesuit-trained Roman Catholic before he joined the Klan and a member of the Knights of Columbus as well?"

"No, I didn't," Hoover admits.

"And I could not have made a better choice," Taft muses. "Otherwise I wouldn't be the Chief Justice today." With that, the supreme grand master breaks out into such a rumble of laughter that tears pour from his eyes. It is obviously an inside joke to which the young Hoover is not privy. "So you see, Edgar," Taft continues, "you must always be willing to be unconventional and unpredictable. Read your Machiavelli, my boy."

"Yes, your supreme worship," Hoover agrees dutifully.

"Now with respect to Garvey," Taft chuckles, "you have said it yourself, the concern is 'niggers with guns,' isn't that right?"

"Yes," Hoover replies.

"As a matter of fact, didn't you report that some of those niggers during some of our activities, in Chicago and in Washington, in particular, started to shoot back?"

"Yes," Hoover replies again, "but I don't see how that . . ."

"Show me in your report where those people shooting back belong to Garvey's 'Universal Negro Improvement Association,'" Taft says. "Go on, show me."

But Hoover knows that he can't. As many UNIA divisions as there are across the country and for all of Garvey's rhetoric, no member of the UNIA has ever fought against Klan raids.

"And the beautiful thing about this organization is that the more the Klan attacks them, the more of those niggers join Garvey's organization," Taft gloats. "So why wouldn't we want him as a member?" The oversized grand master starts to laugh. It begins with an infectious chuckle that is accompanied by a silent trembling of his huge paunch. Then a gigantic grin slowly spreads across his face until it contorts and twists as if the big man is in actual pain. A gulp escapes his mouth and then another and another until the chuckles give way to such waves of laughter that even the normally reserved and humorless J. Edgar Hoover cannot resist. Hoover cackles, but his is a dry, stuffy, humorless laugh without merriment or joy.

"And what does it really matter?" Taft asks Hoover. "Just because you are a mason doesn't mean that you can enter any lodge, does it?"

"No sir," Hoover answers.

"Even niggers have their Prince Hall lodges, but they aren't able to gain entrance to any Scottish Rite lodge, are they? They don't even have access to the lodges belonging to the operative masons working in trade unions. As a matter of fact, a nigger has a better chance of getting into a speculative lodge than he does getting into an operational one. Isn't that true?" Without pausing, Taft goes on, "And yet they still stay on the level and on the square, which serves our purposes. Look how well things turned out in Florida. Where was that place where the niggers tried to vote? Ocoee?"

"Yessir."

"I understand that one of the colored masons in Rosewood flashed the sign asking if anyone would help the widow's son. Do you know what happened?" Taft asks his young seneschal.

Hoover shakes his head.

"One of the Klansmen told him, 'You're right, boy, you're in a heap of trouble!'"

Hoover laughs at that, even without being prompted.

"And then they hung the nigger and burned down his Prince Hall lodge. They burned down the whole nigger town." Taft breaks out into another one of his infectious laughs with tears running down his face. "You know what they call those colored masons down in Florida now, Edgar?" Taft gets out between his guffaws.

"No sir," Hoover replies.

"*Niggers!*"

Hoover joins in the laughter. They laugh so hard that tears pour down their cheeks and their sides ache.

It takes several minutes for Hoover to regain his composure. But when he does, the future FBI director fully realizes the significance of the supreme grand master's logic. Hoover admires his teacher's wisdom and foresight. And, once again, he realizes the great honor that Taft has bestowed on him in explaining the proper approach to solving the great American dilemma. Hoover vows to show himself worthy of his supreme grand master's blessings. Taft turns his attention back to the documents. After awhile, he asks the Justice Department executive, "How many ships does Garvey's Steamship Line say that they have now?"

"Four," Hoover replies, "The *Yarmouth, Kanawha, Shadyside* and *Phyllis Wheatley.*"

"Excellent! We must encourage Negroes to support Garvey's 'Back to Africa' plans."

"So while our friends burn these niggers out of their homes, they join Garvey's UNIA and he takes them back to Africa," Hoover nearly shouts out, believing that he now fully understands the master plan.

"Not exactly, Edgar," Taft says. "Our friends with colonies in Africa will not like that. Besides, Garvey really doesn't have any ships, at least none capable of crossing the Atlantic." Then picking up some of the papers on his desk, Taft says in a dismissive tone, "You may leave your reports. Keep in touch, young man. You're doing a fine job; I believe that you have a sterling career ahead of you." Taft turns his full attention to the reports on his desk. Hoover jumps from his chair, bows respectfully and, giving the required sign, quickly departs the wainscoted office. Magog, dread overseer of the Aryan "brotherhood of death," all powerful exalted ruler over the Knights Templar, the former president of the United States and current chief justice of the Supreme Court, contemplates the next step in his campaign to impose white supremacy upon the world.

PART TWO

*After the European war, during the "red summer of 1919," whites in-
vade Negro communities across the nation intending to put the "niggers" back in their place. The Ku Klux Klan's answer to the question,
"How You Gonna Keep Them Down on the Farm After They've Seen
Paree?" is with fire, ropes and bullets.*

*In July, several white men are shot in Longview, Texas, attempting to
lynch a black schoolteacher. The teacher angers whites when he sends
the Chicago* Defender *a picture and description of another Longview
lynching that took place a month earlier. After the shooting, whites invade Longview's colored neighborhood, burning down homes, lynching
residents and publicly—and fatally—whipping the black principal of the
segregated school.*

*The same month, whites drown a twelve-year-old black boy in Lake
Michigan for swimming in the "whites only" section. For thirteen days
whites and blacks attack each other all over the city. An organized
white mob invades black neighborhoods and firebombs over a thousand
homes. Putting up a heroic defense, blacks make many whites pay for
the outrage with their lives.*

*In Washington, D.C., mobs of white soldiers, sailors and marines
engage in a three-day orgy of burning and killing in Negro neighborhoods. On the third day, when the white servicemen vowed to "burn
down every nigger's house in the city," blacks retaliate, killing a number
of white servicemen. With Negro resistance stiffening, military and civilian authorities halt the invasion.*

*In Knoxville, Tennessee, a white woman falls while running, causing
a fatal concussion. A rumor circulates among whites that she was trying*

to escape a black man. Whites invade Knoxville's Negro neighborhood, killing and burning at will. Federal troops, called in to restore order, use machine guns to shoot down unarmed Negro residents while the white rioters burn down their homes.

In Omaha, Nebraska, a mob burns down the courthouse to grab a black man accused of raping a white woman. He is shot over a thousand times while being dragged through the streets. His mutilated and disfigured corpse is hung at the busiest intersection of town. For the rest of the night, whites ran riot throughout Omaha's colored neighborhood, beating Negroes and burning down their homes.

In Elaine, Arkansas, black sharecroppers, having been denied their wages for over a year, meet to discuss how to force the landlords to pay them. The local sheriff and his deputies break into the meeting and begin flailing away at the sharecroppers with horsewhips. The Negroes resist, and during the melee, one of the sheriff's deputies is killed. Whites from all over Arkansas initiate a full-scale riot, shooting every Negro on sight and burning down their homes until their fury exhausts itself. After the riot, Negro sharecroppers who had not been killed are hunted down and forced to stand trial for the death of the white deputy. A white jury finds twenty Negro sharecroppers guilty and the state of Arkansas hangs them.

In response to the whites' orgy of violence, Negroes all over the country begin to organize themselves into self-defense groups. The African Blood Brotherhood recruits over five thousand Negro ex-servicemen from all over the country, many of whom saw action in the European war. The African Blood Brotherhood figures prominently in organizing resistance to the white invasion and bombing of the Negro community known as Greenwood located in Tulsa, Oklahoma.

Chapter Seven

"Congratulations, Commander Jenkins, we are pleased to offer you a position with the *Negro World*."

Although Hudson Price, the associate editor of Garvey's *Negro World*, offers Pete the job, it is the UNIA civil service commission that reviews his qualifications. All those seeking work with Garvey's Universal Negro Improvement Association and its subsidiaries like the *Negro World* weekly newspaper must undergo a thorough screening by the UNIA commission. Every detail of an applicant's personal life, religious beliefs and political affiliations is scrutinized. The Garveyites screen out infiltrators and agents, or so they believe. But, as in most organizations attempting to challenge white supremacy, spies are everywhere and occupy the most important positions inside the UNIA. These agents insulate the Association's rank and file from its leadership.

Pete is an exception. The battle between the various Negro organizations is beginning to heat up, especially within the pages of the major Negro weeklies. T. Thomas Fortune's venerable *New York Age*, now under the control of Fred Moore, criticizes Garvey's program at every opportunity, while in issue after issue of *Crisis* magazine, DuBois hammers at Garvey personally as well as his program. But on the streets, the battle takes a nasty turn. Garvey's competitors seize entire deliveries of the *Negro World* from drop-off points and dump them into the Harlem River. Newsstands above 110th Street are attacked and Garvey's papers are destroyed. Pete's record as a commander in Garvey's African Legion and a UNIA policeman brings him to the attention of Hudson Price, so when William Ferris, the *Negro World*'s managing editor, decides to hire a security chief, Commander Peter Jenkins is high on the list of candidates.

Pete is overwhelmed. This is an opportunity he never expected to come his way.

"You'll earn $25 per week," Price tells Pete, "and you'll have access to the Royal African Motor Corps."

Twenty-five per week is almost twice the $60 per month he earns as a messenger for the bank, most of which goes to trolley and subway fares.

"So, Commander Jenkins, when can you start? We want you to start guarding our delivery trucks as well as our newspapers as soon as possible."

"Well, sir, I will have to give Mr. Cronin at the bank notice," Pete replies, hoping they understand his position.

"How much notice do you think he will require, commander?" Price asks with a frown. "We need to fill this position immediately. Every day we delay, the *World* loses newspapers and the Association loses money."

"I understand, sir," Pete replies. "I'm certain that Mr. Cronin will accept two weeks notice."

"*Two weeks*!" exclaims Price. "We need you now, commander."

"Yessir," Pete replies instantly. He doesn't want to lose this job. On the other hand, he feels some obligation to the bank. Cronin always treated Pete fairly. Pete knows that when he leaves, Cronin will not have any dependable messengers remaining. Who will deliver the bank's high-priority packages, Pete asks himself. Pete doesn't consider the fact that if he had been tardy completing any of his routes or failed to make any of his urgent deliveries on time, Cronin would have fired Pete without any notice. Still, Pete feels obligated to give Cronin and the bank some notice. In reality, Cronin and the bank will adjust to Pete's departure just fine. There are plenty of faithful darkies who would deliver their mail. It is Pete's own sense of self-importance that makes him believe he is indispensable.

"We expect you to report here for work next Monday, commander," the *World's* associate editor says with finality. "Otherwise we will offer the position to one of our other candidates."

"Yessir," Pete replies immediately. "I'll be here, sir."

When Pete informs Cronin of his departure, his boss shakes his hand in congratulations. "Pete, you've been one of my best messengers," the old Irishman says. "I wish you the best of luck." When Pete picks up his final pay envelope, he discovers that Cronin has given him a week's extra pay.

Pete knows absolutely nothing about the *Negro World* and the newspaper business. Learning the job means starting from scratch, from the beginning. Pete must learn that the newspaper business means composing, printing and circulating a newspaper. Even though he is hired specifically to eliminate the vandalism and destruction of the newspapers that are distributed to the newsstands and left at drop-off points for the paperboys, once Pete is on the payroll, everyone—the editors, writers, advertisers as well as circulation—makes a special claim on his time. He is asked to run errands, deliver copy, do proofreading and editing, ink rollers and assemble newspapers. In time, Pete becomes familiar with the *Negro World* and its operation.

"Ah, there you are Pete," Ferris, the *Negro World*'s managing editor calls out. This has become a daily routine. Ferris gives Pete every type of job he can think of. "I want you to report to our warehouse at 3 AM tomorrow." The warehouse is where Garvey's Fairhaven and Favorite presses churn out the weekly issues of the *Negro World* newspapers in several different languages. "Take some trucks out and get us some roll ends."

Pete is confused. Tomorrow is Wednesday and they normally deliver the *Negro World*'s papers on Fridays, not Wednesdays. And roll ends, what the heck are roll ends?

"Roll ends?" Pete repeats, not wanting to betray his ignorance.

"Roll ends," the boss shouts back with a hint of exasperation.

"Yessir," Pete answers.

"And don't come back here half full; get as many as you can find," Ferris shouts at Pete's retreating back.

The next morning, Pete makes his way to the front of the printing warehouse where several UNIA trucks are parked with their drivers lounging at the entrance.

"Ready?" one of the truckers asks, meeting Pete at the door by the loading docks.

Pete nods.

"How many trucks do we take?" the trucker asks. His name is Josh. Taking one look at Pete, Josh knows that the new security chief doesn't have a clue about what they're about to do.

"How many do you think we should take?" Pete asks back.

Josh eyes the security chief and frowns. "Well that depends," he says.

"Depends on what?" Pete knows Josh is sizing him up, deciding whether the truckers will help Pete out or let him flounder. Originally the truckers were responsible for security. When the newspaper wars started, they were on the front line. The truckers were stopped, assaulted, and even shot at. The truckers suffer abuse from the *Negro World*'s paid staff, as well. Though few Garveyites can even drive, the truckers are held in low esteem.

In part, it's because the truckers are contractors who serve the UNIA for a fee. It doesn't matter that most drivers are loyal UNIA members; they are like cabbies accused of charging unfair rates for their services. Never mind that they are responsible for keeping the UNIA vehicles in running order without compensation. Never mind that a UNIA official in the Royal African Motor Corps can and often does take away a truck from one driver and gives it to another. Never mind the threat of violence that continually hangs over them. Garvey's African Motor Corps truck drivers are not treated very well.

"The number of trucks depends on how lucky you feel," Josh replies. There is something about Pete that makes Josh want to trust him. Maybe Josh realizes that Pete is just like him and the other truckers, just trying to make it, and not a boss ordering them about like so many of the other paid UNIA staff do.

"Before I got this job," Pete says, "I was a messenger. I had to deliver letters and packages by foot. I thought that getting a bicycle would be a luxury."

"You were one step below a truck driver," Josh laughs. "You can't get much lower than that." Josh sees Pete is asking for help and Josh responds. "You see those presses in there," Josh says.

"Yes," Pete replies.

"Those are offset presses. That means that the paper it uses is cut *before* the newspaper is printed," Josh explains. "Not like those big newspapers downtown that print from big rolls of newsprint."

"Okay," Pete says.

"So about this time every Wednesday morning we go out to the large papers, like the *Tribune, Post, Times,* even the *Wall Street Journal,* and collect newsprint roll ends."

"What are *roll ends?*"

"The roll ends are remains of the rolls of newsprint the big newspaper presses don't use," Josh explains.

"Newsprint?" Pete murmurs almost to himself.

"Yes," Josh says. "There is a lot of newsprint remaining on those roll ends. We collect it and bring it back here. The paper cutters use the newsprint from the end rolls to feed those offset machines." Josh looks at the bemused security commander. And answers the obvious question. "And the best part is that all the roll ends are *free.* All we have to do is take them away."

Pete whistles. "Wow, that must reduce printing costs dramatically."

"It does. But that's also where luck comes in," Josh continues. "We're not the only ones who use roll ends. So not only do we have to be lucky enough to get them before anyone else, we also have to be lucky enough to keep what we get."

"So that's why security is needed," Pete says.

"Yep, you've got it," Josh agrees. "There are a lot of end rolls out there. How many do you think you can get . . . and keep?"

"What do you think?" Pete asks.

Josh has been a Garveyite since 1914. He is loyal to the cause and dreams of the time when black men can stand shoulder to shoulder in unity and purpose. He knows many share his dream, but others don't. Their reasons for joining are different, more sinister. Josh senses that Pete shares the dream. "A couple of the big daily newspapers always try to save their roll ends for us," Josh says. "With the others, it's first come, first serve. Like I said, it's just a matter of luck. You might get more if you send a separate truck to each location, but it's always safer to convoy. If you have too many trucks in the convoy, though, you waste gas and attract attention."

"So what do you recommend?" Pete asks.

"Let's just use three trucks this morning," Josh suggests. "Let's take the Pierce-Arrow and a couple of those Fords." The association's growing fleet includes a 1918 Chevrolet one-ton canopy, several 1921 Buick pickups, world-war surplus Ford Model TT trucks and even a 1917 Menominee one-ton express truck. This latter is named for a Wisconsin Indian tribe. But of them all, the 1918 Pierce-Arrow flat bed truck is the fastest, best made and most reliable. That's Josh's truck. And he keeps it in perfect running condition. Josh turns away and goes over to the knot of drivers. Minutes later he returns with others. Pete sees that they are old timers and veterans. "Meet Spade and Hoss," Josh tells Pete. "They know the run as well as I do."

Pete nods to the leathery drivers. "Heard you were over in France during the big war," the one called Hoss says.

"Yeah," Pete replies, "I was in a services company for the 93rd."

"Graves?" Hoss asks sympathetically.

Pete nods. "And you?"

"Transportation," Hoss says. "Me and old Spade, here, were the ones who brought you bodies." Spade nods. He is a good deal shorter than his friend. Both wear tattered clothes, indicating their impoverished circumstances. Spade still wears his regulation campaign hat, while Hoss has tossed a checkered slouch cap carelessly on the back of his head. Neither man can be more than thirty, though each looks far older.

"Hoss and Spade drove Ford trucks over in France," Josh confides to Pete as they climbed into the Pierce-Arrow. "There's nothing about Fords the two of them don't know. And on your first tour of these printing houses we don't want you to have to worry about a breakdown, do we?" Josh laughs, guns the Pierce-Arrow and lurches away from the Harlem river warehouse at a quick 15 mph speed, heading toward downtown Manhattan, the two Model TT Ford trucks following close behind.

"Stay away from the *New York Post*," Josh warns Pete as they head downtown. "Unless you want to start a war."

"Why is that?" Pete asks

"That's *Messenger* and *Crisis* territory."

"Oh."

"The first place we go is the *Wall Street Journal*," Josh explains, "They always save several roll ends for us."

At the *Wall Street Journal*'s yard, they quickly ties the loose paper to the three available roll ends so that the paper will not flap and put them on Spade's flatbed, securing them under a canvas cove with rope. Then they're off again, this time heading to the print warehouse for the *New York Herald*.

"Two years ago the *Herald* merged with the *Morning Sun*," Josh tells Pete. "That's probably why they always have more roll ends available than any other printing shop."

But by the time they arrive at the *Herald*'s gates a number of trucks from other smaller presses are already lined up. Josh decides not stop.

"Just a matter of luck," Pete says to Josh.

"Yep," the veteran driver replies. "We should have come here first."

From there they go to Joseph Pulitzer's *New York World* and pick up several more roll ends. These they load onto Hoss's truck. From the *World*, they make a final run over to Hearst's *New York Journal*.

By the time Hearst expanded into New York with the purchase of the *New York Journal*, his publishing business that began in San Francisco had grown into an empire. Once in New York, Hearst immediately waged and won a circulation war with his former mentor, Joseph Pulitzer of the *New York World*. Hearst revolutionized the newspaper business using his now legendary tactic of "yellow journalism."

Yellow journalism increased the *Journal*'s circulation so dramatically that Josh usually takes away as many roll ends as he can carry—that is, if the yard boss will let them through the gates. Many mornings, the yard boss will simply say, "not lettin' no niggers in here today." And they will have to move on. Sometimes a bottle of liquor might help get them into the yard. But in reality, what does it is the stack of roll ends that the *Journal* is forced to dispose of if someone doesn't take them away. The yard boss must decide whether to deny the *Negro World* trucks access and run the risk of letting the roll ends build up, jeopardizing the his own job. This morning the yard boss gives the *World*'s three trucks access without any problem. Pete, Josh, Hoss and Spade stack roll ends until the trucks are loaded to capacity.

"Your first morning out and you bring back a load," Josh congratulates Pete. "We could have brought three more trucks." And it is true. With the three trucks, they have enough newsprint for several *Negro World* editions. But that's when their luck runs out.

"Oh no!" Josh grunts, looking at the side view mirror.

"What?" Pete asks.

"I think we've got company. See that car behind us?"

"Yes."

"It looks like someone doesn't want us to deliver this paper. Hang on." Josh gives several rapid hand signals and the two Fords peel off, each going in separate directions. "That's going to make it hard to stop all three of us," Josh laughs bitterly. "Let's see who they follow." Josh guns the Pierce-Arrow's engine to a speedy 25 miles per hour.

"Are they still with us?" Pete asks, shouting over the engine's increasing clickety-clacking sound.

"They're still on our tails!" Josh answers. "By the way, do you have a gun with you, by any chance?"

"No," Pete shouts back.

"Great, just great," Josh says. "Just what type of security are you going to provide anyway?"

Pete gives Josh a helpless look, but he makes a mental note never to go unarmed again. Josh is a veteran. More than once he has faced goons sent out to hijack his deliveries. Josh knows the streets of New York like the back of his hand. In 1921, no car in New York can outrace or outmaneuver his Pierce-Arrow. Before long, Josh loses his pursuers and pulls up to the *Negro World* warehouse, just as Hoss and Spade begin unloading their Fords.

"Have any trouble losing them?" Hoss asks Josh with a laugh.

"No trouble," Josh replies. "Unless you mean the extra dead weight I was carrying." He glances over his shoulder at Pete, whose chocolate face now burns crimson. This morning, Pete has learned a lot about providing security for the *Negro World* and its drivers.

Chapter Eight

"Hey, old-timer," Grady Jones hails Pete as he enters Candy's Café.

"Hi there, Grady," Pete replies. "Haven't seen you around lately. Still in the Army?"

"Yes! Doggone it, they won't release me!"

Grady flushes. He tried to catch himself, but the words just poured out. Realizing he just gave himself away, the would-be intelligence agent makes a feeble attempt at covering up. "They can't release me," he quips. "I'm having too much fun."

"Having fun?" Pete repeats. "What are you doing for Uncle Sam, boy? You must not still be digging graves, are you?"

Pete is a cop. Like all cops, Pete suspects everyone, even when they don't give themselves away. Grady popping up at the strangest times, without warning, makes Pete very suspicious of his old friend.

"What does the Army want with a trifling Negro like Grady?" Pete wonders.

Captain Gaines warned Pete about military intelligence agents. "You know Joel Spingarn is a captain in the Army assigned to military intelligence, don't you?" Gaines told Pete.

"Doesn't Spingarn and his brother run the National Association for the Advancement of Colored People?" Pete asked his commander.

"Yes," Gaines replied. "And you can be certain they have their people in our Association watching us."

As hard as it is for Pete to believe that Grady is spying for the Army, his behavior is rather suspicious. Pete fixes Grady with a penetrating stare. Grady shifts uncomfortably under his friend's gaze, then throws Pete off track by asking, "Seen Julia Duncan, lately?"

"Julia?" Pete says. "No, I haven't seen her since *Shuffle Along*."

Pete can also say that neither has Julia been out of his mind since that night, not her face, not her smell, not her touch. As a matter of fact, just the mention of her name causes Pete's mouth to dry up and he grabs a glass of water. Now it's Pete trying to dissemble under Grady's steady gaze.

"Interested in knowing where she is?" Grady asks.

"Why would I be interested?" Pete replies, trying to assume an air of indifference, but without success, especially since he is certain that Grady can hear Pete's wildly beating heart. "The woman walked out on me with another man, a white man. She's not interested in me, whatever she's doing. So why would I be interested in her?"

"Maybe you're not," Grady says, "but I've heard that Van Vechten got tired of her and her father put her out. Now she's down and out with nowhere to go." Grady watches the concern play across his friend's face. "Just like a book," Grady thinks. But the Army's agent takes no satisfaction in what he sees. He knows how much we are all slaves to our passions. Some more than others. Grady observes Pete silently and soberly. He still owes Pete much. Julia loves and trusts him. And now Grady is about to take advantage of them both. Being a compassionate person, Grady says to himself, "No, my friend, don't be ashamed that you love her." Then he pauses before proceeding with his plan. He rationalizes, "It's either them or me."

For all the devilment he causes, Grady Jones isn't really one those mean, low-down street hustlers. Grady's downfall, his fatal flaw, is that he actually loves women, too much. Had it not been for his own good looks, light skin and wavy hair, and the fact that women always throw themselves at him, Grady might have been just like Pete, someone who believes in love, honor and family values. Grady might have been the type of Negro man that women refer to when they say: "Find a fool, bump his head." Someone like Pete. In his own way, Grady wants to make things right for the two of them, or at least try.

Looking into his friend's suspicious eyes, Grady says, "I just thought you might want to know where Julia is, that's all." Then he gets up as if to leave.

"Where you going?" Pete asks. "Why don't you join me for a beer?" He motions to Mabel to bring them two cold ones.

"You know how tough it was in France," Grady says in a matter-of-fact manner. He sits back down. "When I got back to the States, there were lots of women available. So when Julia came around, I just wasn't ready for someone like her."

Pete looks at his friend and wants to believe what Grady is saying is the truth. No one can have done what they did—burying torn, mangled, bullet-riddled bodies, bodies without heads or arms or legs, pieces of bodies, day after day—and not become a little crazy. That's why Pete tried to take care of Grady and the others; it was therapy for him as well. "You're right," Pete admits. "None of us are ready for anyone like Julia."

Mabel brings the beers over to the table. Grady brightens up and, once again, assumes his role. He's still on the government's payroll; they still want him to recruit Pete. But Pete's no fool. Grady can't afford any more lapses or he will be staring into Lieutenant Smitz's laughing eyes while that cracker tightens a rope around Grady's neck.

"Was it so wrong for me to try to get the man I owe so much to together with a woman who is both beautiful and in need of a friend?" Grady asks.

"All I can say is that you make a terrible *shadchen*," Pete says.

"Say what?" Grady laughs. "That's a good one. What does it mean?"

"It's Yiddish for 'matchmaker,'" Pete tells his friend.

"I can use that one on Nadine," Grady says. "She'll be surprised."

"The two of you seem pretty close," Pete observes.

"As thick as thieves. When did you start picking up Yiddish?"

"The Association believes that we need to understand other people's culture so that we can better understand ourselves. Pimps and whores can only teach Negroes how to degrade themselves. Sometimes it's necessary for black people to become humble and learn from others." Pete wonders whether Grady catches the hint. "You'd be surprised how much you can learn working at a newspaper."

Since taking up his responsibilities at the *Negro World*, Pete has tried to learn as much as he can. The *World* is printed in several languages.

Its international focus requires Association employees to learn about the world at large. Pete enrolls in a French class, and his teacher, a Jewish linguist, often throws phrases at the class from other languages, including Yiddish.

"But you're changing the subject," Grady says. "What do you intend to do about Julia?" Once more arousing Pete's suspicions.

"He's a little too insistent," Pete thinks, but then he thinks, "Maybe it's me. Maybe I'm the one who's just a little too excited just hearing the sound of her name. *Julia*!"

"There's nothing I can do for Julia, personally," Pete says quietly, "but if she wishes to join the Association, I can help her find shelter and employment."

Grady looks at his friend; he knows he's got him.

"I'll get word to her," Grady promises, noting the hopeful look in Pete's eyes.

Pete goes out of his way to help the Jamaican beauty. Pete respects Julia; he loves her; he doesn't know what he feels. Just the sound of her name makes Pete as giddy as a schoolboy. Maybe it's good that Pete doesn't know Julia like Grady knows her. There is a fire inside Julia that blazes deep, a fire that burns with desire and passion and lust. Grady has satisfied his own passions in her fire, in her lust, in her wantonness. On more than one occasion, Julia has all but consumed Grady in her frantic need to satisfy her wanton passions and quench her fire. To satisfy Julia, Grady must not succumb. He must remain cold to her heat, calmly riding out her frantic passion. Together Julia and Grady are fire and ice, passion and rejection, love and hate. Neither Julia nor Grady like the other very much, which is why their lovemaking is so furious and intense, lacking the tenderness that Pete wants, that Pete *needs*.

"Come on baby," Grady says to entice Julia up to his apartment. "You know you want me just like I want you. You've got that body and it's made for just one thing and I've got that one thing it's made for."

It never fails. Julia is his whenever and wherever he wants her. She can't resist him. The first day Grady met Julia, she let him make love to her for free, even though she knew that Jacko, her pimp, would be awfully mad if he ever found out. And then Jacko just disappeared and there was no one other than the handsome, rich Grady Jones, who treated her better than Jacko ever did. Grady makes love to her better than Jacko ever did, even though Jacko was her first. Julia always does what Grady wants, and always will.

But her lusty nature is not the only reason Julia submits to the handsome, wavy-haired soldier. Grady has contacts, important contacts, contacts in the white world. If Julia is to escape Harlem and poverty, she needs Grady's help. "So," she thinks, "why not keep him around and keep him interested. That's the way, isn't it?"

But Julia doesn't fool Grady. He knows that she needs him to come alive, to be a woman. He is the man. He is her man; the man who takes what he wants. When Grady wants her, Julia has to give in. Grady doesn't love Julia, he doesn't need her, at least not in the way a man needs a woman. He doesn't even respect her, but it makes no difference. Carl Van Vechten doesn't respect or love her either, and she goes with him without hesitation. Julia does everything Grady asks her to do. When he tells her to leave Van Vechten, she does that as well. One day, Julia wants to feel that she is in charge, that she is calling the shots, that she is in control. And then, she vows, she'll give up the life. Until then, Julia uses Grady, just as Grady uses her. And now Grady is using Julia to control Pete because that is what military intelligence wants.

Later in the week, Grady arranges for Julia and Pete to meet. Afterward, Pete takes Julia over to the UNIA's membership office, where it seems that the entire Garveyite organization embraces her. Since Julia is homeless, the Association gives her a room at one of their settlement homes located in the 1500 block of Harlem's St. Charles Street. They offer her a job as a proofreader for the *Negro World*, due, in no small part, to the efforts of the *Negro World*'s head of security. Julia quickly settles into a comfortable routine, living the life of a Garveyite insider.

Pete and Julia see each other several times a week. Julia goes out of her way to show Pete how grateful she is, especially after the way she treated him in the beginning. For his part, Pete remains as aloof and distant as his heart will allow. For all her arrogance, Julia is a playful person. Gradually she breaks down his defenses and in the process her feelings of gratitude begin to change into feelings of a deeper, more passionate nature. Eventually she is unable to tell whether her present feelings for Pete stem from the fact that he rescued her from the streets, or if she felt this way all along, beginning that night at Cora's rent party when he held her close, or when she thrilled at his touch while watching *Shuffle Along*. Try as she might, Julia still can't understand why she left Pete that night. Grady wanted Julia to make Pete jealous, not to leave him. But somehow reality interfered. Now Julia feels that Pete is the man she wants to be with. It is just that Pete is so poor. Julia's feelings are as confused as ever. She takes advantage of any excuse just to be near him. This is not the plan. Julia's supposed to make Pete want her, not the other way around. Besides, her feelings for Pete are nothing compared to how she still feels, or thinks she feels, about Grady. Julia trusts Pete; he makes her feel safe. Pete commands respect. All of Garvey's followers, including many women inside the Association, believe Pete is a man to look up to and to admire. Julia finds herself believing it, too.

"I've got some good news," Julia cries, bursting into Pete's office. It's been over six months since she joined the *World*'s staff. Before Pete can react, Julia runs around his desk and throws herself into his arms, her hypnotic green eyes overwhelming him with affection. Pete can hardly believe she is the same person who left him at the Kentucky Club. Every time he sees her, Julia finds a way to come close enough to touch and feel. Pete wants to pinch himself just to be certain he isn't dreaming. Gone is Julia's sullen, arrogant attitude. In its place is a happy woman transforming herself into a "New Negro." Gone is that self-centered individual and in her place is a bright woman who is developing a racial consciousness. Now Julia is committed to the ideals of unity, self-de-termination and cooperative economics. Had Pete not personally seen Julia's transformation, he would not have believed it possible that such a vain, self-absorbed person could have changed so dramatically.

"Or have you misjudged her all along?" Pete asks himself.

Hadn't Julia always shared his belief in a future where Negroes re-spect their race, strive for intellectual development and challenge white supremacy? Pete didn't know. For Pete, it's enough that there has been a transformation and that his love for her is more than just a physical attraction.

"Possibly, it has something to do with night school," he thinks. Julia continually talks about how much she enjoys taking evening classes. She even developed a close attachment to one her teachers, Grace Campbell. "Or maybe it's just that I'm in love with her." As she cuddles in his arms, Pete doesn't even care.

"Well, are you going tell me?" Pete asks good-naturedly. "What is it that's so important that you came all the way down here in the dungeon? I hope you make it quick before you crush me to death."

"I got the job at the library," Julia announces. "They want me to start next week."

"Congratulations," Pete says. He tries to show more enthusiasm than he feels.

The announcement doesn't come as much of a surprise. No one believed that Julia would remain at the *Negro World* for very long, especially Pete. A job at the New York City public library, now that is something. Of course, it probably meant that he wouldn't be seeing much of her.

"It's not much," Julia continues. "I'll just be reshelving books, but I'm really excited about it."

"You should be," Pete says. "I know that this is just the first step. It's a great opportunity."

"Actually," Julia confesses, "Grace Campbell got me the job."

"Your teacher?"

"Yes!"

"Grace is West Indian. Her family and mine are good friends," Julia tells Pete. "You know how West Indians believe in helping each other. Grace is politically active. She has connections." Grace had promised Julia's parents that she would get Julia out of the street life.

"Young lady," Grace had lectured, "it matters not what you look like on the outside, it's what's on the inside that counts. Your beauty will only last for so long, and when it's gone, it's gone forever. Take advantage of it now." Julia had listened as if Grace was an older sister. Grace is a ranking member of the African Blood Brotherhood. She had hoped to interest Julia in the *cause* and to further the brotherhood's goal of promoting active resistance to the Ku Klux Klan. The brotherhood has planned to infiltrate Garvey's organization and take it over. Cyril Briggs has wanted to recruit Julia into the brotherhood from the first time Grace introduced him to Julia. Of course, Grace has never divulged Briggs's plan to Julia and Julia has never told Grace about Grady.

In a sense, Pete is relieved that Julia is leaving the *Negro World*. It is hard having her around, seeing her face, smelling her body, gazing into her green eyes. Julia deserves a life of ease and comfort and is likely to get it. She isn't interested in love. She wants wealth and security. Her fair skin and good looks entitle her to good life, at least to a life better than what Pete can give her.

"Looks like you'll be moving on up," Pete says, deliberately moving Julia's body away from his. "I guess I won't be seeing much of you from now on."

"You'll still see me," Julia laughs. "You can't get rid of me that easy."

"I'll bet," Pete replies. "You'll be so glad that . . ." But he doesn't finish his thought. Josh interrupts him.

"Commander Jenkins, Mr. Ferris wants you in his office, right away."

"Thanks, Josh," Pete answers, somewhat embarrassed at the smug look on the truck driver's face. Pete wonders if Josh suspects that he and Julia are more than friends.

"Well, Miss Duncan, duty calls," Pete says in a formal tone. "Congratulations on your new job. Maybe you'll let me buy you a farewell dinner."

"I'd like that," Julia replies.

"Commander," Josh says, "Mr. Ferris said right away!"

"Okay, Josh. I'll be right there," Pete replies. On the way up the stairs to Ferris's office, Pete notices the veteran trucker wears a grim look. His jaw is set and his eyes smolder with something approaching hate. "What's the matter, Josh?" Pete asks. "Has there been another attack?"

The struggle between the *Negro World* and the other Negro papers for the hearts and minds of the Harlem community continues to escalate. In recent weeks, the rhetoric in print is matched by battles in the streets. Garvey vows that they will no longer simply defend themselves; the Association is taking the offense. Pete is told to plan the hijacking of an entire issue of *The Messenger*. Pete assumes that the look on Josh's face means that Ferris is going to tell him that another truckload of the *World*'s newspapers has been hijacked.

"Have we been hit again?" Pete asks.

"Yes," Josh says, "but not here in New York."

"Where then?"

Josh's face turns a whitish grey. "The whites bombed and burned down the entire Negro section of Tulsa, Oklahoma," he says.

The managing editor's suite sprawls across the third floor. From this office, Ferris oversees correspondents, reporters, informants and UNIA officials from all over the world. Messengers stream in and out with the latest reports from all the *World*'s wire service feeds located in the newsroom. Through his wire services, Ferris accesses the same up-to-the-minute reports available to major metropolitan newspapers including the New York *Times*, the Washington *Post* and the Boston *Globe*. Inside his corner office, Ferris hunches behind a great mahogany desk piled high with newspapers, letters, clippings, books and assorted office materials. On top of the pile three candlestick telephones ring furiously. His messengers deposit the wire service reports on top on his desk, where they become lost in the clutter.

Pete strolls into his boss's office, noting the chaos that he has come to expect. It is absolute, total bedlam. Ferris is yelling into one telephone while screaming at Eve, his personal secretary, to answer the others. The *World*'s editor motions his security chief to take a seat, but where, Pete doesn't know. There is paper everywhere, even in the chairs.

"Right chief!" Ferris says finally, slamming the phone back down on its cradle. The *World*'s editor nods to Pete. "Hear about Tulsa?" Ferris asks.

"Josh just told me," Pete answers.

"We're sending some of our people out there. We're gonna cover the riot and the bombing. And I want you to go with them."

A lot of the staff had come up to the third floor and are crowding inside the executive suite. Through the shuffle, Pete sees Julia pushing her way in.

"Me!" Pete exclaims. "I'm not a reporter."

"I know that," Ferris responds, "but our reporters want you along for protection."

"Do you really think that'll be necessary?" Pete asks.

"Don't know," Ferris replies. "But I think they'll feel better about you going."

Pete has a gentle manner, but everyone at the *World*, especially the drivers, are impressed with his toughness and his resolve. After that first experience picking up roll ends, Pete is never caught unarmed again. He keeps a forty-five-caliber Army Colt with him at all times. During his rides with Josh and the other truckers, Pete brings along a duffel bag containing a 1920 model Thompson submachine gun. Although the weapon only fires twenty-two caliber bullets, it is lethal enough to dissuade any would-be hijacker. All of Pete's men wear sidearms and take weapons practice on Pete's makeshift firing range behind the *World*'s building. Pete uses the noise of the printing presses to drown out the sounds of gunshots. The Garveyites observe the security officer's growth in confidence and knowledge. They like his professionalism and integrity. In dealing with the ongoing street violence, Pete is exact in his planning and calm in execution. Over time, Pete has built a solid reputation among the truck drivers, his security staff and the Garveyites in general.

"If it's so dangerous, why are you sending them?" Pete asks calmly.

"Because the *Messenger* and the *Crisis*, not to mention the Chicago *Defender*, will have reporters there. I just talked to the chief. He wants us to send someone to Tulsa, now. And you're going with them."

"Who are you sending?" Pete asks.

"I've got a photographer and a cub," Ferris replies, "but I could use another reporter. I'll take anyone who'll volunteer." The editor shouts loud enough so that everyone on the third floor can hear him.

The staff outside begins to buzz. Some even move back out the door and down the stairs, making plenty of room for a volunteer, whoever it might be. Sending a news crew to report on the Tulsa riot is unprecedented for the *World*. Garvey's weekly never sends a news crew to the scene of a riot. Ferris uses the wire services to get the facts and then has one of his reporters give the story the proper slant before running it. "I wonder who the boss is going to send," someone whispers. "Well it won't be me," comes a response. Few, if any, of these reporters are brave enough, or foolhardy enough, to take on this assignment. The Klan is no joke. Just because the riot is over doesn't mean that the white folks will stop killing Negroes. Those redneck honkies especially don't like uppity niggers from northern newspapers. Whites in a Texas town went on a killing spree just because a Negro teacher sent a picture and description of a lynching to the Chicago *Defender*. No, sir! None of Ferris's reporters is volunteering to go to Tulsa.

"*Send me! I want to go!*" Pete looks up to see Julia pushing her way into Ferris's office. The *World*'s surly editor looks up, and after the briefest consideration, says, "Okay Miss Duncan, you can go."

"Bill," Pete protests, "for Christ's sakes, you can't send Julia. She's not even a reporter, she's a proofreader."

"Julia's been here six months. It's about time she got a promotion," the managing editor replies. "Now that settles it. You've got Bif Meadows as the photographer; he's got plenty of experience. That kid we hired last week, Clarence something or other, the one they call 'Windows,' is the cub, and Miss Duncan here. That's your crew. Now get going. I want you all on the first train to Tulsa."

"But," Pete pleads.

"But, nothing," Ferris growls. "They go with you or without you. It's your choice. But get out of my office, now!"

Chapter Nine

The rhythmic clicktey-clack of the railroad tracks competes with the sounds of the engine as the Santa Fe railroad train roars westward toward Tulsa, Oklahoma. Pete and Julia sit across from each other in the Jim Crow passenger car. They're on the third leg of the three-day trip that began at New York's Grand Central Station aboard the Union Pacific to Buffalo. From there they took a train to Chicago, where they boarded the Santa Fe on the final leg of their journey. Occasionally, their eyes meet. Julia gives Pete a slight smile—or is it a smirk, Pete is never quite sure—Julia's face made all the more appealing by her lovely green eyes. They hypnotize Pete as if he is a bird being stalked by a cat. The rhythm of the train only enhances the beating of his heart and the shallowness of his breathing. Julia's beauty causes Pete to suffer physical torment and the long train ride is excruciating. At times, the smell of her breath and the rise and fall of her breasts influenced by the locomotion of the journey makes Pete even forget to breathe. Then he will suddenly start coughing, his lungs gasping for air as if he were a fish that jumped high in the air after an insect and landed in the shallows.

"Are you alright?" Julia asks him after it happens several times. "Can I get you some water?"

"No, no, I'm fine," Pete replies, rather sheepishly. "I just got something caught in my throat. But I'm okay now."

"Are you sure?" she asks, taking hold of one of his hands.

"Really," he says, quickly pulling back, "I'm okay." Pete's hands are rough and hard, the way cop's hands get from spending so much time of the firing range. Practicing at least twice a week with his forty-five-caliber

Army Colt has turned Pete's hands into steel claws, claws that tingle at Julia's soft, delicate touch.

They have spoken very little since leaving New York. Julia becomes intrigued with the endless number of stories that Bif Meadows tells about the Association, how it began and all the cities and towns Bif has visited over the years spreading Garvey's message of One God, One Aim, One Destiny. Bif is an old time Garveyite and is very close to the Association's leadership. Garvey calls Bif by his first name and Ferris runs the *World* on many of Bif's recommendations. Bif is one of the few Jamaicans who stood by Garvey in the early days when most of the West Indians left the New York Association. Bif is not only Garvey's photographer, he recruits UNIA members in more than a dozen cities. Bif is Garvey's most loyal and trustworthy follower. Bif projects Garvey's image of the New Negro.

Bif is short and squat, barely five feet seven inches. Height is something he shares with Garvey. However, while Garvey is dark-skinned, Bif is light complexioned. Bif's color comes not from his mother, a dark-skinned Jamaican, but from his father, who was born in Nigeria. Bif regales Julia with UNIA stories, beginning with Sam Duncan splitting from Garvey and taking almost the entire New York chapter with him to form what became the West Indian Protective Society of America.

"Sam Duncan is my uncle," Julia replies.

"Your father's brother?"

"Yes."

"Don't you find it strange being a Garveyite?" Bif asks.

"Not really," Julia says. "Dad and Uncle Sam don't really get along that well. Besides, you stayed with Garvey, didn't you?"

"I had my reasons," Bif replies.

"Tell her about the first break-up of the organization," Clarence Payne pipes in. The cub reporter is fresh out of Howard. He wears glasses with lenses so thick they look like the bottoms of Coke bottles, which is why Bif calls Clarence "Windows." When Windows joined the *World*'s staff he attached himself to Bif. Now the two are inseparable.

"That was really nothing," Bif says, barely hiding his irritation with his young protégé for interrupting his train of thought. "It had to do with Garvey not supporting the war. Anyway, he was able to bring all new people back into the fold." Bif leans toward Julia and, almost whispering, says, "Actually the Association was rebuilt from all of Booker T. Washington's people who came North without friends or family."

"Including his father," Windows blurts out.

"Whose father?" Pete asks,

"Bif's father," Windows answers. "Tell them about it, Bif. It's a really interesting story. It had to do with Bif's people from Nigeria who opposed the war. They were being tortured and murdered by the British who wanted them to fight against the Germans."

"That was some time ago," Bif retorts, his irritation clearly showing. "Our friends probably need to know more about where we are going now than about what happened in the past." Pete notices that this is not a subject Bif wants to discuss. Once again, Pete's suspicions are aroused, but he decides to let the matter drop, at least for the time being. "I covered more than a dozen of the race riots in 1919. Negroes called it the 'red summer,'" Bif continues. Bif draws closer to Julia and launches into another one of his tales. Pete decides to listen to Bif's stories more closely even though Bif makes it clear that his stories are for Julia only.

As if on cue, Windows bombards Pete with questions about the Army, France and the European war. And so, all Pete and Julia can do on this final leg of their journey to Tulsa is steal glances at one another, which does not escape Bif's notice. Later in the day, the final day of their trip, Pete and Julia take advantage of an opportunity to be alone. Pete begins to cough once again. Excusing himself, he walks out to the platform between coaches. A short time later, Julia gets up and follows him.

"Are you sorry you came yet?" he asks her, not knowing what else to say and feeling very uncomfortable with Julia's green eyes concentrated on him.

"Oh, no," she replies. "I was concerned about you. Besides which I needed to stretch my legs."

"And they're such beautiful legs," Pete comments playfully.

"How do you know?" Julia asks with an air of mock hostility. The fashion of the day is for young women to wear ankle-length dresses. Pete never has seen just how shapely Julia's legs are. "Do we have a 'peeping Tom' aboard this train?" Julia asks, her eyes fluttering in a look of feigned innocence.

"Not unless this 'peeping Tom' can see with his mind and his heart," Pete replies.

"Well, that's the first time you've ever told me about it," Julia says, turning her back to him, leaving Pete to draw his own conclusions about what she means.

"I never knew it mattered to you," Pete says shyly. "You've always seemed so cold and aloof. I've always felt intimidated."

"Intimidated!" Julia says. "That's one excuse I haven't heard before."

"Excuse?" Pete asks with genuine surprise.

"Yes, excuse," Julia says as she turns back toward him. The railroad clatter swallows up the sound of her voice, and at that moment fate takes a hand. The train makes a sudden lurch, throwing Julia off balance and suddenly she finds herself falling into Pete's arms. In order to keep the lurching train from toppling them both over, Pete reaches out and grabs her. Their bodies crush together, their faces are but inches apart, hot blood courses through their veins. Julia makes no effort to free herself from Pete's embrace.

"Why do I need an excuse?" Pete says, her scent taking his breath away. He musters all the will he possesses trying to resist his passionate urges, even though it seems that Julia wants him to succumb.

"You have so many women running after you I knew you'd come up with some kind of excuse not to forgive me," Julia says. Her voice is soft and sensuous.

Not knowing anything else to say, Pete blurts out, "Is that one of your jokes?"

Julia turns her face fully up to Pete, her imploring eyes begin to turn misty green like the glassy surface of a quiet pond. And, then, before he knows it, tears begin rolling down from her beautiful green eyes onto her honey-colored cheeks.

Completely outdone, Pete attempts to comfort Julia by pressing her close. She snuggles into his arms. Her eager lips, tasting of salty tears, press against his. There, standing on the platform with the noise of the train roaring in their ears, they lock themselves together in an intimate embrace, and, for the first time, Julia's soul awakens and she feels true

love. And both realize that, from the night they first held each other at
Cora's rent party, they have been deeply in love.

"Oh, Pete," Julia cries. "Why have you treated me so mean?"

"I've never . . ." Pete tries to speak above the noise of the train as well
as the sound of his own beating heart. But he is too overwhelmed, too
bewildered to continue.

"I knew you cared for me," Julia says. "I just couldn't get you to
admit it."

"But I didn't think you had any feelings for me," Pete answers.

"Why do you think I followed you all the way out to God knows
where?" she says looking up at him.

Pete shakes his head dumbly. "I don't know," he answers.

"I wanted to be with you, you big dummy," she says. "I didn't want
to lose you." Julia pulls back and gives Pete a look that melts his heart. It
is a look that tells Pete that Julia is his forever. But it is also a frightened
look. It is a look that says, "I am yours but you must always care for me
and protect me, no matter what."

At that moment not only does Pete learn about love, but about fear
as well. Like so many other courageous men, Pete never feared for his
own life. Now he is fearful that something might happen to Julia, and it
is a fear that is almost unbearable, so great is his love.

They remain between the passenger cars for some time, communicat-
ing in those special ways that people in love have always communicated.
They communicate without words, only with looks and touches, discov-
ering the one heart and one soul they share between them as if the train
is speeding them toward some magical place. All too soon, the magic
ends, and the couple rejoins their companions.

"So where have you two been hiding?" Bif asks once Pete and Julia
resettle into their seats, this time next to each other. Bif leers at them.
Blind to Julia's lack of interest and heedless of his own reputation as
being an old billy goat, Bif actually believed that Julia held a romantic
attachment for him. "Windows, why didn't you tell me that these two
were making goo-goo eyes at each other," Bif asks.

"You didn't ask me," Windows replies, secretly enjoying Bif's dis-
comfort.

"Well, I just think they're trying to make me jealous," Bif says.

"Think what you please, old man," Windows retorts, "but you might want to borrow my glasses." Everyone has a good laugh, which clears the tension.

A while later, Julia looks at the young Howard graduate and asks, "Clarence, do you *like* being called Windows?"

The cub reporter blinks a couple of times, seemingly relishing this attention from Julia. "I don't mind," he says. "As a matter of fact, yes, I do kind of like it."

"Okay, Windows it will be," Julia declares, looking over and giving Pete a knowing smile. "From now on you will be Windows to Pete and *me*."

That settles that. Julia makes her declaration: she and Pete are a couple. Bif is nothing if not a realist. In all his years as a photographer, he has seen all manner of vanity, whether in film, on stage or in politics. One thing Bif understands very well is that the ways of the heart are fickle at best. He has loved many women, and many more remain to be loved. Later on, demonstrating that he really bears Pete no hard feelings, he gently awakes the couple, Julia sleeping contentedly against Pete's shoulder.

"We should be arriving in Tulsa soon. Better get ready," Bif says. The four of them prepare to face the tragic events that have brought them to the devil's own plantation, also known as Tulsa, Oklahoma.

The news team gathers their belongings as the train makes its final approach toward the Santa Fe depot. "You've covered a lot of these things," Pete observes. "What should we expect?"

"Expect the unexpected," Bif replies. "When I covered the Chicago race riot, there was fighting all over the city, but it was done by small groups of whites and blacks. I avoided most of the trouble by staying on the South Side."

"I remember the riot in D.C.," Windows says. "I was still in school."

"Where did you go to school?" Julia asks.

"Howard," Windows replies.

"That's right, you told me that, but I thought Howard was in Boston," Julia says.

"That's Harvard. Howard is a black school," Windows says. "Anyway, there were white soldiers and sailors . . ."

". . . and Marines," Bif interjects.

"Yes and Marines, all over the place," Windows continues. "They were shooting colored people all over D.C. Killed a lot of them. Some Negroes fought back, though. The African Blood Brotherhood had veterans with guns. They knew how to use them. The whites went into the colored neighborhoods and tried to burn down colored folks homes. They never came to Howard, though. Most of the students stayed on the campus, trying to keep from getting killed." Windows is quiet for a moment. "But you know," he continues, "I think the government was behind the whole thing."

"Why do you say that?" Pete asks.

"Because as soon as the Brotherhood started killing white folks, the government stepped in and the sailors, soldiers and Marines disappeared off the streets." Windows remembers how frightened Howard's students were. "The riot lasted almost a week," he continues. "They could have stopped it the first day."

"What are you talking about?" Bif lashes out. "Everyone knows that the Ku Klux Klan is behind the attacks against colored people."

"But who is the Ku Klux Klan?" Windows asks. "It's the government."

"You've got a lot to learn about white folks, kid," Bif replies. "Who do you think is behind these attacks, Pete?" Bif asks. "Do agree with our young friend here? Do you think the government is behind all the mess we colored folks have to put up with?" He looks Pete straight in the eye.

Pete hesitates. "I honestly don't know," Pete replies. "But I've seen white people wage war, and they kill without mercy. If the colored people get in white folk's way, the government will plan our elimination. That's why they have an Army."

"I agree with Bif," Julia says, repeating what Grace Campbell told her. "I've heard that the Ku Klux Klan is behind all the violence."

"Before we get too deep into this," Pete says, "I think we need to decide what to do here in Tulsa. I want to make certain that I can give you as much protection as possible. You all need to get in there, get your stories and pictures so that we can all get back to New York safely."

"You don't have to worry about that," Bif chimes in. "Tulsa is like New York. Maybe it doesn't have as many black people here, but they have quite a community. I'm sure we'll be all right here." He gives Julia a reassuring pat on the knee. "Tulsa has two Negro newspapers, the Tulsa *Star* and the *Oklahoma Sun*. I know the *Star*'s editor, A. J. Smitherman. He's on the square; he'll help us as much as he can. We'll probably get everything we need without having to lift a finger."

"Then why am I tagging along on this picnic?" Pete asks. His cop's mind is beginning to wonder whether this is some sort of wild goose chase. All they were told is that there had been a racial disturbance in Tulsa, Oklahoma. They don't have any information about the magnitude of the disturbance. They don't know how many or even if any colored folks have been killed. For all they know, this is just a fishing expedition.

"Look," Bif says "we'll just stick to the black section of town; it's called Greenwood. Some folks call it Black Wall Street. We'll be okay. And I think you'll be surprised."

"Surprised?" Julia asks. "Surprised by what?"

"The Stradford Hotel, first of all," Bif says. "It's very nice, very modern. The dining room serves the best steaks anywhere. There's also Lily Johnson's Liberty Café. People line up for Lily's home-cooked meals. That's where I intend to go before I leave here." Bif continues, "And there are two theaters in Greenwood. The Dreamland Theater features live musical and theater performances, as well as movies."

"Do tell," Julia almost laughs. "Do you think they might show *Shuffle Along* while we're here." She casts a sidelong look at Pete. "I really didn't appreciate what a beautiful production it was the last time I saw it."

"I don't know about that," Bif replies, "but they're certain to be showing something while we're here."

"That's good," Julia says. "Pete, will you take me to a performance? We could pretend that it's our first date."

But before Pete can answer, Bif speaks up. "If he doesn't, I'd sure like to."

"Sounds like you really like Tulsa," Pete says.

"Yep, sure do," Bif replies nonchalantly. "And you will, too."

"Well, since you're so familiar with this fair city, I'm certain you'll be able to find someone to accompany *you* to the theater," Julia teases, still looking at Pete.

"I'll go with you," Windows blurts out. Then all four of them burst out laughing. Their merriment is cut short by the conductor marching officiously down the aisle and announcing in a loud voice, "Tulsa, next stop, *Tulsa*."

Chapter Ten

Garvey's news team can hardly disembark from the train for being jostled and shoved about by a mass of black humanity, all trying to cram into the Jim Crow passenger car at once. Even after they reach the Santa Fe platform, more wild-eyed Negroes stampede from the platform trying to board the train. Most are dirty and disheveled. Their clothes are torn in some places, spotted and soiled all over, hardly more than rags. Frantic, the black mob raises a frightful din. They are crying, shouting, cursing at each other as they push forward, and cramming themselves onto the train like sardines. It's as if some powerful force has deprived them of their senses and has driven them stark, raving mad.

"Look," Julia whispers to Pete, pointing down. Pete can't hear what she is saying over the noise of the crowd. Bif and Windows are too busy trying to retrieve their bags and negotiate their exit against the wild mob to notice what Julia is saying. Finally, after all four have pushed themselves through the exit, off of the train and down to the platform, Pete hears Julia say: "They're not wearing any shoes! *They're not wearing any shoes!*"

Pete looks down. So do Bif and Windows. No wonder some of these people are so angry. Not one of them wears any shoes. And had it not been so tragic, it would have been comical to watch men, women and children walking gingerly over wooden planks filled with splinters and sharp nails. Their feet bleed from gashes and punctures received not only at the station, but also from their long trek from the internment areas where most have been held prisoner for over a week. These are the fortunate ones. They are Tulsa's middle-class colored residents, the ones with white people willing to vouch for their docile, respectable behavior, members of Tulsa's NAACP. The majority of Tulsa's Negro population will remain interned for over a month. Though these fortunate few have been released and are able to afford a railroad ticket, they are subjected to a final humiliation before being permitted to flee Tulsa with their lives: the rednecked Okies of Tulsa mock their victims by depriving them of their shoes. Thus is the *Negro World's* news team introduced to the aftermath of what they will remember as the slaughter in Tulsa, Oklahoma.

On the station platform, with chaos whirling all around him, Windows sees a colored gentleman who seems calmer than the rest and is better prepared for train travel. He wears a three-piece suit with a high button collar and tie. A handsome, middle-aged woman stands next to him, dressed in a fashionable style complete with hat and gloves. Both seem rather more exasperated than intimidated by the whole affair. But the gentleman holds onto a leather suitcase as if his life depends on it. Windows approaches them and asks, "Where are all of these people trying to go?"

"I suppose they're trying to go anywhere away from here," the colored gentleman replies, "at least that's where we're going." The couple continues on their way, disappearing in the sea of pushing, stumbling Negro humanity.

The New Yorkers negotiate their way down the station platform toward what seems to be a rather ramshackle train terminal. Bif should have noticed that there is something unusual about the building, but he doesn't. He's too busy with his cameras, preparing to take pictures of the colored refugees. Pete sees it right away. No, that's not right. Pete doesn't see it, he feels it or remembers it. He has seen mind-numbing fear on the faces of refugees before, in Europe, in the Great War. He saw eyes of soldiers bulging from their sockets and terrorized faces of civilians drastically contorted. It is the same look on the faces of these colored people. Terrorized, they writhe in the grip of cold, merciless fear as if they have gazed into the face of Hell and have witnessed demons engaged in their ghastly deeds. As Pete approaches the station, he actually smells it. The smell he will never forget—the unmistakable scent of gunpowder, the pungent odor of gelignite, and the acrid smell of dead bodies. One can never encounter a battlefield and forget the cloying nausea that accompanies the smell of rotting flesh. Even a corpse buried underground without a coffin exudes an odor. Pete remembers those smells only too well. The smell of death, the smell that indicates that somewhere, quite near, dead bodies are rotting in the sun.

Pete also notices the train station. It's not ramshackle; it's been shot to pieces. There are bullet holes everywhere. The train station was a war zone and from the number of bullet holes it must have been a ferocious battle. In this place, living, breathing, thinking human beings have been turned into lifeless chunks of mutilated flesh. There is a saying that there are no atheists in foxholes. Pete believes it has a corollary: there are no Christians on battlefields. Pete never met anyone willing to die so that they could go to heaven. Certainly not after seeing the tortured, painful faces of war dead twisted into their hideous death masks.

As the last black refugee pushes and shoves his way onto the train, the conductor signals "all clear," and the giant locomotive slowly pulls out of the station and heads down the tracks and westward toward the Oklahoma oil fields.

The news team is facing south. Their first view is of white Tulsa with its tall orderly buildings, theater marquees and lofty church spires. But as the Santa Fe train departs the station, it leaves an unobstructed view of northern Tulsa, the section across the tracks, the area known as Greenwood, home to 10,000 Negroes. A section that *was* home to 10,000 Negroes. Now, as the *Negro World* news team discovers, Greenwood is a neighborhood, a community that no longer exists. In its place lay blackened ruins, skeletal remains and still-smoldering fires, all that remains of a community that has been burned completely to the ground. Looking out over the once prosperous community, the New Yorkers see stone foundations with chimneys rising up like ghostly sentinels into the bluish gray haze of smoke and ash. In the streets, the tortured metal frames of automobiles stick out grotesquely in smoking pools of tar that once had been tires. The desolation and ruin stretch as far as the eye can see. What was Black Wall Street is now a blackened burial ground. The others, Bif, Windows and Julia, become aware of the ghastly smell. They wrap their faces in handkerchiefs. Julia can only gasp, "My God, *my God!*"

"God has nothing to do with this," Pete curses under his breath. "This is the devil's work. This is how the white man exerts his power, without honor, without shame and without mercy."

"What did these people do to deserve this?" Julia asks.

"This is what they tried to do to Negroes in D.C.," Windows blurts out, "but they fought back."

"They must have tried to fight back here, too," Pete observes.

"Why do you say that?" Windows asks.

"Look at the bullet holes in this train station. There was a hell of a fight here, before that happened," Pete says, indicating the devastated area.

Bif Meadows sinks to his knees. Silent tears glisten from his heavy-lidded eyes and stream over his chubby yellow cheeks onto the hairy stubble he calls a beard. He blinks hard and rubs at his eyes as if trying to awake from a dream, trying to make his nightmare disappear. Then Bif slumps over, he's unconscious. Pete leaps over to the photographer's unconscious body. His breathing is labored.

"Get him some water," Pete shouts to Windows.

Bif has gone into shock. Pete has seen it before. In France, many soldiers—some fresh from the United States, some long after their initial encounter with war and death—have a similar reaction. Some recruits, even before seeing mangled corpses, smelling burned flesh and hearing the screams of dying men, went into shock just at the sight of the battlefield itself, with its smell of gunpowder and death. Some of these men, who did not receive immediate attention, never recovered.

Pete saw soldiers go into shock when they got bad news from home. He even saw one of his men go into shock after killing a French woman. They were recovering bodies from a field when a French woman just appeared. Jones, a black soldier recently assigned to their unit, just a teenager, really, began fumbling for his rifle when it fired, accidentally. The woman fell and lay writhing in the mud, the bullet from Jones's rifle entering her side, penetrating her liver. Jones went into shock and died a week later. The rumor was that the Army ordered Jones killed.

"Here's some water," Windows says, handing over a tin cup. Pete splashes water on Bif's face and chest and begins to rub his arms and legs.

After several anxious minutes, Bif begins to move and his eyes flutter open.

"Feeling better," Pete asks, alternately sprinkling Bif's face and giving him the cup to drink.

"Yes, I guess so," Bif replies sheepishly. "I feel like a kid on my first assignment. That should have been Windows passing out instead of me."

"Well, if you don't need any more nursing," Pete says, standing up and returning the tin cup to its owner, "I think we'd better get on about our business." Bif wobbles to his feet but is still woozy. Windows supports him until Bif can stand on his own. Then they all troop into the train station. Pete takes the precaution of hiding Bif's cameras and equipment inside one of their party's two valises.

Though the news team members are the only Negroes to get off the train, several white men disembarked into the "Whites Only" terminal. Some are also news reporters intent on getting a first hand account at what they will call Tulsa's "Negro Uprising." Others represent oil companies. Their corporate headquarters want a first-hand assessment of any damages to Tulsa's extensive oil industry. In 1921, more than four hundred different oil and gas companies called Tulsa home. Oklahoma had witnessed a phenomenal growth in the oil refining and oil supply business. In little over a decade, Tulsa had become the oil capital of the world. The corporate offices back east that control America's oil industry need to assure themselves that the riot doesn't threaten continued oil production. The suffering of the Negro community is of little concern to these white men.

"Look at those darkies," one of the white passengers remarks to his companion. "They behave just like the savages I saw the last time I went on safari. No wonder people around here have got to keep them in their place."

Inside the waiting room, Pete takes charge. "I don't think it's a good idea to let these white folks know who we are; nor should we take any pictures." He directs his last remark at Bif, but the photographer is in no condition to do much of anything.

Nodding at Pete, Windows steps up to the counter and queries the lone white ticket agent. "Where might I inquire about my missing relatives?" Windows asks.

The white stationmaster leaves his desk and comes up to the counter. "May I help you," he asks with a degree of politeness that he usually doesn't show Negroes. An embarrassed look on the white man's face tells the story.

"Our grandparents live here in Tulsa," Windows says. "How can I find their whereabouts?"

The stationmaster appears willing to help these strange coloreds find their missing relatives. "If you want to learn about anyone who lives in Greenwood, I mean who used to live in Greenwood, I'd start with the Red Cross tent across Archer Street over near Standpipe Hill. They'd know which of the detention centers your kin is in."

"Detention centers?" Windows exclaims.

"Yup," the stationmaster says, glancing at the four Negroes one at a time. "During the uprising, they hauled every nig . . . I mean every colored person in Tulsa off to one of the detention centers. There's one at the fairgrounds, at Convention Hall and at McNulty Baseball Park. But there ain't no use in you trying to look for them at those places."

"Why not?" Windows asks.

"They ain't releasing no coloreds from detention unless a white person vouches for them and says they weren't involved in the killings hereabouts," the stationmaster says. The white man gives Windows a look that might have passed for a good-natured grin had not his beady eyes betrayed his hate lying just beneath the surface. "Who did you say your kinfolks are?"

"We didn't," Pete replies, stepping up to the counter. Pete is a good deal taller than the stationmaster and gives the white man a hostile look, a cop's look.

"Well, that's alright by me," the stationmaster chuckles. "I just thought I might know if any of your kin has already been released, since I know most of the nig . . . ah, colored folks in these parts. But suit yourself, you'll find the Red Cross right there on Archer Street, like I told you." The stationmaster returns to his desk.

The white ticket agent glances around at his boss. Then he says to Windows in a hushed voice, waving at the sea of black refugees crowding into the railroad terminal, "All these people here have just been released. Folks around here are pretty upset; some want to hang those nig . . ." It is the ticket agent's turn to correct himself this time. ". . . those *Negroes* who started this ruckus. Why don't you ask some of these people; they might know the whereabouts of your kin folks."

"Thanks," Windows mumbles.

The four of them step outside of the colored waiting room and huddle around. Bif is still trying to clear his head. Windows repeats what the stationmaster told him, even though they had all heard the conversation. "I don't think it's a good idea to talk to anyone around here," Bif volunteers. "These people are scared. And whatever we ask them they'll certainly tell the white folks."

"If you don't think it's a good idea to let that cracker stationmaster know why we're here," Pete suggests, "let's go over to Archer Street. We might learn something from the Red Cross."

The others agree. The *Negro World*'s team of journalists leaves the railway station and heads north across the train tracks and onto what is left of Greenwood Avenue in the direction of Archer Street. It's fortunate that Bif knows his way around Tulsa, since white people keep them under the surveillance the whole time. Anyone with relatives in Tulsa, it is assumed, would know where Archer Street is. On the way, Bif pauses briefly in front of what had been A. J. Smitherman's *Star*. On his last trip, Bif told A. J. that he planned to retire in Greenwood.

"Be sure to come see me when you do," A. J. told the veteran photographer. The Tulsa *Star* can use someone with your background."

"I certainly will consider your offer, A. J.," Bif said to the likeable newspaperman.

"Consider?" A. J. Smitherman laughed. "You haven't been talking to that old fool at the *Sun*, have you?"

"No sir, I surely haven't," Bif said with a straight face.

But A. J. Smitherman knew Bif was lying. "Well, you just be sure to come see me when you get settled," he told the Garveyite.

Now Bif can do nothing but stare at a pile of rubble, twisted metal and concrete foundation that had once housed Smitherman's *Star*. Shards of broken glass are strewn everywhere. Despite Pete's warning, Bif takes out his camera and shoots some photos. It seems to have a therapeutic effect because Bif marches off toward Archer Street at a more deliberate pace.

They pass from the commercial area into the residential neighborhood. There the full magnitude of the devastation hits them. Everywhere they look the neighborhood's former residents can be seen huddling about in twos and threes in front of the ruins that once were their homes. Some sift through the debris looking for personal belongings, mementos, pictures, anything to remind them of what had been. The white mob systematically looted the neighborhood house by house. They stole everything of value, then piled all the other personal belongings outside and burned them. Everywhere can be seen twisted and contorted metal from bed frames and bed springs as if fashioned for some macabre festival by demons from the underworld. Cotton mattresses still smolder, materializing Dante's inferno into reality. Some chairs and tables, though scorched and burned, are still serviceable. Women can be seen collecting a few pitiful belongings and sticking them into drawers of chests or desks that have somehow survived the flames. What had been toys, photo albums, clothes, bedding, and Bibles now lie about in bits and pieces. Broken glass and pottery and silverware and pots and pans and tools . . . and the unmistakable smell of death emanates from charred remains that had once been human beings.

Frozen in their final agonies, ghastly shapes still cry out their terrible shrieks from gaping mouths now silenced by death. Some are burned and mutilated beyond recognition, beyond even the idea that the clump of charred flesh had ever been human. Others, quite recognizable, lie rotting and stinking, repelling even the crows that have gathered to enjoy their ghoulish feast. Here and there black women sit on the stoops of their former homes, crying, moaning, raising their voices to the heavens in their pain to that white God whom, even now, they faithfully serve and hopefully petition, never fully comprehending "the victim's guilt." But it is not their prayers to which he listens, but those of his "chosen" living across the tracks. The only survivors of the white mob's carnage are the wooden outhouses, giving mute testimony to the systematic and planned destruction of Tulsa's Negro community.

Spotting the group as they trod through the destruction, one old black woman sits in a rocking chair, her eyes filled with sadness as she moans over and over, "They all gone! They all gone! *They all gone!*"

"Who's gone?" Julia asks, her eyes filled with sympathy.

"All of them, my husband, my son, his wife, their children. They all gone! Gone to heaven." Then looking right at Julia, she says, "I guess I'm ready to go, too." She lets out a cry as if she had been pierced straight through to her heart, a cry that cuts deep into Julia's soul.

"I can go on," Julia repeats over and over to herself. "I must go on." She tries to keep pace with the men. Julia reaches into one of the valises and she pulls out another handkerchief and wraps it around the first one, covering her nose and mouth, but it's hopeless. The stench of burned flesh, gunpowder and dynamite has burned into her lungs and her nausea is overwhelming.

Pete stops and waits for Julia to catch up. "You all right?" he asks.

She nods, but just as he turns to start up the street again, Julia calls out, "I can't . . ." She doesn't finish her sentence before her body makes a half turn, and, with her head turning toward the sky, she collapses in the middle of the street.

The three men hurry to her side. Luckily, Windows has brought some water.

"It's the smell," Pete says after they are finally able to revive her. "It's making you sick." Then looking over at Bif, he asks, "How far do we have to go?"

"Not far," Bif says, "possibly another four, five blocks."

"Then we'll have to carry her," Pete states. And picking Julia up, they continue through the desolation and grief. Pete prides himself on his strength and stamina. He sets an example for his legionnaires. He keeps in excellent physical condition and expects the same of them. But the next five blocks, shouldering Julia's 125 pounds, stretch the limits of Pete's endurance. By the time Bif leads the party through the debris and litter to the Red Cross's emergency tent, Pete is on the verge of collapse. Of their party, only the cub reporter has not been crushed by the ordeal.

"If you've come here for tents," an amiable white man, in his mid-thirties, says, "we've run out. Try to make yourselves as comfortable as possible over there with the others. I should have more tents before nightfall."

He motions them to join a crowd of Negro men, women and children huddled together in the section of the Frisco railroad yard that the Red

Cross has staked out for the refugees. Blank, vacant looks reflecting their uncertain future are painted even on the faces of children. Fearing the hate of Tulsa's whites, the refugees wait meekly for the tents that will be their only shelter for the next several years. These survivors of the worst mass murder of black people in the twentieth century, until the slaughter carried out by the United States Army in 1943, do not know what fate has in store for them. Back on the other side of the tracks, white Tulsans, and, indeed, whites all over America, applaud the recent events. And the Ku Klux Klan enjoys unprecedented popularity. It recruits members in droves by promising that its "Tulsa Solution" will be applied all over America.

Chapter Eleven

Tulsa was planned perfectly. The timing, the setup, even the cover was perfect. "So what went wrong?" Taft asks himself over and over again. "How did those Negroes put up such resistance?" Taft doesn't like it; he doesn't like it one bit. He's planning a race war. He's planning a race removal. And good white Americans getting killed aren't a part of his plans. No sir. "History isn't going to brand William Howard Taft as a murderer," the chief justice vows. He loves America and he loves Americans. No sir, no Americans are going to die at the hands of these darkies, not if he has anything to say about it. That is why it is so important to get them out of America and back into Africa, where they belong. "If it wasn't for those damned British," Taft swears vehemently. "Well, no use crying over spilled milk." But in Tulsa, more than three hundred *white men* lost their lives. Tulsa is supposed to be the answer, the way of building up the Klan all over the country, the way of eliminating the darkies everywhere except in the largest cities, like New York, Chicago and Los Angeles. Even there, after Tulsa, the Klan can exert tremendous pressure. We can wipe out the entire Negro population within the decade. What made those darkies in Tulsa put a fight, even after the planes dropped the dynamite. *Three hundred white men killed!* Nobody can learn about *that*. What made those niggers fight back?

The white mob that invades Tulsa's Negro community numbers in the tens of thousands. They come from as far away as Oklahoma City. All of them are heavily armed. The Oklahoma National Guard, the state militia as well as local law enforcement join in the attack. But still the fighting is fierce. Inside the railroad yards, Negroes take such protected positions that they force the Guard unit to withdraw, leaving a number of Guardsmen dead and wounded. The battle rages from six in the evening until noon the following day, with the Negroes fighting to the very end.

In the northeast section of Greenwood by Sunset Hill, black men barricade themselves in a concrete store. Well armed, they kill many of the whites foolhardy enough to storm the building in a frontal attack. This concrete building is the first target in the whites' aerial assault. Dynamite dropped from the air kills most of the black defenders in the building. But a few escape. Another group under the leadership of Peg Leg Taylor, an ex-serviceman, conducts a running gun battle with the white mob. Finding secure spots, they ambush a number of whites. Then they race away before the mob can overwhelm them.

The final skirmish occurs between the Negroes dug in at the Santa Fe railroad tracks by the Section Line, off of Peoria Street, and thousands of whites reinforced by elements of the Oklahoma State National Guard. Armed with hunting rifles, shotguns and pistols, the Negroes hold off the whites for several hours. Under the directions of former soldiers, they concentrate their fire into the mob with deadly effect. Dead and dying whites, who came to Greenwood for sport, are destined never to return to their families or loved ones again. They lie in black Tulsa's streets, killed by the Negroes they hated. Other whites arrive with high-powered rifles and a 50-caliber machine gun. This firepower is too fierce and the Negroes must give ground and are finally slaughtered. It is in the railroad yard that Peg Leg Taylor and many other black heroes meet their deaths.

Taft has not planned on the Negroes offering any resistance. They are not men, after all, they're animals.

"Now, Edgar, listen to me," Taft tells his deputy. "There can be no doubt that someone in intelligence leaked information to those niggers in Tulsa. That's why they were ready for us. Some white man is behind all this and I want to know who."

Hoover brings Taft an intelligence report that states that Cyril Briggs and the African Blood Brotherhood claim responsibility for defending Tulsa's Negro community.

"But most worshipful master," J. Edgar Hoover quails, "how could the African Brotherhood have known? No one knew of the plan outside our circle." Hoover trembles before Taft. The FBI operative knows what happens to anyone Taft even suspects of treachery.

"You would have me believe that a loose band of West Indian niggers called the African Blood Brotherhood—where do these niggers get these names?" Taft asks. "A group whose only organizations are in New York, Chicago and Baltimore—just happens to choose to come to Tulsa, Oklahoma at the exact time that we have planned our little diversion?" Taft is annoyed with his minion. "Edgar, do you know how long I've been planning Tulsa?"

"Years?" the Justice Department official quavers.

"Many years!" Taft says sternly. "My plan was perfect. I picked the right location. I picked the right people. *I had the perfect plan.* Do you understand me?"

"Yes, your most worshipful eminence."

"Now are you telling me that my plan was not perfect?"

"No, most excellent supreme grand master."

"Then how did they know about it?" Taft raises his voice only so slightly, but to Hoover it echoes like thunder. The fat man continues without waiting for a reply. "The answer is that someone must have told them."

"But grand master," Hoover dares to reply, "there has been a lot of Klan activity in Oklahoma recently."

"You dare tell me something I already know?" Taft booms.

"No, grand master," Hoover responds quickly. "I just meant that the African Blood Brotherhood might have been attracted to Tulsa because of those lynchings."

"A few niggers being strung up here and there in Oklahoma didn't cause these fellows to come out and organize," Taft responds. "We're stringing them up all over the country. No, they came to Tulsa because they knew."

But there were more than just a few lynchings in and around Tulsa. Whites lynched several Negroes in Okmulgee County in March, Oktaha County in April, and in Hugo County in May, all of them but a few miles from Tulsa. It is probable that whites from Tulsa participated in all these lynchings and it is certain that whites from these counties joined in the attack on Greenwood. There is also the hanging of Laura Nelson off of the Arkansas River Bridge. The black woman tried to stop white teenagers from castrating her small son. The teenagers hanged her, castrated her ten-year-old child, and then hanged him as well. They took pictures of their ghastly deed to show their parents. Yes, there are plenty of reasons why the African Blood Brotherhood might have suspected that Negroes in Oklahoma needed defense, Hoover believes. But he holds his tongue. It doesn't serve to contradict the infallible supreme grand master.

"Edgar, I want you to find the leak," Taft says. "And I want it done quickly. Do you understand?"

"Yes, most worshipful excellency," Hoover replies.

"Check for double agents," Taft orders, looking over some of the files on his desk marked Top Secret. "I want to know about this Captain James Wormley-Jones and William Pickens. The leak could have come from any of our agents, especially from our *Negro agents*."

"Pickens?" Hoover says. "Sir, Pickens has top clearance from the military. Surely you don't suspect him."

William Pickens, a field secretary for the NAACP, had the highest security clearance of any Negro in the United States. Pickens, the son of a South Carolina sharecropper, graduated from Yale in 1904 and became the first black member of the Skull and Bones Society and as well as confidant of Taft, himself. As a recruiter for the NAACP and later its national field secretary, Pickens enjoys a successful career as an intelligence agent. His undercover work includes befriending Garvey and becoming a contributor to the UNIA's *Negro World*. Much later, when his days as a government spy are over, Pickens will become a dean of a college and a high-ranking official in Franklin Roosevelt's New Deal, helping to woo Negro voters from the Republican Party to the Democratic Party.

"I don't trust any of these niggers," Taft says with a snarl. "Just because we use them doesn't mean we should trust them. They're selling out their own people for goodness sakes, how can you trust them? Any of them could be a double agent."

"Yessir," Hoover responds.

"And while you're at it, check on Spingarn as well. I don't trust that Jew."

"Yes, most worshipful grand master," Hoover responds.

With a wave of his hand, the supreme grand master, the dreaded and terrible Magog of the Tomb, dismisses his Justice Department minion. In turn, Hoover gives his required obeisance and, flashing the familiar hand signal, moves toward the door of the office on Yale's campus.

"And Edgar," Taft says.

"Yessir?" the frog-faced man says instantly, bowing to the behemoth sitting behind the desk.

"Remember, I'm depending on you."

"Yessir, you can depend on me," Hoover replies devoutly.

Taft feels reassured. "Edgar will find the leak," he says to himself. "Of course there was a leak. My plan was *perfect*."

The plan to steal and sell off the naval oil reserves at Elk Hills in California and at Teapot Dome in Wyoming is perfect. The plan—hatched while Taft is still president, with his co-conspirators, Albert Fall, the United States Senator from Arizona, and Henry Sinclair, the oil industrialist—is the theft of all of the oil that lies beneath government property in California and Wyoming. The liquid gold is worth hundreds of millions, even hundreds of billions, of dollars. The conspirators scheme to privatize the public oil reserves and distribute the oil through an international oil cartel, the Continental Trading Company, incorporated in Canada, away from prying eyes. The cartel includes the most powerful oil conglomerates in the world: Standard Oil, Midwest Oil, Prairie Oil Company, Pan American Oil Company and the Sinclair Oil Company of Tulsa. Sinclair Oil provides the airplanes that bomb and strafe the Greenwood business district and Tulsa's Negro residential community. As president, Taft issues the executive order to withdraw and turn over to the Navy 69,000 acres of public land containing the Elk Hills oil reserve located in Kern County, California, as well as the 29,000 acres of public land containing the Teapot Dome oil reserve located in Natoma County, Wyoming. When Taft is defeated for re-election, the cartel's plan is neither delayed nor abandoned. During the Wilson administration, overriding the presidential veto, the Republican-dominated congress, under Taft's control, passes a law authorizing the secretary of the Navy to develop, operate, lease, sell and exchange petroleum products from the Elk Hills and Teapot Dome oil reserves. Then orchestrating the election of the naïve, yet totally corrupt, Warren G. Harding, Taft engineers the greatest theft of public resources in the history of the United States. Harding appoints Taft to the position of chief justice of the Supreme Court, recently vacated by the incumbent in a surprise move. Albert Fall is appointed secretary of Interior; Edward Denby, a political neophyte, secretary of the Navy; and the corrupt Klansman, Harry Daugherty, Taft's 1916 campaign manager, is appointed attorney general of the United States.

On that fateful day, May 31st, 1921, Harding, by executive order and at the request of the secretary of the Navy, directs the secretary of the Interior, Albert Fall, to assume all administrative responsibilities for the United States' strategic oil reserves, including the reserves at Elk Hills and Teapot Dome. Fall is given the authority and power to develop, operate, lease, sell and exchange petroleum products from the Elk Hills and Teapot Dome oil reserves. Fall promptly passes this authority over to Taft's international oil cartel, the Continental Trading Company.

It is in the very nature of Taft's plot to steal the United States strategic oil reserves that utter secrecy be maintained throughout. So in order to cover up the theft, Taft decides to create a diversion. The slaughter of thousands of Negroes and the destruction of a community housing 10,000 residents is just the kind of diversion the Tomb's dread and terrible Magog has in mind.

Taft and Richard Lloyd Jones, editor of the Tulsa Tribune, both sit on the board of directors for the creation of the Lincoln Memorial. They share similar views on the Negro. On February 4, 1921, Jones writes in his newspaper:

> Oklahoma's secret order, the new Ku Klux Klan will be a living, lasting memorial to the original Klan members who had saved the South from a Negro empire. The Klan's guarantee of the supremacy of the white race in social, political and governmental affairs of the nation is welcomed.

Later that same month, Jones writes:

> A bad nigger is about the lowest thing that walks on two feet. Give a bad nigger his booze and his dope and his gun and he thinks

he can shoot up the world. And all four things are to be found RIGHT HERE in Tulsa's Niggertown: booze, dope, bad niggers and guns.

On the fateful night of May 31st, 1921, while the president of the United States hands over billions of dollars in public oil to Taft and his cronies, Richard Lloyd Jones issues the directive to destroy the Negro community of Tulsa in his Tulsa Tribune. *A front page headline and an editorial of the Tulsa* Tribune *directs the whites of Tulsa, Oklahoma to:*

NAB NEGRO FOR ATTACKING GIRL IN ELEVATOR AND LYNCH THE NEGRO TONIGHT.

And that is why the grossly overweight supreme master of the Scottish Rite Masons, master and guardian of Graves, and exalted cyclops of the Ku Klux Klan knows that, since his plan had been perfect, there must have been an informant.

Julia does not know where to turn or what to do. The four of them returned from Tulsa nearly two weeks ago. Grady expects to see her *soon.*

"Look here, girl," he tells her on the telephone, "I kept my part of the deal, didn't I? You're where you wanted to be, all prim and proper. Working at the library and with a nice apartment on the Westside. Now it's time for you to deliver."

Grady wants Julia to submit to questioning by military intelligence. Before leaving for Tulsa, she had promised to meet him when she returns.

"It won't be that bad, sugar," he promises. "And afterwards we can go up to my place. I've got some stuff that will blow your mind. You won't come down for a week. You just have to go down to Ellis Island and talk to a few government people and that's it."

Now Julia is sorry she committed herself.

"What kind of questions?" she asks Grady.

"They're just interested in knowing who was behind the Negro uprising in Tulsa," he says.

"All those poor people," she exclaims, feeling nauseous just remembering the ghastly sights and smells. "But really, I don't know anything about who was behind it."

"I know you don't, honey," Grady says smoothly. "All you need to do is tell them that."

Julia thinks about Bif's friends. A few lucky ones got out alive and uninjured. But they lost everything they owned: their homes, personal possessions, furniture, jewelry, clothes, everything. She remembers seeing babies and small children wandering about, crying for parents whose bodies are rotting in one of the many mass graves the whites hurriedly dug to control the awful smells—smells that refuse to obey their segregation laws. For weeks white Tulsans, those unable to flee the city, are forced to protect their mouths and noses from the incredible stench that settles over the entire community. A swarm of insects invades the town. Flies and gnats are so thick that the white people continually brush, fan and swat at the pests, but to no avail; the insects take over. Not being prejudiced, they feast on live white flesh just as well as on dead black corpses. Julia recalls the heartbreaking sight of Greenwood's survivors, young and old, wandering through the burned-out buildings calling out the names of family pets, tears streaming down their faces. Every once in awhile, a pet dog or cat returns. What joy the surviving pet brings. The elderly and sick sleep on the bare ground with little more than threadbare covering. Long soup lines provide a minimum amount of nourishment, the survivors' only source of food. Exposed to the elements, even during the relatively moderate summer period, causes many, especially the very old and very young, to become sick. There is an outbreak of typhus. Inadequate medical facilities and supplies cause many more to die, most of them children. Julia sees no such animal as a good, white Christian in Tulsa. There are only mean, white devils, gloating over the evil they had wrought.

Tulsa's all-white city council passes an ordinance depriving Negroes access to the land where their houses once stood. The council announces a "fire sale" for Tulsa's white commercial interests. Land that once belonged to Negroes is sold to whites for little or nothing. The real estate developers swarm into Greenwood just like insects and gorge themselves on dead flesh. Even before the news team leaves Greenwood, people begin calling it "Deadwood." After all this wretchedness, Grady wants her to inform military intelligence and the Bureau of Investigation about which Negroes are responsible for the uprising. She just can't do it.

How strange her new feelings are. Julia was never concerned for Negroes before. She hasn't really cared for anything or anyone but herself. Hadn't her mother told her that her looks were her ticket out of Harlem? Hadn't her father always talked about how lazy and shiftless those American Negroes are? "Wouldn't move out of their own way for a dime," he would say.

"So why shouldn't I help these white people Grady introduces me to," Julia asks herself, playing the devil's advocate. Even if they do seem strange and standoffish, like Carl and Nadine, I'm helping myself. I'm moving ahead. That's what Grady promised. But that was before Tulsa. Now everything is different. She feels different about a lot of things. And there is Pete.

Before, Pete was just another darkie who looked at her like a piece of meat. "No, that's not true," Julia scolds herself. "Pete has always been a perfect gentleman, a bit shy, maybe too shy, but always courteous." Sometimes he can be, how can she describe it, a bit distant, cold, sarcastic even. "Yes, that's it, Pete can be very sarcastic." And he actually hurts her feelings on occasion. No other man can do that, not Grady, not even her father. And the good Lord knows that her father tried often enough. Sometimes Julia wonders how her mother can stand all her father's abuse. Maybe Pete, like her father, is really just trying to cover up how he feels about her. Julia knows Pete loves her; she'd be a fool not to know. But she really didn't care before. "What changed?" Julia asks herself. "I have," comes the answer. "I love him. I love Peter Jenkins."

Pete is strong. He's so strong that even though he loves her, Julia knows he'll never allow her to crush him or make him less than a man. There are so many other women who want him, women just as pretty, or maybe prettier than her. Pete always has women after him, the women at Garvey's Liberty Hall as well as those working at the *Negro World*. They'd do anything to get Pete's attention.

When Julia first joined the Garveyites, she didn't care how many women were interested in Commander Peter Jenkins of the African Legion. Julia was there for one reason and one reason only: to provide information on UNIA activities and to use Pete to get it. And use him she did, without any compunction. To make it in New York, one can't have a conscience. Besides, Julia had loved Grady then, or at least she thought she did. To make it out of Harlem, one has to be absolutely predatory. The fools who believed in race pride and the "New Negro" deserve to be taken advantage of. *Find a fool, bump his head.* Harlem is filled with numbers runners, pimps, landlords, speakeasy proprietors, dope dealers, ministers and other hustlers who live off their prey. Idealism does not live in Harlem; the rent is too high. Everybody hustles for the white man. The only difference is that some, like the gangsters and dealers, are straight up while others like the "race leaders" and preachers lie. But even that doesn't matter because fools are always looking to be taken advantage of. Either they are too lazy, too dumb or too complacent to get out there and get something for themselves. They want someone to give it to them. *Everyone wants to go to heaven, but no one wants to die.* The so-called Negro leaders are the worst liars of all.

"But Pete's different," Julia sighs. "He's noble and idealistic and brave and he treats me like I'm an innocent little girl," she thinks. "And I love him." Thinking about Pete allows Julia to take her mind off of Grady for the time being. "I wonder what Pete would think, if he knew how much I love him," she wonders. But that is a question that will never have an answer, because Julia vows never to let Pete know how very much she does love him.

"Oh well," she says out loud, "after these last couple of weeks, he might even suspect it by now."

Julia is at her new library job. In front of her is a cart filled with books needing to be restacked. They should have been put up a day ago. But Julia continues to daydream. Pete saw her leave with Carl. Suddenly she feels ashamed of herself. Pete also knows about Grady. "Pete's no dummy," she thinks, "he's just different from the others."

As she stands there daydreaming, she must have conjured him up, because suddenly Pete's standing in front of her.

"Hi there," he says. "Got time for lunch?"

"Oh, is it lunch time, already?" Julia replies.

"Yep," he answers. "I've got a couple of sandwiches and some lemonade that the ladies at the Hall made. We can go over to the park."

"Okay," Julia answers. "Let me check out. I'll meet you out front."

Out front, without needing to say anything, they start out toward a little park off of 135th Street where they can eat their sandwiches. Ever since Tulsa, Julia continues to notice little things about him. He is tall, but not really tall, just a little less than six feet. Julia is tall herself, at least she's tall for a woman, almost five feet eight inches. She likes his broad shoulders and great strong arms. Those arms carried her through the desolation and destruction of Tulsa. When she closes her eyes she can still see where airplanes had actually dropped dynamite on buildings and shot at fleeing women and children. She saw craters where the bombs exploded and she saw horribly charred corpses, unrecognizable as being human with missing limbs and heads. The only accurate description being the "remains." They are the "remains" of what used to be a human. Pete's so strong and tender. If it had not been for him, she would not have survived the ordeal, nor would Bif, for that matter. Julia makes a decision. She will definitely not speak with Grady's superiors.

"Pete," Julia starts.

"Yes," he replies, looking at her with that detachment that infuriates her.

"I've got to tell you something."

"Okay, tell me."

Julia begins to speak, haltingly at first, and then the words come more quickly and then come a torrent, an outpouring of secret thoughts, inner fears and personal feelings. She tells him thoughts even she was unaware of until now. It is as if a dam has burst inside her soul and the real Julia, a different Julia, breaks free from bondage. She not only tells Pete of her secret arrangement with Grady to provide information on the UNIA and the *Negro World*, she tells him about how she had let Grady use her, exchanging Grady for Jacko, a local pimp she had known since she was fifteen. She tells Pete about her father and his mistresses and how her mother drowns her sorrows. She tells Grady about her dreams and her nightmares and why she really never liked men nor had any close friends. She talks about why she doesn't believe in God but fears the devil and how much she wants to live in a nice apartment and have nice things and be treated like she is somebody. Julia tells him how she hates Harlem with all the junkies, hustlers, pimps and low-lifes who never want anything more than to live in "nigger heaven." She talks about how she doesn't like music and doesn't like to dance and how surprised she was when he touched her at Cora's rent party and held her close. Her body tingled as if he was the first man she had ever known.

"When it happened," Julia says, "I hated you for it . . ."

Pete gives Julia a look that says nothing and everything. But he keeps silent.

"Did you know that it had been arranged that I leave you for Carl Van Vechten at the *Shuffle Along* after party?"

"No, I didn't," Pete replies.

"Do you know that it hurt me more than it seemed to hurt you?" Julia asks.

"It hurt, all right," Pete says quietly.

"It didn't seem so to me," Julia replies. "I watched you even after I left. You didn't seem to mind my going at all."

Pete grunts an unintelligible reply.

"After all that I've told you, is that all you can say?" Julia asks. "I've told you more than I even told my mother."

"Well," Pete says, "I'd love to stay here all day and talk, but don't you think you'd better get back to the library. We've been here over an hour." He glances at his watch. "I know I've got to get back."

"But, but . . ." Julia stammers. Her green eyes, like emeralds lovely and alluring, begin to well up with tears. The protective shell Julia developed growing up on Harlem's tough streets, cracks, making her feel vulnerable, a little foolish and even a bit angry. But Pete takes her hand and pulls her from the park bench into his arms. Then slowly, tenderly, he bends down and places his cheek against hers.

After holding her for a long while, he says, "I'll see you after work."

Then Pete leaves. Julia wonders if she has done the right thing. Julia knows she loves Pete, but a woman has to be practical, Julia tells herself. After all, a man is just a man.

Pete is not really surprised at what Julia tells him, especially about the spying. He never trusted Grady. Grady always was a player; Grady plays everyone. Pete is a cop. And, even in an organization like the UNIA, an organization with over 80,000 members all over the United States, being a cop means being suspicious. And Pete is naturally suspicious, if not downright paranoid. He was suspicious while in the Army. It was his suspicions of Grady that led Pete to save the fool's life. Grady is always doing something that can get him or one of the other fellows killed. Grady cares about nothing and no one but Grady. All cops are suspicious. The reason cops have high divorce rates is because they don't trust their wives, and the reason that they have high suicide rates is because they don't trust themselves.

So as Pete ponders what Julia has told him, he becomes suspicious not only of her but of himself. He wonders whether or not he really loves her as much as he thought he did and whether she loves him at all. One thing he knows now, whether or not she loves him, she needs him. She has gotten involved with Grady Jones and Grady cannot be trusted to keep his word about anything. That Julia decided to trust Pete now means that they are in this thing together. Julia answered one question: why had Pete been sent to Tulsa? But now there is a myriad of other questions. Who inside the UNIA set it up? Who inside the UNIA is working with military intelligence? Most importantly, assuming there is mole inside the UNIA, what did military intelligence want to know about the UNIA or the *Negro World* that the mole—who arranged that Julia and he take the trip to Tulsa together—can't tell them?

As soon as he gets back to his office, one of the staff bawls out at him. "Pete!"

"Yeah," Pete growls back.

"The boss wants to see you."

When he walks into Ferris's office the *World*'s boss flashes him a smile. "I've never congratulated you on the way you handled that Tulsa assignment," Ferris says.

"Thank you sir," Pete replies. "But I haven't read any of the stories Windows or Julia wrote about what we saw there."

"I know, I know," Ferris repeats himself. Pete thinks Ferris seems nervous. "Well, you know how these new reporters are, we have to check their work for accuracy. It doesn't pay for us to run stories that are inaccurate because we'd just have to run a correction."

"Yessir," Pete says. After an uncomfortable silence, Pete asks, "Is that all, sir?"

"Yes, yes, that's all, my boy. Fine job, great job."

Back in his office downstairs, Pete asks himself another question, "Why would a newspaper send four reporters a thousand miles away to get a story that it didn't intend to print?"

Chapter Twelve

The Roaring Twenties sanction bootleg whiskey, gangland violence and political corruption. Vice runs the country, and virtue, well, what the hell is that? With the patriotic creed of nationalism and racism sanctioned by the followers of Jesus Christ as well as hooded Klansmen, America remains securely in the control of the robber barons whose antecedents are European aristocracy. Even with slavers, rumrunners and opium dealers as their models, the shameless deeds of the Republican administration under Warren G. Harding, the twenty-ninth president of the United States, writes a new chapter in the annals of corrupt political practices.

Under Harding's administration, the business of government is graft. It disperses alien property, valued in the millions of dollars, to political cronies; it appropriates timberlands, power sites and oil reserves out of the public domain for the use and exploitation of private corporations. In return, the highest government officials line their pockets with the "boodle."

The government's rackets operate out of the office of United States Attorney General Harry Daugherty, the political crony and campaign manager for William Howard Taft as well as Harding. Daugherty organizes the operations, collects the graft and apportions the payoffs to Harding, Taft and everyone else involved.

Under the authority of the Justice Department, Daugherty modifies decrees of federal judges, dismisses civil and criminal actions against industrial and corporate lawbreakers, modifies prison sentences, sells paroles and pardons, auctions off federal judgeships and district attorney appointments, removes whiskey from bonded warehouses and sells it to mobsters, extends the protection of the federal government to bootleg-

gers and underworld syndicates of all types, and creates a black market for property seized by federal agents. Daugherty's power is as audacious as it is unlimited. He answers only to his co-conspirators, the president of the United States and the chief justice of the Supreme Court. The three of them split an estimated "boodle" of seven million dollars each month.

Daugherty protects his operation by appointing his crony, William J. Burns, director of the Federal Bureau of Investigation. Burns owns the Burns Detective Agency. During the Great European War, Burns and confederate Gaston Means act as double agents. One gathers intelligence on the British for the Germans while the other spies on the Germans for the British.

Daugherty orders the FBI director to protect the administration's rackets and collect the graft. Responsible for eliminating any and all opposition by any means necessary, Burns runs the FBI like he ran his detective agency, employing career criminals and corrupt cops as federal agents. Burns attacks anyone daring to threaten Daugherty's criminal empire. FBI agents investigate congressmen, senators, government departments, congressional committees, critics of Daugherty, critics of the Justice Department and even critics of the government in general. Burns operates a highly sophisticated blackmail operation. Critics of the administration find their own affairs being scrutinized and made public. Federal agents reveal information from the personal files, private telephone conversations and personal mail of their critics, their children, their families, their friends, even their neighbors. Anyone threatening Daugherty's rackets, payoffs and threats receives a visit from the FBI. And if Daugherty wants someone eliminated, which happens quite often, the name is passed to Burns's gangland associates and the unfortunate victim—and possibly his spouse and friends—are ticketed for a one-way ride.

When Senator Burton Wheeler introduces a resolution to investigate corruption in the Justice Department, Burns sends FBI agents to the senator's home state of Montana and secures an indictment against the senator. When Senator Robert La Follette becomes hostile to Daugherty, Burns has La Follette's office looted and his files seized. When Elias Mortimer, the commissioner in charge of pardons, challenges the collection *of graft for presidential pardons, FBI agents harass him into resigning. Burns details an agent to snoop on Colonel Jim Darden when he threatens to interfere with the multi-billion-dollar oil deals. When Thomas Walsh presses for an investigation of the Teapot Dome Scandals, FBI agents find an attorney who swears that the Montana senator is himself involved. When B. C. Baldwin, one of the few honest FBI agents, discovers the illegal trafficking of guns and booze in and out of Mexico and arrests the federal marshal responsible for the operation, Burns has Baldwin transferred to Montana, closes the FBI's El Paso office and issues a directive withdrawing the federal agents' authority to investigate any other federal agents without obtaining Burns expressed permission. When the United States Senate called Burns's private secretary to testify before the committee investigating charges against the Justice Department, J. Edgar Hoover, then Assistant Director of the FBI, promptly fires her, after which she disappears without a trace.*

"Private," Captain Hansen says, "you've fouled up again. Can't you ever carry out an assignment?"

The military intelligence officer stares at the hapless operative like a plantation master might look at one of his slaves.

"But sir . . ." Grady stammers.

"Never mind," the officer cuts him off. "We know who it was."

"You do?" Grady replies tentatively.

"It was your friends from the African Blood Brotherhood. The ones you filed your report on."

Grady feels a chill running down his spine. Is Hansen bringing another charge against him?

"We've known about them for some time."

The white intelligence officer stares at his Negro agent and wonders whether Grady is the double agent they are searching for. But after a moment's reflection, Hansen knows that Grady can't be a double agent. He isn't smart enough to be a single agent. According to Nadine's reports, the only thing this Negro is good for is servicing women, and if Nadine's reports are to be taken literally, he isn't all that good at that. "Besides," Hansen thinks, "this man doesn't think in those terms. The only thing on this Negro's mind is pimping women and that's not a particularly ideal vocation for an intelligence agent, particularly since there are so many female spies." Hansen smiles as he flips through Nadine's progress report on Grady. She recommends advancement. Hansen almost laughs out loud.

"In the great game," Hansen's West Point teacher constantly reminded the cadets, "the only winning strategy is controlling behavior. If you know when and how your enemy will behave, you cannot fail. The use of accurate and reliable intelligence has been the key to America's successful military exploits. The people you will be going against cannot succeed against you as long as you understand that we maintain the most extensive intelligence network in the world. And when you go against the colored races, remember that they have no intelligence at all."

No, Grady is not intelligent enough to be the double agent Hoover is looking for. Neither is he what Hansen needs.

"Your Negro will never be a player in our 'great game,' " Hansen told Nadine in their debriefing. "He doesn't understand the anomaly that a successful agent always must keep in mind: that he must have thorough and absolute understanding of the values that he must readily betray. Your Negro has no such understanding; you can trust that he will do as he is told because he's too stupid and cowardly to do anything else." Hansen smiled. "Of course, that's why the white race is on top and will remain there."

At which point, Nadine smiled back. "And do you include 'Jews' when you speak of the 'white race' staying on top, captain?"

Hansen gave the female spy a deliberate stare, trying to decide whether to burst out laughing, but in the end, he merely replied, "Why of course not, my dear."

"Private," Captain Hansen continues to Grady, "I'm changing your orders. We don't need to interview Miss, ah, what's her name?"

"Miss Duncan, Julia Duncan," Grady says.

"Yes, Miss Duncan. We want you to use Miss Duncan to find out more about the African Blood Brotherhood. We want to know how they knew about Tulsa. We want to find the leak. Is that clear?"

"Find the leak?"

"Yes, find the leak. Does the Brotherhood have someone inside of the intelligence community? If so, I want you to find out who it is. Is that clear?"

Grady looks at his commander. "He's got to be kidding," Grady thinks. "Is this just another test? How can Negroes, West Indian Negroes at that, have someone feeding them information from inside military intelligence? That's really dumb." But Grady decides it is best not to speak. "I'd better listen and find out what this white boy has on his mind," Grady thinks.

Grady isn't aware of the top-secret memo on Hansen's desk that says the African Blood Brotherhood organized the Tulsa resistance movement. The memo is written by James Wormley-Jones, the Negro Army captain assigned to the same Army intelligence section as Joel Spingarn, both of whom report to Hansen. Wormley-Jones infiltrated Garvey's organization and got a position at the *Negro World*. Wormley-Jones also joined the African Blood Brotherhood and took his oath of loyalty from Cyril Briggs. The Brotherhood believed that Wormley-Jones is their spy in the Garvey camp. Briggs trusted Wormley-Jones with most of the Brotherhood's secrets. However, try as he may, Wormley-Jones could not get Briggs to tell him how the Brotherhood knew about the plan to hit Tulsa. Wormley-Jones couldn't even find out whether Briggs actually knew about the attack beforehand. Military intelligence believes there is a leak, but Wormley-Jones can't find it. Furthermore, he doesn't believe one exists. But that's not what the higher-ups want to hear. They need Hansen to find the leak, and find it he will, Hansen vows. Although he has very little faith that Grady will turn anything up, who knows. Since God is a white man, Hansen believes, wonders never cease.

Grady discusses his new assignment with Nadine. Again, he is worried.

"If I don't get what they want, they're going to think it was me," Grady says.

"Don't be ridiculous," Nadine laughs. "What do you know?"

"Don't forget, I gave them a report straight from the Brotherhood's leaders."

"That is true," Nadine says, trying to keep a straight face. "But I wouldn't worry about it if I were you."

"Why not?"

"Your assignment's not so difficult," Nadine says. "You're going to give them what they want. Don't worry about these little changes. It's always something with these *spooks*."

Nadine pats Grady's shoulder and gives him a cigarette.

"You know Julia will do anything for you. Just take her to bed, lover boy, and after that everything will be all right."

"I don't see how," Grady begins.

"Look, don't worry," Nadine interrupts. "I'll contact Carl, if you want. He'll take your little Julia off your hands for a while. Then we'll put her on one of those Brotherhood 'brothers.' Simple, okay."

"I guess." But Grady isn't so sure.

"Don't worry," Nadine says. "Now come on over here and let Mama take care of you."

Julia looks up from her desk to see Grady Jones's grinning face staring down at her.

"Hi there, sweetheart."

Julia looks up from her desk. "What do you want?" she asks. Grady annoys her the way he just appears, no call, no announcement, nothing. It's as if he owns her. She doesn't like it and doesn't mind letting him know it.

"I thought I'd come around here, since I haven't seen you lately," Grady says, charm oozing from his every pore.

Now, however, his charm merely adds to Julia's annoyance. She wonders why she found Grady so attractive before, with his ridiculous little mustache and his slicked-back hair. "Probably has to have his scalp burned every week getting it konked," she muses.

"I thought you were going to come down and give us a report about your little trip to Tulsa," Grady says. "Or did you forget?"

"No, I didn't forget," Julia replies, using a belligerent tone to tell him that she's busy. "I just haven't felt like remembering all those horrible things done to those people." Julia looks past Grady to see whether her supervisor, a matronly woman with old-fashioned ideas about not socializing in the workplace, is watching. Her supervisor, a library employee for over twenty years, takes a dim view of the unattached female staff being too familiar with the patrons. "Now Miss Duncan," her supervisor had once lectured, "the library understands that a certain amount of communication is necessary between the staff and library patrons, since this is a public facility. But I must tell you that this communication must be strictly professional and limited. The library frowns on fraternization between patrons and staff."

"Yes, ma'am," Julia had responded, trying to keep a straight face.

If her supervisor is around, Julia can use her as an excuse to get rid of Grady. He notices Julia glancing over to her supervisor. "Oh, you don't have to worry about Miss Prim and Proper over there," he says.

"And why is that, may I ask?"

"You're quitting this dump. I've got something else I want you to do, something more important, something more appropriate for your, ah, talents."

"What makes you think you can come in here and order me around?" Julia's face turns beet red and her eyes narrow. "Who do you think you are, Mr. Grady Jones?"

"Be cool, baby," Grady says. "You don't have to raise your voice." Suddenly all his bravado vanishes and Grady begins to feel nervous. This is not going to be as easy as Nadine had said, he thinks, but keeping up his front, Grady tries the soothing words that normally calm Julia down. "Don't worry, baby," he says, giving her a reassuring pat on the hand. "I promised that I'd take care of you, didn't I. I knew you didn't want to talk about Tulsa. So now you don't have to. I cleared it for you. You know I'm always thinking about you."

"If you're always thinking about me, why are you with Nadine?" Julia says.

"Baby, you know that's business. How can I take care of you in the style you want without Nadine? How could I have gotten you this job?" He can see that Julia is warming up to his rap and his confidence returns.

"You know that it has all been for you from the very beginning. Ever since I met you, all I wanted was the best for you," Grady croons. "But you know a poor nigger like me has to hustle. You know that's right, don't you?"

Julia anger simmers down. "I guess," she replies.

"That's right. And I've got a special surprise for you."

"What's that?" Julia asks, once more under the spell of Grady's charm.

"Carl, you know Carl Van Vechten," he says.

"Oh, him," Julia says with visible distaste.

"Don't be like that, honey," Grady says. "Carl told me to bring you to the club tonight. He might have a job for you. Something with a little more class than this library gig."

"Oh, Grady," Julia says, "I don't know. I kind of like it here."

"No, baby," Grady says in his hustler's voice. "This isn't for you. Besides, if you don't like his offer you can always come back. Come on, now. It's okay, I've fixed it with your boss."

When Pete returns for Julia that night, she has already left. She didn't even leave him a note.

"Why did Miss Duncan leave early?" Pete asks Julia's supervisor.

"She quit," the matron replies.

"She *quit*?" Pete gasps as if the words had stuck in his windpipe.

Since he is, after all, a cop, it doesn't take long for Pete to learn that Julia has returned to Carl Van Vechten. Even for a man with Pete's strength and pride, the news shakes him to his very core. That night, in the dark stillness of his empty room, where no one else can see, silent tears fall from his eyes. Heart-broken, he cries himself to sleep.

Chapter Thirteen

Several weeks later, with Nadine's and Carl Van Vechten's assistance, Grady insinuates Julia into the African Blood Brotherhood. "Find out how they knew about the Tulsa plans," he tells her. But Grady has the bad luck that always follows dumb people. Grace Campbell, who sits on the Brotherhood's executive committee, is responsible for screening new members.

None of the African Brotherhood executive committee members, including Cyril Briggs, is more dedicated to the cause of the New Negro than Julia's former night school teacher. Perceptive and shrewd, Grace has been a New York City parole officer with contacts in the courts and in the police department. She even knows federal agents working for William Burns's FBI. Grace knows how to pump her sources for information. "White men always fall for the accent, don't you know," she tells Julia. "They listen to the sounds and not the words." If Grace believed in reincarnation, it would not surprise her in the least to discover that in a past life she was the famous Voodoo queen, Marie Laveau.

"So tell me, Julia," Grace says. "Why's a nice girl like you getting involved with this Ku Klux Klan scum?"

"The Ku Klux Klan?" Julia says.

"Yes, your boyfriend, Grady Jones, is supplying information to the Ku Klux Klan."

"But, but, Grady works for the military," Julia stammers.

"Where do you think the Klan gets its information?"

Afterward, Grace reports her findings to Briggs.

"Now we have what we need to get Garvey to work with us!" Briggs exclaims. "Call a meeting of the executive committee."

One of Grace's blind spots is Cyril Briggs. She agrees with everything Briggs says. It doesn't matter how farfetched and wild his plans, Grace will go along—she exemplifies the old adage: Behind every great man, there is a woman in love. Briggs dreams of the Brotherhood infiltrating and taking over Garvey's Association, believing the UNIA can propel Negroes into the mainstream of American economic and political affairs under his direction. But Garvey has foiled Briggs at every turn. He has rebuffed Briggs's attempts to merge their organizations and has identified every Brotherhood member who has joined the UNIA. Garvey also knew that Briggs was meeting with UNIA dissidents intent on removing Garvey from office at the next UNIA convention. No information Briggs has will get Garvey to trust the Brotherhood leader. Grace, as smart as she is, goes along with Briggs's plan.

The executive committee meets at Lafayette Hall, located in Harlem at 121st Street and 7th Avenue. The hall was a donation of a leftwing political group. If Cyril Briggs expects his Brotherhood executive committee to rubberstamp his recommendation to pass Julia's information over to Garvey, he is greatly mistaken.

"You cannot be serious about giving Garvey this information," Harry Haywood explodes.

Of all the Brotherhood, there is no one more opposed to Garvey and the concept of the New Negro and race consciousness than Haywood. A West Indian, Haywood maintains a whole-hearted belief in Marxist-Leninist ideology, in which proletarian brotherhood is of a higher order than black nationalism. Haywood believes Garvey to be the greatest menace to the Brotherhood's work.

"Negroes are an oppressed national minority, just as Jews and Irish are oppressed national minorities," Haywood insists. "Garvey does nothing but cheat gullible Negroes—he serves those same white folks who are doing all the lynching and murdering of coloreds."

"The executive committee has already discussed this issue," Briggs thunders. "We need Garvey's organization."

But other members support Haywood's position. The wrangling continues into the evening. Julia sits in an anteroom outside the executive committee meeting. Grace wants her available in case any of the members have questions. As they argue and shout at one another late into the evening, Julia lets her mind wander.

"Grady working for the Klan," she thinks. "Not possible." But then she begins to think about Pete. "What had he said?" Julia tries to remember.

"I'll see you after work and don't worry!" Julia remembers. "Oh why did I let Grady talk me into leaving him?" she asks out loud. Tears start to well up in her eyes and tumble down her cheeks. Julia never cries. Not when her father did everything he could to shame her. Not when her mother slapped her after Julia refused to apologize for calling her father a rag picker. Not even Jacko could make Julia cry. But now she cries every time she thinks about Pete. She has made such a mess of things. Julia misses him; she misses the feel of his arms around her. She misses the way he makes her feel safe and protected. Julia has deserted the man she loves and respects to take up with Grady and Carl—two men she not only dislikes, she despises.

"Oh Pete, Pete," she cries out, looking to blame him for her situation, "why did you leave me?"

Chapter Fourteen

Pete develops a tiny knot in his stomach. It is where he hides the pain, as far away as he can push it. But it isn't far enough. Every once in awhile, he will think of her and the pain comes back. Lately, the knot of pain stays in place. Not that he doesn't miss her. It is just that life has gotten hectic and Pete just doesn't have time to miss Julia.

Vandalism and theft of *Negro World* newspapers continue to increase dramatically. Delivery trucks are being shot at. Newsboys are being beaten. "Don't carry the *World*, if you know what's good for you!" the proprietors of Harlem's newspaper stands are being told. Many of them listen. "The little I make off of Garvey's weekly ain't enough to get hurt or to lose all my other newspapers," they tell Pete. Not only does Pete carry his Army Colt forty-five, but he keeps the duffel bag with his Thompson close by as well. Pete practices assembling and disassembling the Tommy gun so often that he can put it together in the dark. But providing security is not his only job

When Garvey leaves town, all dispatches to and from Garvey to his New York headquarters are in code. And since the UNIA is always in need of funds and Garvey is continually on speaking tours to replenish the organization's overdrawn accounts, each day, hours are spent coding and decoding messages. Ferris gives this job to Pete. Soon, Pete becomes responsible not only for Garvey's personal messages but also for all the encoded messages sent and received by the African Legion as well. These, and his security responsibilities, give Pete little opportunity to moon over Julia. Women still seek him out, invite him to dinner and try every means at their disposal to lure Pete into their arms—and their beds. One of the Black Cross nurses, Eva Darling, makes it impossible for Pete to resist.

Eva is a chocolate bouquet of female charm whose freckled nose gives her a look of innocence—belying her statuesque body built for sin. Eva's pert breasts and a heart-shaped behind drive men wild, but her heart and soul belong to Pete. No man can resist Eva. Try as he did to tell Eva his true feelings, neither can Pete resist nights of passionate lovemaking that end inevitably with Eva sobbing uncontrollably in his arms.

"You still love her," she cries. "You still love her . . . and I love you so much, it hurts."

And there is nothing Pete can say. He can neither deny his feelings for Julia nor give up Eva.

"Do you want me to leave?" Pete asks her gently.

"I never want you to leave me," Eva says, sobbing all the more because she knows that, one day, no matter what, Pete will leave. Julia will ask Pete to take her back. Eva knows Pete can no more help himself then can she. Who can resist the power of love?

"I think our Brotherhood friends are going to cause us some problems," Ferris tells Pete. Lately, Garvey depends more on his *World* editor than his Minister of the African Legion. Ferris, in turn, gives Pete more responsibility. "We just fired Domingo."

W. A. Domingo, a member of the Brotherhood's executive committee, has been an editor and writer on the *World*'s staff for several years. Garvey has Ferris order Domingo off the *World*'s premises abruptly, without notice.

"He must have expected it," Pete tells his boss.

"I don't know," Ferris replies. "It was the president-general's idea, not mine." Pete shakes his head as his boss continues. "Garvey decided to purge every known member of the Brotherhood from every UNIA division."

"Whose idea was that?" Pete asks.

"It was Gaines's idea," Ferris says, shrugging.

"We haven't got enough problems with the *Messenger* crowd and the NAACP, now he's turning friends into enemies, as well," Pete observes.

"Remember," Ferris says, lowering his voice, "Captain Gaines is still your superior. And he still has Garvey's ear."

"Not as much as he did before he went to L.A.," Pete says.

"Make no mistake," Ferris says, "Gaines is still number two around here. He's the one that does all the dirty work." Ferris gives Pete a knowing look. "I certainly don't want to get on his bad side, and neither should you."

"You're probably right about that," Pete replies. Pete had made a miscalculation. He knew that Garvey had recalled Captain Gaines after the Minister of the African Legion had bungled the Los Angeles situation. Garvey had sent Reverend Easton to replace Gaines. In his naïveté, Pete believed that Gaines had lost favor—which is why many decoders have short careers. *They know too much for their own good.*

The Los Angeles division has been in open revolt since the Black Star Steamship Lines failed to honor their commitment to Californians who purchased tickets to Liberia. The Californians, many of whom were members of the Los Angeles division, lost everything and are still stranded in New York. Division president Noah Thompson demanded an audit of the Black Star Line account. He also instituted a "dump Garvey" movement, meeting with other dissident division presidents from around the country. Cyril Briggs attended some of these meetings. Garvey sent Gaines to Los Angeles and elsewhere to dispose of dissidents like Noah Thompson. But Gaines failed. The Los Angeles division gave Thompson their solid support. To make bad matters worse, the co-president of the Los Angeles division, Charlotta Bass, owner and publisher of the *California Eagle*, is also the president of the Los Angeles chapter of the NAACP.

"Gaines is back in New York trying to recover. That's why he told Garvey to purge brotherhood members," Ferris remarks.

"The man's an idiot," Pete states.

Ferris sighs. "You're right; the man is an idiot. But he's not the reason Garvey purged the Brotherhood."

"Why'd he do it, then?"

"The reason Garvey fired everyone connected to the Brotherhood," Ferris begins, "was because of a letter he received from Briggs."

"Did Briggs threaten him?" Pete asks.

"Not quite."

"Then what?"

"Briggs sent a secret message to Garvey telling him about an attempt by military intelligence to insinuate an informant into the Brotherhood."

"And what did Garvey do?" Pete asks.

"Do? He did nothing. Exactly what I recommended that he do. Nothing. Some of the others, including your friend McGuire, wanted Garvey to talk with Briggs. But what would that get us. Associating with those agitators will bring us needless trouble. If Army intelligence is infiltrating the Brotherhood, they've infiltrated us already. We have enough problems with the Black Star Line and the Liberian mission. The Brotherhood would have us involved in an all-out race war."

"And . . . ?" Pete asks.

"Well, afterward, Briggs ran that article in his *Crusader*, you know, the one I showed you."

"Are you talking about the one where he says that he had sent a letter to Garvey offering to cooperate?" Pete asks.

"Not only telling the world that the Brotherhood and the UNIA should cooperate, but also admitting that the Brotherhood was involved in that Tulsa uprising," Ferris says heatedly. He goes to a file cabinet and withdraws a *Crusader* paper.

"Ah here it is:

'*We were in Tulsa! The Associated Press says that the African Blood Brotherhood takes responsibility for the Tulsa riot. The Brotherhood said that it agitated, supplied leadership and ammunition.*' Furthermore, they make the claim, '*We were there to support you, now it's time for you to come and support us.*'"

"You can see why Garvey was concerned," Ferris says.

"Yes," Pete says quietly. "But he shouldn't have purged all the Brotherhood members. It's going to be an all-out war."

"Yes," Ferris agrees. "And we think they're plotting to disrupt our convention."

"Nice timing," Pete observes.

"The Brotherhood might have had enough delegates to oust Garvey," Ferris nearly shouts. "We didn't want to run the risk. Now what I want from you is security."

His boss is getting worked up. Pete's intuition tells him that there is another side to this story. "I wonder what Bill's not telling me," Pete asks himself. For one thing, Pete still cannot understand why the *Negro World* sent a news team to Tulsa but didn't run the story of the riot. Now there is this thing with the Brotherhood. Cyril Briggs can go off the deep end sometimes, but he always supports the same things Garvey claims to support. The Brotherhood never attacks Garveyites or vandalizes the *World*'s papers. "The Brotherhood is not our enemy," Pete thinks. "So why are they being treated as if they were?"

"I'll tighten security," Pete tells his boss.

"And keep it tight," Ferris replies. "Remember that Brotherhood members have been credentialed as convention delegates. Don't do anything that looks like we are keeping them away. We must maintain our policy of being open to all Negroes. But keep them under surveillance at all times."

"Okay," Pete agrees. "I guess I'd better alert the others."

Pete liked Domingo. Domingo always came down to Pete's basement office for a chat. "The people upstairs are crazy, man," Domingo would say. Often he and Pete would discuss the source of friction between the West Indian and American blacks.

"For the first time in their lives colored people of Spanish, French, Dutch, Arabian, Danish, Portuguese and British ancestry meet and move together," Domingo told Pete. "This is only possible within Harlem's seventy or eighty blocks. And in this first encounter with each other and with large numbers of American Negroes, the only thing we have in common is being subjected to white racism."

"So why the hatred between the foreign-born and native-born Negroes?" Pete asked.

"You see," Domingo replied, "the foreign-born generally close ranks against you American Negroes because they blame you, fairly or unfairly, for white racism."

"I don't understand why," Pete said.

"Native-born Negroes," Domingo said, "think only about themselves. You don't have any racial or family pride. You don't value family or tradition. And having no pride, you Americans have no shame and will do anything your master tells you."

Being thoughtful rather than argumentative, it took Pete awhile to respond. "There may be some truth in what you say," he observed, "but I'm not so certain that you foreign-born Negroes are exempt from serving the white master. I've known members of the West Indian community who love white folk's dirty drawers." Pete recalled Edward Duncan's pride at having a picture of the King of England. "The antagonisms between native-born and foreign-born Negroes," Pete told Domingo, "are caused by white folks exploiting the differences between us, which in reality are just a matter of where you were born."

Pete admires Domingo and is sorry to see him go. Pete puts his legionnaire unit on standby and alerts other legion commanders to expect trouble from the African Blood Brotherhood. Surprisingly, the Brotherhood's response to Garvey's purge, all things considered, is rather mild. Apart from a well-orchestrated letter-writing campaign criticizing Garvey and the UNIA leadership to Negro newspapers all over the country, the Brotherhood does little else about the purge.

In August, delegates representing UNIA divisions from across the United States and all over the world descend on Liberty Hall for the Association's annual convention. Pete is given the responsibility for overall convention security. In addition to his African Legion, Pete employs a corps of Black Cross nurses as additional eyes and ears. The nurses are instructed to mingle with the conventioneers and report any suspicious behavior to their commander. In turn, the Black Cross commander reports all incidents directly to one of Pete's security officers. Employing extra eyes is a brilliant idea. Numerous incidents from petty theft to fractious debates are handled expeditiously. Security is dispatched before any minor incident becomes major.

"Commander Jenkins, the President-General has added Rose Pastor Stokes to the convention program for this evening," Captain Gaines informs his subordinate. "Be prepared for anything."

"Yessir," Pete responds. And waiting until Gaines squeezed out of the pantry-sized command post, Pete picks up his telephone and calls Bill Ferris.

"Who is this Rose Pastor Stokes?" Pete asks.

"She's a communist and the wife of J. Phelps-Stokes," Ferris says. "He's a multimillionaire. You should see their home. It's on Madison Avenue."

"What does he do?" Pete asks.

"He owns a lot of banks, railroads and mines. And he's one of the founding members of the NAACP."

"What?" Pete exclaims. "Why is Garvey allowing Rose Pastor Stokes to speak at this afternoon's session of the convention?"

"Don't know, but I'll get back to you," Ferris says hastily. And then Pete hears a click and then silence. The little knot at the bottom of Pete's stomach, quiet for so long, once again begins to make a nuisance of itself.

The President-General is about to open the afternoon session, so Pete decides to make a tour of the convention hall.

Ladies and Gentlemen: We have with us a lady visitor who has been widely made known to the public by the press the world over as belonging to that class of agitators who are endeavoring to free struggling white humanity . . .

Standing at the side of the stage, one of the Black Cross nurses approaches Pete.

"Captain Jenkins, sir," the nurse begins. Approaching the commander of security, in full view, inside the auditorium, is a breach of discipline and protocol for any of the nurses. The nurses's instructions are specific: "Report anything unusual to your commander." One thing the Garveyites maintain is protocol. In this situation, protocol means that all security personnel, including Black Cross nurses, adhere to the chain of command and report directly to their own commander. No one goes over the head of a commander. To do so is to invite stern discipline if not dismissal. If a member of the Association is also an employee, dismissal also means separation from employment. No one disregards protocol. So Pete is annoyed at being approached in this manner. But when he sees who it is, his annoyance disappears.

"Yes, Nurse Darling," Pete replies, trying hard to maintain professional distance. Everyone under Pete's command is watching. As he looks into Eva's wide brown eyes, professionalism is the last thing on his mind.

"Did you know that the Brotherhood is here in force, commander?" Eva asks discreetly.

"Not really, but I suspected it," Pete replies.

"Well, they are," the Black Cross nurse says. "Some of them are even outside selling the *Negro Congress Bulletin* and copies of the Chicago *Defender* newspapers."

"Nurse Darling, why is this information so important that you have decided to break protocol?" Pete asks more harshly than he intends. "This information certainly could have been reported directly to your commander."

"She is one of the newsboys, Captain," Eva says, staring directly into Pete's eyes.

"Who, Nurse Darling?" Pete asks. "Who is outside selling newspapers?"

"Julia Duncan," the nurse says with a parting bow.

Eva's comment could not have made its way more deftly into that secret knot in Pete's stomach. Eva still loves Pete. It is love that motivates her to tell him, as quickly and as discreetly as possible, that Julia is outside.

Making his way from the convention floor to the vestibule and then outside, Pete hopes that no one will notice the eagerness in his step. A few of his security guards see his haste and signal him, asking if he needs assistance. Pete gives them an "all clear" signal. They return to their posts. As well trained as his men are, Pete realizes they know something is amiss. Even at their posts, their eyes continue to follow him.

Outside Liberty Hall, there is plenty of activity. Garveyites who are not delegates to the convention, hundreds of them, mill about the building, hoping to catch the latest news or see one of the dignitaries from distant lands attending the convention. Women of the African Motor Corps in their powder-blue chauffeur uniforms stand by a fleet of shiny automobiles available for shuttling out-of-town delegates back and forth to their lodgings. Black Cross nurses, dressed in white, mingle with the crowd, monitor activities and assist anyone with a medical emergency. African legionnaires in suits and ties maintain their vigil. Up and down, vendors line the street, selling everything from hot dogs and sodas to pictures of Marcus Garvey and Jesus Christ. Pockets of onlookers stroll in front of the convention, gawking at the crowd, straining to catch a glimpse inside Liberty Hall. Protesters carry placards and signs, the noisiest of which are the twenty or more former Garveyites from California, proclaiming GARVEY IS A THIEF! BLACK STAR LINE IS BOGUS! SEND GARVEY BACK TO AFRICA! Periodically, the protesters chant: GARVEY MUST GO! GARVEY MUST GO! GARVEY MUST GO! Across the street soapbox speakers harangue the crowd. One speaker representing the NAACP criticizes Garvey for meddling in international affairs. *"Why hasn't he protected Negroes here at home? Why is he so concerned about sending you 'Back to Africa'? Garvey has the same agenda as the Ku Klux Klan to send Negroes back to Africa!"*

Pete is interested in none of them. He concentrates on the dozens of newsboys, mingling with the crowd, hawking their papers. Pete decides to calm his men's suspicions by conferring with the commander of the outside guard.

"Any problems," he asks casually, as if on a routine inspection.

Trained for discretion, the commander signals his answer, as if he had not heard the question. "All is clear; everyone is in position." Before Pete moves on, he notices a hint of pride in his officer's eyes. These are good men, Pete thinks to himself. Very good men, and this is about all we can expect. He steps down to the street deliberately, slowly; his movements intended to tell the alert legionnaires their leader is making a routine inspection. "A good African Legion commander," they will say to themselves. "He really knows what's going on." Then Pete spots her.

Julia's garb makes her almost indistinguishable from the numerous street urchins whose daily survival depends upon the number of papers they sell. She wears faded knickerbockers patched at the knees, woolen socks darned so many times that the various colors of yarn make a crazy pattern around her shapely legs, and a tattered long-sleeved dark woolen shirt under a threadbare coat, even though the sultry autumn day makes a coat unnecessary. Her hair is stuffed into a well-worn woolen cap with a short visor, the style worn by most of the newsboys. Even dressed in mufti, Julia's face is unmistakable. Pete instantly recognizes the honey-colored skin and pouty lips, full and shapely like those on the mask of Queen Nefertiti. Her eyes, those green almond-shaped eyes once so inquisitive, so seductive, so haughty, now seem older, sadder, less certain.

Nonetheless, it is his Julia. And as soon as Pete sees her, Julia sees him and for an instant time merges into eternity.

With as much discretion as he can muster, Pete signals Julia to follow him across 138th Street and down Seventh Avenue. Then turning around and walking right past her, Pete whispers, "Meet me at Candy's." He continues back to Liberty Hall, where he tells his deputy commander to take charge until he returns.

Pete gets to Candy's before Julia. Even though the diner is a discreet place for them to meet, just to be certain, Pete grabs the booth farthest in the back with the vantage of seeing everyone coming into the diner. Julia arrives soon after, still dressed in her newsboy outfit and carrying copies of the Brotherhood's newspaper.

Pete cannot help himself; he all but leaps out of his booth and pulls her to him. She does not resist; instead, Julia melts in his arms, her supple body fitting into his firm one. Encircling one another, they become as one. Leaning down, his lips touch hers. They quiver with a passion that sears his mouth, sending a fiery explosion coursing through his body. She nestles deeper into his embrace. Then, suddenly aware of Candy's other patrons staring at them with amusement, they separate and sit on opposites sides in the booth—their lips parted but their eyes still locked together.

Pete tries to speak, but before any words can tumble out, Julia reaches over and, taking his hand, says: "I know I've hurt you and I've some explaining to do, but before I do I need to tell you something."

"What's that?" Pete asks, quickly looking at her left ring finger to see whether Julia is engaged or has gotten married.

Seeing his look, Julia says, "No, there's no one else."

"Not even Grady?" Pete asks.

"Not even Grady." Julia stares at Pete for a long time and slowly tears begin to fall. Blinking them back, she begins, "Pete, I think I have found something to believe in, something that's important to me."

Pete decides that no matter what, he will not let that small, tiny knot in his stomach grow and take over this moment. Whatever Julia has done, wherever she has gone, whomever she has been with, it is her business. All that really matters is at this time and in this place and, for however brief the moment, they are together once again and nothing matters other than the fact that he loves this woman more than anything.

Pete looks at her, thinking how attractive she is, even in the second-hand garb of a street urchin. Then he just blurts out, "Gee, honey, if I'd known that selling newspapers was so important to you, I'd have gotten you a job selling the *World*. We can always use good paperboys."

Pete gives a little chuckle. Julia begins to laugh. Then they laugh together. They continue to laugh and laugh as if a thousand clowns are tickling their funny bones. Their laughter is so contagious that even Candy and Big Mabel begin chuckling. Pete and Julia laugh until the months of tension and anxiety that have built up between them dissipates, replaced by a simple joy and a peaceful contentment.

Once again they are Pete and Julia. Once again they are . . . But no, they are more than just Pete and Julia; they are something else, something new, a single being connected by some intense, indefinable thing that many call love. That thing they found on the train to Tulsa, or in the park before Julia ran away with Grady, but in reality, the thing that was born the first time Pete held Julia in his arms the night they met, that night so very long ago. The night Pete was overwhelmed and the night Julia fought hard to forget, but the night that love was born and continued to grow and mature despite everything. That special and unique love the two of them had for each other, that love that would remain for the rest of their lives.

So after the laughter, they sit staring at each other—her lovely, long delicate fingers cradle his strong black hands. They want to just sit and stare, but Big Mabel interrupts and asks: "Are you two love birds going to order something or just sit there mooning at each other all night?"

The big woman startles them.

"I'm really not hungry," Julia says.

"Neither am I," Pete echoes. "Let's go for a walk."

Nestled arm in arm, they walk out into the Harlem twilight. It is seven o'clock in the evening and the deep purple shadows just begin to reach out toward the Hudson River as the final rays of the autumn sun retreat behind the Jersey shore.

"I'm listening," Pete says quietly. They had only gone part way down one of Lenox Avenue's long city blocks.

"What?" Julia replies.

"You said that you would give me an explanation."

"Oh, yes," Julia says. "Of, course. But let's find someplace to sit, first."

"That's a good idea," Pete agrees. Then looking down at her, says, "We could go to my apartment, if you like."

Julia stares at Pete's face, looking for any sign of what, she doesn't know.

Pete immediately begins to explain. "I didn't mean," he stammers. "I only thought."

"Don't worry, I understand," Julia responds, grabbing his arm more tightly. "I understand," she says once again, imperceptibly, almost to herself. Of course, Julia doesn't understand, she doesn't understand at all. How can she? Julia has never been in love before.

Much later, after they have made passionate love like only those in love can make love, Julia begins to talk. At first, she speaks in halting words, wanting desperately not to hurt Pete's feelings but needing to bare her soul and tell him everything. And she does, sparing nothing, telling Pete about Grady Jones and his work with military intelligence, the military's need for information on Garvey's association, about her joining the African Blood Brotherhood. Julia needn't have worried about Pete's feelings. Pete had suspected most of what Julia tells him anyway.

"I don't understand why they wanted you in the Brotherhood," Pete says, shaking his head.

"Grady said they wanted to know who tipped them off about the Tulsa riot," Julia answers. She has told Pete the same story several times now.

"I understand what they wanted," Pete says. "What I don't understand is: why you?"

"Why not me?" Julia bristles.

"Well for one thing, you hadn't a very good track record. You told me that yourself. None of the information I gave you about the Association was of any interest. You joined the Association, but they aren't interested in what you learn. Someone inside the Association sends you to Tulsa to do a story on the riot, but the *World* doesn't print it."

"And when we get back and write the story, it's never published," Julia breaks in.

"I just said that," Pete says, giving Julia one of those looks she neither understands nor likes. "Now Grady and that cracker, Van Vechten, get you in the African Blood Brotherhood," Pete continues, "to find out the Brotherhood's contact in the intelligence community, but your cover is blown from the very start. I wouldn't say that you had a very good track record as a spy, would you?" Pete asks.

"I told them everything, that is, I told Grace Campbell everything, because I think the Brotherhood's sincere," Julia exclaims.

"Don't you think the Association is sincere?" Pete asks. "Don't you believe in Garvey?"

"Yes," Julia answers, "but . . ."

"But what?"

"I don't know. These people are different."

"Yeah, they're different all right," Pete observes. "They all look like they're white."

"Not all of them," Julia protests.

"Cyril Briggs certainly does and so does Grace Campbell."

"Do you think that's what this is all about?" Julia flares up. She doesn't think about the African Blood Brotherhood in that way. She is angry with Pete because she thinks there might be some truth in what he says. She resents him for saying it. But when she looks over at her man, Julia knows that it is not color, not for her. For the others, possibly. She just isn't sure. "Were all Marxist, communist and socialist Negroes just trying to be accepted by white people because of skin color?" she wonders.

"Tell me about this Rose Pastor Stokes," Pete demands.

Julia is happy that he breaks into her thoughts. "That woman's bizarre. She's right up there with your potentates, nobles and the other assorted grand poobahs in your Association," Julia laughs.

"It used to be your Association, too, when you needed it," Pete observes.

"Oh, you can't take a joke about your precious Association?" Julia laughs. "That's the problem with all of this."

"What do you mean?" Pete asks.

"All you New Negroes take yourselves so seriously, as if you really believed in the fantasy."

Julia looks at Pete and takes his hand. "Don't you know that we're the only ones who are real? Just you and me."

"Maybe you're right," Pete agrees. "But tell me about Rose Pastor Stokes anyway."

"Rose is a founding member of the American Communist Party and a good friend of Grace Campbell," Julia begins. "She and Grace invited some of the Brotherhood to Rose's home for a meeting."

"None of this make any sense to me," Pete states. "Why does Garvey invite this white communist to his convention, a woman who is associated with the African Blood Brotherhood?"

Julia just looks at him. She isn't a cop and doesn't have a cop's suspicious nature. They all sound so sincere even if they are living in a dream world. Julia believes that they really can work together. But Pete knows better. White people—whether communists or capitalists, Jews or Catholics, soldiers or pacifists—work for, cooperate with and trust other white folks, period. They use Negroes when they want something. What all whites want is a world dominated by and for white people. Their only disagreement is over which white group will run it. All white men and women, for that matter, see Negroes as a means to an end, that end being white supremacy. Pete frowns.

"Who is Rose's husband?"

"J. Phelps-Stokes," Julia replies. "He's a multimillionaire."

"What does he do?" Pete asks.

"He owns banks, railroads and mines. He's one of the founding members of the NAACP."

"And yet, Marcus Garvey invites Rose, a leading communist, whose husband supports his most hated rival, W. E. B. DuBois, to speak at his UNIA convention? This is making less and less sense."

"Well, if none of it makes sense," Julia says seductively, "why even worry about it? Isn't there something that we can be talking about other than politics?"

"Like what?" Pete asks.

"Like us . . ."

Chapter Fifteen

For the next several weeks, Julia and Pete are oblivious to everything, everything except each other. They live in their own little world, unhampered by friends or family. The political events swirling around them are nothing. Julia wants to move out of the apartment she shares with two other women and move in with Pete. Her roommates work in Harlem nightclubs. They usually get back to the apartment between six and seven in the morning just as Julia prepares to leave for work. She hardly knows either of them.

"You'd better stay there," Pete counsels, "at least for the time being, for the sake of appearances." Julia frowns. "Who knows?" Pete continues. "You might want to make up with your family. It won't help matters if you're living with me." As things turn out, they are fortunate that she keeps her room.

Julia gets her job at the library back. Each evening, Pete meets her after work and they stroll over to a delicatessen, where they buy something to eat back at Pete's apartment. Every once in awhile they even get around to eating. Sometimes they visit one of Harlem's cafés. Pete calls them "greasy spoons." One evening, Julia suggests they dine at a midtown restaurant.

"I don't know about this, baby doll," Pete says as they board a midtown trolley.

"Don't be silly," Julia laughs. "It's on Bleecker Street. Grace and I go there all the time. You'll like it."

But when they arrive, the headwaiter sniffs indignantly and tells them that the restaurant is booked solid. "You should have called for a reservation, madam," he says. Somehow Pete believes that reservations would not have made any difference, since the restaurant is half empty.

"Don't worry, honey," Julia says, putting on a brave smile but fixing the headwaiter with an icy stare. "I know the headwaiter at another place that is just as nice, perhaps even nicer. It's not far from here." She takes Pete's arm, turns and marches out the door. However, they have no better luck at the next restaurant. "Hi, Max," Julia sings out merrily, putting on a brave front. "A table for me and my sweetheart, here."

Looking as if he had been slapped, Max replies, "Ah, Julia, is he with you?"

"Yes, Max," Julia replies, "he is with me."

"Well, I don't think we a table left in the house," Max says. Then shrugging his shoulders, he continues, "You know it's not me, Julia. If it were up to me, of course, I would seat you. But it's my other patrons, they might object to eating next to a . . . ."

"A Negro," Pete completes the sentence for him. "Come on, Julia, let's go."

On the way back to Harlem, they don't speak. Julia can't look Pete in the face, afraid of what she might see. Pete thinks Julia just wants to be a part of the white world, to be accepted by them, and to live among them. So, for the life of him, Pete cannot understand what Julia sees in him. Pete doesn't express his feelings, however; it really doesn't matter whether they're served at a white restaurant. What does matter is that Pete doesn't realize that Julia had the best of intentions. All she wanted was to treat him to a meal that wasn't a "greasy spoon."

Pete's suspicions continue to get the better of him. He cannot help wondering, "Is she still playing the spy?" That evening and several others pass without incident. But as always happens with young love, sooner or later, they have their first quarrel.

Actually, to call what happens a quarrel is like calling the Grand Canyon a hole. Essential truth can be lost in understatement. Pete and Julia do not quarrel, they war. Words explode in salvos of spite and recrimination. Each one tries to wound the other with shots of un-kindness. Then, they blast with a name-calling barrage that degenerates into an onslaught of the foulest language and blasphemies that, had either of them been Catholic, would have had them on their knees saying "Our Fathers, Hail Mary's" and "Acts of Contrition" for a solid month.

They only thing that saves them from ending the relationship right then and there is that Julia has the good sense to return to her own flat, giving her time to contemplate how fragile a black man's ego is, particularly after the many times she, herself, has damaged it. When she returns to Pete's apartment several hours later, at three AM, both of them apologize to each other until dawn. In a way, their first, but certainly not their last, quarrel prepares each of them for the trials that are to follow later. Even though Pete and Julia shut out the world and concentrate on the perilous enterprise of making a life together, the "real" world refuses to be abandoned. It comes crashing back into their lives with the force of a jealous lover intent on revenge, which isn't far from the truth. One morning, as Julia is leaving her apartment, Grady Jones meets her in the hallway.

"Do you know how much trouble you're in," the government spy asks, "not to mention the trouble you got me into?"

"What kind of trouble?" Julia wonders what she ever saw in this pasty-faced weakling standing in her doorway.

"You told the Brotherhood about your assignment and my people are not happy."

"They're not?" Julia responds, her green eyes widening in a look of innocence.

"No, they're not!" Grady says. "Don't think that, because you're a woman, they won't hurt you. Don't you know how much danger you and Pete are in?"

"Pete?" Julia says. "What about Pete? What has he to do with this?"

"He has everything to do with it," Grady states. "Pete interfered with their plans; they are not happy about that either. The only way you can fix things is for you to come with me, right now!"

Grady is telling the truth, at least part of it.

"They began rounding up the small fry in the Brotherhood as soon as Garvey kicked them out of the convention," Grady says.

"What for?" Julia asks.

"Some were arrested for selling the *Negro Congress Bulletin* outside of Liberty Hall," Grady tells her.

"I was selling the *Negro Congress Bulletin* outside of Liberty Hall!" Julia gasps.

"Exactly," Grady says.

"But why?" Julia asks.

"The official line goes like this. The Communist Party of America, headed by Mrs. Rose Pastor Stokes, is working with the African Blood Brotherhood, headed by Cyril Briggs, W. A. Domingo, Richard Moore and Arthur Reid, all of whom are aliens. The *Crusader* magazine, an organ of the African Blood Brotherhood, spread dangerous propaganda among Negroes in Harlem, especially during the Garvey Convention. They are being arrested on charges of violating the Alien and Sedition Law. Garvey disavows any connection with the Brotherhood. In ejecting their delegates from his convention, Garvey said that the Brotherhood only pretends to be interested in the cause of Negroes. The Brotherhood really advocates Sovietism, Bolshevism and Radicalism."

Rose Pastor Stokes, the pseudo-radical, provides J. Edgar Hoover with a list of every radical socialist, labor agitator and international conspirator in the United States. Her list includes members of the African Blood Brotherhood. Hoover is ecstatic!

"Good!" Hoover exclaims when he receives the list. "Now they'll start running scared and we'll find out everything we want to know about this little band of revolutionaries. Soon I'll be able to give the Grand Master the Brotherhood's source of information about Tulsa."

A purge of the Brotherhood begins. Brotherhood members without U.S. citizenship are being rounded up and deported. Others are arrested on a variety of charges. Still others simply disappear. Julia's name is on Hoover's list.

"This is serious, isn't it?" Julia quavers.

"Yes, it is," Grady agrees. "Especially since you betrayed me and joined them." Seeing how shaken Julia becomes, the military agent pushes her harder. "Of course, it hasn't helped that you have been seen midtown with Pete."

"I thought Pete was your friend," Julia stammers.

"Baby, both you and I know that in this business, you don't have friends. I'm the closest thing to a friend that you've got. I'll put in a good word for you, but you must come with me and talk with my superiors. They've been wanting to meet you ever since you returned from Tulsa."

Julia tries to think. She knows one thing, for certain; she isn't going anywhere with Grady, not this time. "But I'd better play along," she decides.

"All right," Julia responds, as if giving in, "why don't you pick me up here at my apartment, later tonight, after I get off work."

"I think you should come now," Grady says.

"If you straighten this out for me, I still want to work for the library," she reasons. "I should at least let them know that I might be gone for a day or two."

Grady thinks it over for a couple of minutes. He doesn't want Julia to think he's unreasonable. "I have to get her to trust me," he tells himself. "I need her to cooperate. One day shouldn't matter that much." Grady makes a decision. Believing he still controls his former mistress, he says, "Okay, I'll meet you at the library after work this evening."

"Why don't you meet me here?" Julia suggests. "You wouldn't want to run into Pete at the library, would you?"

"No, you're right," Grady says, his face contorting into a frown. It is only now that Julia becomes aware of just how much Grady fears Pete.

"Okay, then," Julia says. "I should be ready by eight o'clock tonight. How long do you think the interview will take?" Grady shrugs. He knows that military intelligence plans to work on her for a long time. There's no sense in frightening her any more than necessary, he thinks. "Maybe I should arrange for a couple of days off," Julia says, without waiting for Grady's reply.

"Yeah, a couple of days should do it. You're a smart girl," Grady says. "I'll see you at eight then." Turning back down the hall, he slinks out the door.

Julia is frightened. She wants to call Pete immediately, but decides to keep her composure. "Pete's going to meet me after work. He'll know what to do," she tells herself. "So that's where I'd better go, just in case Grady's watching me."

That day becomes the longest day of her life. Time seems to drag by. Julia prays that Pete will call or pick her up for lunch, which he sometimes does, but he does not come by today. Her supervisor notices how jumpy and nervous Julia seems. "Is there anything wrong, dear?" she asks.

"No, not at all, madam," Julia replies. "I am just so thankful that I'm back with the library. I want to do a good job." White folks are always fond of docile Negroes whose only interest is to serve. Julia's supervisor feels secure that order is restored and this arrogant Negress is properly contrite.

Finally five o'clock comes. Julia hurries to meet Pete at their usual spot. Quickly, she tells him of Grady's visit. Julia is right; Pete knows exactly what to do, or at least what not to do.

"You can't go back to your apartment," he decides, "and you can't come back to mine, either."

"Where will I go?" Julia wails.

"You have to go back to your parents," Pete tells her.

"My parents," Julia says. "I can't go back there." There is no conviction in her voice. "Why can't I go to Grace's? I know she'd help me."

"Do you trust Grace in this situation?" Pete asks. Julia thinks about it.

"I don't know whom to trust," she says finally.

"You can trust me," Pete says, "and you can trust your parents." Julia knows Pete is right. "Do your parents have any close relatives living nearby?" he asks.

"My mother has a couple of brothers and a sister," Julia replies.

"Then you must go to one of them until we can straighten this mess out. In the meantime, I will see what I can learn from the Association."

Even though she hates the idea of returning to her parents' home, even for a brief stay, Julia knows that Pete is right. It's a good plan. Julia's mother will protect her daughter, especially if she thinks that Julia's problems have to do with an unwanted pregnancy rather than unacceptable politics. Edward and Sharon Duncan won't be too happy that a Garveyite like Pete will be the father of their first grandchild. She has a momentary anxiety attack, but after repeating to herself, "Pete will protect me," it goes away. The next day Julia finds herself safely ensconced in a room at her wealthy aunt's home on Striver's Row.

Chapter Sixteen

Gaston Means hails from an old plantation family where his grandfather was a slave driver. His father, whom everyone calls Colonel, is mayor of the rural town of Concord. Means's uncle is Concord's police chief. The Colonel and the police chief educate young Means, at an early age, in the noble cause of defending white culture and white supremacy. Means joins his father and uncle in the Ku Klux Klan and proudly participates in lynchings, learning that violence is the acceptable method of preserving the natural order of things.

This lesson was not lost on the young Means when he found himself in financial difficulties. Marrying a widowed heiress from New York, Means takes his week-old bride on a hunting trip for their honeymoon. He leaves his naïve bride in the woods of North Carolina with a bullet in her head and takes for himself sole possession of her considerable wealth.

Under the Colonel's and the police chief's tutelage, Means proves himself such an adept knight that he is raised to the exalted position of grand dragon for the entire state of North Carolina.

The talented Means continues to rise from obscurity to prominence until he reaches the pinnacle of power inside the Harding Administration, where he is appointed a special federal agent for the Justice Department and Daugherty's "bag man." FBI Director Burns has every confidence in Means. Burns used Means to spy on both the British and Germans during the war; Means could be trusted. Means collects boodle from bootleggers, gunrunners, influence peddlers, and all the other assorted criminals with whom Attorney General Daugherty and FBI Director Burns do business.

True to his heritage, his beliefs and his oath to defend the purity of the white race, Means hates Warren G. Harding with a passion. It matters little that Harding gives Means unlimited power. Nor does it matter that America's most secret societies admit Harding into their inner sanctums. The Marion Lodge of the Scottish Rite admits the president and raises him to the sublime degree of master mason. Weeks later, the same lodge raises Harding to a thirty-third degree mason. Nor does Means care that Harding receives his red fez as a member of the Columbus's Aladdin Temple of the Ancient Arabic Order of Nobles of the Mystic Shrine. Nor even does Means care that Harding receives the mark master, most excellent master, and royal arch degrees. Three days before his inauguration as the twenty-ninth president of the United States, the supreme grand master directs the Order of the Red Cross, the Order of the Knights of Malta and the Knights Templar to induct Harding into their societies. None of these investitures matter to Means, grand dragon of the Knights of the Ku Klux Klan. What matters most was that the supreme grand master orders Means to participate in a solemn White House ceremony conducted by the imperial wizard, Colonel William J. Simmons, that admits the president of the United States into his own noble order, the Knights of the Ku Klux Klan. This is a duty so distasteful to Means that he swears to wipe away this insult to the white race, since he, and everyone else, knows that Warren G. Harding is a nigger!

Nadine eyes Grady from across the room: the smoke from her freshly lit cigarette drifts lazily into the air. This nigger's really beginning to bore me, she thinks. Oh well, she has her orders. It isn't as if he occupies all of her time. Their sex has become rather mechanical and routine. Grady arouses Nadine only when he performs some special little something dredged up from her own wanton imagination. Nadine needs constant stimulation. Even when he is in the mood, which is seldom, Grady just can't satisfy Nadine's erotic needs. Grady is seldom in the mood. No matter, she sighs, in this business it doesn't pay to get too close to someone you're eventually going to harm.

Nadine is exploring sex with female friends. She finds that her voluptuous body responds to their gentle touching and kissing. Even now, the nipples on her breasts begin to swell and her thighs quiver in anticipation. Interacting with multiple female partners unleashes her passions. While male sex still thrills her, Nadine now finds herself swept up in the ecstasy of feminine eroticism. Nadine's female partners set a fire deep within her loins and then leave it to slowly burn. If only they had the basic equipment, she grumbles. "Oh well, that's why I still need Grady," she thinks, even though she knows Grady isn't going to be around much longer. "He fails his assignments, miserably, and he knows too much," Nadine tells herself. This is the worst situation imaginable if you're a spy.

"So what are you going to do?" Nadine asks.

Grady is morose. He sits in the only comfortable armchair in Nadine's apartment. Decorated in the art deco style that is all the rage, her apartment embodies a feeling of elegance, jazz and power. None of which concerns Grady right now. All he thinks about is Captain Hansen's last remarks.

"Private, you are the sorriest piece of crap on my staff," the military intelligence officer growled. "I ordered you to bring in one of your tramps and you can't even do that." Hansen glowered at the Negro private. "Do you take me for a fool, private?"

"No, no sir," Grady Jones stammered.

"Then why have you been treating me like a fool?"

"Sir," Grady said, "I tried to explain. She wasn't at her apartment, but I'll find her. There's nowhere she can go. All I need is a little more time."

"More time," the intelligence officer thundered. "You've been fooling around with this woman since June. It's now October. How much more time do you need? I need some information and I need it now, do you understand me?"

"Yessir," Grady replied.

"Now get out of here and bring that whore in for questioning," Captain Hansen shouted. "And I mean right now."

Grady has no idea where Julia has gone. And Nadine doesn't seem interested in helping. Nadine has grown distant and aloof, lately. He can't please her anymore, not even in bed. "How did everything get so fouled up," he asks himself. Then he gets up and goes over to where Nadine lounges.

"What do you think we ought to do?" he asks.

"We?" Nadine stares with pitiless eyes. "Don't look at me. You're the one who lost her. It's up to you to find her."

"You've got contacts," Grady says half-heartedly. "Couldn't you ask them?"

"Look, nigger," Nadine says blowing cigarette smoke in his face, "you've got your orders. Get out there and find Julia Duncan."

Nadine almost becomes sexually aroused watching the dejected figure of Negro manhood slink out the door. He used to be so arrogant, so proud, she thinks. Now look at him, a little adversity and he's reduced to a whimpering dog. Nadine almost bursts out laughing. It's all such a farce, she thinks. It's so funny. The joke is on Grady. Nadine knows that Julia Duncan doesn't know anything about the information leak to the Brotherhood. In fact, there is no leak, not unless they consider Rose Pastor Stokes the leak. Because it was Stokes—or rather, her shadowy billionaire spouse, J. G. Phelps-Stokes—who told Cyril Briggs about the plans for the Tulsa riot.

"I love this game," Nadine murmurs to herself. Stubbing out her cigarette, she goes into her bedroom to dress for her afternoon's entertainment with the girls.

Rose Harriet Pastor was the daughter of working-class Polish Jewish immigrants. She was her family's primary breadwinner.

James Graham Phelps-Stokes traces his roots back to Puritan New England. His family is included as a charter member of the Social Register. J. G., as he is known, sails, rides horses and plays polo. At Yale, J. G. was a track and tennis star. J. G. owns the Nevada Central Railroad and the State Bank of Nevada. A large part of his extensive wealth comes from the Austin Mining Company, the Manhattan Silver Mine and the Ione Gold Mine. J. G. and his brother Anson share a vision of an Anglo-Saxon–dominated world with their close friend and collaborator, William Howard Taft. In fact, Anson is Taft's staunchest supporter inside the Skull and Bones Society. J. G. heads the highly secretive organization known as the United States Russian Information Bureau, a group closely allied with the China Society as well as the Royal India and Pakistani Society. These secret societies collect the great stores of vital intelligence

required to further Anglo-Saxon domination. Through their member-
ship in the super-secret Pilgrims Society, J. G. and Anson help Taft plan
a stock market crash for 1929.

J. G. is unhappy. The organization he founded and now funds, the
NAACP, fails to exert any influence over West Indian Negroes. So J. G.
uses his wife, Rose, and the Communist Party of America, to send the
Brotherhood to Tulsa. Neither military intelligence nor the FBI is aware,
but Nadine knows. Nadine has contacts. She decides not to share this
information with Grady. He wouldn't know how to use it, even if she
did. It will make little difference to Grady, Nadine reasons. His fate is
already settled. Turning toward her wardrobe, she exclaims, "This outfit
should drive the girls wild."

Not unlike Sir Percival, the mythical knight on an elusive quest for the
Holy Grail, Grady continues his vain search for Julia. He questions his
other women as well as her roommates. He puts the word out on the
streets. He even goes to Van Vechten, hat in hand.

"Why don't you watch her parents' store?" the Harlem impresario
suggests. Grady spends the next several days watching the Tinker Street
flat. Julia doesn't show up there. Out of desperation, Grady turns to his
"friend," Pete, for help.

"I knew I'd find you here sooner or later," Grady says, sliding into
one of Candy's booths.

Pete notices that worry lines have taken possession of Grady's face.
"What do you want?" he asks.

"Is that any way to treat a friend?" Grady says, managing a weak
smile. "I just want to keep touch and see how you're doing. After all, I
still owe you my life, and Grady Jones never forgets his debts."

"Something's got him spooked," Pete thinks, seeing through Grady's
pretense.

"How you been? Haven't seen you since you got back from Tulsa,"
Grady continues.

Pete munches on Big Mabel's fried chicken special.

"I heard that was some kind of slaughter, almost like France all over
again."

"Where did you hear that," Pete asks. "Did you go out there?"

"No," Grady replies. "Julia told me."

"She did?" Pete says casually. "It must have been when you took her back to Van Vechten."

Grady gives Pete a frightened, almost pitiful glance and then looks away.

"So how's she doing?" Pete asks casually.

"I guess she's doing all right," Grady replies, hesitatingly. "To tell the truth, I haven't seen her lately. I thought maybe you had."

"Me?" Pete snorts. "I may be slow, old buddy, but I've learned my lesson by now."

"What do you mean?"

"You've been using Julia to get information from me, haven't you?" Pete says sharply. "You, of all people, should know how she feels about me."

Pete fixes Grady with his cop's stare. Pete's unblinking eyes bear into Grady's counterfeit soul.

Grady wilts. Pete is his only hope. "I'll offer Pete a chance to get even," he thinks. Quickly he formulates a plan to confess everything, hoping to enlist Pete's support.

"You're right," Grady admits, "I did try to use her to get information."

"Oh?" Pete arches his eyebrows.

"Yeah, but she never told me anything," Grady adds quickly.

"So what information did you need about me?" Pete asks, trying to appear uninterested, but Grady notices a telltale flicker in Pete's eyes. My plan's working, Grady decides. So he begins from the beginning and tells Pete how the Army threatened to execute him for murder if he didn't agree to work for military intelligence. Grady describes how he recruited a number of women, including Julia, to supply the military with information about what went on in Harlem. Before he realizes it, Grady tells Pete the entire story, including why he desperately needs to get Julia over to military intelligence. Grady feels relieved. Maybe confession is good for the soul.

Being a cop, Pete listens in silence, withholding judgment, keeping his suspicions and cynicism in check. It is like France, all over again. Grady is in a jam and expects Pete to rescue him. If Pete believes Grady's story, the Army doesn't know who actually killed those white boys. As far as the Army knows, Grady did it. That is, if Pete can believe his old Army buddy.

The trouble is that Pete doesn't trust Grady. Even if he has withheld their names from Army intelligence, which seems unlikely, Grady now has a trump card that he can play at anytime. On the other hand, Sam and Willie have been missing for some time; now Pete knows why. Pete believes there is a New Negro in most black men, but this is not the time to trust Grady with Julia's life, nor his own. Too many Uncle Tom, handkerchief-headed Negroes sell out race men for a dollar and offer seventy-five cents in change—particularly those cute-looking Negroes who think they're better, the ones like Grady.

"Sounds to me like you're in a bad situation," Pete observes.

"Yeah, but if I find Julia, everything will be all right. I know you don't care what happens to that Jamaican witch the way she's treated you. She left you for that white boy, not once but twice."

"Of course, you didn't have anything to do with that, did you?" Pete cannot resist the jibe. Grady lets it pass; he needs Pete's goodwill.

"No, man," Grady stammers, "not me."

Grady doesn't know about Pete and Julia. How can he know? His degenerate relationship with Nadine, and the way he uses and abuses black women, prevents Grady from being intimate with any woman. Grady's a spy for the military, an agent and a user. He doesn't understand human emotions like love and trust. He can't understand that the black man's duty is to protect his woman to the best of his ability, even if it means his own death. Grady is no man; he is a thing that can't be trusted. Pete, on the other hand, values honor and integrity over everything else. This is why Julia chose Pete over Grady. She knows, in the end, Pete will protect her, while Grady will betray her, just like those African chiefs of old who sold their women into slavery.

"I'll tell you what," Pete tells his so-called friend, "give me a couple of days and I'll ask around. If I locate Julia, I'll let you know. How's that?"

"That's great!" Grady says. Grady thinks, "This might work out okay after all."

"Where should we meet?" Pete asks.

"Why not back here at Candy's next Sunday?"

"Good, I'll see you then."

Grady slides out of the seat feeling better than he had in weeks. See, he says to himself, good things come to good people. I guess I'll go up and see if Nadine's home. I feel a bit frisky and sometimes that woman can drive me wild. Grady heads for a midtown trolley.

Chapter Seventeen

President Harding's Birmingham Centennial Celebration speech surprises and angers white people all over the United States. A New York Times *editorial rails: "We are against the president's theory that the races can be intermingled because we know it is impractical, it is unjust and it is destructive to the best ideals of America. Give the Negro economical and political equality with the white man or woman and the friction between the races will be aggravated. The president is right in that the race question is a national one and is not confined to any section, but this unfortunate and mischievous utterance on the subject will be deprecated by people in every section of the country and by people who are dedicated to the preservation of the white civilization."*

Harding's Birmingham speech might have been unfortunate, delivered in any section of the United States, but the president delivers it in the deep South, in the heart of Dixie. This makes the speech unfortunate in the extreme. Not for the Negroes who clap and applaud it. For them, Harding's speech is like "manna from heaven." But for Harding, himself—less than a year later, the president is poisoned. Some suspect that Gaston Means administers the fatal dose. Means claims that Harding's white wife, Florence, does the deed.

"Hi, boss!" Pete steps into Ferris's office. "You wanted to see me?"

Once the convention has ended and challenges to his leadership have quelled, Garvey faces serious financial difficulties. The UNIA is afflicted by numerous petty larcenies and thefts; much of it involves staff. They feel entitled. Garvey is not meeting his payroll. Employees go months without a paycheck. Corruption at the Black Star Line is notorious. The organization continues to receive money from the sale of Black Star Line stock, *much of it in cash*, but little goes toward the company's debts. Corruption affects other segments of the Association, as well. Garvey's various retail outlets underreport their revenues. The *Negro World* staff underreport as much as 50 percent in newspaper revenue. Even as newspaper vandalism is reduced, theft increases dramatically. Rumors circulate about the Association's worsening economic woes. Legal actions threaten to send Garvey and other officers to prison. Pete expects that Ferris has called him into his office to discuss the Association's worsening finances.

"Yes, come in, Commander Jenkins," the *Negro World*'s managing editor says formally. "I'd like you to meet James Wormley-Jones."

"Jim, this is our head of security, Commander Peter Jenkins."

A small, impeccably dressed light-skinned Negro rises from his chair and proffers his hand.

"Commander Jenkins," Wormley-Jones says.

"Mr. Jones," Pete responds.

"Wormley-Jones," the visitor corrects the security chief.

"Wormley-Jones," Pete repeats.

There is something about the man that Pete doesn't like. Possibly it is Wormley-Jones's clammy handshake, wet and moist like a limp dishrag. He has no grip at all. Pete notices how the visitor avoids making eye contact, preferring, instead, to glance about the room. In France, during bombardments soldiers were continually searching for cover. That is the way Wormley-Jones keeps looking around.

The visitor resumes his seat. Pete takes another.

"The reason I've called you in," Ferris continues, "is to tell you to prepare for some additional security problems."

"Oh," Pete responds. "Why?"

Ferris looks over at his visitor and says, "Maybe you'd better explain, Jim."

The little man turns fully to face Pete. He's got a rat's face, Pete thinks. But he listens to the visitor and tries not to betray his feelings.

"President-General Garvey has decided to go after Cyril Briggs and the entire African Blood Brotherhood," Wormley-Jones begins. "Today he delivered a letter from Cyril Briggs to Justice Renaud of the 12th district Magistrate Court. In this letter, Briggs invites the President-General to use the Association to help the African Blood Brotherhood and their communist friends overthrow white governments. The President-General wants authorities to know that we are not revolutionaries or Bolsheviks and that we do not support organizations that seek the overthrow of legitimate governments."

"So you expect that when the Brotherhood learns that the President-General sent Briggs's letter to the magistrate, they will want to retaliate?" Pete asks slowly.

"That's not all," Ferris responds. "This will be in next week's issue of the *Negro World*." He passes over a front-page proof with headlines that scream:

White Man
Negro for Convenience
A White Man in New York by the name of Cyril Briggs
has started the
"African Blood Brotherhood"
to catch Negroes, no doubt. To make it succeed he claims to
be a Negro, and continuously attacks the Universal Negro
Improvement Association and its founder Marcus Garvey.
Negroes take notice and govern yourselves accordingly.

Pete is speechless. Many criticize Briggs for being reckless. His recent statements have possibly been too rash. Some even blame Briggs for the terrible massacre in Tulsa. "Had they not fought back, possibly the devastation would not have been so great," the argument ran. But Briggs, a white man masquerading as a Negro, now that is really far-fetched. Garvey is attacking the only Negroes in the United States who defend blacks against lynchings and murders. The Brotherhood puts itself on the line while others merely write self-serving newspaper editorials. The Brotherhood is in the streets while others hide in their offices. Meanwhile the slaughter of Negro people, across the country, is running into the thousands.

Pete looks from Ferris to Wormley-Jones. This is nothing short of treachery against the entire Negro race, Pete thinks. But he is smart enough not to speak out. His cop's mind knows this came from the top and objections will not be tolerated. The rumor mill completely missed this one, Pete observes. He will mention it to Josh. Meanwhile Ferris and Wormley-Jones, believing they have his complete approval, counsel Pete about the precautions he is expected to take.

"Be certain that all your people can be trusted," Wormley-Jones advises. "The worst thing that can happen is that, after this thing becomes public, the Brotherhood finds someone willing to tell them about our plans. There must be no leaks!"

"That's right, Pete," Ferris reiterates. "Make certain that all your people are absolutely trustworthy. And even then tell them only what they need to know."

Pete nods his agreement. The pair bombards Pete with additional suggestions. All the while the chief of security maintains a straightforward demeanor. Finally, Wormley-Jones and Ferris satisfy themselves that Pete is on the team and ready to do what is expected of him.

"Will that be all, sir?" Pete asks his boss.

"Yes, commander," Ferris replies. "Just remember," Ferris says as Pete makes for the door, "The President-General is counting on you."

"Yessir," Pete responds.

Pete feels betrayed and confused. He pours out his soul to Julia.

"I just can't believe it," Pete keeps saying.

"Believe it," Julia says, her soft green eyes filled with compassion.

"What is even more disgusting than those headlines," Pete murmurs, "is the fact that Wormley-Jones sat there giving the orders for the war on the Brotherhood like he was enjoying the idea that black men are going to die!"

"He's a member of the Brotherhood," Julia says. "I was there when he took the oath."

"You told me that," Pete recalled.

"And Cyril put him in charge of our entire New York section," Julia exclaims. "Oh, Pete! What are we going to do?"

"I don't know." Pete shakes his head slowly. "Doesn't Cyril suspect anything?"

"How can he suspect anything," Julia asks. "How can anyone? I was never a true believer in Garvey and still I can't even believe Garvey would do this."

"Right after the convention, I remember Garvey saying that Thomas Dixon, the author of the *Klansman*, endorsed the UNIA," Pete says. "I remember at the time I thought that Garvey was just being his usual outrageous self. But now . . ." Pete lapses into thought.

Then after awhile he says, "One thing I do know."

"What's that?" Julia asks.

"Our James *Wormley*-Jones is well named," Pete observes.

"Oh!"

"Yes, he is a *worm*!"

"We have to warn the brotherhood," Julia decides. "I'll call Grace."

"I think you should go down to her office," Pete recommends. "You never know who is listening." It turns out to be good advice. Hoover has already begun listening in on telephone conversations involving the Brotherhood's leadership.

Pete tells Josh what Garvey plans to do.

"Get this order out to everyone," he instructs his subordinate. "There's to be no fighting with the Brotherhood, no matter what. Do you understand?"

"Yessir," Josh responds. "Don't worry. I'll make certain everyone gets the word. No fighting with the Brotherhood."

Even though Pete and Julia give the Brotherhood ample warning, Briggs simply could not, would not believe them. So when Garvey's article hits the streets, Briggs and the Brotherhood executive committee, all except Harry Haywood, are dumbfounded. Yet their response is immediate. Briggs prepares an editorial in the *Crusader*; the others prepare for the street battle that is certain to follow. Grace Campbell calls every Brotherhood chapter in the country advising them of Garvey's attack. She tells them to lie low.

"We're going to fight this thing in the courts and not the streets," Grace tells chapter leaders.

For the Brotherhood's rank and file, Grace's warning is already too late. The FBI begins its roundup. Brotherhood members are arrested on sight and charged with everything from possession of firearms and bootlegging to violations of the Alien and Sedition laws and advocating the overthrow of the government. Briggs files a criminal libel suit against Garvey and the *Negro World*. Garvey retaliates by having Briggs arrested. New York prepares itself for an all-out shooting war between the Brotherhood and the Association. Both sides accuse the other of treachery. Partisans arm themselves. Harlem holds its collective breath.

Pete and Julia meet surreptitiously with Brotherhood and Association factions, trying to explain the inexplicable and trying to defuse a situation ready to explode. Finally, when it becomes apparent that all that remains to be done is pray, *mirabile dictu*, quite literally, their prayers are answered by Garvey's Chaplin-General.

Bishop George Alexander McGuire's prestige inside the Association is only matched by the admiration he enjoys within the Brotherhood. Bishop of Garvey's African Orthodox Church and Chaplain-General for the Association, many religious Garveyites hold McGuire in even higher esteem than the President-General. McGuire's concern is for his suffering flock. The bishop feeds the hungry, treats the sick and finds employment and housing for those who had nowhere else to turn. He uses Garvey's Association to address the many ills afflicting a suffering Negro race. Bishop McGuire translates Garvey's rhetoric into a practical ministry and, for that, Bishop McGuire is universally praised.

So just as it looks like an all-out shooting war is about to erupt between the Association and the Brotherhood, Bishop McGuire announces that he is severing his ties with Marcus Garvey and the UNIA and joining Cyril Briggs and the African Blood Brotherhood.

"I invite all who still believe in our cause to join me," McGuire announces, "but only under the conditions that you respect those on the other side and that there be no bloodshed."

McGuire's announcement is electric. It forces Negroes on both sides to reconsider what is happening and, most importantly, it helps avert the bloodshed threatening to engulf Negro communities across the United States.

Chapter Eighteen

Justice Renaud in the Twelfth District Magistrates Court, New York City, sustains the charge of criminal libel brought by Cyril Briggs, editor of the Crusader, *against Marcus Garvey, President-General of the Universal Negro Improvement Association. Through its American headquarters at 56 West 135th Street, the UNIA made public the following statement of Marcus Garvey, editor in chief of the* Negro World:

"*For over a year, Cyril Briggs, editor of the* Crusader *and the executive head of the African Blood Brotherhood, has been trying to gain notoriety by attacking me and corporations I represent. Recently he sent inflammatory copies of his magazine and circulars to the members of the Universal Negro Improvement Association in different parts of the country. Three weeks ago the* Negro World *carried an announcement that Briggs is a white man. This statement caused Briggs to issue a summons for my appearance in court for criminal libel. Those trying the case seized upon it as a splendid opportunity at getting back at me for my uncompromising stand for the Negro.*

"*I hold that Briggs is a white man. Briggs's mother, who gave testimony for him, states that she is a colored woman and that she lived with a white man in St. Kitts, British West Indies, but she is not married and that Briggs is an offspring born in St. Kitts. Briggs bears his mother's name. The judge claims that one drop of black blood makes a colored American, and therefore holds that Briggs is a colored American and not a white man.*

"*I submit that 'white man' is not proper terminology, such as colored American, but that 'Caucasian' is. Briggs, being white in color, is a white*

*man even if one drop of black blood makes him a colored American. I
hold therefore that Briggs is a white Negro."*

News article, Washington Bee

A short distance south of where Spuyten Duyvil Creek connects the East
and Hudson Rivers, making Manhattan an island, three dingy buildings huddle on uptown 135th street. Inside, their bustling energy belies
their decrepit, run-down appearance. Surrounded by the largest black
population in the world, these buildings serve as a nerve center for the
Negro race. At least that's what the Garveyites who occupy the buildings believe.

Here are housed the offices of the Black Star Steamship Lines, the
Negro World and the Universal Negro Improvement Association's international headquarters. Here plans are made and executed, orders
are given and carried out. And here, the rule of one man is as impla-
cable as it is absolute. Though the empire might quiver from external
assaults, Marcus Garvey will countenance no challenge to his authority.
Garvey will not allow Bishop George Alexander McGuire to bring him
down.

"McGuire has contacted every division in our entire organization,"
Garvey shouts. The President-General is furious. "He stole our mailing
lists. He's supposed to be a man of the cloth and he stole from us."

Garvey paces back and forth, then shouts to his secretary, "Get Bill
Ferris and Wormley-Jones in here. I'm gonna deal with that traitor."

A little later, after his two henchmen arrive, Garvey settles down.

"Don't worry about him, chief," Wormley-Jones replies. "You're covered. He can't harm you."

"He's stopping me from raising money," Garvey shouts. "He's telling people not to buy Black Star stock or contribute to the redemption
fund. Hell, since he began his letter-writing campaign I've lost over 700
members from the Philadelphia division alone."

"And more than twice that number from Chicago and some of the
other divisions," Ferris comments.

"You see," Garvey declares. "I'm losing members . . . and money."

Ferris and Wormley-Jones are silent for a while.

"And Cockburn, that traitor," Garvey says. "He's talking about all that booze the *Yarmouth* ran in and out of New York and Boston."

"Don't worry about that," Wormley-Jones says. "It was just another one of the Association's businesses. Besides, Cockburn's not crazy enough to talk about the bootlegging business. He knows that's not a healthy thing to do."

"Well, why's he dealing with McGuire then?" Garvey asks.

"Why else?" Ferris replies. "He wants his back wages. He's already sued the Black Star Line and gotten nothing. His claim is just one of those included with the Hudson Towboat Company and the Irvine Engineering Company."

Neither Joshua Cockburn, captain of the *Yarmouth*, nor any of the crew has been paid in two months. The district court had ordered the sale of Garvey's ship, the *Yarmouth*, to satisfy the National Dry Dock and Repair Company's liens. But Garvey couldn't satisfy any of the other lien holders. Captain Cockburn, his crew and all of the gullible black families who sold all their belongings to book passage with the Black Star Line for passage to Africa have no recourse against Garvey's fraud. He doesn't have to nor does he intend to pay them a dime.

"What about Gordon?" Garvey asks. "He knows everything."

"Again, who's he going to talk to?" Wormley-Jones answers. "And who is going to believe him. Your people believe what you tell them. They read the *Negro World* and believe in Marcus Garvey. If you're worried you can always contact Johnson's man. Burk says he can fix anything for twenty thousand."

Lincoln Johnson is the Negro Republican whom Harding appointed as Washington's Recorder of the Deeds. With his direct connections to Attorney General Dougherty, Johnson advised Garvey that all his legal difficulties could be eliminated for twenty thousand dollars.

"Where can we get twenty thousand dollars?" asks Amy Jacques, Garvey's private secretary.

Neither Ferris nor Wormley-Jones are surprised by the secretary's intrusion. Jacques hears everything discussed in Garvey's private office and expresses her opinion about everything as well.

"We don't even have two thousand dollars!" she says.

"Let's stick to the issue," Wormley-Jones says, "which is Cyril Briggs and the African Blood Brotherhood. That's what we've got to deal with."

"What more can we do to Briggs?" Garvey asks. "We had him arrested and his followers bailed him out of jail."

"Which wasn't easy," Ferris says.

"His case is thrown out of court," Garvey continues, "while they force me to print a retraction. I wonder just who has the juice around here anyway."

"That's better than having to pay damages," Ferris blurts out.

"Don't worry. It won't be long before Briggs and his whole gang will be out of your hair for good," Wormley-Jones states. "More importantly, the Brotherhood will no longer concern our friends."

"How long will that be?" Garvey asks.

"Briggs is telling his people that the time has come to concentrate on building his organization," Wormley-Jones says. "He and McGuire plan to get your people to desert the Association and join his Brotherhood."

"I knew it," Garvey exclaims. "That's been Briggs's plan all along. He sent that fake letter telling me how he wants us to join forces and work together. The man must have thought I was a damn fool. I guess I showed him."

"Well now he intends to recruit from our lists by holding mass meetings all over the country," Wormley-Jones continues. "He intends to begin here in New York with Gordon, McGuire and Cockburn speaking at the Rush Memorial Methodist Church. Briggs believes that these traitors will fill his Brotherhood with our people. After that, Briggs intends to take those traitors to Philadelphia, Boston and Norfolk as well."

"What can we do about it?" Garvey asks.

"I believe we should have some of our members attend this meeting," Wormley-Jones smiles. "Especially some of Minister Gaines's Legionnaires."

"You've got to convince Cyril not to hold this meeting," Pete tells Julia. "It's a bad idea."

Briggs and Bishop McGuire plan to hold mass meetings all over the United States, beginning in Harlem, to expose Garvey's rackets.

"I can't tell Cyril what to do," Julia replies. "Besides, your friend Bishop McGuire will be there, and he thinks it's high time that people learn about Garvey's swindles."

"Bishop McGuire is a good man. He believes that there is a Divine Providence watching over us," Pete says. "His belief blinds him to the evil in man."

"His beliefs allowed him to see the good in you, don't they?" Julia observes. "And if it hadn't been for those beliefs, he wouldn't have helped you get where you are in the Association."

"George is a kind man," Pete agrees. "He's helped a lot of people. But just because the bishop is a good man doesn't mean that he'll be able to stop what Garvey is planning."

Pete pleads with Julia.

"You've got to trust me," he says. "Most of Garvey's people don't believe in any religion, and they especially don't believe that some white Jew is their god."

"How can you say such a thing?" Julia exclaims.

Although she isn't a particularly religious person, Julia is as deeply indoctrinated into Christianity as are most Negroes.

"If you'd seen what we saw in the European war," Pete states, "you'd understand. Most New Negroes reject the Christian devil and his lies. A long time ago, David Walker said that one of the basic reasons for black people being enslaved everywhere was because of lying Christians."

"So what are you saying?" Julia asks.

"I'm saying that you've got to get George and Cyril to call off their meeting." Pete repeats himself, this time louder, as if the increased volume will make Julia understand. But, of course, it doesn't.

"Garveyites know that McGuire is a good man," Pete continues. "But that doesn't mean that all Garvey's people will follow him, especially now that he has joined in the Brotherhood's fight against the Association. Garvey has made this thing a white and black issue and it doesn't matter what the courts say. To Garveyites, Briggs is a white man."

"Cyril is not a white man," Julia almost shouts. "He is as much a Negro as you and me."

"As much of a Negro as *you*?" Pete laughs. "You've never considered yourself a *Negro*."

"Then what am I?" Julia asks angrily.

"I have no idea what you think you are, with your green eyes, light skin and straight hair, but I'll bet it's not a *Negro*," Pete declares. "That's why Grace, Domingo, Haywood and your other West Indian friends believe that Marxists are the 'good whiteys.' You believe in that socialist crap, in a Marxist heaven, the same as those other niggers believe in a Christian heaven, because you all want to be accepted by white people. You are just not strong enough to handle a world where blacks are running things and telling you what to do."

"What do you mean by that?" Julia asks, her green eyes flashing with anger.

"You're ready to die to get into the white man's heaven rather than live in a world run by Negroes, that's what it means," Pete says.

"You're just mean," Julia flashes. "That war made you crazy in the head."

"I may be crazy, but neither Marxist whiteys nor Christian whiteys plan to give you niggers anything in this life," Pete says. "And if there is a heaven, they plan to have you serving them there as well. Otherwise it wouldn't be heaven for the white man, now would it?"

"How can you say that?" Julia sputters, her face turning beet red in anger.

"Marxists are just as racist as the other whites. They want a world run by white folks. They're just using you the same way the Christians use you. And when they're done using you, they'll treat you just like the Christians treat you, just like any other nigger, *nigger*!"

Julia looks at Pete, her eyes ablaze with anger. How dare he call me a *nigger*? She fumes. He's just jealous because he and all those other so-called Negroes are descendants of slaves, too dumb to live in anything but mud huts, sold out by their own people.

"I'm not a nigger," Julia shouts defiantly.

"Being a nigger and being treated like a nigger are two different things," Pete observes. "You believe that because they treat you different, they think you're different. You think because you can slip downtown and go to the white man's theater and eat in his café and sleep in a white man's bed he thinks you're different. West Indians, half-breed Negroes, even Africans, you all think you're better than Negroes born here in the United States. You think because you're the white man's whores that you're not his niggers. But if any of you'd been in Tulsa when the Klan came in, you'd know better. There's no difference between you and me as far as the whites are concerned. It's not your color or your education or what you look like that matters to them. *It's whether or not you serve him and how well you can keep him entertained*!"

With that Pete gave Julia a wink and wry smile.

"I've heard quite enough from you," Julia shouts. "Get your black nigger ass out of here."

Cyril Briggs peers out from the sacristy at the crowd filling Rush Memorial Methodist Church. Even though it's only a little after four in the afternoon, the pews are almost completely full. Briggs looks confused. The announcement of the Brotherhood's first anti-Garvey meeting stated that the mass meeting would begin at four thirty PM.

"No matter," Briggs remarks, puffing up with satisfaction. "With this many people arriving early, I know we're going to have a full house. I've got him now."

"You certainly do," says the light-skinned, rat-faced Negro at his side, the one who has helped Briggs make all the arrangements. "You've got Marcus Garvey right where you want him." James Wormley-Jones wears a look of complete satisfaction.

In the sacristy, Bishop George Alexander McGuire and Captain Joshua Cockburn prepare themselves. Each pore over their prepared speeches. J. D. Gordon, the UNIA's former American president, is expected momentarily. Gordon was ousted at Garvey's last convention. He criticized the President-General's mismanagement of Association funds and the defrauding of the Negroes who purchased stock in the Black Star Steamship Line. Gordon was the dissidents' choice to succeed Garvey. A rigged vote was all that Garvey needed to have Gordon expelled from the UNIA. Tonight all was in readiness for the Brotherhood to deliver the most effective blow against Marcus Garvey since Stephen Duncan left the UNIA in 1910, taking over seventy percent of the membership with him.

"Don't you think it's a bit dangerous for you to be here?" Briggs asks his secret conspirator. "If Garvey should discover that you've helped me, he'll fire you from the *World* or worse."

"Don't worry about me," Wormley-Jones answers in an amused tone. "After tonight there's only going to be one organization speaking for Negroes." Wormley-Jones gives Briggs a reassuring pat on the shoulder. "And the Brotherhood will be it."

"You remember Julia Duncan, don't you?" Briggs asks.

"Of course," Wormley-Jones. "She's a real beauty. Isn't she one of Carl Van Vechten's women?"

"Yes, but she's also a member of the Brotherhood," Briggs boasts. "You remember her; she's been at several of our meetings with Grace."

"Ah, yes," Wormley-Jones says, a cold chill running down his spine, realizing Julia could blow his cover. "I do remember seeing her." Wormley-Jones's palms begin to sweat.

"She's very close to Pete Jenkins, Garvey's top security guy," Briggs says confidentially. "Julia said that Jenkins is trying to get me to call off tonight's meeting. He told her that something might happen."

"You don't say," Wormley-Jones says, feigning surprise. More perspiration runs down the back of his head onto his neck. "Did she tell you anything else?"

"Not really," Briggs replies. "She said it had something to do with a color thing. She was kind of upset when she told me. Apparently they had had a lovers' quarrel."

"A *lovers'* quarrel?"

"Yes, they have been seeing each other for a couple of months," Briggs laughs.

"Well that *is* interesting," Wormley-Jones remarks. "Oh! Here is Dr. Gordon. Don't you think we should start? You don't want to lose any of your audience, do you?"

Briggs steps up to the pulpit. He is filled with great expectations for himself and for the future of the African Blood Brotherhood. Behind him in the first row of seats, normally reserved for the ministers, Bishop McGuire and Captain Cockburn have taken their places,

"Good evening, friends," Briggs began in a halting manner. "It is wonderful to see that so many of you have joined us this evening."

Briggs is plagued by a speech impediment that prevents him from speaking effectively. The Brotherhood executive committee warns Briggs against speaking at all. But Briggs cannot pass up the opportunity to introduce his guests. He can already see masses of Garveyites defecting to the Brotherhood's banner.

"It's your triumph, your victory," Wormley-Jones tells Briggs, "you should be the first person your new members see. You are going to be their new leader. They're used to seeing Garvey, now they must see you." Briggs cannot resist the opportunity.

As soon as Cyril Briggs begins his opening remarks, the rather quiet gathering becomes restless and noisy. The unexpected disturbance throws Briggs off.

"Tonight, I ah . . . I wish to introduce," Briggs stammers.

Hoots from different sides of the church ring out and the general murmurings became louder and boisterous even.

"Bishop Alexander McGuire is well known to many of you . . ." Then the boos began.

"Boo! Boo! That traitor, that Judas! Hiss!"

Catcalls and boos echo from every part of the church, increasing in volume until it becomes impossible for Briggs to be heard above the din.

"Please, my friends," the Brotherhood leader pleads. "We must have order."

But his pleas go unheeded. He calls for silence in vain. His pleas seem only to encourage the crowd to become more boisterous and rambunctious. Many are on their feet, shouting. In desperation, Briggs turns and motions Bishop McGuire up to the pulpit.

And at first, the sight of the stately, dusky-hued prelate striding to the pulpit seems to quiet the crowd.

"My brothers," McGuire begins, "often I have spoken to you . . ."

But hardly do the words leave his lips before the crowd begins to howl like hounds who have treed their prey.

"TRAITOR! LIAR! You're the white man's flunky!" A verbal barrage rings out assaulting the minister from every corner of the church. Invective follows upon invective like a gladiator's net enveloping the hapless prelate in its snare. Bishop McGuire is determined to continue, but the crowd is even more determined to prevent his being heard. The outcome in this contest of wills is never in doubt. The booing crowd shouts McGuire off of the pulpit.

"Go get the cops," Briggs shouts at Wormley-Jones.

The yellow-face double agent nods and, slipping through the crowd, exits the side door. By now, many Harlemites who actually came to hear Bishop McGuire and the others speak, begin to arrive. They are too late. Burly Legionnaires bar all of the entrances. No one can get in. Several men dressed in suits who seem accustomed to controlling crowds guide the newcomers back outside and onto the street. These are Garvey's security guards, trained by Pete. They divert the newly arriving Brotherhood supporters, who greatly outnumber the Association's hecklers, away from the church. So expertly is the crowd handled that even though all of Harlem wants to hear the true story about Garvey and the UNIA, none of them gets access to the church that evening.

"All the seats are taken," Garvey's security guards tell the late arrivals, redirecting them back outside.

Inside Dr. Gordon rises to give his address. Briggs believes that, since Gordon had been second in charge of the Association, Garvey's assistant president-general, even the Association members would want to hear what he had to say. But the crowd affords Gordon no more hospitality than is accorded Bishop McGuire. Once again the words TRAITOR!! and LIAR!! resound throughout the church.

Finally policemen arrive. The six patrolmen, under the direction of a sergeant, in their unmistakable blue uniforms, complete with nightsticks and side arms, deploy inside the church. Even so, the crowd continues to howl, as groups of them attempt to outdo each other's hooting and howling at the pulpit. The policemen stand by and watch. After a time, it seems as though the policemen, themselves, urge the crowd to be even more abusive and disruptive, if that is possible.

"You must clear out these rowdies," Briggs begs the police officers.

But the police seem disinclined. Finally, the pastor of the church rushes in and announces that the program is cancelled.

"Everyone must leave," the anxious minister tells the police.

With that, the police are galvanized into action. "The program is over," the cops shout. "Everybody out!"

They each take a row and move everyone out of the pews, into the aisles and up toward the exits. Within minutes the police have cleared the church and the streets as well. The people of Harlem will not hear the truth about Marcus Garvey this day.

"You've been a good Legionnaire," Ferris tells Pete, looking around nervously. "You been honest and loyal. So I'm going to tell you something that you need to know."

"What's that, boss?" Pete had been called into Ferris's office as soon as he arrived at work the next morning.

"You're in trouble, Pete. Big trouble," Ferris says.

"What do you mean?" Pete asks. But he already knows what Ferris meant. Josh has warned him that Wormley-Jones told Garvey about Pete's relationship with Julia.

"I don't know what you've done or who you crossed, but the word is out that you and your woman have some important enemies," Ferris says. "I think you ought get away as soon as possible, like today. The President-General has added you to his enemies list, right along with Cockburn, Gordon and Maguire."

Pete hurries to Julia. "We've got to leave," he tells her.

She doesn't question why, she merely asks, "Where?"

"Los Angeles," Pete replies.

Looking into his eyes, Julia asks, "I can trust you, can't I, Pete?"

"I love you and you can trust me to love you till the day I die," Pete answers.

Julia says, "Give me a minute to pack and I'll be ready."

While packing, Julia tells herself, "Yes I love him and need him, so I'll go to California with him. I'll even marry him and have his brats, but one day I'll get even with Peter Jenkins for calling me a whore."

"The chief wants to congratulate the Bureau on its operation against the African Blood Brotherhood."

They meet in a private suite in one of Washington's more exclusive hotels: J. Edgar Hoover, William J. Burns, Harry Daugherty and Gaston Means. The marbled entryway opens into a paneled living room, whose centerpiece is a cavernous fireplace. The furnishing includes sofas, ottomans and easy chairs sunk into thick Persian carpeting. A great crystal chandelier bounces rays of light against the gilt-edged walls and satin drapery. To the right is a game and billiard room and to the left through a set of glass doors a great dining room. The suite, occupying an entire floor of the hotel, boasts a private elevator and a vestibule manned by handpicked FBI agents. For the convenience of the four guests, a battery of colored servants sees to their every need. This evening, they prepare a report for the chief justice and supreme grand master. Hoover conveys Taft's directives.

"The chief," Hoover continues, "is satisfied that the leak to the African Blood Brotherhood has been sealed, thanks to Brother Means, here."

Means clearly enjoys his work. He is a pure assassin. Like his late wife, people around Means wind up dead.

"You must be referring to that nigger soldier boy, the late Grady Jones," Means says, recalling with delight the frightened look on Grady's face just as he slit the black man's throat. After which, the Klansman indulged himself in that bloody ritual he had learned from his father and uncle while on their hooded forays.

"Why are you congratulating me?" Means asks. "It isn't over yet."

"As far as the chief's concerned, it is over," Hoover says, glaring at Means.

"We didn't get the Brotherhood leadership," Means replies. "There's still Briggs, Domingo, Campbell and the rest. We didn't even get those other two working with the nigger soldier boy, Duncan and Jenkins."

"Those two have left New York and headed for California," Burns says.

"If they go to Los Angeles, nothing should be done. Nothing!" Daugherty states emphatically. "Our friend needs those chapters on the West Coast for revenue. He needs as much money as he can raise, and so do we." It is enough that the chief believes that the leak to the African Blood Brotherhood has been closed and that they have been effectively disbanded. "Edgar, how many Brotherhood members are in jail?"

Hoover rummages in his papers and then comes out with a report. "From the names of about 4,000 brotherhood members, compiled from all known sources," the assistant director of the FBI states, "we have arrested fifteen hundred, of which seven hundred have been deported and one hundred and twenty-five have been killed."

"I think that effectively dismantles what was formerly known as the African Blood Brotherhood," Daugherty declares.

"I'll tell the chief that we have successfully completed our activities and that the Brotherhood will never again interfere with our plans," Hoover says.

Means is unhappy, but he dares not disobey his orders, at least not directly.

PART THREE

The Pan African Congress meets for the first time in Paris. Fifty-seven delegates represent the United States, the West Indies and various parts of Africa. They propose a set of amendments to the League of Nations Charter calling for civil rights guarantees, abolition of slavery and native African participation in colonial governments. Their most important proposal is for the League of Nations to take control of Germany's African possessions. In accepting the urging of the Pan African Congress, the League of Nations give the Allies, Britain, France, Italy, Spain, Belgium, the Netherlands, Denmark and the United States a mandate to rule over the African continent.

W. E. B. DuBois leads the Pan African Congress. The Congress supports, without debate or discussion, DuBois's agenda. In other words, the Pan African Congress supports the agenda that Joel Spingarn, of U.S. military intelligence, and William Pickens, William Howard Taft's eyes and ears, give DuBois. Taft has been Pickens's benefactor since the Negro's student days at Yale. During his tenure as a field representative for the NAACP Pickens repays Taft.

DuBois's Pan African Congress accepts, as reasonable, European control of Africa. Whites might consider self-rule under a federated association of African states at some future date, possibly in the next millennium, but only after the African bounty of gold, diamonds, oil, rubber and other treasures are firmly under the control of whites. DuBois prevents the Pan African Congress from raising any issues like mob violence, terrorism, malnutrition, inadequate healthcare, substandard education, limited access to tax dollars and public resources, lack of employment and union discrimination. "This is not the forum for such issues," he declares. His congresses are occasions for a general exchange of the ideas that will prevent race war and racial strife. For his coopera-tion, DuBois receives assurances that opportunities for a peaceful and accelerated development of the Negro "talented tenth" will continue through financial support to Negro colleges from wealthy white patrons like J.G. Phelps-Stokes.

Marcus Garvey is furious. DuBois has obstructed his plans once again. Garvey wanted the League of Nations to turn Germany's African terri-tories over to the UNIA. The British know that the Germans are behind Garvey. A memorandum to the British secretary of state for the colonies states: "It is possible that the whole movement underlying the UNIA and African Communities League was originated by German propaganda and money, and probably is still supported by German Americans. On this point it seems to me that His Majesty's Ambassador at Washington should be able to make enquiry and give advice."

Charlotta Bass, publisher and editor in chief of the Los Angeles–based California Eagle *is a member of DuBois's first Pan African Congress and serves both as president of the Los Angeles chapter of the NAACP as well as president of the Los Angeles Division of Garvey's Universal Negro Improvement Association.*

Chapter Nineteen

In 1920, New York is a great city whose 14,000,000 inhabitants come from all over the world. The predominantly black community of Harlem has almost 80,000 people jammed into a small geographical area. In 1920, Los Angeles is little more than a large trading post where the San Fernando Valley land barons, who own thousands of acres of Southern California land, come to advertise, distribute and sell their great stores of cattle, wheat and oil reserves. Los Angeles has always been the place to buy and sell. This is perhaps the reason why *los angelenos* developed the marketing technique known as advertising—which was why Los Angeles became the radio and movie capital of the world. *Hooray for Hollywood*. Compared with New York's massive population, Los Angeles is a country town whose population barely tops 500,000. And yet, 70,000 Negroes live in this land of adobe huts, Catholic missions, sprawling ranches and desert, only 10,000 fewer than in New York.

Even though it sits next to the thunderous Pacific, Los Angeles blossoms in the southwest corner of the great Mojave Desert. It has served the collective needs of the surrounding land barons for all manner of stores, shops, markets, trading areas and, most important, access to transportation to ship their vast herds of beef, bushels of wheat, bales of cotton and the many other farm and ranch products that are the produce of California's bounty. Los Angeles, as a gigantic marketplace, sends goods to the four corners of the world by rail, ship, and truck—and, increasingly, by air. In order to induce the purchase of their products, Los Angeles creates images and displays them in every possible medium. All the images emanating from the great southern California marketplace on radio and billboards, in the movies and in newspapers convey one single, solitary message: BUY! BUY! BUY!

Negroes, driven by the inexorable scourge of white supremacy, make their way out west and settle in Los Angeles. Here they discover one absolute fact, one mighty truth, and one finality. Any Negro fortunate enough to have made it all the way to Los Angeles ignores this fact, at their own peril. The absolute fact of life for any Negro living in Los Angeles in the 1920s is that Los Angeles is the last and final stop. Negroes fleeing the brutality of Mississippi, re-enslavement in Arkansas, murderous mobs in Oklahoma, marauding whites in Indiana, economic deprivation in New York, lying lawyers, crooked judges, rent-gouging landlords, joblessness, nonexistent health care—these Negroes, who settled in Los Angeles, survivors of countless atrocities, threats and betrayals, had to realize that Los Angeles is where the Negro is forced to make his final stand. *There is nowhere left to run.*

Charlotta Bass meets Pete and Julia at the Union Pacific railroad terminal. She wants to fall to her knees. To Charlotta, they appear to be young gods from the motherland: Ogun and Yemaya.

Pete's body, toughened from years of physical training with the Army and with the African Legion, radiates strength and vitality. His sharp features and muscular five-foot-eleven-inch frame forces women to catch their breath. Pete's unblinking, brown eyes, which complement the velvety dark hue of his skin, miss nothing. Seemingly at odds with his calm, quiet demeanor, they dart about, observing his surroundings, taking mental notes on everything. Charlotta, a newspaper publisher since 1912, has seen a lot. When Charlotta looks into Pete's eyes and sees their cynical detachment, their icy stare, the publisher of the *California Eagle* notes, "He's as tough as they come."

As striking as Pete appears to the *Eagle*'s publisher, Charlotta cannot turn her eyes from the most beautiful woman, white or Negro, she has ever seen. Julia's lovely green eyes captivate her. From that moment on, Charlotta's commitment either to Marcus Garvey or W. E. B. DuBois will always be secondary to the loyalty she will give to Julia and Pete.

Their flat is angled, quite accidentally Pete believes, so that in the morning the rising sun pours light and life through their bedroom window, and in the evening the last flickering rays of the sun settling into the

Pacific are painted against their living room. The living room is ample enough for their spare furnishing—thinly covered sofa and a floor-model radio. The radio, a Philco, never fails to impress Julia's frequent female visitors even though its reception of their favorite radio programs leaves much to be desired. Compared to the bulky Philco, the smaller table-model radio in the kitchen has better reception and can pick up more radio stations. The kitchen radio is the main reason why Pete and Julia spend so much of their time there. This evening Julia finds Pete reading the evening paper just after arriving home from duty at the Newton Street police station.

Pete looks up just as his wife of six months drifts into the kitchen of their flat.

"Domestic life agrees with her," Pete thinks.

Julia wears a gingham apron. She walks with bare feet across the well-scrubbed wood floor, which smells slightly of ammonia. Her golden glow, or rather her afterglow, makes Pete fall in love all over again. Julia is happy. She loves her husband and she receives the attention of Los Angeles's tight-knit Negro community.

Julia insisted on getting married as soon as the couple arrived in Los Angeles. Pete arranged a quiet courthouse ceremony, with Bif Meadows and Clarence Payne, both working for the California *Eagle*, as witnesses. Then they moved into a two-bedroom flat that squats against a dusty hillside on New Jersey Street in Los Angeles's Boyle Heights district. There, Pete and Julia spent their honeymoon—neither will ever see Manhattan again.

The flat is affordable, especially compared to the exorbitant rents Harlem landlords charge. The neighborhood is pleasant. And as long as one remembers that most of Southern California is desert, one can admire the aesthetic character of Boyle Heights, including the abundance of dust, dirt and dry heat.

Nothing in her flat reminds Julia of her parents' apartment, and that is exactly how Julia wants it. She doesn't want her home to look like her mother's place, like the inside of a second-hand thrift shop. Her father prides himself on possessing white people's junk. Not Julia. Before purchasing second-hand furnishings, Julia will do without.

When they purchase their floor-model radio, Julia tells Pete, "I want a new one." She knows that, left to himself, Pete will just search the thrift shops for a second-hand radio, like her father.

"I don't want my home looking like my mother's place with second-hand clothes, second-hand dishes, second hand-furniture, even second-hand thoughts," Julia tells her husband.

"Second-hand thoughts?" Pete shakes his head. "What do you mean by second-hand thoughts?"

"What do you think I mean?" Julia replies. "Second-hand thoughts from the *Negro World*, second-hand thoughts from the *Crusader*, second-hand thoughts from *Crisis*."

Second-hand thoughts. Is Julia claiming originality for all her thoughts? he wonders. But Pete decides not to press the point. They converse best when they keep it light, Pete believes. Actually, they converse best when Julia does all the talking.

"I talked with Grace today," Julia announces casually.

"Your friend in New York?" Pete asks. He returns to his Los Angeles *Evening Herald* newspaper.

"Yes," Julia replies. "I only know one Grace."

"I wish the only one you knew lived in Los Angeles," Pete says under his breath, but aloud he asks, "How's she doing?"

Since coming to Los Angeles six months ago, Pete and Julia have been forced to make adjustments. One of the adjustments for Pete is getting used to Julia's long-distance telephone calls to her mother, to Grace and to anyone else she can think of. Another adjustment is that he has to pay for them.

"She's alright."

"Is she still upstate?"

"Yes."

Grace Campbell and many other Brotherhood leaders decided to go into hiding in order to escape Hoover's dragnet. The FBI was reeling in as many Brotherhood members as possible. The decision was made to break up the organization for good.

"She says that she sees Moore, Briggs and some of the others," Julia continues. "But they're not meeting regularly. Apparently, Briggs had gotten an issue of the *Crusader* printed, but they all got together to keep him from distributing it."

"Briggs just doesn't want to give up, does he?" Pete comments.

"Grace says that after Garvey busted up Cyril's second mass meeting, most of the membership, those who hadn't been arrested already, went completely underground or, if the FBI let them, renounced their membership."

Pete puts down his newspaper; his cop's instinct is working again. He complains so often about the telephone bill that he knows that Julia will never voluntarily make him aware of her using it unless she wants to tell him something.

"Did Grace mention anyone else?" Pete asks.

"They found Grady Jones, at least what was left of him." Julia sounds small, like she is a child whose voice is about to crack when performing in front of adults for the first time.

Pete gets up from the kitchen and walks over to his wife. He puts his arms around her and holds her close.

"It's all right," Pete says softly. "You can let it out."

"Oh, Pete," Julia sobs, "they cut him up and they castrated him."

Pete holds his sobbing wife in his arms, and, too, tastes the salty tears flowing unbidden down his cheeks. He remembers Grady had once been his friend, and now he is dead. After releasing his own sorrow, Pete begins to realize that neither he nor Julia is safe. But he comes to the same conclusion all Los Angeles Negroes must understand: there is nowhere left to run. This is the final stop.

"Grace said she attended Grady's funeral. There weren't many people."

"Where did they bury him?" Pete asks, trying to control his feelings.

"In the military cemetery in Queens," Julia replies.

"I guess from the night at that French farmhouse, Grady was just living on borrowed time." Pete looks over at Julia and smiles. "He had a job to do."

"What was that?" Julia asks.

"His job was to bring us together."

A faint smile brightens Julia's sad face.

"Yes, darling, you're absolute right. Grady was meant to bring us together."

She nestles even closer in his arms. "And I do love you," she whispers. "Even though you don't believe me, I love you, my strong handsome, prince."

Pete says nothing. He can't. He's too choked up with emotion.

After awhile, after a very long while, after having left the kitchen for the bedroom, Julia asks the question that has been bothering them both all along.

"Do you think they'll still come after us?"

Pete rubs his fingers through her hair and stares out into the darkness of the night sky.

"I don't know sweetheart, I just don't know."

Chapter Twenty

"The guests of honor have arrived," Windows says, opening the door to a distinguished English Tudor–styled home. The home belongs to Jim Dukes, a short, balding black man, whose distinguished bearing and precise manner of speech might identify him as a college-educated professional rather than the chauffeur that he is. In 1902, when he moved his family into their home located at Hooper Avenue and 33rd Street, their white neighbors paid the Dukes an unfriendly visit.

"We don't want no niggers around here," the neighbors said.

Though Dukes was quiet and respectable, he was not to be run out of his home. Dukes had fled from Texas, where hooded nightriders terrorized his parents. The chauffeur produced a gun and told his neighbors that they had better get off his property. From then on, the Dukes family and their home came to symbolize the determination and spirit of black Los Angelenos. Their family home became one of the centers of social activity for the New Negroes of Los Angeles.

After six months Charlotta Bass has decided the time has come to introduce her two friends to Los Angeles society.

"What have you newlyweds been up to?" Windows asks as he escorts the pair into a living room packed with guests who are eager to meet the celebrated New Yorkers. From the time Julia arrives in L.A. society, women cannot stop talking about her beauty and those mysterious green eyes. And Pete, as the newest addition to the Los Angeles Police Department, is already a legend.

"It's nice seeing you, Clarence," Julia replies.

"Clarence?" Bif Meadows shouts out, breaking away from several guests. "You mean Windows, don't you?"

"Julia's not like the rest of you morons," the former cub reporter lashes out. "She's a lady and knows how to treat people."

"People, yes," Bif laughs. "But you're not people. You're one of those pop-eyed creatures who should be in a circus, isn't that right, Pete?" This is Bif's way of showing how happy he is to see the couple, especially Julia. Bif is a man of the world. He is hardened to the facts of life and is not above making a deal or two, especially if it puts money in his pocket or makes him a friend in high places. Tulsa had completely depressed him. Bif had a woman in Tulsa. They had made plans. But that's all Windows knows. Bif had been unable to work for months. He drank heavily and had it not been for Windows, he might even have slid into an alcoholic abyss. He still isn't fully recovered, but he's getting better. And there is no place like Los Angeles for a veteran photographer like Bif to start a new life.

Bif pushes through the crowd and leads Pete, with Julia on his arm, through the living room, by a den with a stone fireplace off to the right, past a dining room set up for a buffet of salads, meats and all sorts of tasty dishes, through a hallway lined with guests representing the cream of black middle-class society, through swinging double doors and into the kitchen where Charlotta is supervising a number of cooks.

"My dears," Charlotta says, reaching out to embrace first Julia and then Pete. "We are so happy you are here."

Then taking both Pete and Julia's hands and leading them through the swinging doors and back into the living room, Charlotta announces: "Everyone, your attention please, everyone, our guests of honor have arrived."

The throng, which had been noisily engaged in conversation, quiets down.

"Everyone, I want you to meet Officer Peter Jenkins, newly appointed to the Los Angeles Police Department, and his beautiful wife, Julia. Our guests come to us from New York where Officer Jenkins headed security for the *Negro World*. Mrs. Jenkins is originally from Jamaica." Then turning to Julia, Charlotta asks, "Isn't that right, my dear?"

Nodding in agreement, Julia replies, "My parents were born in Jamaica, but I was actually born in New York."

"Well, we are very proud of your husband and happy that you both could join us, isn't that right everyone?" Charlotta drops their hands and begins to clap. Everyone in the room joins her. The applause goes on for some time. "We will begin the receiving line now." Charlotta guides Julia and Pete into the den. One by one, the guests enter. Charlotta introduces everyone present, important and not so important, to Pete and Julia. Even before every guest passes through the receiving line, Pete realizes that Charlotta has assembled an important array of guests. Members of the Los Angeles UNIA Division 156, including Division President Noah Thompson and his wife lead a procession of Los Angeles Garveyites. Many of them remember Pete from the convention, while others know of his reputation. Rumor and gossip operate as effectively in Los Angeles's Garveyite circles as it does in New York. The Los Angeles division is still in disarray since Noah Thompson's accusations at the convention.

Pete and Julia also meet leading members of the NAACP, local businessmen and members of the L.A. black press, not only those working for the *Eagle* but also friend and rival, the publisher of the *New Age*, Fred Roberts.

Joe Bass, Charlotta's husband, in addition to being a deacon of the Second Baptist Church, is active with Los Angeles County's top Republican leadership. Many colored Republicans and religious leaders add their presence to the festivities. And of course, members of the Colored Women's Club, the arbiters of Los Angeles's Negro society, are in attendance. Only Charlotta could bring together such a social array of colored *los angelenos*.

Following the introductions, both Pete and Julia make short speeches expressing their gratitude for the welcome they have received. Afterward, the guests partake of the feast that has been prepared. Pete and Bif stroll out the back door into the patio area. A great fishpond takes up the entire right side of the yard. Large, golden fish swim lazily to and fro between green lily pads and giant fronds shooting out of the pond's still, murky waters. Every so often a fish will leap into the air trying to catch a flying insect. Pete and Bif plop down into a large comfortable yard swing and eye the guests as they troop by.

"So level with me Bif," Pete says confidentially.

"What do you want to know, old chap?" Bif responds, drinking his iced tea, which has been doctored from a pocket flask. Pete could not imagine Negroes living as well as the Dukes. Los Angeles seems too good to be true.

"Is all this real? I mean, a chauffeur lives like this?" Beyond the pond a two-car garage houses a Pierce-Arrow limousine owned by Jim Dukes's employer, a well-known Hollywood producer, as well as the Dukes's family Ford.

"It's as real as it gets, my friend," Bif says.

"I can't imagine heaven being much different than this," Pete observes.

"That's because when you wake up every morning, you see that angel lying next to you."

"Yes," Pete muses, "you're right about that. I can't quite believe it myself."

From the time Bif first laid eyes on her, the photographer has been obsessed with Julia. Pete knows Bif envies him. But in a town where Pete hardly knows anyone, Bif passes as a friend.

"That's not what I'm talking about," Pete says.

"Well, what do you mean?" Bif grins, the "tea" having put the older man into a mellow mood.

"Is Los Angeles really a black man's paradise or am I missing something?" Pete asks seriously.

"I don't get your meaning," Bif says. "You don't really think Los Angeles is paradise, do you?"

"Well, maybe not paradise, but . . ."

"Well, L.A. certainly isn't paradise by a long shot," Bif retorts. "What makes you ask something like that?"

"When I was in New York, some folks came out from California with tickets on the Black Star Line to sail to Africa. Of course, there wasn't any ship to sail on, so I had to find places for them to live and . . ."

"So?"

"Well, I got the impression, since they were from Los Angeles, that California was a hard scrabble place, where Negroes faced hard times and have no prospects," Pete says.

Bif looks hard at his friend, before breaking out in a great laugh. He laughs and shakes all over until tears pour from his light brown eyes and over his sallow cheeks.

"Now I've heard everything," the veteran photographer says, trying to control himself. But a second later, Bif is attacked by another fit of laughter. He must grab his stomach to keep it from hurting.

"They kept telling me that you were totally in the dark. I couldn't believe it. You seemed in the know when we were in Tulsa," Bif says once he is finally able to control himself.

Pete shrugs. A maxim he learned from Ferris was that it was better to keep one's mouth shut and be thought a fool than to open it and remove all doubt. This is one of those times when Pete needs to keep his mouth shut.

"First of all, who in their right mind do you think would want to leave California to go to Africa?" Bif asks.

Pete thinks about Bif's question. "But those people seemed," Pete starts to say, before remembering to keep his mouth shut.

"How many of them had a pot to piss in or a window to throw it out of?" Bif asks.

Pete thinks about the stranded Californians for whom he provided housing.

Without waiting for a reply, Bif continues, "Where did they buy their tickets?" Bif shakes his head as if talking to a young schoolboy. "You know about DuBois's campaign to discredit Garvey, don't you?"

"Of course," Pete answers.

"Well, then," Bif says matter of factly. "What do you think the NAACP does with the people asking them for help? You know they don't do nothing to help black folks with practical problems. All they do is talk."

"Then you're saying . . ."

"I'm saying that any time DuBois's crowd gets in a pinch, where they are forced to help some poor black folks, they always find a way to dump them on Garvey. DuBois knows that we won't turn anyone away, no matter where they come from or who sends them. DuBois and those white folks he works for don't care about black folks and they certainly don't help black folks get jobs, housing or medical help. L.A. is no paradise, but you can't judge it by what DuBois told some 'grifters' to do or say."

Bif takes another sip of his "tea" and studies Pete's face.

"Look here," Bif continues. "The homes here in L.A. are palaces compared to what blacks live in back east. They have lawns and back yards and cost as little as $2,000 down with a monthly payment of $10 a month. There are jobs for anyone who wants to work; the jobs aren't great, but they pay better than anywhere else in the country. Los Angeles is a great place to find a job. Black men can work in the iron and steel mills as well as the shipyards and automobile plants. And there are schools here for Negro children. No this isn't paradise, but it's a lot better than anyplace else I know of."

"What keeps Los Angeles from being a Negro paradise, then?" Pete asks, not without some sarcasm.

"I want to say something about that." It was Joe Bass who spoke. The managing editor of the *Eagle* has just come outside and catches the tail end of the conversation. "I don't quite agree with Bif about the employment situation here. Sure there's employment but the unions are the enemies of colored workers. They're run by the Klan and a colored man can't get a decent job." Joe pauses as if lost in thought. Then he continues. "You remember when we upgraded our printing presses, Bif?"

"Three or four months ago as I remember," Bif replies.

"Well, the typographer's union here in Los Angeles kept our typesetter from getting the training he needed to become a certified linotypist. He wasn't a member of the union, they wouldn't let him join, nor would they give him the training he needed. We had to send Dan up to San Francisco for training and certification."

"And there's another thing," another guest joins in. "Negroes can't own or even occupy property on the westside. Nor can we go down to the beach . . ."

"There's lots of places we can't go . . ." someone else says.

"We can't get our fair share of the taxes, either," Joe continues. "The banks won't lend us money for developing our businesses. Anytime Charlotta rides the streetcar, she runs the risk of being accosted by some white person demanding the right of Jim Crow seating. I can be beaten or arrested by a white cop for no reason other than my dark skin. No, Officer Jenkins, Los Angeles certainly isn't paradise, but it's better than any other place in this country."

"Well, I can promise you that no colored man will be mistreated by the police as long as I'm around," Pete vowed.

A lively discussion ensued. Everyone congratulated Pete on coming to Los Angeles and being accepted by the LAPD.

Later, when they are once again by themselves, Bif continues their discussion. "It's the problem of light-skinned versus dark-skinned Negroes," Bif says. "The good jobs, professional jobs, go to the light-skinned Negroes. Even if a dark-skinned Negro has a college degree, the nod will always go to the lighter-skinned Negro. All the social positions that have any meaning in the Negro community, except preaching, go to light-skinned Negroes. A lot of people around here won't say it, but those are the facts."

Pete starts to tell Bif how wrong he is. How did Pete get his job with the Los Angeles Police Department, if Bif is right? Pete certainly isn't light-skinned. Once again, he decides to hold back. Besides, Pete already knows how he got his job with the LAPD.

"In 1867," Bif continues, "when the Pullman Company made it a policy to hire only blacks as porters, the company decided to discriminate by color. The dark-skinned porters carried luggage, shined shoes, cleaned berths, made beds and did everything the white passenger wanted, all on no sleep and with a smile. Pullman paid these porters $27.50 a month plus tips. Light-skinned Negroes were given the waiter and cook jobs that paid $50 a month. This skin-color caste system has prevailed among Negroes ever since."

Pete looks at Bif. His forehead furrows and his eyes narrow as he realizes something he should have known all along. "Well, I'll be," Pete tells himself.

Within Garvey's African Legion, in addition to the security section, there is another section of Legionnaires who only report to the Minister of the African Legions Captain E. L. Gaines, Garvey's spymaster. Pete realizes what he should have known all along: Bif Meadows is one of Garvey's spies.

Bif smiles as if he has read Pete's mind.

"So now you know," Bif says, laughing. "It took you long enough. You don't have to worry. If we had wanted, we could have gotten you and the missus at any time. We're not your enemy."

"Oh, no?" Pete replies, his cop's mind now on full alert.

"No, no," Bif repeats. "The chief still has a great deal of respect for you. He thinks it was smart of you to get out of New York, protecting your missus and all. He wasn't the one who was after the African Blood Brotherhood."

"You sure could have fooled me," Pete says sarcastically. "I guess those court scenes between Garvey and Briggs were being staged."

Bif shrugs.

"I'll bet you want to know why the chief didn't publish any of our reports about Tulsa in the *World*, don't you?" Bif is probing. He waited for Pete's answer, but it didn't come. "Well?"

"Well, what?" Pete asks, realizing Bif wants something.

"Well, why didn't the *Negro World* report on the Tulsa riot?"

"We were there to provide a first-hand report to the chief and his brass, not to report anything in the press, I guess," Pete replies.

Bif eyes Pete defiantly as if to make Pete forget how deeply Bif was affected. "I get it," Pete tells himself. "This spy wasn't in the Army and didn't see any action. Now he's embarrassed over how he behaved in Tulsa." Pete studies the old Garveyite for awhile, wondering exactly who Bif is working for. Pete says, "Tell me something."

"What is it?"

"Who killed Grady Jones?"

Bif stares at Pete. "Did you know your friend worked for military intelligence?"

"I suspected it."

"Then you know he didn't have any protection since he wasn't in with DuBois or Spingarn and he was too close to the government's fake communists."

"Fake communists?" Pete asks. "Who are they?"

"You should know who they are. After all, Julia was involved with them. You know, the ones around Rose Pastor Stokes."

Pete stares at Bif, trying to penetrate his meaning. "Sometimes I wonder whether it's just because I have some inside information or because people, Negroes and whites, are so stupid," Bif exclaims.

"What do you mean?"

"Well, ask yourself, 'Why would people in the African Blood Brotherhood and those other whites believe that Rose Pastor Stokes is a legitimate communist?' Didn't she have ideological differences with the other communist party, the Wobblies? Her husband, J. G. Phelps-Stokes is a multimillionaire; he owns mines, railroads and banks. He's the major financier of the NAACP, a government-run intelligence agency, as well as most of the Negro colleges."

"You mean that entire episode at the convention was to set Briggs up?" Pete asks naïvely, more to himself than to Bif.

"Well, let's put it this way," Bif says. "One of the closest friends of William Howard Taft, is Anson Phelps-Stokes. This Phelps-Stokes is the power behind Yale University and a member of the Pilgrim Society. Anson Phelps-Stokes is J. G. Phelps-Stokes's brother."

"How do you know all this?"

"Rose Pastor Stokes, a Russian Jew, and her husband were 'outed' by legitimate Marxists in 1918 during the war."

Bif's eyes narrow and his shoulders hunch over.

"Those New Negroes in the African Blood Brotherhood, following that fool Briggs and looking for solidarity with their so-called white friends, didn't have a chance. Many of the ones that weren't deported ended up like your friend Grady Jones!"

"Who killed Grady?"

"Does it really matter who killed him?"

"It does to me," Pete says evenly.

"Well, now that you're one of LAPD's finest," Bif says indifferently, "there might be a time when you will have some information I might be willing to trade you."

But before they can finish their conversation, Julia appears.

"Oh, there you are," she says. "I've been looking all over for you. There are so many people dying to meet you. You must meet Noah Thompson before he leaves."

Julia puts her arm through Pete's.

"You don't mind if I steal my husband, do you?" she says to Bif.

Before Garvey's West Coast agent can respond, the two of them are heading into the house.

"I thought you might have needed rescuing," Julia confides to Pete as they join the other guests in Dukes's living room.

"That's why I love you," Pete says, steeling himself for another round of idle chit-chat with the cream of black Los Angelenos.

Much later, back in their Boyle Heights flat, Pete and Julia review the events of their "coming out" party. Julia, flush with excitement, recounts, almost word for word, the conversations she had with almost everyone at the party.

". . . and since Charlotta encouraged me to join the National Association, I just can't decide which group to belong to. What do you think?"

"Think of what?" Pete yawns.

"I have just been explaining to you that there are two groups in the local NAACP," Julia says. "Haven't you been listening?"

"Yes, but . . ."

"Well, both groups were at the party. The Junior Branch is not really for juniors; they are college students and young professionals. Next year, the Junior Branch intends to produce DuBois's play, *Star of Ethiopia*, at the Hollywood Bowl. I think it's exciting."

"It sounds like it," Pete says.

"So you think I should join the Junior Branch?"

"I think you should do what you think is best."

"DuBois will be coming to Los Angeles to oversee the production," Julia continues happily. "Although it's been shown in New York, D.C. and Philadelphia, I was told that this production will be the best. Who knows, they might make it into a movie."

"It'll probably be better than *The Birth of a Nation*," Pete observes.

"Why do you say that," Julia asks, the gaiety now out of her voice.

"Because I have been assigned to the Garrick Theater," he says.

"You mean the theater that's showing *The Birth of a Nation*?" Julia asks, trying to keep the alarm from her voice.

"That's right." Pete hesitates and then continues. "Bif told me that he knows who killed Grady Jones."

"He does? Who was it?"

"He didn't say who did it," Pete replies. "Just that Grady was a dead man as soon as he began working for the government."

"Does that mean that I'm still in danger?" Julia asks, trying to be calm.

"No! Bif doesn't think so. He says that it was a good move bringing you here to Los Angeles."

"I do love it here," Julia says with a sense of relief. "But I'm kind of concerned about you."

"Don't worry," Pete states. "I can take care of myself."

Chapter Twenty-One

Los Angeles is a party town, a modern day Babylon, wide open for fun and frolic. Big-time spending and conspicuous consumption is everywhere. L.A. is the world's biggest marketplace. Anything can be had for a price. Hollywood projects glamor and pageantry. College students party around the clock.

Jazz and night clubs sprout up throughout the Central Avenue community, like the classy Cadillac Club, which caters to the Hollywood crowd, or the fleshpots like the Apex Room, where pimps and drug dealers ply their trade. A shooting or a stabbing occurs every night.

Yet Los Angeles does not experience the gang violence that plagues Eastern and Midwestern cities. Mobsters like Al Capone, Dutch Schultz, Legs Diamond and Lucky Luciano do not control L.A.'s streets. Even if L.A.'s mayors, district attorneys and city councilmen take campaign contributions from madams, bootleggers and gamblers, and the vice squad is on the take, criminal syndicates and mob-dominated rackets cannot gain a toehold. California, and Los Angeles in particular, is Ku Klux Klan territory. This fact, and Joe Bass's city hall contacts, was how Pete got the opportunity to join the Los Angeles Police Department.

"How would you like to be an L.A. cop?" Joe Bass stared at Pete. In spite of himself, Joe liked Pete. The handsome New Yorker reminded Joe of the son that he never had (he and Charlotta have no children). "Before you answer, you should know that being a Negro cop in Los Angeles could be very dangerous."

"I've faced danger before," Pete replied.

"Not like this," the dark-skinned editor of the *Eagle* declared.

"Tell me more," Pete said.

"Have you ever heard of the film, *The Birth of a Nation*?"

"*The Birth of a Nation*," Pete replied. "Isn't that about the Ku Klux Klan?"

"Yes," Bass said. "When it came out in 1915, it was called *The Clansman*."

"What does the film have to do with the police force hiring me?"

"I'll get to that," Bass said, "but let me tell you something about the film."

Pete and Julia had been in Los Angeles less than a week. Julia and Charlotta were out shopping. Pete and Joe were sitting in the *Eagle*'s offices waiting for their wives to return. Pete was telling Joe how much he needs to find a job.

"*The Birth of a Nation* is a devilish movie," Joe said, and, lighting a cigar, began to describe the film:

"The Birth of a Nation *begins with the portrayal of an idyllic South representing white chivalry and culture. Negroes are happy in their natural condition of slavery. However, during the Civil War, the Union Army turns these happy slaves into soldiers, who, freed from the kindly slave master, look and behave like apes. The ape-like Negro soldiers brutalize an innocent Confederacy. They loot Southern homes and hunt down white women. After the war, the Negroes leave the Union Army to become lawmakers responsible for 'reconstructing' the Southern way of life. Eating chicken on the statehouse floor while passing laws that legalize interracial marriage, the Negro legislator is a pawn in the hands of Northern carpetbaggers and Southern scalawags. In the movie's final scene, a virtuous white woman flees in terror from her former Negro slave. His lust transforms the Negro man into a beast bent on rape. In order to escape her former slave's clutches, the white woman must leap from a cliff. When her rescuers arrive, too late to save her, with her dying breath, she identifies her Negro assailant. The film ends with heroic white men forming a Ku Klux Klan party that hangs the black culprit.*"

Pete looked at his host. "I'd heard that this film got the white folks rioting all over the country."

"The original director's cut had the Klansmen castrating the Negro before they lynched him," Joe said. "Charlotta and I demanded that scene be removed when Griffith first showed *The Clansman*, in 1915.

But even as it is the film is despicable." Joe clenched down on his cigar and scowled. "When we denounced *The Birth of a Nation* in the *Eagle*, Negro actors criticized us for interfering with their jobs."

Pete just shook his head. "What does this have to do with me?"

"The Ku Klux Klan is reshowing *The Birth of a Nation* at the Garrick Theater downtown," Joe said. "Although the council and the city commissioner tried to close it down for public safety reasons, a court order permits it to be shown."

"But I don't see how," Pete interrupted.

"We told the folks downtown that as long as that film was being shown, our community is in danger," Joe continued. "They promised that the police department will defend our community against the Klan. And I got a personal commitment that any Negro the *Eagle* recommends will be hired onto the police force. Now are you interested?"

"Certainly."

Thus Pete became a member of the Los Angeles Police Department. What Joe didn't tell Pete, because he didn't know, is that the historic Hollywood partnership—between Thomas Dixon, author of *The Clansman*, and D. W. Griffith, the producer who turns *The Clansman* into *The Birth of a Nation*—is a government plan. Woodrow Wilson, Dixon's classmate and friend at Princeton, called the film a moving depiction of historical truth. The president of the United States and former president of Princeton University saw the movie as a call to arms. All the glamour, pageantry and mind-altering symbolism that Hollywood can generate is used to portray the Klan's historic mission and recruit new members. The leaders of Los Angeles's Negro community can take little solace in the hiring of one Negro police officer to protect them against the Klan's nationwide designs.

"Didn't take you long to get on with the department, did it?"

Chip Winters is one of those all-American white boys who doesn't believe coloreds should have any civil rights or privileges. This California native cannot believe that the Los Angeles police force would hire a man like Pete. It matters little to Chip that he, himself, had been hired right after dropping out of college.

"It took me as long as anyone else, I guess," Pete responds.

At first, Pete likes the idea of being a police officer. But he wonders how he is going to deal with these white folks. It has been a long time since his days as a bank messenger. A long time since he had to buck and skin so he wouldn't offend some white man. A long time since he had to feel like he was less than a man.

The first few days aren't so hard. The first day, along with the other recruits, Pete is given a badge, billy club and a special police revolver. He is directed to Wilson's store on Second and Wilshire, where he can purchase his police uniform. The following day he and the other recruits are directed to the desk sergeant.

"You recruits," the sergeant bawls out, "have the privilege of working for the finest police department . . ."

The orientation is a rah-rah session meant to instill pride in the recruits. The private Los Angeles Police Revolver and Athletic Club that functions as L.A.'s police academy will not be established for another five years. Los Angeles's recruits were expected to learn on the job. There is no formal training. For the next several weeks, Pete works with an assortment of veteran police officers, most of whom willingly show him the ropes and try to overlook the fact that he is a Negro.

Now Pete has been assigned to work the Garrick Theater with Patrolman Chip Winters, a rookie, like himself, on the force less than a month. The Garrick Theater, a modest one-floor building that seats 650 patrons, is located at the southwest corner of Eighth and Broadway in the heart of downtown Los Angeles. Pete's partner tries to pull his subtle, "Me Tarzan, you boy" routine.

"Don't get me wrong," Chip says. "I don't mind you. I really don't have anything against the coloreds. I just meant that . . ."

"Look, skip it," Pete says, deciding to put this youngster in his place right away. "We're both cops and we both do what we're told and neither of us have very much experience. And that's why we've been given this assignment."

"I guess you're right," the rookie cop concedes.

Even though Chip is all-American in his attitude, he is all-American neither in looks nor in brains, which is why he dropped out of Los Angeles City College. Chip had dreams of becoming an attorney. It is his father, who works in the city maintenance department, as well as

Chip's hulking 6-foot 5-inch, 250-pound frame that gets Chip into the LAPD. Chip has a huge head with bushy eyebrows set over dull brown eyes and a full handlebar mustache, reminding Pete of a Viking raider of Norse lore. Chip, a Los Angeles native, looks far older than his 22 years. His looks, as well as his slow, hesitant speech, betray his low IQ, which accounts for Chip's failure with the ladies, even in a town like Los Angeles.

Pete is assigned to the Newton Street station, located just off of Central Avenue, while Chip works out of the central station. Pete's instincts tell him this is unusual, especially since the Garrick Theater is not part of the Newton Street precinct station's responsibilities. If he is assigned to patrol downtown Los Angeles, he should be working out of the central precinct station.

"So how did your day go?" Julia asks. It was his first day patrolling the Garrick Theater and Julia has been worried. Pete is noncommittal; he isn't certain how he feels about his assignment and he doesn't like his partner. He wishes Josh was here. No matter, it is just the first day of another assignment.

"It's a job," Pete responds.

"Well, sir, if you do your job as a police patrolman as well as you have done your job as a husband," Julia beams, "you're going to be a great success."

Pete is tired. Walking a police beat for ten hours is tiring work; he needs to build up his physical stamina. "I don't want Winters reporting that I can't keep up," he tells himself. So he isn't really concentrating on what Julia was saying.

"What do you mean by that?" Pete asks.

"What I mean," she says, "is that I may have to postpone my plans to work in Hollywood for awhile because of you."

"Because of me?" Pete asks quizzically.

And then noting the broad grin across Julia's face, it slowly dawns on him.

"Do you mean that . . . ?"

Before he can finish his sentence, she flies into his arms.

"Yes, my big, strong husband. I'm pregnant."

Pete stares at his wife for several minutes, emotion and love welling up in his heart. He could never believe Julia was his wife, not really. When he wakes up in the morning, he fully expects to find Julia gone and when he returns from work, he is surprised to find her there. Pete continually fights against loving her too much. But now, Julia is going to have his child. Pete is happier than he has any right to be.

"Have you told your mother, yet?" he asks, not knowing what else to say.

"Of course, silly," Julia smiles at him. "She wants to come out to Los Angeles as soon as possible."

"What about your father?"

"I don't think he is quite over the fact that you 'stole' me away from him and Mother," Julia laughs gaily, "but I think Mother is working on him. I'd like him to come with her."

"That will be an interesting family reunion," Pete observes.

"He won't stay long, of course; he's too worried about his business."

"He should sell the store. Then they could move out here permanently," Pete says. "I'm sure that Joe and Charlotta could help them open up a store here."

"You think so," Julia says. "I'd be so happy. I miss my mother."

"Then you need to start working on it now. As stubborn as your father can be, I'll bet he won't be that difficult to convince once he sees L.A."

"Great," Julia exclaims, giving Pete a long kiss on the cheek, "I'll call Mother now."

Me and my big mouth, Pete chastises himself silently. And then out loud, he shouts, "You know the Post Office is still in operation. We need to save all the money we can, don't you think?"

"You are absolutely right, dear," Julia agrees. "I'll make this a quick call and give her the details in a letter. Just think, if they move to Los Angeles, we can eliminate all those long distance calls. My father should be happy about that."

"Well, if they move out here," Pete observes, "I'm certain you'll find someone else in New York to call."

When Charlotta hears the news, she can't control herself. She and Joe have no children of their own, but this will be their first godchild.

Charlotta is only a little jealous when Julia explains that she wants her parents to move to Los Angeles, permanently.

"One thing is for certain," Charlotta states. "They are going to need a place of their own. Your flat will not be large enough for you and your parents. Especially when the baby gets here." Charlotta begins planning for the arrival of Julia's parents and for the baby. And L.A.'s social scene buzzes happily over the glad tidings of the blessed event.

Pete remains on his special assignment observing the Garrick Theater. Daily crowds of white people, mostly white men, troop in to watch *The Birth of a Nation*, only to emerge frustrated, angry and ready to join the Klan. Local radio broadcasts begin praising the Klan and their fight against niggers, Catholics and Jews. Then, one day, the Garrick's theatergoers include men wearing white bed sheets and white hoods.

"Where is he?" Pete asks himself, looking around anxiously for Chip. On duty for several weeks now, Pete and Chip begin to settle into a routine. Julia is beginning to show and Pete is more concerned about her than he is about the Klan.

"I need to take a break," Chip had said. "I'm going over to Hamburger's department store. I'll be right back."

"Make sure you do," Pete told his partner. "You know the afternoon showing is about to let out."

"Don't worry about me," Chip had growled as he stomped down Broadway toward Fifth Street. Pete still doesn't like his partner. He especially doesn't like Chip's surly attitude, as if the world owed him something.

"It's that jazz music that's done it," Chip exploded one day. "People have gone crazy for that jazz music. 'Nigger music,' I call it. It gives people rickets and makes them fidgety and restless. One day, your people are gonna have to pay the price for all this jazz music."

Chip has no problem using the word "nigger" in front of Pete. He seems to enjoy it, as if he is trying to annoy Pete. Though he doesn't realize it, Chip is successful. But Pete refuses to give his partner the satisfaction of knowing and refrains from commenting. He wonders what Chip means about "Negroes having to pay for jazz music."

The Garrick's midday showing has just let out and Chip has yet to return from Hamburger's. Several-white robed Klansmen mingle in the crowd. Suddenly one of them shouts, "Look at that nigger across the street. Let's get him!" Twenty or more stare menacingly at Pete and, following the hooded leaders, begin to cross the street. Pete does not run—instead he blows his whistle and, drawing his revolver, stands his ground. Shocked at his boldness, the crowd stops its charge.

"Kill the nigger!" someone shouts out. Pete fires his revolver into the air. The crowd moves back.

"You men disperse," Pete shouts, "or some of you are going to get hurt."

"You hear that," one of the white-sheeted Klansmen shouts. "This coon's threatening to kill a white man."

Still, Pete holds his ground. Remaining as calm as possible under the circumstances, he blows his whistle once again.

"If you men don't disperse, you'll be in lockup before long," he shouts at the crowd.

"Yeah, and you're going to be one dead nigger!" one hooded Klansman, who seems to be the leader, shouts back.

Many of the crowd want no part of this drama. They begin to separate themselves from the hooded fanatics and, backing away, the mob begins to disperse almost as quickly as it formed. Behind the crowd, from several different directions, police whistles begin sounding, accelerating the crowd's dispersal. White-robed Klansmen begin running in all directions. Then Chip appears next to Pete.

"You all right?" he asks.

"I'm fine," Pete replies.

The white cop glances at the white men, racing away in all directions, their sheeted costumes flapping about as they run. He tries to hide the frustration that is gnawing at his innards. Pete can tell that his partner's beefy face is red not only from exertion but also from embarrassment.

The colored community does not ignore the attack.

"WHITE MOB ATTACKS NEGRO OFFICER" newspapers headlines blare.

"No longer is the urge to lynch a colored man somewhere off in some distant place," a Los Angeles *Times* editorial states. "The spirit of the mob is found right here in Los Angeles." It is a warning that does not sound on deaf ears, especially in the Central Avenue neighborhood. "The

Klan is re-emergent," the *California Eagle* declares. "Their numbers are increasing all over the country." But if the Los Angeles Negro community believed that this incident would decrease the Klan's boldness, they were mistaken. In Southern California, especially in Los Angeles, this incident helped the Klan capitalize on its dramatic increase in popularity.

Racial tensions in Los Angeles reach a fever pitch. Fights break out all over the city. Several racially inspired murders, suspiciously resembling lynchings, are reported. Los Angeles is on the verge of a full-fledged race war. The mayor, city council and chief of police all agree, *The Birth of a Nation* has got to go.

Meanwhile, Pete's superiors commend him for not firing at the mob of would-be lynchers.

Chapter Twenty-Two

"Our friend is in serious financial trouble!"

"So what does that mean to us?" the fat man asks, sitting behind his oaken desk, sipping his usual glass of milk. When he was president, Taft's dairy cow grazed on the White House lawn.

"He didn't pay his twenty-thousand-dollar installment," Hoover says quietly, "nor did he pay Johnson."

Lincoln Johnson, a life-long Republican, is one of Harding's few Negro appointees. Johnson, the District of Columbia's recorder of the deeds, serves as a go-between for the administration's payoffs from Negroes.

"Postmaster General Hayes is going to proceed with the mail fraud indictment unless Garvey comes up with his payment."

"What's that nigger doing with all the money he's collected?" Taft asks.

"I don't know, sir," Hoover responds.

"Well, find out!"

Taft can't afford to get angry. Anger causes his blood pressure to rise, and at over 350 pounds, his doctor tells him that even a slight increase in blood pressure can cause a heart attack. "I guess I should try to lose some weight," Taft often tells himself. Right now, he makes a deliberate effort to calm himself.

Taft says, "You know we still need our friend and his organization, don't you?"

"Yes, most worshipful grand master," Hoover replies.

"Then use your agents to pass the word. Tell Garvey to contact our friends. Hell, tell him to contact Fall and even Harding. *Get him some money!* I want Garvey working with our people in Atlanta. Everything depends on it."

"Shall I get Daugherty to stop the indictments?" Hoover asks.

"No, no, no!" Taft replies sternly. "When this is all over, I want Marcus Garvey discredited and in prison. But for now, we need him. You understand that, don't you?"

"Yes, grand master."

"How is the work progressing?"

"We have increased our membership all over the country."

"Out West?"

"Especially out West."

"Splendid! Our people have them scurrying out of the South like rats, leaving everything behind. Just last week we ran over fifteen hundred of them out of Georgia. Most of them owned acres of good Georgia land. Soon we'll have the coons either on their way back to Africa or hanging from every tree between here and Los Angeles."

The grotesque supreme grand master of the Scottish Rite slips into another one of his frequent states of narcolepsy. His aide can do nothing but wait, not knowing whether Taft will be unconscious for a minute, ten minutes or an hour. After several minutes, Taft awakes and continues.

"What about that African Blood Brotherhood?"

"We have rounded up most of the organization," Hoover responds. "According to intelligence, some remain of value to us, most of the others have been disposed of."

"I don't suppose there are any trophies available?"

"Sir?"

"Oh never mind. You can go. Keep me informed, mind you. Especially about our progress in the West."

"Yes, most worshipful grand master."

On his way back to Washington, the assistant FBI director muses about his meeting. Wouldn't have been wise, he thought to himself, to tell him about those loose ends. Julia Duncan, now Julia Jenkins, and Peter Jenkins, now Officer Jenkins of the Los Angeles Police Department. They should have been taken care of by now.

"Oh, well," Hoover sighs to himself, "our friend wants the go-ahead, and I suppose it's time."

"Miss Smith!" Hoover shouts into his office intercom as soon as he settles in.

"Yes, Mr. Hoover?"

"Find Gaston Means and have him report to me, immediately."

William S. Coburn looks out the window of his Orange County office. Coburn has a brilliant legal mind. When working out of the Imperial Palace, the Klan's national headquarters in Atlanta, Coburn had been the organization's leading attorney. Now Coburn—tapped by Imperial Wizard William Joseph Simmons for one of the most prestigious positions within the Klan's Invisible Empire—is Grand Goblin of the Klan's Pacific States Division. It's the kind of position that will rocket his career into the stratosphere of political power and authority. Success in bringing the West completely into the Klan's fold could mean a congressional seat, or even a federal judgeship. The possibilities are endless, even if some in Atlanta still blame him for the breakup of the Oakland organization. California's largest Klan division still is in Oakland; they just don't report directly to Atlanta.

"That couldn't be helped," Coburn tells to his superiors. "Some of Oakland's members didn't want to be identified as Klansmen. Besides, the breakup resulted in an overall increase in Klan membership." Coburn knows, but doesn't tell his superiors, that the real reason for the split was that Oakland Klansmen didn't support the national headquarters when word of the Imperial Wizard's drinking and sex escapades became generally known. Elsewhere in the Pacific region, however, the Klan's popularity is at an all-time high. Coburn's job, to ensure that the Klan gains power in the city, county and state governments throughout the West, is a complete success.

The office of the Klan's Grand Goblin shows more sophistication than his political affiliations might suggest. There is no ten-foot Confederate flag tacked to the back wall. Instead, a small state flag of Georgia is discreetly displayed on a standard to the right of his desk, balanced off by the American flag to the left. The Goblin's office is tastefully furnished in the manner of an important executive, even though he dislikes his high-backed armchair because it will not swivel.

Coburn's tried and true method is to recruit Klan members from the existing secret societies, primarily the Masonic brotherhood. In California, every city has a lodge, and the annual Masonic ritual known as the Rose Parade has been a New Year's Day pageant in Pasadena, California since 1910. Coburn knows that soon Klan membership will include every political jurisdiction and every law enforcement agency in the Pacific States Division. The white men out West understand the Klan's message that it is the duty of every white man to protect his heritage by keeping America out of the clutches of Jews, Catholics and niggers. But the Klan's newly installed Grand Goblin for the Pacific States Division is somewhat mystified by the recent events in Los Angeles.

"Excuse me, sir," Coburn's secretary breaks his train of thought. "Mr. Winters is here to see you."

"Show him in, Miss Cooper," Coburn says.

Chip Winters thrusts his bulky frame into the office of California's top Klansman.

Motioning the L.A. cop to a chair, Coburn gives him a stern look. "Brother Winters," he asks, "why is that nigger still alive?"

"Well, sir," the red-faced recruit starts out, but the Grand Goblin interrupts.

"Listen, son," Coburn says, "we all must carry out our orders. Do you understand me, boy?" Coburn was a little older than Chip but certainly not old enough to be his father. Yet the rookie policeman accepts the Klansman's tongue-lashing.

"Yessir!" Chip replies meekly.

"We will not allow white people to be threatened by niggers with guns. I don't care if the Los Angeles Police Department or the great Almighty, Himself, has hired them. We *won't allow it!* Is that clear?"

"Yessir," Chip stammers.

"Now I'm gonna tell you what you're gonna do and there better not be any slip-ups. You hear me, boy?"

"Yessir!"

The Grand Goblin of the Pacific States lays out his plan to handle the uppity nigger, Officer Peter Jenkins, exactly as his friend and mentor, the Grand Dragon of the state of North Carolina, has instructed him.

* * *

Stung by the newspaper rebukes in the Los Angeles *Times*, the Klan unleashes a propaganda war. Radio broadcaster Bob Schuler reaches millions of southern California listeners with his racist diatribes praising the Klan's fight against niggers, Jews, and Catholics. He discusses how the Klan is the only organization willing to take on the bootleggers, while the federal government fails to enforce prohibition. Hearst's Los Angeles *Examiner* joins in the war. The *Examiner* prints a front-page story calling for a citizens' committee to assist the Los Angeles Police Department in the manhunt for a Negro accused of assaulting a white woman. For days, the police department is swamped with calls from white men wanting to know where to go. A white southerner, A. J. Davis, recently arriving in Los Angeles, circulates a flyer that reads:

"The niggers are invading every possible avenue that they can, they crowd into our street cars, plant themselves next to some neatly dressed white maiden, they infest our amusement places and are a nuisance on our streets. Louisiana, Texas, Alabama and Florida, in fact all the southern states, have separate areas for them with this inscription 'THIS END FOR NIGGERS.' But here in Los Angeles, not only must we whites lower ourselves to their level to abide them, other whites even employ them.

The sooner there is a move to stop this rapidly growing condition of contamination and stop the evil, the better it will be for our beautiful city, our homes, our families, and especially our daughters! See what the South has suffered from the BLACK MONSTERS in The Birth of a Nation! *They are a menace to any locality, they are different from any other race for they insist in mingling with the white population, so let us start at once to better conditions, BEFORE IT IS TOO LATE!"*

Anxious businessmen, laborers and even political leaders flock to the *California Eagle*'s offices, disturbed by escalating events. The Basses do all they can to counteract the Klan attempts to intimidate Negroes in L.A.'s Central Avenue district. Joe especially urges restraint.

"We have friends downtown," he tells anyone who would listen. "They understand what's at stake. They'll stand with us when the time comes."

But what about these threats, Joe is asked.

"This is not the time to give in to fear," Joe tells the daily gatherings.

Joe delivers the same message time and again. Joe has faced a white mob before. A drunken group of white men, bent on lynching him, ran Joe out of Montana. Had it not been for a kindly white storekeeper, Joe's body would certainly have decorated a telegraph pole and his eyes and flesh been food for the crows. Joe's efforts to organize Montana's colored cowboys upset the whites. So when he came to Los Angeles, Joe made certain he made friends with the white men who ran the city. That's who Joe believed would save them from the Klan.

"We need to think of something," Charlotta tells Pete one evening. Julia had come into Los Angeles from Boyle Heights to do some shopping. Pete meets her at the *Eagle*'s offices, which are just a few blocks away from the Newton Street station.

"We're working with the mayor and others to get the Garrick Theater to shut down that film," Joe says.

He still believes that the political process will save the Negro community from the racial explosion everyone is expecting, but no one knows how to prevent.

"Once that devilish film is gone, all this will blow away."

"I'm not so sure," Windows pipes in.

The young reporter always barges into his publisher's office whenever he sees Julia there.

"I've heard that the Klan intends to hold a parade through downtown Los Angeles on July Fourth."

"Where did you hear that?" Joe thunders.

"It's just a rumor I heard," Windows mumbles. "But I heard that the parade will signal an attack on the colored people living in the West Jefferson area. They're talking about a Tulsa solution."

"You'd better keep those kind of rumors to yourself until you can verify them," Joe lectures his reporter.

"If you go downtown to Broadway and Eighth Streets, you'll see Ku Klux Klansmen parading in and out of the Garrick Theater," Windows says quietly. "That's proof of their intention."

"Our police department can handle that situation, isn't that right, Pete?" Joe replies.

Julia's pregnancy is reaching full term and the baby is due next month. Sharon and Edward Duncan are planning their trip to California for the arrival of their first grandchild. Charlotta has plans and she is not happy that Windows raises issues that might spoil them. "What if it frightens Julia into returning to New York with her parents after the baby's birth?" Charlotta asks herself. "Don't you have anything to do?" Charlotta gives Windows a sharp look that says his presence is no longer welcomed.

"Yes, ma'am," Windows replies. And nodding to Julia and Pete, the reporter makes a hasty exit.

"What do you think, Pete?" Charlotta asks after Windows leaves. "Is there anything to this threat of a Tulsa solution?"

"That's just silly twaddle," Joe thunders, not giving Pete the opportunity to answer. "This is Los Angeles, California not Tulsa, Oklahoma."

Pete and Julia give each other knowing looks. There is no getting around it; the situation is dangerous. Once white folks start to riot, there is no stopping them and it doesn't matter whether it is Tulsa, Oklahoma, Des Moines, Iowa or Los Angeles, California. White folks are armed and they believe it is their God-given right to kill black people. The Klan's threat of a Tulsa solution in Los Angeles is very real.

"Why don't we go have dinner," Charlotta suggests. "I want to tell you about the nicest little home that I found on Jefferson just a block away from the high school. It has four bedrooms. You can move in and your parents can stay with you when they arrive."

The rumors persist and threats continue. Others don't share Charlotta's optimism in Joe's city hall contacts—neither do they share his conservative views. Hugh Macbeth, the *Eagle*'s city editor, disagrees with his boss.

"Joe, you don't seem to get the point," Hugh explodes one day. "It doesn't matter whether or not the rumors are false or the cops can handle the situation downtown. Once the violence starts, once a riot occurs, the ignorant masses of whites will have a free hand on our community. All these redneck Okies, Arkies and Texans living here in L.A. are going to have a field day."

"Our friends downtown won't let it happen," Joe retorts.

"Joe, Los Angeles is not that much different from Tulsa," Hugh says.

"Like Tulsa, Los Angeles has a lot of prosperous colored folks. Negroes here have nice homes and successful businesses. Poor whites, whether in Tulsa or Los Angeles, don't like it. The whites in the labor unions and in the Democratic Party don't like it. They'll riot at a moment's notice. Jealousy over what we've got is enough to set these dumb rednecks off. They're flooding into southern California by the thousands. You'd better tell these black people here in Los Angeles to get prepared. They need to arm themselves. There is nowhere else left for us to go."

"I don't believe that," Joe says. "And I've got the proof right here."

Joe Bass digs inside his desk and pulls out a paper.

"This letter," he says, "was sent to Charlotta and me just last week by the Watts Police Department."

"Who sent it, boss," Windows asks, always around to hear the latest news.

"It was sent here anonymously. But the letter is from G. W. Price, Imperial Representative of the California Klan, to the Klan's Grand Goblin for Pacific States."

"What does it say?" Hugh asks skeptically.

"It says that the Klan is interested in taking over public offices. And it gives their strategy for getting Klan members elected. They plan to use this strategy in Watts."

Bass throws down the letter with a satisfied grin.

"If they plan to play politics," he says, "we can beat them. This is not the South. We can go to the polls and vote. They can't keep us away. This letter gives us the names of the Klan's candidates. They also name those willing to take money and work for Klan candidates, *coloreds and whites*!"

Joe Bass looks around triumphantly at his listeners.

"Then why don't you publish the letter?" Hugh asks.

"You know what, Hugh," Joe replies, "that's a good idea. I think I will publish the letter."

The following week's issue of the *California Eagle*, the one in which the Klan letter is published, has its largest circulation in the weekly newspaper's history, more than five times its normal circulation. Calls for copies come from up and down California and across the United States. In its wake, a controversy follows that nearly shuts the paper down, permanently. Not only does the Klan sue the *Eagle*, as well Joe and Charlotta Bass, for libel, but the colored politicians named as Klan stooges organize a boycott of the *Eagle*. They urge the Central Avenue business community to withdraw their advertisements and tell the community to stop their subscriptions. Black *los angelenos* are urged to switch to Fred Roberts's *New Age* newspaper, the *Eagle*'s local competitor. Roberts opposes the Basses's conservative approach to the Klan menace. The *New Age* editorializes: "The Klan's threat of a Tulsa solution for the Central Avenue neighborhood is real." The Negroes accused of supporting the Klan hide behind the hysteria that sweeps through the Central Avenue community.

"The Basses are the real supporters of the Klan," they cry. "They and their cronies downtown want to keep Negroes defenseless."

Joe is crushed. He has been duped. With one newspaper issue, Joe has toppled from the position as the voice of black Los Angeles and is at a low point in his career as a respectable race leader and reliable newspaper publisher. But Charlotta believes in her husband and makes it a fight. "If Negroes take to the streets," she writes, "not only will they face armed white mobs eager for a final solution, but they will lose the support of those whites who, as of yet, are not committed to mob violence. It is these whites that the Klan fears."

"Looks like your faith in the downtown crowd was misplaced," Hugh tells his beleaguered boss. Hugh must report the loss of over six hundred subscriptions. In addition, advertisements from white as well as Negro businesses have decreased. The publication's income has dropped almost twenty five percent.

"We're not done yet," Charlotta exclaims. "Get me Fred Roberts on the telephone."

"Fred," Charlotta pleads with the *New Age* publisher, "you've got to tone down your articles about the Klan."

"Why?" Roberts asks.

"You know as well as I that once this thing starts, there's no telling what will happen."

"Look Charlotta, we've been friends a long time and I'm not out to take advantage. It's no secret that you and Joe were set up by that Klan letter." Roberts has a reputation for being on the square.

"Then why don't you join us?" Charlotta asks. "What we need is reason."

"Reason?" the publisher of the *New Age* says. "People know, although they won't admit it in public, that Klan money finds its ways into a lot of these Negroes' hands. Even some of those Negro preachers aren't above taking gifts. We've got to take a stand against the Klan, but Joe should have known better. He got caught like some greenhorn reporter writing his first newspaper story."

"You're right," Charlotta admits. "We knew better. Joe even waited a week before publishing the letter."

"What made you do it?"

"We've been getting pressure about trying to keep the lid on this thing," Charlotta explains. "Now it's up to you, Fred. You've got to tone down the rhetoric. We can't give the Klan an excuse."

"We're not the only newspapers that Negroes read," Roberts observes. "What about all that propaganda put out by the *Examiner*? Who's going to counter their lies?"

"We know what you're up against, Fred; we're under the same kind of pressures. All I'm asking is for you not to pander to those who want to see blood in the streets. Can I get you to agree?"

"I've always admired you, Charlotta," Roberts declares. "The *New Age* will stand behind you against the Klan's civil suit."

"And your news coverage?"

"We will urge everyone to calm down and put aside groundless racial animosities. But," Roberts says, "we won't change our opinion about the city hall crowd. Negroes must find a way to protect themselves. They can't depend on white folks to protect us. It's not going to happen."

"Thank you, Fred," Charlotta replies. "I knew that we could count on you."

"Look Pete," Chip says in his friendliest tone, "I know I let you down out there."

"Let me down?" Pete replies in a quiet, understated manner. "I think it was more like you deserted me under fire. You're my partner; you're supposed to back me up."

"I know. Don't you think I feel bad about it?" Chip says softly. "But look how things turned out. You're off that shit detail and a hero to boot. And I'm still there and in the doghouse with my sergeant. And my new partner kicks me around so much I'm beginning to think that I'm a can of corn."

"So what do you want from me?" Pete asks.

"Well, I thought you'd help me redeem myself."

"How's that?"

"There's some bootleggers in Inglewood that the Klan intends to raid," Chip says hesitantly. "If you and I were to stop them, my sergeant might let me out of the doghouse."

Pete eyes his erstwhile partner suspiciously. "What's in it for me?" Pete asks.

"What do you mean? You'd be a hero again."

"I don't care about that."

"What do you mean? I know you and your wife are expecting a kid. This could mean a promotion and a *pay raise*. Now don't tell me you couldn't use some additional cash. I don't see a fellow like you down on the take on Central Avenue. Or am I wrong."

"No, I'm not on the take," Pete says quietly.

"Well, then," Chip says. "If you're not on the take, then you had better get yourself a promotion. And the best way to do it is by helping me. You can't lose. Besides, don't you want to get even with those bed-sheet-wearing bastards?"

Pete eyes the redneck cop. He knows at a glance that Chip can't be trusted. But he is right about one thing. If Pete wants to get ahead in the Los Angeles Police Department, he will need lots of exposure. The Negro community is depending on him. If mob violence in L.A. is to be averted, they've got to see cops like him doing the job. And, yes, Pete did want to get even with those honkies. An opportunity like this didn't just come everyday. Even if he can't trust this white boy, Pete decides to take the chance. No guts, no glory. If he survived the big war in France and the gangs in New York, he can survive L.A. He just needs to be careful. These white folks are some sneaky devils.

"Okay, white boy," Pete says, "give me all the details."

"The Klan announced that it intends to run all the wetbacks out of Inglewood, starting with Mexicans they have identified as bootleggers," Chip begins.

Pete listens without commenting.

"One Mexican family received several death threats. Last week they got a note saying that unless they stopped their bootlegging business and got out of town, they would receive a visit from the KKK."

"A visit from the Klan?" Pete asks.

"A visit from the Klan."

"Why didn't they report it to the Inglewood Police Department?"

"They did, but the cops told them to go home. That it was just their friends playing a joke on them. The cops warned the family not to spread rumors around or they'd get into trouble."

"So how did you find out about it?" Pete asks.

"I have a friend in the Inglewood department," Chip replies. "He knows this was no practical joke. These people are serious."

"So why doesn't he do something about it?"

"He is," Chip says. "He promised to give the family some protection, tonight."

"So why does he need us?"

"My friend is like me, a California native. He doesn't want the Klan to take over Inglewood. But he's got to be careful. A lot of the cops around here are sympathetic to the Klan. He doesn't know who to trust. He just wants to do the right thing, so he asked me to give him some backup."

"Why you?" Pete asks.

"He heard about our little ruckus with the Klan outside the Garrick Theater," Chip says. "He read about you in the papers and, since you and I are partners, he figured that he can trust us."

"He does, does he?"

Pete gives Chip a look that says, "I know you're lying. I don't trust you or your friend." But Chip doesn't get the message. White folks don't believe that Negroes know anything. White folks think all Negroes believe every lie coming out of their mouths. A lot of Negroes do, but not

Pete. Besides, who would trust a dumb cracker like Chip Winters, Pete asks himself. But Pete can't help himself. He's curious and wants to find out what this white boy is up to.

It is an eerie night. The harvest moon has long since sunk below the northeastern horizon marked off in the distance by the San Gabriel Mountains. When Chip drives his black-and-white up to the Newton Street station, Pete tosses a duffel bag into the rear before climbing into the front seat.

"What's that?" Chip asks.

"You never know about these things," Pete replies. "I brought a thermos with some coffee and a blanket."

"That's a good idea," Chip says.

Inglewood is a sleepy suburb southwest of Los Angeles. Sitting on the "shoestring" corridor that gives Los Angeles access to its Long Beach harbor, Inglewood is another white enclave thoroughly covered by the restrictive covenants that prevent Negroes from either buying or residing there. These covenants didn't prevent Mexicans from living in Inglewood. It was up to the Klan to correct that oversight.

It is as if Pete is back in France again. Men assert their manhood. Armies march purposefully, for power, for glory, for purpose. A Negro cop daring to be a man. Pete just couldn't stand it. He couldn't stand the fact that all of this destruction and this death would not change the status of the black man one iota. They were subhumans that did not count. During the war, he saw the corpse of a black man, hanging from a tree, castrated and brutalized. Pete vowed from that day onward he would have his revenge, not in a rage, not in an emotional outburst, but coldly, calculatingly and deliberately. That was why he kept his eye on Grady Jones. He knew that cocky Negro would certainly run afoul of some white crackers who were just looking to lynch a nigger. It was just a matter of time. All Pete needed to be was patient. Then, one day, one of his fellow soldiers told him about some whites on leave who had seen Grady with one of the mademoiselles. They were boasting how they intended to teach the nigger a lesson. Pete and his boys followed Grady and caught the would-be lynchers. That is what Pete intends to do tonight. He also intends to keep a sharp eye on Chip as well.

"That's it," Chip declares, having checked the Inglewood address.

He parks his black-and-white a block away from single-story Spanish house in the middle of the quiet residential neighborhood. Inconspicuously, they walk back down to the Mexican bootlegger's property. The street is dark and the house was quiet. Pete wonders if the occupants are asleep. He can't imagine they are. They're probably huddled inside, scared to death, he thinks. Pete pats the duffle bag making certain his Thompson is there.

From out of the gloom a pale beam of light sends out a dim signal.

"That's the Inglewood cop," Chip announces.

When Officer Raul Ramirez approaches them, Pete can see why this member of the Inglewood Police Department doesn't trust any of his fellow officers. Raul's swarthy complexion and heavy accent betrays his Hispanic and Catholic background. He and Pete instantly recognize their brotherhood in the common struggle. Introductions are brief. Then the three policemen take up their vigil. Raul stations himself in the bushes next to the house near the driveway. Chip and Pete take up positions in a vacant lot on the opposite side of the street and several houses down. Pete crouches down where the lot is closest to the house; whereas Chip sits on a couple of orange crates farther back, almost directly behind Pete.

In the darkness, Pete opens his duffel bag. He removes a blanket and thermos filled with hot coffee. In addition, Pete removes the parts and magazine of his .22 caliber Thompson submachine gun.

The 1920 "Tommy Gun" fires .22 caliber bullets at a rate of 30 rounds per minute with deadly effect from a range of 200 yards. The white man's superiority, Pete has always believed, is based upon his superior ability and willingness to kill, and nothing more. This night, Pete intends to prove another point.

Their vigil lasts hours. Long after his thermos is empty and the cold has penetrated his blanket, Pete shines his flashlight at his watch for what seems the thousandth time. It is just a little after three AM. Beginning to believe that, indeed, the whole matter has been a joke, Pete raises himself up, intending to walk over to where Chip still perches on the orange crates. Before he can take a step, however, two cars come sputtering down the street. The first one, a 1914 Model A Ford sedan, carries five passengers and the second, a 1921 Hudson convertible, carries four. As the vehicles stop in front of the Mexicans' home, Pete can see the pale white of their costumes shimmering against the gloomy darkness of the night.

Silently, the men climb out of the cars and form a knot on their intended victims' lawn. Solemnly they plant a four-foot tall cross, wrapped in a white cloth, into the ground. Then dousing it with a flammable liquid, they set the cross afire.

Brandishing their weapons, shotguns, rifles, revolvers and whips, the nightriders spread out in front of the house. Two of them run around to the back. Their leader boldly marches up to the front door and shouts, "Come out here, you wetback bootleggers, and face your judgment."

Pete checks his weapons, his .38 police special, his trusty Army Colt .45 and his Thompson. Glancing around, he sees Chip still sitting on the orange crates to his rear. Slowly Pete begins his approach, making certain to keep Chip in his field of vision. The Klansmen, themselves, seem less concerned with flushing out their quarry than preparing a defensive perimeter for themselves. Pete can see that Raul had taken an ideal position on the flank of the Klansmen in front and outflanking the two in the rear.

"Come on out here," the leader shouts again, "else your women and children are going to get hurt."

Then Raul shouts out, "Inglewood police! Drop your weapons and step away from the house!"

The fiery cross illuminates the Klansmen's robed forms against the front of the house. As Pete watches, they move, taking up defensive positions with military precision. Pete realizes that these guys know exactly what they're doing. Two Klansmen peel off to face Raul. The two robed figures who had moved to the rear now reappear and Ramirez has the four of them facing him.

But in their arrogance, the Klansmen completely underestimated the resolve and experience of their adversaries. As soon as Raul realizes that the Klansmen are making defensive maneuvers, he cuts loose with his 10-gauge pump action shotgun. Two quick blasts catch the two in the driveway completely unaware. One goes down writhing in pain as the lead pellets tear through his white sheet, searing and mutilating the white flesh beneath. Seeing his comrade fall to the ground, the other Klans-man drops to one knee and begins firing at Raul with deadly accuracy. In the flickering light of the burning cross, Pete sees surprise register-ing on Officer Ramirez's face as two .45 caliber slugs explode into his chest, spinning his body around in a macabre dance of death. But even before the courageous Inglewood policeman realizes that he has been hit, Raul's body tumbles into the bushes lining the driveway. And as his severed aorta pumps out his life's blood, the last sight he will ever have in this life is the home of those citizens Officer Ramirez had pledged to protect. Then he dies.

The other Klansmen turn to face Pete's charge, as if they knew exactly where he would be. The masked raiders formed a skirmish line behind the burning cross, expecting Pete to expose himself to the light. Their revolvers and shotguns start barking with deadly intent, but their aim is off. He is not where they thought, where Chip told them he would be.

Pete has crossed the street and appears to the left of their skirmish line. He fires his Tommy gun at his hooded adversaries. Twenty-two caliber bullets trace a path through the fiery cross and it falls backwards toward the house. The bullets begin chewing up the lawn, searching and find-ing the white flesh under those white robes, which afford no protection against their fury. The Tommy gun continues spitting fire in Pete's hands and within minutes, it is all over. The vaunted knights of the Ku Klux Klan lie on the ground, some crying out in surrender, other screaming in pain, all pleading for their lives.

During the melee, Chip remains frozen in place. Shocked, he cannot believe what has happened.

"That no-good nigger brought a Tommy gun," Chip curses under his breath, shaking himself out of his stupor. "I'm gonna kill that son-ovabitch."

Dropping to his knees and bending low, Chip watches Pete approach the wounded and bleeding Klansmen, who raise their hands in surren-der. "They're going to blame all this on me," he thinks. He wastes too much time. That is his first mistake. Had he circled around Pete's back immediately, he might have gotten the drop on him and lived to tell the tale. But Chip isn't very smart; it takes time for him to figure things out.

The Negro war veteran has not forgotten his white partner. Pete knows that Chip is skulking somewhere behind his back. His choice of firearm is Chip's second mistake. In a gunfight between a .38 caliber police special and a Thompson submachine gun firing 30 rounds a minute at close range, the Thompson is at a decided advantage. Only a dumb redneck like Chip could have believed he had any chance at all. As Chip takes careful aim, planning to drive a bullet into the hated nigger's head, Pete whirls about, sending a spray of .22-caliber rounds in Chip's direction. The shots that tear into Chip's legs and arms are not lethal, but those that hit him in the chest and his face end his life even before the his body hits the ground. By the time Pete walks over to where his former partner lies, Chip is nothing more than a bullet-riddled corpse.

Chapter Twenty-Three

"Can you tell me what the hell is going on in California?" the supreme grand master thunders through the telephone at his heavy-jowled minion.

"Well, most worshipful grand master, we followed your instructions completely," Hoover stammers. He didn't want to say too much over the telephone. "But do you think we should discuss this now?"

"We shouldn't be discussing it at all!" Taft explodes. "How were all those names revealed to the L.A. district attorney?"

"Sir, the Knights involved in the Inglewood affair were all police officers."

"So?"

"There was a grand jury investigation."

"How did that happen?"

"Someone turned over a list naming three hundred Klansmen to the Los Angeles *Times*. The *Times* threatened to publish their names unless the D.A. investigated police in the Klan," Hoover replies. "As soon as the investigation began, the district attorney office seized all California Klan records. There were a thousand Knights in the various police departments and sheriff's offices all over Los Angeles County. The D.A. purged them all. And . . ."

"And? You mean there's more?"

"Yessir, most worshipful master."

"Tell me!"

"In addition to the Knights arrested in Inglewood, thirty-six police officers, including the Los Angeles 'Kleagle,' who was a deputy sheriff for Los Angeles County, have been indicted for the Inglewood raid."

The telephone goes silent. The assistant director of the FBI does not know whether the chief justice has fallen asleep or is just thinking. After several minutes, Taft says quietly, "Now you listen. I want this entire mess cleaned up. Do you understand?"

"Yessir."

"Those indicted I want exonerated at their trial. Do you understand?"

"Yes grand master."

"They're heroes, defenders of white womanhood. They're to be treated as such. Understand?"

"Yessir!"

"The dead police officer. What's his name?"

"Officer Chip Winters, sir."

"Officer Winters will be remembered as a martyr—a hero fallen in the struggle against degeneracy and crime."

"Yessir."

"Edgar," Taft speaks quietly, "this has been a terrible setback, but I do not intend that it disrupt our plans for California, do you understand me?"

"Yessir."

"We have come too far to fail now. We've got them on the run and the only place they can go is back to Africa or into the Pacific Ocean. And I don't care which!"

Hoover's telephone makes a loud click and then goes silent.

"Do you think it will be safe for my parents to come out to California now with the indictments and all?"

Julia and Pete begin to relax for the first time in weeks. After the Inglewood incident, Pete began getting death threats at the police station as well as at home. The constant stream of vile curses and racist epithets forced Julia to stop answering the telephone. Pete was given administrative duties at the precinct and the department assigned two police officers to watch Pete as well as Julia.

"Nothing better happen to either Office Jenkins or his wife," the district attorney informs L.A.'s police chief, whose name mysteriously disappears from the list of Klansmen employed by the LAPD. The chief passes the word, "No one is to touch Jenkins, *yet.*"

The mayor, as well as the city council, back the order. It is only after Pete and Julia move from their Boyle Heights apartment to a three-bedroom bungalow in the Central Avenue neighborhood that the couple begins to feel safe. When the trials are concluded, all the cops involved lose their jobs—however, none are convicted and none serve any jail time. In the precinct, so many promotional opportunities open up because of Pete that resentment and hostility give way to tight-lipped professionalism. Some cops, a very few, even give Pete a modicum of respect. A large proportion of the cops who lost their jobs because of their Klan affiliation occupied the LAPD hierarchy. Good cops, those whose careers were on permanent hold because they were not a part of the "good old boy" network, suddenly find themselves being promoted to sergeant, lieutenant and detective. Of course the top spots, the watch commanders, the captains and deputy chiefs, remain unaffected. These officers are permitted to let their Klan memberships quietly lapse.

Nearly a month after the incident, Pete and Julia can go days without a threatening letter or an obscene telephone call. They even begin to venture out with friends.

Six months into Julia's pregnancy, the doctor discovered two heartbeats. She is having twins. The babies are due soon and Julia's parents are rushing their travel arrangements. They want to be in Los Angeles when the babies arrive. Julia did not want Ed and Sharon to come during the Klansmen's trials. It was enough that she had to go through that terror. All during the trials, Julia ran up huge long-distance telephone bills between Los Angeles and New York, talking to her mother and Grace every day and sometimes twice. Now her parents and Grace are all on their way.

"Aren't you scared sometimes? I mean aren't you worried that something might happen to Pete?" Grace asked her.

"No," Julia responded. "Pete can take care of himself. He's really quite a man, a little arrogant sometimes and a little scary. L.A. is like the wild, wild west. Pete was meant for this town. I worry more for you and Mom and Dad."

"Well, I don't know if I could handle the fact that my husband has been attacked twice by the Ku Klux Klan," Grace said.

"How many other black men do you know who have come out on top of the Klan?" Julia asked.

"None," Grace responded.

"Well?"

"Well what?"

"Well if you don't understand, you of all people, then I can't explain it," Julia said.

"Try," Grace demanded.

"Okay. Every other black man I know is always looking over his shoulder, worrying about this or that. Trying to recapture his lost manhood by drinking more than he should, flashing fancy clothes or diamond rings or even an automobile. Pete is just Pete. Everyone knows who he is and what he stands for. And I'm his wife and soon I will have his children. And there is no more to it than that. Truly, Pete is the only New Negro that I know."

But Julia continued to fret about her parents. She believed that they can be targets of Klan retaliation.

"Sweetheart," Pete said, "your parents will be fine. They will have their own flat and your father has had a lot of experience protecting his family."

"I guess you're right," Julia said, smiling at her husband.

"I'm more concerned about them," Pete said patting Julia's bulging belly. This is their bond that cements their love. Julia is delighted to give her hero husband a family of his own, sons to carry on his name. Oh, yes, they both know the twins will be boys. New Negroes who will be race leaders. Pete's chest swells with pride whenever he thinks about it. Julia feels sorry for Charlotta and Joe. It is the one thing missing in their relationship. They have no children.

But right now, the Basses have more pressing problems. With the Inglewood incident driving members out of the Klan, the organization presses its lawsuit against the Basses even more vigorously. If the Klan is successful, the suit will bankrupt the Basses and close down the *California Eagle* newspaper. The gathering at Lincoln Park this Sunday is to support the Basses by raising a defense fund for their pending court case.

"Folks, this is a beautiful day to visit Lincoln Park and enjoy nature's beauty."

Fred Roberts is speaking. The publisher of the *New Age* organizes the Basses' defense despite the backlash. The Negroes on the Klan's payroll are relentless in their denunciation of the Basses. But Roberts, true to his word, is determined to defend Joe and Charlotta to the end. Roberts knows how much black Los Angeles owes them. But his support is not entirely altruistic. Roberts will become the first Negro to sit in the California State Assembly, elected by Los Angeles's Central Avenue community. This is the seat Joe believes should have been his but is now lost to him forever. Hounded from public life by Negro lackeys of the Ku Klux Klan, Joe becomes a bitter recluse until his death not many years later.

"There's an important reason for us to be here," Roberts says to the more than two hundred people gathered at the park. "We are here because Los Angeles is the final battleground against the Ku Klux Klan. Negroes have nowhere else to run."

A shout goes up. "And we're not running. No sir." The audience applauds.

"Now Charlotta and Joe are involved in a lawsuit that we know has been sponsored by our hooded enemies. They are being attacked because they stood up for you just like Officer Jenkins over there stood up for you in Inglewood."

The crowd erupts in applause. It takes several minutes to quiet them down. Roberts continues.

"We know their chances in court are not very good, not because they are guilty of anything, but because they are colored. And colored people don't get justice in the white man's courts."

Once again there is applause.

"Look at what happened with those Klansmen who attacked those innocent people in Inglewood: the court freed them all. If it hadn't been for Pete Jenkins, here. Stand up, Pete."

Again cheers poured out from the crowd. "Pete stood alone against the white policemen in their white robes and white hoods, burning the symbol of white supremacy on the lawn of those Mexicans, and Pete beat them. Is there any doubt that we are in a battle for our lives?"

"No!" the cry went up.

After Roberts's rousing speech, the Negro leaders, one by one, stand up to give their support to Joe and Charlotta. Represented are the Colored Ministers' Alliance, the NAACP, prominent businessmen from the Central Avenue business district and prominent colored men and women's clubs. All promise to give the Basses financial, as well as moral, support. Noah Thompson, the erstwhile Garveyite president, gives an impassioned plea for support, recounting Charlotta's many years as an unflinching supporter for the cause of the New Negro. Even the black ultra-conservative Jim Alexander, president of the statewide African American Council, pledges his support. Alexander is on friendly terms with the Basses's enemies. During Taft's presidency, Alexander was appointed a collector for the Los Angeles Internal Revenue Department.

Bif Meadows watches the Lincoln Park gathering. He positions himself near Julia and Pete's picnic table. Once the speeches are over and people begin socializing, Pete finds himself surrounded by well-wishers and hero worshippers. Black *los angelenos* have never had a genuine hero before. Pete is someone who demonstrates bravery, honor, and self-sacrifice, the virtues to which New Negroes aspire. Many came to the Lincoln Park gathering just to shake his hand.

Sidling over to Julia, Bif speaks quietly, "He's a real hero alright. But just remember, if anything happens to him, I'll be there for you."

Julia looks over at the older man. "What do you think will happen, Bif?" she asks, not certain whether to be angry or relieved.

"I have no idea," the veteran Garveyite shakes his head, "but one thing is certain. This thing is not over."

"Thank you for your concern, Bif," Julia says, fixing her penetrating green eyes on him, "but I'm certain that my husband can take care of himself, as well as his wife and children."

"I'm sure you are right, Julia," Bif says.

She wonders whether the lines crisscrossing Bif's yellow, moon-shaped forehead are an indication of his concern or his age. Bif's chin sags, displaying an unexpected frown that Julia finds both sinister and frightening. The look startles her. It reminds Julia of the look on Bif's face as he lay stricken by the Tulsa horror. She turns away, hoping to rid herself of this harbinger of evil, this person her mind to tells her to fear, but her instincts tell her to trust.

"By the way," Bif continues, seemingly unaware of his impact on the pregnant woman, the woman who has been the object of his desire from the moment he first laid eyes on her, "did you know the chief was coming to California?"

"Who?" Julia asks, happy to change the subject.

"Marcus Garvey," Bif says.

Indeed, Marcus Garvey needs money and is coming to California to get it, just as he was instructed. First he goes to San Francisco, then to Oakland where the Golden State's largest Klan organization does not turn him away. In fact, when Oakland Klan No. 9 split from the national Klan headquarters over the vice and drunkenness reportedly taking place at the Imperial Palace, several Klan organizations vie with Oakland Klan No. 9 for membership, including the East Bay Club, the Knights of the Invisible Empire and the White Cross. At one Klan demonstration, more than 2,000 hooded and robed members of the not so Invisible Empire parade through Oakland's city streets. So large was Oakland's Klan membership among white workers that Klansmen hold dominant positions in the police department and Alameda County sheriff's office as well as in the city commissioner's and district attorney's offices. In fact, the entire city government, including the schools, is completely controlled by Klan members. No prosecution for their terrible deeds is possible in Oakland. Garvey's appearance in Oakland is by Klan invitation. He tells his colored audience to go back to Africa and then collects his money. But his trip to Los Angeles is a completely different matter.

The Los Angeles UNIA Division Number 156 turns out a great throng to welcome the President-General of the UNIA. Charlotta Bass and Noah Thompson organize a grand parade. Beginning at Fourth Street, continuing down Central Avenue to 21st Street, then over to Hooper Avenue and back to Eighth Avenue, a motorcade of over fifty vehicles, all decorated in the UNIA colors of red, black and green, transports UNIA officers and dignitaries from all over southern California. Garveyites from San Diego, Bakersfield and Riverside make their way to Trinity Auditorium, where Garvey receives a thunderous welcome to Los Angeles. Thousands of waving and cheering Negroes lining the parade route go wild when a gigantic float of the Twin Goddesses of Liberty and Africa passes by, accompanied by detachments of Black Cross nurses and African Legionnaires marching in unison to the music of a hundred-piece UNIA marching band. Mounted policemen accompany the parade along the entire route, giving the entire proceeding the official sanction of Los Angeles.

Twelve thousand black *los angelenos* jam Trinity Auditorium to hear the words of the foremost leader of the New Negro movement in the United States, if not the world. But if the Negroes of Los Angeles expect Garvey to support their struggle against the Ku Klux Klan, they are disappointed. "Back to Africa!" is Garvey's theme:

"Two years ago the Universal Negro Improvement Association elected me the first provisional president of Africa. I cannot say why they gave me such a position but I suppose it was because they saw me with shoulders very broad and thought I could measure up to the burdens of such a position. The job, the biggest of this age, is bigger than the job of the president of the United States. I have the job of creating a government out of governments. I believe I can measure up to the job. I am here to reaffirm the declaration that 'Africa Shall Be Free' so long as four hundred million Negroes live."

The disdain black Los Angeles pays Garvey's flight of oratorical arrogance is immediate. Instead of the cheers the President-General expects, the sophisticated crowd reacts with surprised silence. Undeterred, Garvey continues in the same vein.

"I trust you understand the purpose of the Universal Negro Improvement Association. We teach human love with respect to all mankind. I hope you will never do anything to interfere with the white man's government. Remember, this is a white man's country. Some of us flatter ourselves to believe that because we are here we are going to get everything . . ."

"Isn't he under indictment for mail fraud," a staff reporter for the Los Angeles *New Age* murmurs.

"This president of Africa will soon be governing from a federal prison cell," another voice says a little louder than the first.

"Doesn't he know what is going on out here?" another voice shouts.

An elderly gentleman and his wife are the first to get out of their seats and leave the Trinity Auditorium, but they are not the last. Soon the trickle of those departing becomes a flood. By the time Garvey concludes his speech, there is a smattering of applause and even a cheer or two. But the overwhelming reaction of black Los Angeles to Garvey's speech is a stream of people with their backs turned heading for the exits.

After his speech, Garvey, ever sensitive to a crowd's reaction, makes his apologies and absents himself from the planned gala reception being given in his honor. The President-General instructs his bodyguards to take him directly to the Southern Pacific Railroad Terminal, where Garvey catches a northbound train back to Oakland, back to Klan territory.

"Sir, you asked me to contact you as soon as I got word that our friend has complied with our directives," the assistant FBI director speaks confidentially into the telephone.

"Yes," comes the reply.

"Shall I read the memo?"

"Please do."

"Agent Scully says Edward Clarke, acting Imperial Wizard and assistant to the Grand Wizard of the Ku Klux Klan, sent the telegram to Marcus Garvey directing Garvey to attend a meeting with him in Atlanta. It has been verified that Garvey has received the telegram."

"Who gave you this information?"

"Special Agent Andrew Battle, sir."

"Is he trustworthy?"

Hoover takes a quick moment to consider his reply and then answers, "Yessir!"

Taft notices the hesitation in the underling's voice, but lets it pass. "Better to give my ambitious young friend some room," the supreme grand master thinks. "Hoover serves me well. Who knows where we'd be without him." The grand supreme master pauses. Taft knows Hoover's devotion is total.

"Good," Taft speaks into the telephone. "Has Garvey responded?"

"Not that we know of, most exalted grand master."

"Let me know as soon as you find out. I don't like what's happening in Los Angeles and I don't want any more slip-ups. The Negroes in Los

Angeles must not be allowed to interfere with our efforts to expand the Invisible Empire, do you understand?"

"Yes, your exalted worship."

"Have you heard about Garvey's meeting with Klan?" Grace Campbell calls Julia after reading about it in the *Negro World*.

"No. When did this happen?" Julia replies.

"Last month. That man should be whipped and put out of the country," Grace explodes. "Meeting with the Klan. What's gotten into that nigger?"

"Just wait until I tell Pete," Julia says. "He's not going to believe it. He still thinks Garvey represents the New Negro even after what he did to Bishop McGuire."

"And us," Grace chimes in.

"Tell me what the *World* says." Julia demands.

"Just a minute, I'll read it to you." There was clunk as Grace puts the telephone down. Then after several of minutes of silence, she is back. "Listen to this," she says as she begins to read:

"Have this day interviewed Edward Young Clarke, acting Imperial Wizard, Knights of the Ku Klux Klan. In a two-hour conference, he outlined the aims and objects of the Klan. He denied any hostility toward the Negro as a race. He expressed sympathy for the aims and objectives of the Universal Negro Improvement Association. He believes America to be a white man's country and states that the Negro should have a country of his own in Africa. He denied that his organization, since its reorganization, ever officially attacked the Negro. I have extended an invitation to a Klan spokesman to speak at our forthcoming convention."

"Where was this published?"

"It was in the President's Comments section. You know, where Ferris puts all of Garvey's comments telling people how important he is."

"I don't know how important he'll be after this," Julia laughs. "I think he has made one big mistake."

All over the country, the Negro press howls at Garvey for what they call his treachery. *Crisis* magazine declares Garvey to be a pariah. Dubois states, "Clarke, for the Klan, and Garvey, for himself, entered into an evil agreement. The Klan is allowing Garvey to come into the South to sell his worthless stock to gullible Negroes. In return, Garvey promises to oppose any Negro organization who attacks the Klan."

The *California Eagle* and the Los Angeles *New Age* jointly denounce the provisional president of Africa in no uncertain terms. Joe Bass, having successfully emerged from the Klan's lawsuit, thunders: "Mr. Garvey, here is your hat and please be on your way. We want you to understand that the Ku Klux Klan is strictly not only anti-Negro, but un-American. Any Negro who stands for this dastardly institution stands as a traitor to his race."

Garvey, of course, would not suffer the criticism silently and he lashed back in his *Negro World*:

"Negro editors and Negro leaders have gone wild and have started to lambaste the Ku Klux Klan, writing all kinds of things against them. Let me tell you this: the Ku Klux Klan is really the invisible government of the United States of America. There are more people identified with the Klan than you think; there are more people in sympathy with the activities of the Ku Klux Klan than you think; and there is more sympathy in this country for the Ku Klux Klan than these ordinary illiterate Negro newspapermen think."

Garvey let it be known that he is compiling a list of Garveyites who say anything negative about the Ku Klux Klan, and E. L. Gaines, head of security, is paying those on the list a rather unfriendly visit. Pete's name heads Gaines's list.

Chapter Twenty-Four

On August 2, 1923, in the midst of the Veterans Bureau, Alien Property and Teapot Dome scandals, newspapers across the country proclaim that Warren G. Harding, the twenty-ninth president of the United States, is dead. Insiders snicker at the official pronouncement that a cerebral hemorrhage is the cause; they know the president with Negro blood was poisoned. Throughout the Midwest and in every county in Ohio, the Ku Klux Klan conducts midnight services. Robed and hooded members of each Konklave hold up fiery torches while church and courthouse bells toll. The day before his death, Harding sent an aide to Los Angeles to publicly deliver a letter written by him to the Knights Templar of the Hollywood Commandery. Included in the presidential delegation to Los Angeles is Gaston Means.

The doorbell rings several times, but the laughter and noise from all the people crowding into the Jefferson Avenue bungalow prevent anyone from noticing it. So Bif and Windows just let themselves in. The living room is filled with friends and well-wishers, the den loaded with gifts. Of course, Charlotta has already thrown Julia a baby shower, but now that everyone knows that Julia had twins, the people and the gifts just keep on coming.

The twins, Chatsworth and Sydney, are a month old. Edward and Sharon host the christening party that also serves as a housewarming. Upon arriving in Los Angeles, the Duncans decide to make California their home. Julia's parents are pleasantly surprised at how affordable the California market is. They purchase a home on the eastside just a couple of blocks down from Jefferson High School. Once they settle in, the

Duncans know people from New York as well as Jamaica. Los Angeles boasts a large West Indian community, giving the Duncans connections and contacts that rival even the Basses'. A short while after arriving in Los Angeles, Ed purchases a small furniture store on Whittier Avenue in Boyle Heights. With his more than thirty years of retail experience, Ed becomes an immediate success by working with West Indian real estate brokers to satisfy new homeowners' furniture needs. The secret to Ed's success is the free delivery from his store to his customer's new home. Ed forms a partnership with a West Indian drayage company that charges Ed a reasonable rate in return for all his business. The drayage company becomes so successful that it purchases several teams of horses and build their own stable.

Ed and Sharon Duncan's home is filled with well-wishers.

"How do you do," Sharon Duncan greets the two newsmen pleasantly. "I'm so glad you were able to attend our gathering, Mr.?"

"Meadows, Bif Meadows, Mrs. Duncan," comes the curt reply. "This is my friend Windows."

"Clarence Payne," Windows introduces himself. "We work for the *California Eagle* and we are friends of your daughter and Pete."

"Then you are very welcome," Sharon says, her smile stretching across her face.

"Now I see where Julia gets her looks," Bif says, apologizing somewhat for his abruptness.

"Well, thank you for the compliment, Mr. Meadows. And you may put those in the den," Julia's mother continues, noticing the proffered gifts.

"Thank you," Bif replies. "By the way, is Pete around?"

"Yes, he's out back with my husband, cranking the ice cream maker. Just go out through there, you can't miss them."

"Thank you," Bif says as politely as possible. The two go through the dining room doors into the kitchen, where women are preparing a feast. Chicken is frying in a large black skillet on the stove, a ham is baking in the oven, a great bowl of potato salad is being prepared at the kitchen table and a pot of Jamaican-style rice and peas, which Black *los angelenos* call red beans and rice, is being poured into a large serving tureen. Other tasty dishes already sit on the dining room table, having been prepared by some of the women before they arrived. Charlotta reigns over the kitchen, directing, supervising, and answering questions. The women chatter together, laugh at each other's stories and have a great time. Pushing through the kitchen door, into the laundry room and through the back door, Bif finds the men outside, puffing on cigars and watching as Pete labors at the crank of the ice-cream maker.

"Hi there, ole buddy," Bif hails the Los Angeles policeman. "Congratulations. Twins, no less."

"Congratulations or condolences," Pete laughs. "Now Julia really is on me about buying a house on my policeman's pay. By the way, Bif, this is my father-in-law, Ed Duncan."

"Ed," Pete says, addressing the spry fifty-year-old businessman puffing on a cigar in a cluster of men, all of whom who spoke in the distinctive dialect of the Caribbean, "Ed, this is Bif Meadows. He works for the *Eagle*."

Ed holds out his hand and says, "Happy to meet you, Mr. Meadows. Your boss, Mr. Joe Bass, is a fine gentleman."

"It's an honor to meet the father of such a beautiful woman," Bif says, once again showing his jealousy.

"Well, as you can see she got her looks from her mother," Ed smiles.

"Yes, I met your wife inside the house," Bif says. "You are to be congratulated as well."

"Thank you," Ed Duncan says. Then turning back, he rejoins his West Indian cronies, leaving Bif and Pete to themselves.

"Did you hear the latest?" Bif asks Pete.

"The latest?" Pete says. "No, what is it?"

"Jim Eason was shot in New Orleans."

Pete stops turning the crank on the ice maker. "Is he . . . ?"

"Died in the hospital," Bif says.

"Do Joe and Charlotta know?"

"Yeah, and Noah Thompson as well."

The officers of the UNIA's Division 156 have been very close to the Reverend James W. Eason, the UNIA's elected leader of the American Negroes. Among Garveyites, Eason is more popular in Los Angeles than the President-General himself. When the Los Angeles Division directs Thompson to investigate charges of mismanagement and embezzlement,

Eason supports the investigation. Garvey then sends Gaines to Los Angeles to replace the UNIA leadership and intimidate its membership. Charlotta and Thompson counter by withdrawing the entire Los Angeles Division from the UNIA, reorganizing it as the Pacific Coast Negro Improvement Association. Only through Eason's tactful negotiations is the Los Angeles Division encouraged to return to the UNIA fold. Eason promises that he will look into charges of UNIA corruption, personally. Not only does he promise to investigate the mishandling of Association funds but also investigate the alleged stock swindles involving the Black Star steamship lines. Eason begins meeting with other division UNIA leaders who want to oust Garvey. Eason plans to surprise Garvey at the convention with charges that include violation of the UNIA constitution, incompetence in managing the affairs of the Association, and maintaining a secret alliance with the Ku Klux Klan. Eason also tells the dissidents about Garvey's secret negotiations on behalf of the Germans at the Geneva peace conference.

"It would be better for our people to take care of our own affairs than to try to take care of the affairs of others in other countries," Eason confides to them.

Gaines inserts spies into Eason's secret meetings, learning about the plans to remove Garvey from UNIA leadership. When Garvey hears about the conspiracy, not only does he block Eason's investigations but he also kicks the American leader out of the Association. But Garvey is not yet satisfied. The President-General puts a contract on Eason. In a failed attempt at shooting Eason, Garvey's Chicago hit men kill a Chicago policeman instead. But in New Orleans, Garvey's assassins are successful; they gun Eason down on Rimpau Street in front of the Dew Drop Inn.

"Jim Eason contacted Charlotta and Noah two weeks ago," Bif tells Pete. "He wanted to know whether they could offer him any protection in Los Angeles."

"Yes, I know," Pete replies. "I told them that, with all this Klan business, this would be the last place Eason should come."

"I guess New Orleans wasn't much safer," Bif observes. "Anyway, I thought you should know as soon as possible."

"Why is that?" Pete asks.

"Gaines has a lot of names on his list," Bif replies. "Yours included."

"Me," Pete responds with feigned surprise. "Why would I be on Garvey's hit list?"

"Because you're on the Klan's list."

"I don't think even the Klan is going to risk killing a Los Angeles policeman," Pete says, thoughtfully. "Besides, they've already tried and failed."

"Did you know that Charlotta has been getting death threats from the Klan ever since she and Joe won their lawsuit?"

"Joe has mentioned it," Pete replies.

"I'll bet you're getting threats as well."

"I've been getting threats ever since the Garrick Theater incident," Pete says.

"Well, I think you need to know that this thing isn't over yet," Bif says. "Los Angeles is too important to them."

"Do they know who did it?" Pete asks.

"Did it?"

"Killed Jim Eason."

"He identified two of Gaines's security police before he died," Bif says. "They're being held in a New Orleans jail now and will stand trial in a couple of weeks. But they won't be convicted."

"Why not?"

"They've got Klan attorneys who practice in New Orleans."

"Quick Joe," Charlotta shouts to her husband, "go get Pete."

Still assigned to the Newton Street station, Pete now patrols the Central Avenue community. After being on his beat for several months now, Pete knows just about every Central Avenue shop owner from Tenth to 30th Street. Everyone likes Pete's low-key, quiet demeanor. He would need a truck to take all the vegetables, fruit and milk that the storeowners offer his family each day. And it's not just the colored merchants, but the Mexican and Asian merchants as well. They all respect L.A.'s sole Negro policeman.

The Klan's continual threats unnerve the Basses. Pete makes it a special point to tell Joe exactly where he will be on his beat so that they can reach him if the need arises. In fact, the entire Central Avenue community knows when and where to expect him. Pete also gave Joe and Charlotta revolvers for their protection. So when Charlotta tells Joe to find Pete, Joe knows right where to go.

"Another call from the Klan?" Joe asks his wife.

"Yes, they said that they're coming tonight," Charlotte responds, trying to stay calm.

"Get your gun out and I'll be right back." Joe sprints out the front door.

With a trembling hand, Charlotta pulls the .38 caliber pistol from her desk drawer. Charlotta cannot imagine what she will do if she has to use it. Pete tried to get her to the firing range, but somehow Charlotta never had time. Now it is too late. Not only has she never fired a gun before, Charlotta has never even loaded one. This gun is not loaded; the bullets are still in the box.

"Lord, please don't make me use this gun tonight," Charlotta prays.

Several minutes pass after Joe disappears down the street. Then a hooded Klansman appears at the window. Charlotta picks up the revolver and points it at the window. The hooded figure disappears. Almost instantaneously, Charlotta hears the screech of a police whistle and her husband bursts through the door.

"Are you alright?" he shouts, breathless from his exertions.

"I'm fine, now," Charlotta replies.

"Good, Pete's just outside."

Then comes that unmistakable sound, like the sound of a jackhammer digging in the street or the sound that a riveter makes putting together the pieces of a steel bridge. But this sound doesn't come from a jackhammer or a riveter. It comes from a Thompson machine gun spraying .45-caliber bullets—the rat-a-tat-tat barking over the sound of the racing car engine and squealing of tires as the car pulls away from the curb. And then there is silence. Joe and Charlotta listen to the silence for what seems an eternity.

Next come the wails of police sirens and the call of police whistles. Outside the *California Eagle* offices, policemen bend over the prostrate figure of a police officer. His still-bleeding body is riddled with machine gun bullets. Even in the dark, the Basses know that the blood—oozing from the torn police uniform that the patrolman had worn so proudly— pours from the dead body of Officer Peter Jenkins.

PART FOUR

Chapter Twenty-Five

It takes months, years even, before Julia really feels Pete's loss. She is too young; they were both too young. Julia can never quite accept that he is gone. Pete loves her; he promised never to leave her. No matter what Pete would always take care of her. Of course, everyone else does not understand. "They want me to accept the fact that he has gone, that he has left me," Julia tells herself. "They don't know that Pete will never leave me. He loves me."

It is she who never really knew her own feelings. There was a time that Julia believed she loved her husband, but Pete had always been too big, too strong and too distant. Pete was bigger than life. He was a hero; everyone said so. How do you love a hero? Julia had tried, but now he was gone.

When the realization that Pete is gone finally works its way into Julia's conscious mind, it is because she misses how protected she felt with him. When Pete was around, Julia never feared anything. Pete always protected her. She could nestle in his big strong arms and feel safe. Now Julia begins to have nightmares.

"Isn't it just like a man not to keep his promises," Julia tells Grace.

Her friend, who came to Los Angeles to help her through her grief, does not comment. Grace knows better than anyone, better than Julia, herself, how much Julia adored Pete. "Maybe it is a good thing that Julia doesn't remember," Grace tells herself. "People grieve in different ways."

And there are Julia's twin sons, Chat and Sid, to think about. Ed and Sharon, the grandparents, help as much as they can. But the twins need their father. Sydney and Chatsworth Jenkins are fraternal twins.

Actually, using the word twins to describe the two brothers is hardly accurate. Two people could not be more different had they been born on two separate continents. Julia's mother must chide her daughter for saying on more than one occasion that Sid was mistakenly put in the wrong crib and that Chat's real twin brother was given to the wrong family. These unfortunate comments became the source for the rumor, an unfounded rumor, that Chat and Sid are not really brothers. But a rumor never altogether disbelieved by either family or friends. Over time even the brothers, themselves, consider the rumor a plausible explanation for their physical and personality differences, as well as the dislike they feel for each other. Everyone can see that Sid gets his fair complexion, wavy, auburn hair and green eyes directly from Julia, while Chat's dark, handsome face and noble bearing, even as a child, identifies him as Pete's son.

"You must come live with us," Julia's mother insists after Pete's funeral. "You will need us to help you through your ordeal. And we can help with Chat and Sid."

Grace is a great comfort. She stays with Julia and the twins throughout. But when Grace returns to New York, that awful transition and adjustment period begins. At first it is just during the night, the days are so busy. Taking care of twins is not merely twice the work, it is four times the work. After a week alone, Julia decides to move in with her parents.

There is the packing and all those little things that remind her of him . . . his favorite socks, an old shirt. The moving and the taking care of the babies take most of her energy and concentration. Julia doesn't know who spoils the boys more, her parents or Charlotta. The twins get used to always having someone around to care for them. As the hectic days begin merging one into another, days becoming weeks, weeks becoming months, and months becoming years, Julia's realization becomes a certainty that is as real to her as life itself—she really misses him and his love.

For a long time, Julia is unable to shake the feeling that any moment Pete will walk through the door and throw his arms around her, holding her close, in that special way, just once more. But it is just a feeling that she must learn to deal with.

For a time Julia tells Pete all the things she had intended to say from the very beginning, from the time that she knew that she loved him and the he loved her. At night, she pretends to snuggle close and feel his warmth. She knows that he's tired after walking his beat. So she tries not to disturb his sleep, but just lies there and repeats over and over "until death do you part."

Finally comes the time when Julia blames herself for his death. "I held back my feelings," she tells herself. "I held them back from Pete and from myself. I kept him at a distance. He didn't know how much I loved him. That's why he was trying to be so brave, he wanted to prove himself to me." But her confession does not matter because Pete is gone and will never return.

The twins grow up with separate yet interdependent personalities. Even before they are out of their cribs, they find ways to communicate, understood by themselves only.

"Look," Sharon says one day soon after Julia moves into her parents' bungalow in the Central Avenue neighborhood, "they're talking to each other."

"Impossible," Ed responds.

But it is true. If one is wet and needs a diaper change, the other cries. Julia learns they do not like being fed at the same time. When one is making a lot of racket, the other is certain to be hungry. As they get older, Chat begins to talk for Sid.

"Grandma," Chat will say, "Sid doesn't want to go to bed." Or "Grandpa, Sid wants to go to the store with you."

Sid experiences a significant delay in his speech development. By the time the twins are ready for kindergarten, Julia worries that Sid has become retarded.

"Momma, Chat's teasing Freckles again." Sid ambles into his grandmother's kitchen.

"Okay Sid," Julia responds. "Go tell Chat not to tease Freckles."

"Okay, Momma," the youngster says. He runs outside, "Chat, Momma says to stop teasing Freckles . . ."

"You see, Mother," Julia complains, "he's not getting any better. Now the only time he says anything is when he's tattling on his brother."

"You need to be patient, Julia."

"The doctor thinks that I should send them to different schools," Julia tells her mother.

"You can't really consider splitting them up," Sharon protests.

"Why not?" Julia asks. "The doctor says that the separation will be good for them."

"They'll resent you for it," Sharon responds, "especially Sid. He's not as strong as Chat. He needs you more."

"Didn't you tell me that Sid prefers staying here with you and Daddy?"

"Yes, and this may have prevented his development."

"Well I don't see how you can say it would be bad for him. It's not as if he won't see us, we're over here almost every day as it is." Which is true.

"Still Julia," her mother protests.

"Something must be done soon," Julia replies. "You have been telling me for years that there is something wrong. Now that I have sought professional advice, you don't want me to follow it. Don't you want your grandson to live with you for awhile?"

"It's not that," Sharon begins to say before being interrupted by her husband who has just caught the tail end of the conversation. Ed doesn't need to hear more since this running feud has been going on between his wife and daughter for months now.

"I agree with your mother," Ed says. "Give the boy some time. He'll soon come around."

Actually, Sid is Ed's favorite. Sid likes to go outside with his grandfather and help him rake the leaves or watch him water the yard. Sometimes, Ed takes his grandson to the furniture store, which has expanded to the building next door. Now Ed has ten men and two women working for him. Business is so good, in fact, that in spite of the restrictive covenants and other obstacles to Negroes purchasing homes in the upscale Los Angeles neighborhoods, Ed and Sharon have moved into a beautiful Spanish home on the Westside of Los Angeles and have given Julia the Jefferson Street residence. The fact that Ed and Sharon are foreign-born and Julia has made Hollywood contacts explains how they are able to slip over Los Angeles's color line without any problem. Though it is 1929, the stock market has not yet collapsed. The economy is booming and people are still buying houses and furniture. The Klan has been driven underground and money talks louder than color in Los Angeles. When Sid is with his grandfather, or grandmother, in their grand house on the Westside, he has no problem talking. It is only when he is alone with his brother or his mother that his speech impediment manifests itself and his behavior becomes subdued and passive.

"I don't know why you two think you know better than the doctor," Julia says, lapsing into her Jamaican accent. "Where did you get your medical degrees?"

"There is no need for your sarcasm, young lady," Ed replies. "Your mother and I are just thinking about the boy's welfare."

"Are you now," Julia says. "And whose welfare do you think I'm thinking of? Tell me that, will you now?"

"Possibly you are thinking overly much about your own career and what Bif Meadows is telling you," her mother replies, giving Julia a sharp look.

Julia cannot hide anything from her mother. Sharon reads her daughter like a book. It is true that trying to manage two pre-schoolers impacts her so-called Hollywood career, if one can call her film appearances as an extra or the bit parts that Bif has gotten her a *career*.

"That's not a very nice thing to say, Mother!"

"It may not be very nice, but it is the truth, now," Sharon scolds her daughter. "You tell me it isn't so, if you can."

But Julia can't. After Pete's death, Bif Meadows is Julia's most persistent suitor. While other men who courted her respected Julia's grief, Bif unabashly pursued Julia from the very beginning, using all the persistence at his command, which is considerable. After all, Bif is in the news business, and being pushy is his job.

From the very beginning, Bif made himself indispensable. He took care of all the funeral arrangements and saw Julia through the mountains of paperwork. When the police department claimed that Pete's death was not in the line of duty and that Julia had no claim to a police widow's pension, Bif doggedly pursued the matter until the city attorney honored Julia's claim. Although it could not be proven, part of the police department's denial was based on the fact that the Klan still had an immense amount of influence within the LAPD.

Bif and Windows moved Julia to her parents' home off of Central Avenue. Afterward, Bif hung around even though Julia told him time and time again they could never be more than friends. After awhile, however, it became clear that her widow's pension would not meet her living expenses, especially since she had never learned to curb her extravagant lifestyle. Bif introduced her to King Vidor, who was directing his first talking picture with an all-Negro cast. The movie was called *Hallelujah*. Julia got a small role. After Julia's film debut, Bif got her a bit part in the movie *Hearts of Dixie*, the picture that made Stepin Fetchit a star. From then on, Julia hooked onto the film business and became a Hollywood groupie. Bif knew everyone in the film industry. He became Julia's agent. They were inseparable. Chat doesn't mind "Uncle" Bif, but Sid can't stand him. This is why Sharon suspects Julia's motives for separating the twins.

"Well, Mother, if you don't want to help me, why don't you just say so instead of beating around the bush."

"I didn't say that I would not help."

Sharon looks at her daughter, concern pouring from her eyes. Sharon wonders whether Julia cares about the risk she is taking with her sons, especially with Sid. "She's always been such a selfish child," Sharon remembers. But in the end, the mother knows that she will do whatever her daughter asks.

"Then I would like Sid to stay with you and Dad for awhile."

Noticing the look on her mother's face, Julia quickly adds, "Just until Sid has a chance to become his own person and not depend on Chat for so much."

"Certainly Sid is welcome to stay with us," the twin's grandmother says. "But I hope you know what you are doing, for both of their sakes."

But Julia doesn't really understand what she is doing. Not to the twins, not to her parents, not even to herself. All Julia really understands is how much she misses Pete.

Chapter Twenty-Six

The senior class of 1941 celebrates their last days at Jefferson High. Although Chat and Sid went to different grammar schools, both will graduate with Jefferson High's senior class. The family will celebrate with a gala graduation party.

Chat enjoys a stellar high school career. He's been an all-league basketball and football player for the past two years. Chat grows into an exact replica of his father. Handsome, strong, athletic, with a quiet, shy personality, everyone loves him. Julia adores him. She wishes that she had named him Peter. UCLA offers Chat an athletic scholarship, a rare honor for a Negro kid from L.A.'s Central Avenue neighborhood. The university could have offered him an academic scholarship, so high is Chat's grade point average. His future is promising, almost as promising as "Jeff's" most famous alum, Ralph Bunche, who graduated in 1923, the year Chat and Sid were born. Bunche received an athletic scholarship to UCLA as well before making his mark in the field of international diplomacy.

Sid is neither an athlete nor an intellectual. Sid is nearly two inches shorter than Chat and weighs ten pounds less. It is not that Sid is a weakling, but neither is he muscular or athletic. Chat stands over six feet tall. When friends of his family see Chat, the first thing they say is, "If Pete could have seen that boy, he would have been so proud." At Jefferson High, Sid is known as Chat's younger brother. His only school interest is ROTC.

"Sydney," his grandfather tells him, "you will make a fine Army officer one day."

Sid loves his grandfather and likes nothing better than being in Ed's furniture store and listening to his grandfather's stories about Harlem and Jamaica. When he is still a little boy, Sid dreams of working in his grandfather's furniture store. But nowadays, there is little to do. When the depression hit in 1929, Ed's business all but folded. Though Ed keeps it going, the store never again attains its pre-depression success. In his advancing age, the furniture store begins to resemble Ed's Harlem thrift shop on Tinker Street.

The depression that destroys Negro businesses all over Los Angeles contributes to the eventual decline of the *California Eagle*. When Joe dies in 1934, competition from the Los Angeles *Sentinel* and declining subscriptions and advertisements force Charlotta to release her full-time staff. For a while Charlotta struggles to publish the *Eagle* with the help of part-timers. Bif and Windows both find positions with Los Angeles dailies; Bif with the *Times* and Windows with the *Mirror*.

Sharon and Ed sell their Westside home and move back to the house on Jefferson Street. Julia marries Bif Meadows. He buys a home in lower Beverly Hills. Both Chat and Sid live with their grandparents now. While Chat looks forward to college and intercollegiate athletics, Sid dreams of becoming an Army officer in order to succeed at something his father never accomplished. In the meantime, following his grandfather's footsteps, Sid tries to make money any way he can. Sid sells newspapers, serves as a houseboy for Julia's movie actor friends and works whatever odd jobs he can find. Once in awhile, Sid even works in his grandfather's furniture store, although he doesn't consider it work, since he never gets paid.

"Hey, Mary," Sid calls out. "Wait up, where are you going?"

Mary is Sid's girlfriend. She's a senior and very pretty. They meet when Sid transfers from Dorsey High to Jefferson his junior year. At Dorsey, just as in grammar and junior high school, Sid is just about the only Negro in the entire school. When Sid first enrolls in school, his grandparents registered him as Jamaican, positively confusing teachers and principals right along with Sid, himself. When he moves with his grandparents back to the Central Avenue community and transfers to Jefferson High, Sid's records still identify him as Jamaican. Chat is registered as "Negro." So when Chat takes Sid around introducing him as his younger brother, it confuses teachers, students and Sid, himself, even more. In addition to being confused, it angers him.

"Why do you always introduce me as your younger brother?" Sid asks Chat one day.

"Why not?" Chat replies. "You are younger."

"By only three minutes," Sid replies belligerently. "We're twins and we were born on the same day."

Chat looks at his brother and smiles. "We may be twins," he says, "but you don't look nothing like me. You're one of those yellow niggers, high bright, almost white." But Sid can't tell whether Chat is really mocking him or just jealous. In 1941, color really matters at Jefferson High—but what matters more is being a celebrity, and even though Sid has light skin, Chat is a big man on campus. It's ironic. Negroes idolize light skin and straight hair. The bleaching cream and hair straightening business is booming. That is why everyone in L.A. fawns over Julia. But his light skin and wavy hair denies Sid the only thing that really matters to him: his mother's love. Chat's brown skin and coarse hair reminds Julia of Pete. That makes all the difference.

"You look just like your father," Julia tells Chat, holding him close.

Sid sees pictures of his father and it is true. Pete and Chat do look alike. As far as Sid is concerned, his light skin and wavy hair are a curse.

"Grandma, why doesn't Momma love me, too?" Sid would ask his grandmother with tears running down his cheeks.

"Of course, your mother loves you, Sydney," Sharon would say. "And your grandfather and I love you, too."

"But she lets Chat live with her and not me. Why not?"

It was enough to break Sharon's heart, but she knew nothing could be done. Sharon knew that Julia would sooner have sent Chat to live with her parents than allow Sid to move in with her and Bif, which might have been a better alternative than keeping the twins separated. Even had Sid known what the actual relationship between his mother and father was like, he might have eased some of his bitterness. Sid might have learned that he shared far more in common with his father than did Chat. But how could he have known that Julia treated Pete the same way that she treats Sid now? How could he have known that his father often felt un-loved, rejected, unappreciated? Bif, too, is a member of the same club, despite all he has done for the Jamaican beauty and her family. That was Bif's prize for having successfully pursued and won Julia. Won her? Bif can't say he won Julia. Bribed her, maybe. Bif knows that Julia doesn't love him now, nor did she ever. None of this matters to Sid. All that matters is that his mother loves Chat and doesn't love him.

Chat stands in Sid's way. Chat and the ghost of his dead, martyred father. Chat thinks of his father as a hero, but Sid thinks of him as a fool. Why else did he allow that pig, Bif Meadows, to take his wife? What kind of a man would do that? Certainly no hero. His father paid for being a fool with his life, Sid thinks, and so would Chat. For now, if he can't have his mother's love, Mary's love will do.

Mary is slim and tall, with light skin and wavy brown hair. If someone were to tell Sid that he chose Mary because she looks almost exactly like his mother, they would have been right. Mary has everything ex-cept Julia's green eyes. Of course, Mary chose Sid strictly on the basis of color.

"Don't we make a fabulous looking couple?" Mary says to Sid, or to anyone else listening, including her family, friends and clubmates. The only people Mary cannot convince that she and Sid make a perfect couple are Mary's parents. After graduation, they plan to send Mary as far away from Sid as possible, which, in this case, is to Howard Univer-sity in Washington, D.C.

"You're still planning to come to my graduation party Saturday, aren't you," Sid asks. Mary has a bad habit of looking at everyone around, even when she is talking. She just has to see who is looking at her. Mary has the reputation of being flighty and not very bright, the 1940s version of a colored "valley girl."

"Of, course, silly," Mary coos. "You know I wouldn't miss it."

"So, what time should I call for you?"

"Maybe I should meet you at your party," Mary says slowly.

"Your parents again?" Sid asks, his face clouding over.

"You know the problem," Mary replies. "My father wants to send me away to school."

The Reverend Arthur Smith is the presiding pastor at Tabernacle Baptist Church located at the corner of Central Avenue and 12th Street. Tabernacle is a spin-off of the venerable Second Baptist Church, Los Angeles's first all-black church.

"But what's that got to do with you coming to my party?" Sid asks.

"It's not coming to your party," Mary responds, "It's you and me, the two of us dating. He's afraid that if we continue to date that I might decide against leaving you."

"Well, what's wrong with that?" Sid's face brightens and his eyes twinkle.

"I don't know," Mary smiles as she moves closer, entwining her arm through his.

They stop and sit on a bench in front of the school. The afternoon classes have ended and students spill all over the campus. Several of Mary's friends call out to her as they pass by.

"Remember, there is a Key Club meeting at four o'clock, Mary," one of them shouts.

"I'll be there," Mary calls back.

"Not if I have anything to say about it," Sid says pulling her closer.

"That's exactly what my father is concerned about," Mary says stiffening, "and quite frankly, so am I."

"What do you mean?" Sid asks, feigning innocence.

"You know what I mean."

"No, I don't! What do you mean?" Sid asks again. "When I take you for a spin in my old jalopy, you seem to enjoy being close to me."

"I do, but . . ."

"But what?"

"I'm always inviting you to come to church, but you never come," Mary complains. "My parents don't think that you're a man of God."

Sid just looks at her. He doesn't even know what being a man of God is. His family is not particularly religious; they are not even Christians. Not that Sid or Chat can tell. In Jamaica, Sharon practiced Santeria. But in New York, she didn't continue. Neither Julia did receive a religious upbringing.

"Jeez, Mary," Sid responds, "I thought you loved me."

Mary just sits there, a forlorn look beginning to creep down from her furrowed brow into her sympathetic but worried eyes.

"I do love you Sid. You know I do, but that's just the problem." She takes his hand into the two of hers. "You don't seem to understand. I can't even tell my father that you're going to college."

"We've been all through that," Sid says matter-of-factly. "You know that I'm enlisting into the Army after graduation. With my three years of ROTC, I should do just fine."

"That's just the point, Sid." Mary's face definitely begins to cloud over and the moisture that has been collecting in her eyes begins to run down her cheeks. "I don't know where you are going to be and neither do you. What do you want me to do? Wait for you? For how long? My father tells me that we'll be in that European war pretty soon. Then what'll happen to you?"

"Well I just thought that . . ."

But then Sid falls silent. He cares for Mary as much as he cares for anyone. He remembers that a man his mother knew from her African Blood Brotherhood days, Harry Haywood, visited them several weeks ago. He had just returned from Spain where he fought with the Abraham Lincoln brigade against Franco's fascists. Harry says that it is just a matter of time before the whole world would be fighting. Sid knows that Mary is right. He has no right to ask her to wait for him. Sid's not like Chat; he's not going to UCLA in the fall. He looks at Mary and says nothing at all. They just sit there, holding hands, their silence saying more than any words can.

After awhile, Mary gets up quietly and says, "I'd better go or I'll be late for my club meeting."

Sid nods. "Yeah, you'd better go."

Parties are being held all over Los Angeles. The graduating class of 1941 is celebrating. But no party can match the glamour or excitement of the one given by Julia Meadows for her twin sons. Actually, the party is not just being given by Julia. Sharon, Ed, Charlotta, Bif, the colored club women of Los Angeles, the colored actors in Hollywood and most, if not all, of Los Angeles Negro society participate. The soiree is being held at the Elks Hall on Central Avenue and Santa Barbara near St. Patrick's Catholic Church. The young arranger-composer Gerald Wilson, fresh from New York with the Jimmie Lunceford Band, assembles a group of L.A.'s finest local musicians, including an up-and-coming young saxophonist, Eugene Stovall, and his friend, LeGrand Mason, a bassist, both of whom play the local night clubs and live in the Central Avenue district. Invitations are sent to the entire Jefferson High graduation class and they are all present.

"Aren't you glad you came?" Sid yells to Mary.

The wild sounds of the band combined with the laughter, talking and general pandemonium make any conversation impossible. Sid and Mary are swinging on the dance floor. Other dancers hem them in on all sides. The crowd is not limited to Jefferson High graduates. Each invitation admitted a graduate and three guests, so the other revelers include parents, chaperones, friends and everyone else that could finagle themselves into what is being called "the party of the year." It seems that all the Negroes in Los Angeles are crowded into the Elks ballroom at the same time.

Mary doesn't answer Sid. She lets the music take over completely, her body twisting with the rhythm, moving with the beat. The riffs of one soloist after another drive the crowd into a frenzy of excitement and pleasure, Mary and Sid along with them. To and fro, the couples interweave their arms and hips together, swinging in perfect unison to the beating drums, blaring trumpets and crooning saxophones. Mary is completely unaware of everyone and everything around her, lost in the beats and rhythms that mirror the sounds that transport her soul to glory every Sunday in church.

How strange Mary seems, Sid thinks, as they bump and push against each other as well as against the other dancers. It's as if that silly, color-struck schoolgirl doesn't even exist, replaced by an exotic African maiden whose body has been taken over by an Orisha. Mary's a completely different person, like she's a *twin*.

"Well, dear," Sharon says to her daughter, "this certainly has been a memorable graduation."

Sharon shares a grand view of the festivities from the balcony overlooking the Elks' ballroom with her husband, Julia, Bif, Charlotta and Grace Campbell. Grace endured the four-day journey by train just to be here.

"Yes, indeed," Grace echoes.

"I wanted to do something special for the boys," Julia replies. "They've missed so much not having their father and all."

"Umph," Bif snorts.

"Don't get upset, dear," Julia tries to soothe him. "Bif doesn't think I appreciate how much he has done for me and the boys," she says to no one in particular. Sharon gives her daughter a sharp look.

"Yes, Bif," Sharon says, turning to her son-in-law, "you really outdid yourself this time."

It's about time someone thanked me, Bif thinks, indulging in his favorite pastime of wallowing in self-pity. Everyone knows how well Bif has looked after Julia and her sons, not to mention her parents. But it's not as if he hasn't been repaid many times over. After leaving the *California Eagle*, Bif advanced rapidly in the *Times* organization. He is now in charge of the *Times*'s photographic department. Bif is an insider in the entertainment capital of the world. He owns a split-level home in lower Beverly Hills with a Cadillac in the driveway. But it's all because of Julia. Everywhere she goes she is all that people talk about. Bif's connections and Julia's beauty propel them into Hollywood circles as well as to the top of Negro society. These connections are responsible for Bif's advancement, and they also get Chat the scholarship into UCLA. Even though their relationship has often been downright bitter, Bif pulls the strings for Sid's career in the Army. Yet only recently has Julia fully appreciated how much Bif has done for her and her family.

"Bif has been a dear to the boys and me," Julia admits.

"On that note, Ed would you care to join me for some punch?" Bif winks as he rises from his chair and pats the flask in his hip pocket.

"Don't mind if I do, my boy," Ed says, winking back.

Ed shares Sharon's fondness for Bif. He thinks it's a shame the way Julia treats Bif, but he has long since reconciled himself to Julia's ways. Ed owes Bif for saving what was left of his furniture business during those tough years after the crash in 1929. "But all it says," Ed thinks, "is that Bif loves Julia. And she couldn't have done any better."

"After you two finish, you can bring us back some refreshments," Julia says sweetly.

Bif reserves the Elks Hall's parlor area, off of the main auditorium, strictly for the purposes for which he and Ed are now headed: to enjoy some alcoholic refreshment.

"Thanks, Dwight," Bif says, nodding to the burly six-foot, two-hundred-pound security guard hired to guarantee that none of the youngsters gain admittance. Inside, the air is thick with cigar and cigarette smoke. Parents, chaperones and other adult guests sit at cocktail tables, conversing amongst themselves. All heads turn as Bif and Ed walk in. The partygoers nod their heads and tip their glasses to their hosts.

"This is quite a shindig, old man," someone shouts out from one of the tables. It's Windows. He's sitting with two attractive women who don't look like anyone's mother. They're starlets who sing and dance in the chorus lines of some of the Hollywood musicals.

Bif walks over to Windows and says, "Do me a favor when you can."

"Just name it," Windows replies.

"Take some punch up to Julia and her mother, will you? They're sitting up in the balcony."

"Sure thing."

"Charlotta and Grace are up there with them," Ed adds.

"Okay you two," Windows says to his pretty guests, "you're about to earn your keep."

Bif turns and motions Ed over to an empty table.

"I remember when that boy was just a stumbling, bumbling kid," Bif says, watching his long-time protégé escorting the Hollywood beauties out of the room. "Now look at him, a charming sophisticate. Los Angeles is a great town to be young in."

"You should be proud of yourself," Ed comments.

"Some say I'm just an opportunist," Bif muses. He produces a hip flask and two tumblers and pours them each a shot of gin.

"Well, I say more Negroes need opportunities," Ed replies, knocking down his gin and chasing it with punch.

"After this war, there will be opportunities for a lot more Negroes, I promise you," Bif replies.

"What do you mean?" Ed asks.

"There's a Swedish fellow, his name is Myrdal, Gunnar Myrdal. He's in the United States right now working on a plan to give coloreds opportunities for advancement. White folks are planning to integrate the entire American society."

"You don't say," Ed says. Ed is continually impressed with Bif's inside information. One of the reasons Ed was able to survive the crash of 1929 was that Bif predicted the calamity in July, three months before it happened. "But how do you know this?"

"When you're in the newspaper business, you hear a lot," Bif replies quietly. "I just hope the boys can survive to take advantage of it."

They all assemble at Union Station to send Sid off to the Army. "Even Chat," Sid observes. That's uncalled for, he quickly chastises himself. Why wouldn't Chat be here. My brother doesn't dislike me. It's me; I'm the one who doesn't like my brother.

"Now son," Bif pulls Sid aside and says, "whatever you do, just get along with them." Sid reads the worried look in his stepfather's eyes. Bif has not aged well. His short stature is almost equaled by a protruding stomach that continually troubles the *Times* photographer. Bif appears to be one big block of bulging flesh. His heavy jowls sag, pulling the rest of his face down in the sad expression one normally associates with bloodhounds. Sid knows that in his own way, Bif has treated him like a son. Bif got Sid a favorable posting with military intelligence. All Sid has to do is get through basic training without incident.

"Don't worry, Pops," Sid smiles, "I won't let you down."

Both his grandmother and mother cry, as they each hug and kiss Sid goodbye. The last one Sid hugs is Mary.

"I'll write you every day," she whispers. Mary will write a total of two letters, which is one more than Sid writes Mary.

Then Sid boards the Southern Pacific that will roar its way northward to Monterey and the Army induction center at Fort Ord. As he leans out from the chugging train slowly making its way out of Union Station, waving goodbye to his family assembled on the platform, Sid notices Chat comforting his sobbing sweetheart, holding her a little too close for Sid's liking. And in the fleeting moment, Sid finally finds a good reason to hate his twin brother.

Chapter Twenty-Seven

For years the Democratic Party feeds Negroes propaganda. In the South, white Democrats prevent Negroes from voting, while in the North and West white Democrats urge the Negroes to elect Franklin Roosevelt president of the United States. Roosevelt becomes only the second Democrat in the twentieth century to gain the White House. The first, Woodrow Wilson, was a Klansman. After his election, Roosevelt initiates his New Deal. It's a "new deal" for the whites but the same "old deal" for colored folks. The Agricultural Adjustment Administration becomes Roosevelt's very first New Deal program. The program declares Negro-owned farms uneconomic and seizes ownership without giving the Negroes any compensation. The Agricultural Adjustment Administration gives these farms to larger white farmers and calls them cooperatives. Roosevelt's New Deal subsidizes these so-called cooperatives by paying white farmers not to grow certain farm products, making them rich while driving the moderately successful black farmers into bankruptcy. The white cooperatives soon take over all farmland owned by Negroes. Roosevelt's New Deal bans Negroes from sharecropping and drives black families completely off land that they have worked for generations. When the white farmers complain about the lack of cheap labor, Roosevelt has the State Department negotiate a bracero treaty with Mexico, replacing cheap black sharecropper labor with even cheaper Mexican migrant farm labor.

The Social Security Administration becomes another program in Roosevelt's New Deal. It replaces the Post Office Department as the federal agency primarily responsible for domestic intelligence by extending the government's surveillance over the mails to all official public and private records, giving the federal government access to and knowledge about every citizen in the United States. Roosevelt's New Deal enhances government surveillance capability by subsidizing the development of a new technical machine called the computer. Another New Deal program, the Works Progress Administration, gathers information to feed the computer. Intelligence gatherers are hired and organized into the Federal Writers workshop by the Works Progress Administration. One of these domestic spies, Frank Yerby, feeds information into the computer on a new Negro organization known as the Black Muslims.

Though not officially a New Deal program, Roosevelt's administration negotiates and approves military contracts with Hitler's Nazi government. The Roosevelt Administration directs American companies to provide the Nazis with gas and oil supplies, aircraft bombsights and guidance systems as well as the computers used by the Social Security Administration to track American citizens. The Nazis use the computers to track down and expel Jews. The Ford Motor Company provides the Nazis with the trucks and aircraft engines. Ford-manufactured trucks transport German troops into Czechoslovakia and Poland, while war planes—powered by Ford engines, fueled by American petroleum, and equipped with American-made bombsights—bombard European cities into submission. At the conclusion of the Second World War, the Ford Motor Company collects millions of dollars in payments deposited into Swiss bank accounts by the Nazis for services the Ford Company rendered the Third Reich during the war. At the same time that Roosevelt's administration assists the Nazis to appropriate the personal property and land of all those the Third Reich has thrown into concentration camps, his New Deal administration, itself, seizes hundreds of millions of acres of valuable farm and timberland in Washington, Oregon and California from American citizens who Roosevelt interns in American concentration camps. Adhering to a policy that sets aside petty partisanship, the Roosevelt Administration makes an equitable distribution of the land to wealthy Republican and Democratic Party supporters. Harry Truman, Roosevelt's wartime Vice President and a member of the Ku Klux Klan, manages this policy. Roosevelt's New Deal upholds Mussolini's famous dictum, "We fascists pay our debts and make the trains run on time."
WAR!!!

*The New Deal's war comes on December 7, 1941, a day that will live
in infamy, or so Roosevelt says.*

*It is an inevitable war. It is war well-planned by an arrogant colonial-
ism unwilling to die, by propaganda machines spewing hate, by ghouls
whose bloodlust is upon them, by the greedy desiring more wealth, by
Christians whose motto is* in hoc signo vinces. *The war calls for oceans
of blood. The war staggers even the imaginations of the most ardent
militarists. The war is conceived at such a level that only that ancient
sage, Josephus, could have understood. The war renders null and void
any rule of civilized behavior. The war aims at the annihilation of human
life and domination of subject populations. The war unleashes bestiality
and barbarism as twin symbols of the Christian world order. Yes, the
war is well planned.*

Thanks to his stepfather, Sid is in an ideal position to survive in the world
gone mad. Bif's contacts give his stepson an opportunity few soldiers,
colored or white, will ever know, the opportunity to stay alive. All Sid
has to do is follow Pop's instructions, ignore the continual racial slurs
and nigger-baiting and apply every lesson he learned in the ROTC to
his advantage. Thus Sid breezes through basic training and is assigned
to a colored detachment of Military Police stationed at Fort Dix, New
Jersey.

The war affects Chat, as well.

"I've got to join up," Chat tells Julia a week after Pearl Harbor. "I
don't really have a choice. Sid is already in the Army doing his part; I
have to do mine as well."

Like thousands of other young Americans, Chat prepares to answer
his country's call. No matter that he attends UCLA and has a promising
college and athletic career ahead of him. No matter that he is eligible
for a draft deferment. Chatsworth Jenkins, son of hero and soldier Peter
Jenkins, is a patriot determined to do his duty.

"If coloreds don't join in this fight, how can we deserve the benefits
of citizenship?"

"You can't enjoy any benefits if you're dead," Julia replies. "Be sen-
sible. There are plenty of other colored boys available to do the fighting.
But there aren't many colored boys attending UCLA on scholarship.

Do you think that they will find another one to put in your place if you leave college?"

Julia doesn't give Chat the opportunity to answer.

"Of course they won't! It's your duty to stay in college and graduate."

Chat looks at Bif.

"Can't you explain it to her, Pops? This is the colored man's opportunity to serve his country. A lot of the fellows from Jefferson are joining. All my friends are joining. If I don't go, what will they think of me? Besides, Mom didn't try to keep Sid from enlisting."

"That was different," Julia blurts out, her rejoinder giving Chat another reason to want to join the Army.

"Why?" Chat asks. "Why was it okay for Sid to join the Army and not me?"

Chat stares at his mother.

"Sid always said that you didn't care for him very much. I never believed him, until now."

"That's not true, Chat, and you know it!" Bif scolds.

Normally, he didn't get into his wife and stepson's arguments. He knew that neither wanted nor needed his help. Getting involved in their arguments meant that eventually both mother and son would turn on him.

"If it's not true," Chat says smugly, "then you can't object to my joining the Army like Sid did."

Once again, family and friends gather at Union Station to see another son off. This time it was not just off to an Army career, it was off to war. And this time, they are not the only family and friends seeing a loved one off. Union Station is mobbed by thousands of parents, relatives and friends, white and colored, seeing thousands of young men board the troop trains that will take them to far-away lands where they will die on battlefields. All are proud of these young lions, knowing many will not return home again.

Julia cries the whole night before. When they come for Sharon and Ed, Chat's grandmother's eyes are red from tears as well. And at Union Station, the tears flow not only down the women's cheeks but from the men, as well. Ed continually dabs his eyes with a handkerchief, but Bif is inconsolable. Chat's stepfather is so overcome by emotion that he cannot control the great sobs shaking his heavy frame. Neither Julia nor Chat understand how much the crusty old newspaperman really loves his adopted family and how his great heart nearly breaks to see his stepson going off to fight in a senseless war. Julia had seen Bif overcome by this kind of emotion only once before, when he lost those he held dear in Tulsa.

"Is there anything you can do to help him?" Ed asks Bif inside Union Station on the way to the car.

The walk gives Bif time to pull himself together.

"Now that we're at war, my contacts won't even acknowledge they even know me. They won't even return my calls. There's absolutely nothing I can do for him."

"Then he's completely on his own," Ed sighs.

"Yes," Bif murmurs, "God help him."

But Bif knew better than anyone that even God could not help Chat. With the exception of those few like Sid, the Army harbors deadly intentions for the thousands of young Negroes like Chat . . . intentions that make it unlikely that many of those brave young lads, whose sense of honor and valor causes them to enlist voluntarily, will even survive training camp. Army intelligence is determined not to repeat the errors made in the First World War. There will be no Negroes returning from this war who are trained and willing to kill white people.

"Sergeant Cooper!"

An eighteen-year old private stepped through the door of the Quonset hut; his oval face has barely seen the edge of a razor. The Negro private peers at the finely chiseled face of the black soldier seated behind the metal desk, hunching over a mountain of papers. He waits for a signal. The sergeant does not like to be disturbed before he gives his permission.

"What is it, private?" the first sergeant of Bravo Company replies after awhile, without looking up.

"The new recruits have arrived, sir."

"Don't sir me, soldier," the first sergeant bawls out. "You will address officers as sir. You will address me either as First Sergeant Cooper or as Sergeant Cooper. Is that clear, private."

"Yessir, I-I mean, yes, First Sergeant Cooper," the private quavers.

Since the company commander court-martialed and confined to the stockade all the company's senior enlisted men, Sergeant Cooper is forced to use this green eighteen-year-old recruit as his orderly.

Sergeant Cooper raises his head and the private can see the sweat running down his face. The Quonset hut is made of prefabricated corrugated metal, which acts just like an oven in the southern heat. Seymour Cooper, a career soldier since 1918, is happy to be leaving the hell-hole known as Camp Claiborne in Alexandria, Louisiana.

"Have the recruits assemble outside, private. I'll inform the Captain."

"Yes, Sergeant Cooper."

The private disappears back outside. Sergeant Cooper rises from his desk and strides back to the rear of the Quonset hut. He stops and knocks at a door marked *Captain Orval R. Woolsey, Company Commander*.

"Yes, who is it?" questions a gruff voice from within.

"Sergeant Cooper, sir."

"Come in, sergeant."

Coop, as the other noncommissioned officers call him, opens the door, steps smartly inside the company commander's office, snaps off a salute and says in a brisk voice, "Sir, Sergeant Cooper reporting that the new recruits assigned to Bravo Company have reported, sir."

"At ease, sergeant."

Behind the desk sprawls a beefy, red-faced white man who, despite the fact that he has a portable fan and a window-mounted air-cooling system running full blast, also sweats profusely. Woolsey is a career Army officer who looks more like one of those good old boys, a local sheriff of some sleepy southern town. A mass of red hair tumbles across Woolsey's splotched face almost falling into his little pig eyes. His massive frame might have challenged even the most expert tailor had Woolsey sought to give his uniform even a semblance of military smartness, which he doesn't. As the commander of an all-Negro company, Woolsey behaves exactly the way he looks, like a rednecked racist who enjoys the job of keeping his nigger troops in line.

Woolsey eyes his top sergeant with open contempt. Ever since the disturbance that is causing a shake-up in the 367th regiment, Captain Woolsey and his first sergeant have been icily precise in all their dealings. Coop violates his company commander's code of loyalty in defending those uppity buck niggers in Bravo Company. Woolsey wanted them arrested and charged, along with the other rioters. But Sergeant Cooper stuck up for his men and, in the end, forced his company commander to back down. Now instead of waiting to be court-martial, they sit in the stockade until Bravo Company ships out with the rest of the regiment. Woolsey promised the good white folks of Alexandria they'd never set their eyes on those niggers again. And, by God, he intends to keep his word. "But one day, I'm gonna teach them niggers a lesson," he vows. "Them and that nigger sergeant, too."

"You get 'em, Orval," the other white officers in 367th regiment laughed.

"You can laugh if you want," Woolsey said. "But all them niggers is Double Vs and it's them Double Vs that's got the colored troops stirred up."

Coop stands in front of his company commander awaiting Woolsey's response. After several minutes, Bravo Company's first sergeant asks, "Would the Captain like to see their files?"

Woolsey likes to keep the black man standing. But Coop had better things to do than just stand around while his redneck commander played master of the plantation. The Negro first sergeant had no problem letting company commander know exactly how he felt.

"I said at ease, sergeant," Woolsey growls. "The captain will let you know when he wants anything from you. Is that clear, boy?"

"Yessir," Coop responds crisply.

"Now, you get your black ass out of here!"

"Yessir."

The Negro first sergeant salutes and, upon receiving a begrudging acknowledgement, does an about face and makes a dignified exit.

Coop dares not dismiss the new men standing in the hot Louisiana sun without Woolsey's orders, nor could he direct them to their quarters.

Company commanders are responsible for addressing the new arrivals in person. So Coop goes outside to stand with the new arrivals. The men come from Pennsylvania, New York and California. The first sergeant tries to distract them from the sweltering sun by checking their names and asking each one of them about themselves. That is how Sergeant Seymour Cooper first meets Private Chatsworth Jenkins, the son of his old comrade in arms, Peter Jenkins, one of the originators of the group know as the Double Vs.

"And if he's anything like his father," Coop muses, "Orval Woolsey is going to be on his ass like white on rice."

Chapter Twenty-Eight

When war is declared, Army intelligence promotes Elmer Hansen to the rank of major and assigns him to the General Headquarters staff, in charge of GQ's intelligence section. Hansen's first assignment in GQ is to assess the impact that the large number of Negro volunteers have on military morale as well as upon the overall war effort. It takes Major Hansen several weeks to complete his assessment. And when he submits it, GQ is not happy.

"Major Hansen, report directly to the chief," he is ordered. GQ's chief of staff, Brigadier General Lesley J. McNair, wants an immediate explanation of Hansen's report. General McNair is responsible for the organization and training of all Army recruits.

"If Negroes enlist in large numbers," Major Hansen begins, "all the services will face difficult, if not impossible, demands on current resources. The Negroes will create a logistical nightmare. The Army will be most affected since the Navy's and Marine Corps's Negro enlistment policy is severely restrictive and limited."

General McNair gives his intelligence officer a solemn look. "Major, the president made a commitment that Negroes will be accepted into the military. I don't intend to tell our commander in chief that we cannot keep his commitment. When the president tells us to do a thing, we do it. Is that understood, major?"

"Yessir."

"All I've heard since I've taken over here, major," the General says, "is that we can't do this and we can't do that. Hell, major, is there anyone around here that can do something I ask?"

"Yessir."

"Don't make me sorry that I recommended you for that oak leaf you're wearing on your shoulders there, son."

"No sir."

"Okay, tell me about it."

"You see sir," Hansen continues, "aside from the problems of controlling the coloreds, we won't be able to train, transport or house them either. The coloreds require separate facilities; we'll need to almost double our resources. I'm told that there isn't enough transportation, housing and training facilities for our regular enlistees. But you know that better than I do."

McNair nods his agreement.

"What do you recommend, major?" the general asks.

"Reduce the recruitment of coloreds into the Army to a bare minimum."

"That can't be done right now," the general says.

"Why not?" Hansen asks. "The Navy, Marines and Coast Guard have restrictions against coloreds. The Army should be able to implement these restrictions without fuss, as well."

"The president made public announcements about bringing them darkies into the military," McNair sighs. "Any cutbacks will be made public. He can't back out of those commitments now, especially with the war on."

"These darkies," Major Hansen exclaims, "will there be no end to them. Why couldn't our plans to send them all back to Africa with Garvey have succeeded?"

"What plans were those, major?" the general asks.

"Well sir, it was a plan worked out by military intelligence with the Federal Bureau of Investigation to deport Negroes under the Alien and Sedition Laws." Hansen goes on to explain how they had hoped to force Negroes out of America and back to Africa using their membership in the UNIA as a pretext.

"That would have been an excellent solution, major," McNair says. "Why wasn't it implemented?"

"The English, French and Belgians refused to allow that many darkies back into Liberia," Hansen replies. "They were afraid that there would have been insurrections all over Africa."

"That's too bad."

"Yessir. It would have worked, too. Everything was prepared. It probably would have gone a lot smoother than Hitler's program of transporting all those Jews to Israel."

"Yes, it might have been successful. Still, I can see our allies's point," McNair observes. "Can't have a bunch of crazy darkies running all over Africa, disrupting the process of civilization. But that doesn't help us solve our present dilemma, does it, major?"

"No sir."

"The president expects us to resolve it. You work out the logistics, and keep me informed."

"Yessir. But sir."

"What is it, major?"

"The situation is more than just a logistical problem."

"How so, major?"

"Sir, we have been monitoring the colored troops' mail."

"And?"

"The letters indicate that morale among the colored troops is very low. They're complaining about their conditions."

"All soldiers complain about their conditions, major," the general observes. "Why should the darkies be any different?"

"Yessir," Hansen agrees. "But our analysis indicates that the low Negro morale could trigger major riots involving Negro troops before it's over."

Hansen pauses to let his comments sink in, then he continues.

"Already there have been a number of incidents where the coloreds have insisted on equal treatment. Any one of these incidents could have turned into a full-fledged riot."

"Riots!" General McNair says sharply. "The Army will not tolerate any riots."

"Nosir," Major Hansen replies. "A riot would hamper war production. It could even pass beyond the control of civil authorities, and require the use of federal troops now training for the front."

"Do you have any idea where these riots might take place?"

"Yessir. Estimates say that a riot could take place at any of the following cities: Baltimore, Maryland; Chester, Pennsylvania; or Harrisburg, Pennsylvania, sir."

The general pauses, lost in thought.

"And sir," Hansen concludes, "these incidents are in addition to the attacks and firefights that we are already experiencing because of the so-called Double V Brotherhood."

"Double V? What the devil is that, major?" The general, who had been shuffling papers on his desk, now gives his officer his undivided attention.

"The Double V Brotherhood is an underground conspiracy among the colored troops. They seek to overthrow our legal government and the American way of life, sir."

"Is this in your report as well?"

"Yessir," Hansen responds. "There have been outbreaks in New Jersey at Fort Dix as well as at Camp Shenango in Pennsylvania, and reports continue to come in. We try to downplay the problems particularly when the incidents involve colored soldiers and MPs. Sometimes these riots involve civilians and the press is asking us a lot of questions."

"Any casualties?"

"Yessir, quite a number of dead and wounded on both sides."

"I'll pass this information on to the inspector general, major," McNair states with finality, indicating that the interview is concluded. "You may leave your report."

"Yessir," Major Hansen, preparing to leave.

"But, major."

"Yessir?"

"You had better come up with some kind of a plan to handle this situation, do you understand?"

"Yessir."

"The general staff is not going to accept the fact that the United States Army can't deal with this situation. How in hell are we going to beat the Nazis if we can't even control our own niggers?"

"Yessir."

Major Hansen salutes and promptly leaves the general's office.

McNair, who is in charge of preparing the entire United States Army for war, is annoyed with his population officer.

"Come in here with a cock and bull story like that," McNair says out loud. "I'd be the laughing stock of the entire war department if it got out that our niggers dared to oppose us."

Leslie McNair sits in his office and tries to relax. He has a GQ meeting scheduled. Marshall might even attend.

"Calm down," he tells himself.

McNair is a West Point–trained career Army officer. He is experienced and blooded, not only in the great European war, but in the Philippines as well. It is a well-known fact that the colored race is cowardly and lacks the will to fight. General Marshall, himself, has said that the last European war proved that the coloreds are fit only to serve white troops, drive the trucks, load supplies, things like that. Secretary of War Stimson has warned the president several times against placing too much confidence in that cowardly race because they have shown such little initiative in battle.

"Niggers trying to take on the United States Army," McNair snorts. "It's absurd."

Then the answer becomes apparent, at least to GQ's chief of staff, General McNair. These coloreds are being led by a group of agitators and malcontents, he concludes. Probably some holdovers from that Garvey movement Hansen talked about.

"It never fails," McNair exclaimed out loud. "We train one of those niggers to act like a white man and he turns on us."

Then the general opens a gold-plated cigarette box on his desk. The cigarette soothes him.

"Once we identify the agitators," he thinks, "we can put an end to all this unrest and lawlessness."

Believing that he has resolved the matter, McNair turns to the more important matter at hand—winning the war.

"College Boy, again?" Private Harris asks Coop.

Harris, responsible for preparing Bravo Company's daily report, must report another soldier being transferred to the stockade. Coop and the aide play the guessing game: who does Woolsey put in the stockade today. They call Private Chatsworth Jenkins "College Boy."

"Yep, it's College Boy, again," Sergeant Cooper replies.

"The captain sure hates old College Boy," Harris remarks. "This will be the third time since we've been here that the captain has put College Boy in the stockade. What's it for this time?"

"The captain didn't like the expression on his face."

"What?"

"He didn't like the way he looked," Coop explains. "That's about all I can figure out."

Coop feels bad about what's happening to Chat. He blames himself since he made the mistake of letting it be known that he and Chat's father served together in France. Then bad matters got worse. Woolsey read Chat's record and found out that Chat attended UCLA. From then on, Pete Jenkins's son became the special object of his rednecked commander's vindictiveness. Not that any of the other recruits or any of the other soldiers, for that matter, are spared Woolsey's heavy-handed policy of demeaning and tyrannizing. But Woolsey has a special list, and Chat's on it.

When the 367th regiment was reconstituted as the 364th and transferred from Louisiana to Arizona, there was a general belief among the men that things would get better. But they soon found out that, if there is a hell, its name is Papago Park and it is located in Phoenix, Arizona.

"Coop should have known better," Harris tells another solder. "He knew that Woolsey would single out College Boy."

"Yeah," the other soldier agrees. "Why did Coop do it, I wonder?"

Chat sits by himself behind the stockade's barbed wire fence.

"I see you're back again, Chat," Solomon Pugh says.

Solomon is another semi-regular member of Papago Park's stockade. That, too, is to be expected since Solomon has the Double V symbol tattooed on his chest.

"Yeah, Solly, I'm back."

"What did you do this time?"

"Nothing."

"Well, don't you think it's about time you at least did something?"

"Something like what," Chat asks.

"We're meeting over there by the water trough. Come over and join us if you like."

The stockade at Papago Park is nothing more than a rectangular area doubly enclosed by two barbed wire fences. The only structures inside the fences are the water and feeding troughs. Woolsey likes the idea of his niggers feeding and drinking out of troughs.

"Like the animals they are," Woolsey cackles.

The prisoners are forced to endure the blazing desert heat during the day and the freezing cold at night. During the two-week sentence (the normal stay for each inmate found guilty of an Article 15 offense) each prisoner is completely exposed to the elements. Several men have already died. Others, suffering from heat and sun-stroke, must be hospitalized. Never are there fewer than eighty-five colored inmates in Papago Park's stockade at any one time. The stockade's two troughs give the prisoners their only protection from the extreme desert climes. They are the domain of the Double V Brotherhood. Solomon is their leader. None of the other prisoners dare come close to the troughs without his permission, which is only given at feeding time or when a prisoner requests permission for a drink of water. Not all the Negro prisoners request membership in the Double V and not all that request membership are accepted.

"Look who's back," Solly tells the other ten members of the Brotherhood.

"Come to join the Double V, College Boy?" one of the members asks.

"What's the Double V?" Chat asks. Of course, he already knows about them. He would have been a fool not to know about the Brotherhood that sprang up wherever Negro soldiers are posted or stationed. The Brotherhood is so ubiquitous that it is rumored that the colored MPs are routinely screened for any links to the hated and feared Double V. Wisely, Chat allows himself to be recruited by feigning ignorance.

"No one knows when or where the Brotherhood actually formed," Solly begins. "Some say it was organized during the last war. The white folks lynched so many colored soldiers that the brothers got together and vowed to defend each other with their lives."

"Was it called the Double V back then?" one of the members asks.

"I don't know, fool," Solly snaps. "Just let me school College Boy, will you?"

"Okay, Solly," the brother says sheepishly.

"Anyway, as I was saying, I joined the Double V when I transferred into the 367th, back in Louisiana."

"Why?" Chat asks.

"One of the fellows from another company, on a pass in Alexandria, was walking on the sidewalk when a white woman passed by. All of a sudden she starts screaming rape."

"Rape?" Chat exclaims.

"Rape," Solly repeats.

"Cops came from everywhere, started beating the soldier senseless and took him to jail."

"Was he from Bravo Company?" Chat asks.

"No. He was from some other outfit, Able Company, I think," Woodson, one of the other brothers, responds.

"Anyway," Solly continues, "when his buddies hear about it, they go into Alexandria, kill a bunch of those crackers, tear up the town and get the brother out of jail. That's when they broke up the 367th and sent us here to Camp Hell."

"But what about the Brotherhood?" Chat asks.

"They court-martialed and hanged several of those boys. They sent others to jail for ten or twenty years. When some of us supported the ones that were court-martialed, they tried to arrest and court-martial us. They called the Brotherhood a terrorist group."

"I had never heard of it before then," one of the brothers volunteers.

"Neither had I," says another.

"But some of us decide that it was a good idea for us to form a brotherhood for our own protection. That way, if anyone of us gets attacked by these racist crackers, someone will come to his rescue," Woodson adds.

"That's right," Solly says, "Coop gave us the idea. He said that that was how they did it in Europe during the last war."

"After we formed our brotherhood, we were contacted by other groups in the regiment; they formed brotherhoods for themselves."

"You know what," Chat says. "I think my father was a Double V member."

"Oh yeah," Solly laughs, "so you're what? A second generation Double V?"

"Whatever," Chat says thoughtfully. "All the same, I know he was a member. Him and Coop knew each other then. That's where Coop got the idea."

"Yeah. We heard that Coop and your old man knew each other," Solly says. "Coop recommended you."

"So are you going to join us, College Boy?" Charles sneers. Charles is from Oakland and doesn't particularly care for his fellow Californian.

"Yes, I'm in," Chat announces.

"Well, College Boy," Charles speaks out, "it ain't that easy."

Charles looks around to see if anyone will challenge him before continuing. "First of all, we all have the Double V either tattooed or branded on our chests. We don't trust anyone who can't be identified."

"I don't have a problem with that," Chat says. "But it will have to wait until I get out of the stockade."

"Then I say he can't join up now," Charles announces to the group.

Actually Charles opposes Chat's admission to the Brotherhood for a completely different reason. Charles intends to depose Solomon as the Brotherhood's leader and take over himself. When that time comes, Charles doesn't want any opposition, especially from someone like College Boy.

"It's not that we don't trust you," Charles explains. "You've been a down brother with us all along. And no one will forget what you did for Darrell."

"Yeah, College Boy stood by Brother Darrell," Woodson affirms.

During one of the frequent forced marches Woolsey sends Bravo Company on through the rugged Superstition Mountains in the scorching Arizona sun, Darrell Clark, one of Chat's buddies, wears his reissued GI boots all the way through to the sole. Literally walking barefoot, the rocks and bramble shred Darrell's feet so bloody that the Negro private cannot take another step. Chat trades boots and aids the hobbled soldier back to camp where Darrell must be hospitalized for several weeks. Chat becomes an instant hero in the eyes of some, but others, like Charles, resent him. When Captain Woolsey hears about the incident, he gives Chat the Article 15 punishment that results in Chat's first—but not his last—visit to Papago Park's stockade.

Solly shrugs. "The Double V brand is really the only condition for joining," he says. "I guess you'll have to wait." The other brothers reluctantly agree.

"Now get your black ass on away from here," Charles says.

Chat doesn't move. He just sits and stares at Charles, who glowers back menacingly.

"I'll tell you what," Chat says. "Does anyone have a sharp knife?"

"No, but I have a dull one," someone responds. The group laughs.

"I'm serious," Chat says. "You've got nothing better to do. Sharpen up a knife and cut the Double V on my chest."

Solly gives Chat a look and says, "Either you're one bad ass brother, or one crazy nigger. Which one?"

"Probably both," Chat replies. "I'll let you decide after you make the cuts."

Woodson produces a knife hidden away in his boot.

"We're gonna see how crazy you are, nigger," Woodson says.

Chat smiles. "My father was a Double V and I'm gonna show you dumb ass niggers that I'm one too!"

Solly snorts out a laugh. Then he says, "You heard College Boy. Sharpen that knife. I'll do the cutting."

Woodson takes his time and sharpens the knife to a razor's edge against one of the rocks littering the ground. But when Solly takes the blade from Woodson, the Brotherhood leader continues to sharpen it until, with the slightest touch, the knife draws blood from his finger. Then, as Chat opens up his Army shirt, staring straight ahead, Solly makes four half-inch slices into the upper part of Chat's chest, forming the brotherhood's Double V symbol. A profuse amount of blood flows down Chat's chest as the others watch in amazement, but no sound passes Chat's lips.

"You're one bad-assed motherfucker," Solly says as Chat pressed his shirt against the cuts to stop the bleeding.

"Not really," Chat replies. "You're the one that did the cutting. You don't think I'd just let anyone do it, do you?" Solly looks at Chat and then gives him a hug. Although Chat was a good deal taller and broader than the Brotherhood leader, he feels the strength of Solly's wiry body.

But while everyone concentrates on Solly's hands and the bloody incisions oozing from Chat's chest, Charles stands up and gives an unobtrusive signal to one of the MPs in the watchtower. In a matter of minutes, Captain Woolsey comes ambling across the parade grounds and up to the stockade gate.

"Open the gate!" the company commander cries out to the MPs. Woolsey draws his .45 caliber Army Colt pistol. Striding over to the water troughs, he thunders, "You men come to attention. What's going on here?"

"Nothing, sir," Solly replies.

"Nothing! It looks as if you are assaulting this soldier with a knife."

"No sir, captain," Chat speaks out despite the pain. "I cut myself trying to get water from the trough."

The band of brothers, all except Charles, begins moving menacingly toward the redneck officer. The stockade guards, colored MPs, attached to the 364th infantry, are slow to move into the area. So the white officer stands alone, almost completely surrounded by the sullen Negroes he has tormented and imprisoned.

"Don't lie to me, soldier," Woolsey shouts. "The rest of you get back."

He releases his pistol's safety and, aiming at their bare feet, fires off a couple of rounds. One of the brothers lurches forward, hitting the captain in the back of the head. Woolsey whirls with surprising agility for a man with his girth and size. But just as Woolsey brings the muzzle of his gun up to train on the offending Negro, Chat reaches over and grabs Woolsey's arm, causing the weapon to discharge harmlessly into the air. Before the stockade's Negro guards can rescue the white man, the other prisoners are on Woolsey in an instant, pummeling him right and left. Woolsey is knocked to the ground, his gun lands some distance away, and the angry Negroes are kicking and stomping away—all except Charles, who holds back with an amused look on his face.

"You men stand accused of assaulting an officer of the United States Army with the intention of causing great bodily harm and even death. What do you have to say for yourselves?"

The speaker is Colonel John F. Goodman, the newly arrived commandant of 364th regiment. Colonel Goodman is neither a West Point graduate nor a regular Army officer. The new regimental commander is a college professor, who serves in a reserve Army unit that has been activated as a part of the nationwide reservist call up. Because the Army has no other place to put him, Goodman now finds himself regimental commander of the 364th. But the former college professor is distressed by the conditions he finds at Papago Park.

The Papago Park Army Base, located five miles from Phoenix, is an abandoned cattle ranch. The sergeants and the MPs of the all-Negro 364th infantry regiment live in stables and barns. They are lucky. The 3,000 colored troops sleep in tents. They are underfed and malnourished. None of the men has been given a decent issue of clothing. They wear tattered and frayed uniforms from the First World War; their boots are cracked and worn, many with holes in the soles.

The regiment's morale is extremely low. The colored MPs have orders to maintain discipline by using whatever force is necessary. The Negro soldiers resent the Army but hate the colored MPs. The only training these soldiers receive are frequent forced marches under the blazing desert sun over rugged rocky terrain. Not a few casualties and even a number of fatalities result from these forced marches. If there is an American complement to the Japanese death camps, it is Papago Park.

Colonel Goodman reads the files of the soldiers accused of assaulting Captain Woolsey.

"Sergeant, what did Captain Woolsey have against these men?" Colonel Goodman asks Bravo Company's first sergeant in preparation for the pending court martial.

"Dunno, sir," the first sergeant responds. "Captain Woolsey seemed to take a personal dislike to some of the men. When that happened, they would find themselves in the stockade."

"But sergeant," the colonel queries, "some of these men . . ."

"Yessir?"

"Never mind," the colonel mutters more to himself than to the first sergeant. "How many of those men *died there*, sergeant?"

"A couple, sir."

Captain Woolsey is charging the prisoners with attempted murder. He is asking for the death sentence in each case. Charles is a military intelligence agent assigned to the Military Police Company at Papago Park. He files a secret report stating that the Double V Brotherhood planned the assault on Captain Woolsey in retaliation for having been put into the stockade. His report states that the prisoners were being punished for insubordination and breaches of discipline. Captain Woolsey's report recommends leniency in the case of Private Charles Oates.

"It was Private Oates's own action, at great personal risk at the hands of these would-be murderers, that saved my life," Captain Woolsey's report states.

After reviewing the files and the various reports, Colonel Goodman instructs Solly, Chat, Darrell and the other Brotherhood members to report to his office for an "unofficial" discussion prior to charges being formally made. The meeting takes place over the strenuous protest of the Provost Marshall's office. However, the only concession Colonel Goodman makes is to allow Charles to be included with the others in order to maintain his undercover status. Solly speaks for the group.

"Sir, we have suffered unimaginable indignities and hardships. Captain Woolsey treats us like his plantation slaves. We all volunteered to defend our country in this time of need. Some of us gave up comfortable lives, others promising college careers." Solly glances over at Chat, a glance that does not escape the commandant, who has noted Chat's college credentials. "We came because we believed it was our duty to defend America against her enemies. And this is how we are treated. Some very fine men, young men in the prime of their lives, have died at the hands of those they sought to serve. We have done nothing wrong. We are the victims, sir. Captain Woolsey is the murderer. He came into that stockade to murder us. We were defending ourselves."

John Goodman looks at each one of the soldiers.

Then he states, "The mistreatment that you men have suffered will stop. You have my word. I am ordering barracks to be built to provide proper housing for this regiment and I am ordering that you all be fed three meals a day."

Solly and Chat look at each other with smiles, but Charles, a scowl darkening his face, looks as if he'd been slapped.

"I want you men to tell the others," Colonel Goodman continues. "I am instituting an open-door policy. If anyone in this regiment believes he is being treated unfairly, I give him permission to come in to see me."

"Speaking for myself," Solly exclaims, "I believe that you are a good person and the men will appreciate anything you do for them."

Colonel Goodman keeps his word and institutes the changes. He builds barracks to house the men and a mess hall where they can enjoy three meals a day. Every man in the entire regiment receives new uniforms, boots and personal equipment. Goodman systematically replaces his company commanders, beginning with Orval Woolsey, with officers who are sensitive to the plight of the Negro. The new company commanders of the 364th regiment, though white, begin to demonstrate a more benign attitude toward the Negro soldiers. Colonel Goodman charges his company commanders with implementing a regular Army training program for his regiment. Within six months, Goodman reports a dramatic improvement in his colored soldiers' morale. His men begin to think and act as if they are American soldiers, preparing themselves to defend their country. Even the Brotherhood begins to concentrating on "victory against fascism" instead of "victory against racism"— that is until Thanksgiving Day, 1942, the day that the fickle finger of fate imposes doom on the luckless 364th regiment in general, and on Chatsworth Jenkins in particular.

In 1942, Phoenix is a wide-open town. Everything is available for a price. Gambling, prostitution, drugs—the Phoenician city fathers tolerate it all. Other than vice, Phoenix has few avenues for personal and civic advancement.

The biggest market for Phoenix's juke joints, prostitutes and drug merchants might have been the soldiers stationed at Papago Park. The mild administration of Colonel Goodman affords the colored soldiers ample opportunity to discover the many diversions and entertainments

Phoenix has to offer. Unfortunately, there is a stumbling block. In Phoenix, racism is like the air one breathes. Racism is chronic, permanent and pervasive. In 1942, Phoenix is rigidly racist, steadfastly segregationist and wildly white supremacist. No amount of green in the pockets of soldiers from the 364th can offset the blackness of their faces.

Though Phoenix's racial etiquette is less violent than its Southern counterparts, white supremacy, segregation, and economic inequality exist from the day the first white settlers kill off Native Americans and declare Arizona white man's country. Whites enact the first segregation law in the Arizona Territory in 1864, prohibiting marriages between whites and Negroes, mulattos or Mongolians. Furthermore, the law declares any children of mixed heritage must forfeit any legal inheritance rights from either parent.

The Ku Klux Klan finds Arizona a fertile ground for recruiting. Klaverns spring up around the state like mushrooms. Klansmen intimidate and terrorize the relatively few Negroes bold enough to settle there. Residential segregation is maintained by restrictive covenants limiting the sale of Arizona real estate to whites only. The city's parks, swimming pools, theaters, grocery stores, restaurants, and hotels are all segregated, meaning limited to whites only. Phoenix is so racist that it is rumored that dead Klansmen rose up to lynch the ghost of a Negro who tried to haunt the white section of a segregated cemetery.

Black Phoenicians work in low-wage, non-managerial, labor-intensive occupations. They live in substandard housing, amidst deprivation and squalor. They suffer from a lack of medicines and doctors. The only public restrooms available to Negroes anywhere in the city are in the city hall, the bus station, the train station and the county building. Everywhere signs proclaiming "We reserve the right to refuse service" greet the Negro soldiers of the 364th regiment.

"Which means 'nigga' don't come in here," Chat tells Solly.

"Man, I'll tell you," Solly says. "Now that we can come into town, there's nowhere for us to go."

Phoenix's colored population is restricted to the area south of Van Buren Street, the only place the soldiers of the 364th are allowed to go. The soldiers flock there in droves and that leads to another problem. There weren't enough women in the Van Buren district for the 3,000 men stationed at Papago Park. This problem is why on November 26, 1942, Thanksgiving Day, Phoenix explodes in an orgy of violence and death.

"Did you hear about what happened in town?"

Darrell Clark comes barreling into the mess hall. Darrell is naturally rotund, so he looks like a big barrel rolling past the dining tables.

"What's up?" someone asks.

"Two soldiers got into a fight over a woman. When the MPs tried to break it up, one of them flashed the Double V sign. And then they got it on."

"Got what on?" Chat asks.

"The MPs shot the Double V brother."

"Shot him!"

"Yeah, and they didn't stop there."

"No!"

"When some other brothers came to help, the MPs started shootin' at them, too. The MPs started shooting at everyone in sight."

"What?"

"Yeah, man. They started rounded up every nigger in town. Anyone who ran or resisted got shot. They even started shootin' civilians."

"Civilians?"

"Yep, them yellow-assed niggers are going wild. They riding around Van Buren Street in armored personnel carriers mounted with .50 caliber machine guns, shooting up houses and stores and anything that moves. The police won't let anyone in or out, civilians or soldiers."

"How did you get out?" Chat asked.

"One of my homeboys is an MP. He got me out."

"You must be one lucky nigger."

But luck is a matter of perception. More than thirty Negroes, civilians and soldiers are killed in Phoenix's Thanksgiving Day riot. Some of the dead civilians are children. The Army singles out sixteen Double V Brotherhood members and identifies them as the ringleaders who caused the disturbance. The sixteen stand before a general court-martial and receive sentences of 50 years of hard labor at Fort Leavenworth. Though the colored MPs are responsible for all the deaths, none are charged with murder.

After the Thanksgiving Day riot, Phoenix's city fathers demand that the Army transfer the 364th regiment out of Arizona. The Army complies and the 3,000 soldiers of the ill-fated 364th are transferred to—what for many of them will be—their final duty station, Fort Van Dorn in Centreville, Mississippi.

Chapter Twenty-Nine

Fort Van Dorn covers 41,843 acres of mostly uninhabited Mississippi swampland. The camp, located on a part of the old Whitaker Plantation, borders the toe of Louisiana, just at the point where the mighty Mississippi River makes an eastward jog before it tumbles south down toward the Delta region and into the Gulf of Mexico. The Mississippi River marks Fort Van Dorn's southern border ninety miles north of Baton Rouge—ninety miles of the densest alligator and snake-infested swamp imaginable. Five miles northeast of the Army encampment on relatively dry grassland squats the sleepy town of Centreville, Mississippi.

The miles and miles of swamp upon which the Army encampment sits are soggy and damp. Even the ground where the barracks and other buildings sit oozes with mud. Outside the compounds that make up sections of Van Dorn, deep swampy water collects under forests overgrown with cypress, tupelo and willow tress. Overhead Spanish moss, ferns and vegetative mold cling to the trees, creating a dense, leafy enclosure that blocks out the sun. In between the groves of trees, masses of leafy shrubs and prickly bushes shelter slow-moving creeks and marshes, from which blooms an infinite variety of flora including reeds, water lilies and honeysuckle. Vines, green brier, catbrier and pepper creep, crawl and intertwine everything, holding the entire 43,000 acres of swamp forest in a gigantic embrace of active, cloying vegetation that covers the land and blocks out the sky.

Van Dorn is overwhelmed with the smells of plants, flowers and all manner of vegetation, permeating the air with a sweet, pungent odor. At first, the scents are pleasant and one is filled with a sensation of nature's bounty and richness. After awhile the odors become overwhelming—

they fill the nostrils with the smell of rotting vegetation and stagnant water. The swamp smells become nauseating, with its unending process of decay and putrefaction.

Van Dorn's swamp forest teems with wildlife that continually broadcasts its presence in a cacophony of shrieks, howls, whistles, warbles and grunts. Birds, ducks, heron, egrets, and even storks make a loud racket except when they are being stalked by a predator. Then an eerie hush descends upon the swamp. Once the predator moves on, or makes its kill, the racket begins again. While the noisy waterfowl make their home in the watery marshes, their quieter cousins, the eagles, hawks, ravens and owls nest on higher ground. The high ground and marshes host raccoons, possums and wild pigs, who compete with the alligators, water moccasins and cottonmouths for their favorite food of frogs, salamanders and fish found in stagnant pools as well as the rotting logs. Red-tailed deer, brown bears and an occasional cougar also call Fort Van Dorn's swampy forest home. When the 364th arrive at their new Mississippi home, the call of the wild sounds none too friendly.

Upon their arrival the 364th regiment finds that Fort Van Dorn's barracks and buildings can accommodate 39,000 enlisted men, with room for 2,000 officers. The camp hospital has a 750 bed capacity. The company of colored MPs assigned to the 364th regiment does not accompany the Negro regiment to Fort Van Dorn. An all-white regiment of 4,000 military police is already in place.

"I have a bad feeling about this place," Coop says at a meeting of the Double V cell leaders representing the 364th's ten companies. The regiment has been at Fort Van Dorn for a month. The conditions are extreme and rumors abound about the treatment Negroes receive at the hands of the military police and civilian sheriffs. Coop calls the Double V meeting to discuss the situation.

"You men must keep sharp. Share information with each other," he tells the gathering.

But it doesn't take the first sergeant to tell the men of the 364th how serious their situation has become. Upon arriving at Van Dorn, the regiment is isolated in a compound several miles away from the main camp. Within the compound, which is surrounded by a double row of barbed wire fencing, the regiment has its own barracks, mess halls and command posts. The Negro NCOs live inside the compound along with the enlisted men; the white officers are billeted in the main camp. Military police units in armored personnel carriers and jeeps patrol the compound's perimeter. Every gate from the compound into the main camp is guarded by white MPs. Two months pass. The Negroes are given no orders and remain isolated. Seldom do they see their officers and there is no training schedule. Passes are given to any of the Negroes who wish to go into Centreville. But it is rumored that colored soldiers assigned to other units stationed at Van Dorn recommend that the 364th stay away from the Mississippi town.

"What do you think is up, Coop?" Solly asks.

Of all the Double V Brotherhood leaders, Coop knows that Solomon is both trustworthy and committed. Solly is calm and cool-headed. He cares for his men and they, in turn, depend on him. Coop also knows, as does Solly, that half of the Brotherhood's leadership and most of the Brotherhood's membership work for Army intelligence. Solly has no way of knowing whether Chatsworth Jenkins is one of them.

"Why do you think College Boy pulled that stunt in the stockade?" Coop asks Solly.

"I don't know, Coop," Solly replies. "But I think he's a stand-up guy. I like him and trust him."

"Well, he's your responsibility," Coop says.

Like many others, Coop owed Chat's father. When he was young and full of himself in France, Coop also challenged the Army's racial policies against fraternizing with the French mademoiselles, just like Grady Jones. And just like Grady, Coop got caught and needed rescuing. "How long ago was that?" Coop asks himself. It seems like a century or more. It seems to Coop that Pete's Brotherhood group was better organized back then. Not like these brothers, who neither take orders nor follow directions, and will sell their buddies out to the whites without a second thought. "Look who's talking," Coop shakes his head sadly. Anyway, that was then and this is now. Life is not without its ironies, Coop knows.

Still, Coop knows that he should be watching out for Pete's son. He owed Pete that much and a good deal more. But he couldn't; things are different now, the first sergeant rationalizes to himself. You don't get to be "top kick" without making some adjustments, some compromises. Now his job is to see that all his men survive—not just a few of them, but all of them. Anyway, if Pete's son follows directions, he'll be all right. Pete has a smart kid, smarter than most of the men in Bravo Company. It's a shame, what happened to Pete. Coop hadn't even heard about it. Coop will do the best he can for Pete's son, but it is really up to College Boy. And in the meantime, Coop decides to do his job and carry out his orders.

"I learned something from a corporal in the 512th quartermaster regiment," Coop tells the Brotherhood leadership.

"What's that, Coop?" the leader from Charlie Company asks.

"He says they've been fishing bodies out of these swamps."

"Are they colored?"

"Yep, that's what he says."

The men of the Brotherhood are silent.

"He says the Army gives the locals access to all the swampland around here," Coop continues, "with an understanding that if any colored soldier is caught out there, they can kill him and nothing will be said."

"Why would colored soldiers be caught out in the swamps?" another unit leader asks.

"They're trying to escape."

"Escape from what?"

"I don't know," Coop replies. "But anyone trying to escape here by going AWOL gets shot."

This news had a sobering effect on the gathering.

"So what do you think we should do?" Solly asks.

"I think each of you had better draw up some escape plans for your units."

"Escape plans," one of the leaders says. "How are we going to escape from this swamp?"

"That's right," someone else chimes in. "What we should be planning is how to kick some cracker's ass!"

That was what Coop doesn't want to hear. There cannot be a fight. These men have no idea what's being planned. It is suicide even to consider such a move. Already it's too late for certain members of the Brotherhood. Someone in this meeting is bound to report what was said. But there are some who agree. Others dissent. A heated exchange take place between those who want to plan a general uprising and those who believe that each unit should act on its own.

"I don't think this organization should be talking about running and hiding," one of the younger leaders exclaims. Another round of arguments take place.

"I'm making the final decision," Coop says, realizing that no decision can be made at this meeting. "There will be no plans for a general uprising. Whatever plans you make will be strictly for your own group. Don't share either your intentions or your plans with anyone outside your individual units. Of course, you can share them with me. Remember we really don't know who to trust."

"I think we should write down everything that happens and send letters home to make certain they know what's happening to us," the leader from Able Company proposes.

"That's a good idea," Solly agrees, along with some of the others. Coop keeps silent although he wants to say, "Didn't I just tell you fools not to share your plans with anyone else?" But he knows it won't do any good. Doomed men seldom listen.

"Sir, I regret to inform you that there has been another incident with the 364th Regiment."

Major Hansen requests this urgent meeting with General McNair after the shooting of Private Irwin C. Wiley by a Centreville, Mississippi deputy sheriff.

"What is it this time, major?"

Hansen describes the incident.

"Major, I'm in the middle of planning the Louisiana military maneuvers to be held in June and you're bothering me about one dead nigger?" General McNair responds.

The careers of Ike Eisenhower, George Patton and Omar Bradley, just to name a few, were decided by the Army's Louisiana maneuvers held in 1940. The maneuvers McNair plans for 1944 is his chance to reach the upper echelons of the military establishment. Right now, McNair is completely uninterested in the affairs of the 364th.

"Sir," Hansen continues, "the incident has been compromised by a number of AWOLs, letters to relatives as well as letters and an affidavit submitted by the NAACP to Secretary Stimson's office."

"The secretary of war's office?"

"Yessir. The NAACP told Secretary Stimson that the Army is covering up the shooting."

"Hansen, I thought you arranged to have the local sheriff patrol Fort Van Dorn so that no one from the 364th could leave before we finalize our plans."

"Yessir," Hansen replies, "we have the full cooperation of the civilian authorities in this matter."

"Then how in the hell did the NAACP get involved, major?"

"Well sir, some colored soldiers escaped Fort Van Dorn and contacted the NAACP."

"This is another mess, isn't it, major?

"Yessir. I'm afraid that it is, sir."

"What is your recommendation, Hansen?"

"I believe, sir, ah, I think it is time for the general to forward our recommendations to the inspector general, sir."

"Are you fully prepared to implement this action, major?"

"Yessir."

"Well, then, I'll forward your recommendations."

After his officer leaves, McNair summons his aide, Lieutenant Carl Pippins.

"Carl, set up a private meeting between me and General Peterson. Tell him that I am prepared to make my final recommendation for disposing of the 364th."

Major General Virgil L. Peterson is inspector general for the Army's General Staff. The general of the Army and the secretary of war must clear any recommendation on the magnitude being contemplated. Even the president, as commander in chief, should be notified, although in a way that gives him plausible deniability if anything should go wrong. But what can go wrong? General Peterson takes responsibility for securing the clearances.

Two weeks later, McNair walks into the inspector general's office. "Good to see you, Les," Peterson greets his fellow officer warmly. "You're here about the 364th, I'm told."

"Yessir. Hansen recommends that we take action immediately before the politicians make the decision for us."

"How is that, Les?"

"Sir, as you know, the president has made political commitments that he would rather not break. However, even though he is fully supportive of our position, Secretary Stimson is in receipt of an affidavit from the NAACP that he dares not ignore. And, frankly sir, neither can the president. Fortunately, this matter is still under our control. But if word of this leaks out to the colored press, or even the general press, who knows what the result will be. The time to act is now."

"I see your point, Les."

Peterson came to the General Staff as a career officer who is sensitive to the political climate. He knows the Army's sentiment on the matter of the discipline problem involving the colored troops of the 364th regiment. The Army wants to put this colored mutiny down, dramatically and forcefully. Its reputation rests on taking aggressive action against any organized resistance to its authority. This is especially true when the mutiny comes from a regiment the Army brass considers to be made up of semi-literate simian-brained niggers. The entire General Staff is personally affronted that this rebellion has been in existence for as long as it has. They are determined that it continues no longer. Who knows what could result. If the Nazis or even the Russians learn of the nigger rebellion, the consequences could be irreparable.

"What are you recommending?" the inspector general asks his chief of staff.

"Sir, the worst possible solution is to transfer the 364th somewhere else. That just plays into the hands of the malcontents. Anytime they want to move they'd just start making more trouble."

"I agree," Peterson responds.

"What we need to do is identify their leaders, the malcontents who are stirring up all the trouble. That's our aim."

"How do we do that, general?"

"Isolate them, deprive them of liberty or passes. Then we'll send in intelligence officers to identify the malcontents. While we're there we'll identify the followers, too—the ones who would be likely to get involved in mob action to change their situation. We will only spare the

Negroes who accept their condition as the 'American way of life.' After all, that's what this war is all about, isn't it? Preserving the American way of life?"

McNair taps his finger on the desk knowingly, signaling his confirmation and agreement on a matter that doesn't need further discussion.

"I thoroughly agree with you, general, and I like your approach. I think it will sell." General Peterson takes the diplomatic and political approach. He understands how to get the Army what it needs from the civilians.

"Thank you, general."

"Now tell me, Les, what other alternatives did you consider?"

"Sir?"

"Should someone raise the question, I need to be prepared to answer it, Les," Peterson says.

"Of course, general," McNair replies. "We considered breaking up the regiment and transferring the individuals in small groups into other colored units. But that doesn't solve the problem, it spreads it."

"How is that?"

"Those that are fomenting these riotous behaviors will go unpunished. In fact, they will be free to promote unrest and resentment among the other accommodating Negro soldiers. Right now this insurgency is limited to one unit. Wholesale transfers will infect the entire Army and possibly civilian communities as well. That would be like turning the whole country over to the coloreds."

"I see what you mean."

"Besides, we've already isolated individual troublemakers. That strategy doesn't seem to work."

"Why not?"

"New ones take their place. What we must do is impress upon the sounder, more reasonable coloreds that they themselves should identify and deliver for proper discipline the mutinous malcontents among them. That's the only way to suppress this mutiny. If we deliver the message properly, other coloreds, military and civilian, will realize that we will not tolerate any attempt to change the existing social order. Now is the time to teach these people that they must remain in their place."

"I agree with you, my friend," General Peterson states. "You begin the process and I will advise General Marshall's deputy chief of staff, Lieutenant General Joseph T. McNarney, of our decision. Don't delay implementation unless you are specifically ordered not to proceed. I agree that time is of the essence. There is no telling how long the NAACP can keep this thing covered up."

Chapter Thirty

"Sir, Corporal Jenkins, reporting as ordered, sir."

"At ease, corporal."

Captain Ickes barely looks up from his desk. As the officer in charge of the provost marshall's office at Camp Chafee, Arkansas, Ickes has a general disdain for the colored agents attached to his office. He has no sympathy for traitors who betray their own people no matter how useful they are to Army intelligence.

"They have no values," Ickes argues.

"On the contrary," his colleague counters. "They share exactly the same values as you and I. As a matter of fact, they want to be as much like us as possible."

"Then I would question not only their values, but also their sanity."

"Why so?"

"Because a man must be mentally ill to sacrifice his life to be something he is not rather than to risk his life to preserve what he is."

And this is exactly how Captain Ickes feels about Corporal Sydney Jenkins.

"Corporal," Ickes continues, "you are to report to Fort Van Dorn for a special assignment."

"Can the captain enlighten me as to the nature of this assignment?" Sid asks.

"No, the captain can tell you no more than you are ordered to Fort Van Dorn, where you are to report to First Sergeant Seymour Cooper. You have your identity?"

"Yessir."

Then that will be all, corporal."

"Yessir," Sid responds. Saluting and making an about-face with military precision, Sid strides out of the provost marshall's office.

On his last two undercover assignments, Sid worked with another agent attached to a separate military police unit at Fort Dix. The other colored MPs here at Camp Chafee keep their distance; they don't trust him. They call Sid "King Midas." Not because everything he touches turns into gold, but because whomever Sid touches winds up in the stockade. Sid is good at gaining the confidence of unsuspecting colored soldiers and learning their secrets. Some are sneaky thieves; others are homosexuals. Some merely enjoy smoking reefer; others deal heroin. Many of the colored MPs warn their friends about Sid. They say that Sid will even turn on his own snitches. But like the Canadian Mounties, Sid always seems to get his man. All Sid really wants to do is please his superiors and get promoted.

"One day, I'll be an officer," Sid promises himself, "and these thieves, hustlers and malcontents are going to help me."

Sid's normal police assignment is to catch criminals, that is, Negro criminals. In addition, he is to identify leaders, members and sympathizers of the mutinous underground group known as the Double V Brotherhood. Even before he arrives at Fort Van Dorn, Sid knows this will be his assignment. He is good at undercover work and has no compunction against betraying unsuspecting colored soldiers. They are the keys to his success.

At Fort Van Dorn, reveille sounds at 05:30 hours. The men are expected to be up, dressed and in formation outside of their barracks by 05:45 hours. Within that time, their personal area, including bunk and belongings, should be put in inspection order. While standing in formation, Coop gives the men of Bravo Company the day's announcements. Today's announcements include three new recruits.

"Find out whether the new men should be recruited into the Brotherhood," Solly tells Chat. "Also find out if they know anything about what's going on outside the regiment."

"Like what?" Chat asks.

"Like anything," Solly responds with just a touch of edginess. Recently there has been a lot of movement in and out of Bravo Company as well as the 364th. New people are coming in all the time. The Brotherhood is wary of all this movement. Solly can't get any information from Coop other than, "I'll tell you when I learn anything." Many, if not most, of the transfers coming into Bravo Company are from other companies within the 364th as well as from the two other colored regiments that arrived at Van Dorn earlier. Most of the transfers are either Double Vs or, at least, sympathetic to the Brotherhood's aims.

"You got any ideas about what's going on?" Chat asks.

"Not a clue," Solly responds. "But whatever it is, Coop doesn't know anything about it."

Chat likes Sergeant Cooper; he's been like a father to him. But there's something about Coop that Chat can't figure out. Like how upset he was after finding the Double V Solly carved on Chat's chest.

"Shouldn't have ever done that," Coop said shaking his head.

"Why, sergeant?" Chat asked. "You have one. All the members of the Brotherhood do."

"Oh, I guess you're right," the old veteran said. "I guess you didn't have a choice. You are your father's son."

They never discuss the matter again, but, after that, Chat notices sadness in the eyes of the old veteran. After this morning's formation, Chat and the rest of his unit stand at ease, waiting their turn to enter the mess hall. He glances about, searching for the faces of the new men. One of them catches Chat's eye. He has light skin and wavy hair. Chat recognizes his brother immediately.

"*Sid!*" he wants to shout.

But in that same instant, the communication that has always existed between the two brothers, the type of communication that needs no word to be spoken, freezes his brother's name in his throat. Sid spots Chat and signals his brother to remain silent. Unlike the first couple of months at Van Dorn, when the 364th was given little to do and had relatively free access to the base and town, recently the Army has kept the men of the 364th under tight constraints. When they are not drilling and marching, they work twelve-hour shifts. Some of the men perform menial duties, serving as attendants in the officer's quarters, doing their laundry, cleaning their barracks and latrines or pulling KP. These assignments are not given to Brotherhood members; these Negroes are like trustees in a penitentiary. Brotherhood members and sympathizers are assigned to labor gangs, which clear swamps of trees and bushes, build roads and unload supplies. These men are under constant surveillance. White MPs guard the work gangs in Jeeps as well as in APCs with mounted fully loaded machine guns. Several days pass before Chat and Sid can speak privately.

"What are you doing here," Chat asks.

"I'm on assignment with military intelligence," Sid replies.

"*Military intelligence*!" Chat exclaims. "Is that why you're using the name Arthur Lewis?"

"Yes."

"What do you do for military intelligence?"

"Whenever the provost marshall's office conducts any type of investigation, it calls on the military police, who send in people like me to gather information in secret."

"So what kind of information are you getting here?"

"I get information and identify members of a group that you probably never heard of," Sid says.

"What group is that?"

"The Double V Brotherhood."

Chat stares first at the ground and then at his brother for several minutes before he says, "I'm a member of the Double V Brotherhood."

"You mean that you sympathize with these rabble-rousers?" Sid snorts.

"I mean that I'm a member," Chat says. He unbuttons his fatigue shirt and lifting up the khaki colored undershirt, reveals the four ugly scars cut in the form of a double V on his chest.

"Oh no," Sid says. "They're identifying all Double Vs and putting them and their sympathizers into Bravo and Easy Companies."

"What for?"

"I don't know, but it isn't good."

Sid looks at Chat. He has little love for his brother. Chat has stood between him and his mother all of his life. But now Sid knows Chat needs his help. Sid literally holds his brother's life in his hands.

"I report to Sergeant Cooper," Sid tells him. "Anyone for the Brotherhood stays and anyone against the Brotherhood is transferred out."

"Sergeant Cooper," Chat gasps. "He's the leader of the Brotherhood for the entire 364th."

"That's what you think," Sid says. "Sergeant Cooper is military intelligence, just like me. Only he and some of the others are permanently assigned to the 364th."

Chat looks at his twin, trying to figure it out. Finally he asks, "What do you think I should do?"

"You've got to get out of Bravo Company," Sid declares thoughtfully, "although with that scar, it may be awfully difficult."

"That's the same thing, Coop, ah, Sergeant Cooper told me."

"He did?"

"Yes. Did you know that he knew our father?"

"Really?"

"Yes. Apparently the Brotherhood was started during the first European war. And our father and some other Brotherhood members saved Coop's life."

"Let me tell you something, brother," Sid says authoritatively. "The Double V Brotherhood is a group of communists and anarchists. They conduct espionage and sabotage for the Russians and socialists. It's actually a fifth column organization that uses dupes like you to further its ends. How could you be so stupid to join these crazies?"

"Crazies?" Chat explodes. "You don't know what you're talking about. The Brotherhood fights to protect colored soldiers against being lynched and murdered by whites and the Army itself."

"Oh yeah!" Sid shouts. "Well, I'll tell you what I think. I think the Brotherhood is just a bunch of crazy niggers *like you* who never can accept your place in the world and are trying to destroy what others have done to help our people."

"Others!" Chat shouts out. "You mean people like you who are so busy serving the white man that you have no self-respect or dignity?"

"No, I mean others like *me* who make certain that people like *you* don't make things worse for our people."

"Well, if that's the case you better turn me in to Sergeant Cooper," Chat spits out. "Actually, it doesn't matter because he already knows."

Later, Chat tells Solly what he has learned from Sid.

"It looks like the Army is planning to wipe out the Brotherhood," Solly concludes.

"How do you think they're going to do it?"

Solly shakes his head.

"Dunno," he says. "But they rounded up all the Japanese in the United States and put them in internment camps. That's probably what they plan to do with us."

"Yeah. I'll bet you're right. I'm from L.A. and all our Japanese neighbors were picked up."

Chat remembers the Army trucks taking away the Japanese family who lived down the street. He didn't know them very well. Chat remembers that Sam Hiyakawa had tried out for the UCLA football team and how he'd joined the others in ridiculing the Japanese student's efforts until one day Sam just didn't show up for practice. The Hiyakawas' house stood empty after the Army took the family away. The sign saying "Property of the United States Government" was still nailed to their house the day Chat left to join the Army. Bif told him the family had been interned in a concentration camp in Arizona not far from Papago Park.

"I can't believe that Coop is working for military intelligence," Solly says.

"I know how you feel," Chat agrees, "I feel the same way. But I don't think we can trust him, do you?"

"I heard that another couple of boys tried to make it out of here last week."

"Did they make it?"

"No!"

"Have you worked on any escape plans?" Chat asks.

"Yes," Solly says thoughtfully, "but everything I came up with, I shared with Coop."

"General McNair," the orderly called on his commander's intercom.

"Yes."

"General Peterson is on your line."

"Hello, General."

"Les, I want to tell you that deputy chief of staff approves your plans for handling the 364th."

"Thank you, general. Did General McNarney make any comments?"

"No, but he assures me that my report on the matter has been forwarded to General Marshall and Secretary Stimson. And the secretary has the fullest confidence in you and your staff. Do you have any questions?"

"No sir."

"Then I will leave the matter in you hands, Les."

"Thank you, general."

Brigadier General Lesley J. McNair returns the telephone to its cradle. Then speaking to his orderly through the intercom, he says, "Arrange for Major Hansen to meet me in my office as soon as possible."

"Chat, I've been ordered to report back." Sid meets his brother during mess call. "Whatever is being planned will happen soon after I leave."

"How do you know that?" Chat asks.

"Because everyone in the 364th has been reviewed."

Sid looks at his brother. A sensation hits him full in the stomach, like when an elevator suddenly drops and you're in the basement while your stomach is still on the first floor. Sid feels a sense of loss, or is it regret. Memories of him and Chat, many of them of times when they were young, happy and carefree, flit through his mind. There were the times when they talked about anything and everything. And now Sid really wants Chat to know how much he really loves him and how much he wishes that somehow all that had come between them could be swept away. Sid wants to tell Chat that when Sid looks at his brother, he, too, sees his father and how important that's always been. But then Sid realizes something even more important. Sid realizes that it is up to him to save Chat's life. And that Sid might just be too late. So with a renewed sense of urgency, Sid continues with his bad news.

"Those given a positive review in Bravo Company have been transferred. Everyone remaining in Able, Bravo and Charlie companies have been labeled as misfits, malcontents and subversives, including you."

"I didn't receive any evaluation," Chat replies.

"You didn't need one," Sid replies. "They already knew that you're a member of the Double V Brotherhood."

"And that makes me a misfit and a subversive!" Chat almost shouts, forgetting where he was.

"Yes," Sid replies quietly. "It makes you a subversive. They are trying to identify all the members of the Brotherhood as well as those who might sympathize or be swayed by them."

"So now what's going to happen?" Chat asks.

"I don't know," Sid muses, "but believe me it's going to be bad. I want you to come back to Camp Chafee with me. I can get your orders cut. I'll tell them that you have information that is important to Army intelligence."

"And what information would that be?" Chat asks quietly.

"It doesn't matter. We'll make something up." Sid's beginning to feel desperate. "Besides, I've cleared it with Sergeant Cooper. He said that he'd do anything to help you out."

"Help *me* out!" Chat says trying to keep his voice and temper under control. "What about the men in Bravo as well as the other three companies. That's over a thousand men. Are you going to help them, too?"

"What's going to happen to them will happen whether you are here or not," Sid says. "Are you coming or not?"

"I don't think you understand," Chat says slowly. "The reason that the Brotherhood was formed in the first place was so that we could help each other, defend each other. Do you know who was one of the founding members of the Brotherhood?"

"No," Sid says with an air of indifference. "Who?"

"Our father, Peter Jenkins," Chat says proudly. "One of the people he saved in Europe was Seymour Cooper."

"And look where it got him," Sid sneers. "Dead at 27."

Chat looks at his brother. It is as if he was seeing him for the first time. "Look, don't get me wrong, Sid. I appreciate what you're trying to do for me," Chat says. "But these guys here are just like brothers to me and I can't leave them. Can you get some of the others out, too?"

"Not a chance," Sid replies, knowing Chat's chances for survival was nil, which showed that he really didn't appreciate his brother's ability to survive nor Chat's vengeful nature. Several years will pass before Sid learns this lesson.

Work crews from Bravo Company clear roads connecting areas where additional barracks are being constructed. Both Solly and Chat are assigned to the crew. Chat tells Solly what he has learned from Sid.

"Do you trust him?" Solly asks.

"I've got to trust him," Chat responds. "He's my brother. Besides, what reason would he have to lie?"

"You said that he wanted you to go back to Arkansas as an informant," Solly observes. "He also said that Coop was betraying the Brotherhood."

"I see what you mean," Chat says.

"But on the other hand," Solly continues, "if he is telling the truth, Coop knows all of our escape plans."

"But didn't you tell us that it was Coop who told the group to develop some escape plans in the first place?"

"Yeah, you're right. Coop was the one who told us to be prepared."

"All right, you guys," one of the sergeants from the engineering company in charge of road building shouts out. "The Army isn't paying you to stand around gabbing all day, get to work!"

Chat's work group moves rocks, tree stumps and debris to either side of a dirt road. It is just as if they are on a Mississippi chain gang; the only difference being the men of the 364th don't wear chains.

Later in the evening, Solly shares Chat's information with Bravo Company's entire Brotherhood unit. Darrell Clark invites brothers from Able and Charlie companies to join them. They tell their unit leaders. Charles Oates, the informant at Papago Park, is the Brotherhood leader for Able Company. The discussion over whether or not to trust Coop becomes heated.

"How we going to disrespect Coop like this?" Charles asks. "He's the one man in this outfit I do trust. I certainly don't trust College Boy, here."

"Coop is the one who told us to develop escape plans," Angel Carrillo reminds the group. Angel is the Brotherhood leader of Charlie Company.

Angel is from Puerto Rico, but looks like a Negro. "Lots of brothers have gone 'over the hill' since we came to this hell hole."

"A lot of them have been shot, too," Solly reminds him. "You've seen the reports; you know." Angel is Charlie Company's orderly and is responsible for his company's daily reports where an accurate report on soldiers gone missing is filed.

"But some have gotten away clean," Darrell chimes in. "Didn't someone hear from Clarence Johnson, recently. He's back in his home in Atlanta, Georgia. He even contacted the NAACP."

"Oh yeah," someone responds, "what them niggers going to do about this situation?"

"Johnson says that they filed a complaint," Darrell reports.

"A complaint! Man, these white folks are killing niggers down here. What good is a complaint gonna do when these crackers are shooting folks?"

"I think the point is this," Solly interrupts. "Some of those who wanted to get away followed Coop's advice. Some made it; some didn't."

"But nobody knows for certain what happened to them, do we?" someone else says.

"Yeah, but a lot more have gotten caught and wound up dead," a brother from Able Company observes. "And if College Boy here is telling the truth, that's what the Army's got planned for everyone who's a part of the Double V."

There are some murmurs of agreement. "Now I know what one of my teachers was trying to tell me about Homer," Chat tells Solly quietly.

"What's that, College Boy?"

"A bunch of us were complaining about reading Homer. We asked him, 'What can some two-thousand-year-old Greek writing teach us?' "

"What did he say?" Solly asks, faintly amused.

"He said that we could learn how not to make mistakes."

"What did he mean by that?"

"That's what we asked him. We had just finished reading Homer's *Odyssey*, and the teacher asked: 'Now that you've finished this book, what boat would you have gotten in if you were preparing to return home to Greece after the Trojan War?' "

Solly gives Chat a quizzical look and says, "You've got to be kidding."

"That's what I thought at the time, too," Chat says slowly. "And remember, we had just read the book."

By now everyone is listening.

"So what was the answer?" Solly asks.

"Well, the Greeks left Troy in four squadrons. One under Odysseus, another under Menelaus, a third under Agamemnon, Menelaus's brother, and a fourth under a Spartan statesman and diplomat by the name of Nestor. It takes Odysseus twenty years to get home, and all the men who sail with him die. Odysseus is the sole survivor. After ten years, only half of the men aboard Menelaus's ships live to see Greece again. Agamemnon, on the other hand, finds his journey home easy. But once he's there, his wife and her lover have Agamemnon and his entire crew slaughtered. The fourth squadron under Nestor returns to Greece in a timely manner under fair winds and every man arrives home safe, sound and wealthy from the plunder seized from the vanquished Trojans."

Solly looks at Chat and says, "I get your point."

"Well, I don't get it," Charles sneers out. "School me, College Boy."

"The point is this: When your ass is on the line, you need intelligence to make the right decision!"

Chapter Thirty-One

"Sir, some of the mutineers suspect something," First Sergeant Cooper reports to the beefy, red-faced lieutenant who is officer of the day for Fort Van Dorn's provost marshall's office. The O.D. is also an Army intelligence officer who reports directly to Major Elmer Hansen.

"Is that so, sergeant?" the O.D. replies. "What exactly do you think they suspect?"

"Sir, they don't know any details, even I don't know any details for that matter," Coop starts out, trying to make his report as accurate as possible.

"Go on, sergeant."

"Well sir, as you know there have been a lot of transfers between the companies. And your office conducted a lot of interviews."

"Yes, sergeant, what about the interviews?"

"Well, sir," Coop continues, "these men are not stupid. They know something is happening."

"What can they know about anything?" The lieutenant leans back in his chair. "We are separating the 364th into two different groups. The group that is deemed trustworthy, soldiers who can be counted on in battle units, are being sent to the Aleutian Islands for defensive purposes. Those who are less trustworthy, like those in your Bravo Company, will be assigned to work details. We have a swamp to clear and a dam to build. I can't see why this should be of your concern."

"No sir."

Coop hears rumors, not so pleasant rumors. He hears that the MPs are going to provoke an incident at the fort to cause the Brotherhood of the 364th to retaliate. Colonel Goodman has issued orders that the firing pins be removed from all the 364th's M-1 rifles. In addition, Good-man orders all automatic weapons including BARs and Thompson sub-machine guns as well as mortars, bazookas and explosives, removed from the regimental armory. Enlisted men are not permitted sidearms, but Goodman orders his company commanders and platoon leaders to conduct random weapons searches along with their normal barracks inspections.

"We trust you, sergeant," the lieutenant tells the Negro, curling his lips into a malicious smile. "You'll be informed of everything the brass is planning."

"Thank you, sir," Coop says, visibly relieved. "It's just that, you know how the rumor mill works."

"I understand, sergeant. Just keep us informed, everything will be fine."

"Yessir."

"That will be all, sergeant."

"Yessir, thank you, Sir."

"And sergeant," the Lieutenant says as Coop is about to leave.

"Yessir."

"You're doing a fine job for your men. They should thank you for it."

"Thank you, sir."

Coop snaps to attention, gives a salute and wheeling about, strides out of the provost marshall's office.

As soon as Coop leaves, the lieutenant puts a call through to Major Hansen and reports the discussion to his superior.

"Sir!"

"Yes lieutenant," Hansen replies.

"If we want to maintain the element of surprise, I recommend that we move soon."

"Thank you, lieutenant." Hansen is noncommittal. This operation is his, and his completely. Hansen is uninterested in recommendations from some "ninety-day wonder."

"Is that all, lieutenant?"

"Yessir!"

Coop returns to Bravo Company feeling somewhat better. He had been feeling guilty about encouraging the Double V brothers to escape. But, at the same time, the Army has been Coop's life and for twenty-five years Bravo Company's first sergeant has carried out orders to the best of his ability.

"You weren't carrying out orders in France that night when Pete and the others saved your black ass from a lynching," Coop reminds himself.

"I was young in those days," he reminisces. "Since then I've been a good soldier. Besides, the Army needs to know who is likely to desert the battlefield under combat conditions. The black soldier is still under suspicion. If he runs away from the situation at Fort Van Dorn, what will he do on a battlefield in Europe or in the Pacific?"

Coop has a good heart and is genuinely concerned for his men.

"Better they run now than on a battlefield," he decides.

At least that is what he was told. This is the only reason Coop agrees to work with the provost marshall's office and allow Army intelligence agents to interview his men in the first place. Coop has begun to feel a heavy burden. He worries that the dead bodies of young colored soldiers found in the swamp were there because of him. His concerns about what might happen to his men wear on the sergeant more than ever. Now that he knows the men are only being separated into different units, the twenty-five-year Army veteran begins to feel a lot better.

"There's nothing wrong with that," Coop thinks. "That's how they did it in the first European war. Some colored units fought and others worked."

It is like a gigantic burden has been lifted from Coop's shoulders. He feels the way Judas must have felt just before the soldiers led Christ away to his death.

Three thousand unarmed Negro soldiers are cut off and isolated inside a barbed wire compound in the heart of Mississippi. These men are separated from civilization by hundreds of miles of snake- and alligator-infested swamp and marshlands bordering the mighty Mississippi River to the west and south, and by thousands of marauding whites, both military and civilian, armed to the teeth and intent on eradicating the Negro menace in their midst to the north and east. The signs are unmistakable; something is being planned. The Negro soldiers can feel it. The assaults against Negro soldiers found outside the fort, even with valid passes, by MPs and local sheriffs deputies, become a daily occurrence. The colored soldiers are detained and beaten. A white MP asks a sheriff's deputy to shoot a Negro soldier who has been detained for having a button missing from his tunic. The deputy complies and shoots the colored soldier. "Go tell your Brotherhood that we kill niggers around here," the MPs instruct the dead soldier's buddies.

All the Brotherhood units of the 364th meet separately. The dead soldier was from Able Company. Charles Oates, Able Company's Brotherhood unit leader, requests support from the other companies. Double Vs from Able Company want to attack the Centreville sheriff's office. Solly calls a Double V meeting of Bravo Company's Brotherhood unit.

"The other Double Vs have decided that the shooting of the soldier from Able Company is meant to provoke us into doing something stupid," Solly begins.

"Able Company's Double Vs say that if we don't join them, they'll go along," Darrell says. Bravo Company's Brotherhood discusses the issue. Most are torn between supporting Able Company and taking a wait-and-see position.

"And I've got more bad news," Darrell broke in. "Solly asked me to set some rifles aside, and guess what?"

"What?"

"None of the rifles have firing pins and there aren't any automatic weapons, anywhere."

"What!" Solly exclaims. "That's impossible!"

"Go see for yourself. The armory only has rifles without firing pins or ammunition. There aren't any grenades, mortars or bazookas or even bayonets."

"I don't like this," Chat says.

"So that's that," Solly says with resignation. "I say we get out of here as soon as possible."

"I'm with you," Chat agrees. "What's the plan?"

"We head south across the Mississippi River into Louisiana and try to get to New Orleans," Solly replies.

"It must be over a hundred miles to New Orleans from here," one brother says.

"Over two hundred miles," someone else comments. "It's ninety miles to Baton Rouge. And that's once we're out of the fort and across the river."

"Over a hundred miles through that swamp. That's impossible. We won't stand a chance out there."

"Well, let's face it," Solly observes. "If we make a break for it, not everyone is going to make it. Hell maybe none of us will make it."

The brothers discuss whether it makes any sense to leave at all. Only a few believe there is any urgency. Most decide it is better to wait it out at the fort.

"The only ones getting killed are the ones leaving Van Dorn," one soldier observes. "I'm keeping my black ass right where it is."

Others echo his sentiments.

"Didn't Coop just say that they're planning to turn Bravo and some of the other companies into labor outfits?"

"Yes, that's what he said," Solly confirms.

"Well, we're all working on road gangs now. It isn't so bad."

"And it's a lot better than winding up in the belly of an alligator."

"Or being bit by a water moccasin. That isn't a pretty way to die."

"I'm not ready to die at all!"

"Me neither!"

"It's a tough decision whether to stay or go," Solly says finally. "Every man has to decide for himself."

In the end, most of Bravo Company's Brotherhood decide to stay at the fort. Only five of the brothers, Solomon Pugh, Chatsworth Jenkins, Darrell Clark, Squeaky Harris and Woodson Simmons, whose knife Solly had used to cut the Double V on Chat's chest, decide to desert the Army.

"That's it then," Solly concludes.

"We need to start now collecting the things we need—food, shoes, socks, medical supplies and the like," Woodson says.

"And find a safe place to store them," Solly adds. "They're inspecting everything."

"We need guns," Darrell states decisively.

"What for?" asks Chat.

"So that we can fight," Harris answers.

"If you want to fight," Chat says, "stay here. We don't need to walk a hundred miles just to find a fight."

"I agree with Chat," Solly says. "If we don't have guns, we won't make any stupid decisions."

"Also any missing guns will be reported and there'll be an immediate search," Harris, who was the company's orderly, reports.

"Which means all or some of us might get caught before we ever get away."

Within the week, the five Double Vs collect an assortment of clothing, supplies and food. They divvy it up, and by the light of a harvest moon plunge into the Mississippi swamp on a perilous journey for freedom. The United States Army never hears from them again.

Epilogue

Less than a month later, after Chat, Solly and the others take off on their desperate bid for freedom, on another moonlit night in the fall of 1943, a lieutenant from the provost marshall's office directs a convoy of MPs to surround the compound occupied by the Negro troops of the 364th regiment. The unit has been consolidated into five companies. One week earlier, two companies of the 364th are transferred to Alaska. The remaining companies, Able, Bravo and Charlie, of nearly 1,200 Negro soldiers, await deployment to the Pacific. The rumors, according to Coop, are that these men will join labor battalions.

Inside the compound, the few Negro soldiers outside their barracks watch as the officer directs Jeep-loads of MPs heavily armed in combat gear to positions directly in front of each barracks. Armored personnel carriers encircle the entire compound, forming a perimeter just outside the gates. The curiosity on the faces of Negroes turn into alarm as a column of trucks rush from behind the Jeeps and APCs move toward each of the compound's four gates. MPs now swing the gates open and the trucks roar into the compound, coming to a halt just outside the mess hall. Two companies of MPs, 500 white men armed with rifles and automatic weapons, leap from the trucks and are whistled to combat formations in front of each barracks.

Once the assault units are in position, a white sergeant walks up to the first Negro soldier he sees and slams his rifle butt square into the man's face. The surprised soldier, blood streaming from a gaping hole in his forehead and a broken nose, falls senseless to the ground. Other Negroes witnessing the assault charge the MP. The slaughter begins.

First comes small arms and rifle fire, followed by the Thompson submachine guns and the Browning automatic rifles. Then in come Jeeps and APCs; their fifty-caliber machine guns erupt in a staccato of gunfire. The heavy machine guns concentrate on the wooden barracks, systematically raking back and forth across the entire length of the compound. Individual MPs concentrate on killing the Negroes who now are streaming out of barracks' doors, across the compound and into the barbed wire fences. Dazed by the noise, confused and frightened at the sight of the dead and dying covering the ground, men begin to pantomime their final roles in this theater of death. Some fall to their knees and beg for their lives, others throw up their arms in a feeble attempt at warding off the angry bullets that slam into their flesh and rip apart vital organs, still others look for a way to escape. But all escape routes are blocked. Some of them are half dressed, in their skivvies and underwear, others are in full dress, but the relentless hail of murderous gunfire slaughters the men of the 364th all-Negro Army regiment, annihilating every last one.

The initial assault ends and the fifty-caliber machine guns go quiet . . . but the killing continues. Wounded, dying men writhing on the ground, crying out in agony and pain, are shot until their only movement is the involuntary twitches a body makes after death. Others, believing that it is over, pull themselves out of the blood and gore that was once a comrade, raising their hands in surrender, but to no avail. Bullets slam into their bodies and into their faces and they fall, never to rise again. The MPs move forward, their guns flashing, spitting death in every direction, at every black, brown or yellow face. The bodies are shot so badly that they no longer resemble a human form—they are reduced to raw, bloody carcasses. Blood flows everywhere so that every single boot is soaked through.

Next comes the systematic search, barracks by barracks. Jeeps follow individual MPs. Some of the Negroes try to hide. The bury themselves in latrines, they climb into trees, they even cower under a mound of dead bodies, all to no avail. No one escapes the slaughter that lasts until the early morning hours. Every barracks, every latrine and every storage building, every square inch of the compound was covered. No one survives.

The screaming and yelling of men in the final agony of death is blood-curdling and horrible. Black men sink down, begging for their lives as laughing MPs taunt their victims before ripping them apart with the high-powered armaments. Some men pray, others curse, but for most, completely bewildered by what is happening, no words escape their lips at all. Some Negro soldiers break into the armory, only to discover that there is no ammunition and the rifles have no firing pins. When it is finally over, 1,200 black men lay in a river of blood that mingles with all the other dead and dying life making up the Mississippi swamp.

Over the next several days, the mutilated corpses are piled onto trucks and taken to a lime pit. The Army corps of engineers builds a dam over the pit. And there the bodies of 1,200 black soldiers of the 364th regiment lie to this day.

Neither Sid nor any member of his family ever learns what really happens to Chatsworth Jenkins. In a form letter, the Army tells his mother that her son has died in the service of his country in the Aleutian Islands off the coast of Alaska. The NAACP never makes any additional inquiries of the war department or the secretary of war about the disappearance of the 1,200 men of the 364th nor does the NAACP ever tell any other Negro what it knows.